LAST FLIGHT OUT OF OZ

· A NOVEL ·

ADAM SWENSON &
RICHARD A. SWENSON

KNOLLWOOD INK

LAST FLIGHT OUT OF OZ

Copyright © 2011 by Adam Swenson and Richard A. Swenson

Cover design and art by Colin Lammie (lammiester@gmail.com)

All rights reserved. No portion of this book may be reproduced, stored in a retrieval system, or transmitted in any form or for any means—electronic, mechanical, photocopy, recording, or any other—except for brief quotations in printed reviews, without the prior written permission of the publisher.

Published by Knollwood Ink.

First edition, December 2011

ISBN 978-0-9839066-0-5

PUBLISHER'S NOTE
This is a work of fiction. Names, characters, places and incidents either are the product of the author's imagination or are used fictiously, and any resemblance to actual persons, living or dead, business establishments, events, or locales is entirely coincidental.

Printed in the United States of America

For Nico Everett Swenson

7.7.07 - 6.3.08

Abyssus Abyssum Invocat

Ozymandias

Percy Bysshe Shelley (1818)

I met a traveler from an antique land
Who said: Two vast and trunkless legs of stone
Stand in the desert. Near them, on the sand,
Half sunk, a shattered visage lies, whose frown,
And wrinkled lip, and sneer of cold command,
Tell that its sculptor well those passions read
Which yet survive, stamped on these lifeless things,
The hand that mocked them, and the heart that fed;
And on the pedestal these words appear:
"My name is Ozymandias, king of kings:
Look upon my works, ye Mighty, and despair!"
Nothing beside remains. Round the decay
Of that colossal wreck, boundless and bare
The lone and level sands stretch far away.

Table of Contents

1.	A Vengeance Begun	2
2.	Starry, Starry Night	12
3.	Outrun, Outfight, Outsmart	22
4.	Tightly Coupled	35
5.	Ozymandias	49
6.	But Is He Right?	59
7.	Taking Flight	67
8.	You Can Never Go Home Again	76
9.	The Assignment	86
10.	Collateral Damage	93
11.	This Will End in Tears	100
12.	The Relentless Wound	119
13.	Deep Greens and Blues	122
14.	The Genius Is off His Meds	128
15.	Goodwill to Cats	132
16.	Hardball	134
17.	The Smell of Death	145
18.	Nice Doggie	152
19.	A Hole in the Wing Is Worth Two in the Heart	159
20.	Want a Pickle?	165
21.	The Break-In	176
22.	May the Mountains Bring Peace	190
23.	Follow Your Heart	197
24.	Salmon Ella's	206
25.	Must Be Love	219
26.	Bomb!	229
27.	Terrain Denial	238

28. The Nineteenth Icon	245
29. What She Sees	259
30. Fire on the Mountain	266
31. The FBI	273
32. A Million Little Pieces	283
33. Let the Great Axe Fall	290
34. Unexpected Visitor	293
35. Fuel, Meet Fire	300
36. Home Lies Beyond the Road Ahead	302
Acknowledgments	307
About the Authors	309

Chapter 1

A Vengeance Begun

DR. ANTHONY WEISSMAN HAD NEVER BEFORE STOKED THE fire wearing his tuxedo. But special occasions warrant special touches.

It grieved him to think that Susan, even on their anniversary, would not approve of tonight. He put the tux on in hopes it might help. She always liked to see me well dressed, he remembered: "Nothing but the best for my beloved Antoni." Then she'd stand back, look me over, flash a huge smile, pat my chest with both hands, and finish with that big exaggerated kiss. Part of her perpetual affirmation campaign. Not an easy job, this affirming stuff, but she'd known that going in.

He bent over and tossed another log into the fireplace. Then he poked the rising flames with the iron. Almost hot enough.

He began to straighten up, but stopped just in time. His head stayed down. How to do this? I must get to my desk without looking at the mantle. Keep the head down. Avoid those eyes—they'll be a problem. They'll try to stop me. Perhaps if I can just keep my gaze on the floor. Then I can slowly rotate away…

No use. He could never keep anything from her, and it was foolish to think he could tonight. Somehow, she always knew. Harsh words with a colleague? She knew before he walked in the door. When the guest conductor disappointed with a Mendelssohn piece (oh my, Antoni was intense about Mendelssohn), she knew to squeeze his hand and lean into his shoulder and whisper, "I'll make it up to you." When the nightmares came, the demons barely emerged out of their hole before she chased them back with her devastating love.

Even in death she knows. This part is intellectually awkward, of course, since there's no God or afterlife. But, however you dissect it, she still knows. She knows about tonight, you old fool.

OK then. Might as well face it. He slowly straightened up, lifted his head, and looked at her. He smiled. He picked up the photo and held it close. Those eyes. They always won. Glistening and blue, like arctic ice, only warm and hopeful and so impossibly generous. The undefeatedness of those eyes. He'd seen her enter a room and subdue it with her eyes alone.

"Good evening, Susan," he said softly. A gentle name for such a gentle person. She loved all of humanity and all of humanity had loved her back.

"I'm sorry. Please forgive me," he whispered. "Peace and justice will not embrace tonight. Tonight, only justice." He kissed her and placed the picture back on the mantle. He started to pivot away from the roaring fire, then stopped. He reached back to the mantle and turned the picture to face the massive stone chimney.

"Justice," he repeated inaudibly so her eyes would not hear. "Tonight, the great axe will fall."

He crossed the room to his ornate walnut desk. He sat down and put on a pair of latex surgical gloves. Before him lay a blank, cream-colored invitation made of expensive cotton paper with hand engraving in gold at the corners.

He looked over at the champagne. Not just yet.

Weissman took his calligraphy pen and hunkered over the delicate invitation. What came next had been practiced a thousand times. Flowing from the tip of the pen in his own elegant script appeared six words.

He leaned back and surveyed his work with satisfaction. He blew on the invitation, then blotted it. Next he carefully addressed the envelope, slid the invitation in, sealed it, and placed it on a corner of the desk.

He took off his gloves and threw them into the fire. Then the unused invitations and envelopes. The flames reached for each item, flashing brightly. Finally, the entire calligraphy set with its 24kt gold pen tip. He stirred the embers until nothing remained.

The ink disappeared down the sink, chased by five minutes of water, full-stream. Lastly, he put the ink bottle in a thick cloth sack and hammered it into tiny shards, then threw the sack in the trash.

The deed was finished. Now he could have the champagne. He poured two glasses and took them to the fireplace. Setting both on the mantle, he turned the picture to face him again. "Susan, some anniversary champagne for you. It's our fourteenth, remember? Of course you do. Hello, Joshua. I miss you son. I'm so glad you have your mother's eyes."

They were so innocent. They did not deserve to die. Not like that. He felt the tears coming. He lifted his glass: "I will join you soon."

א א א א

Kevin Morgan occupied the passenger seat of Weissman's Lexus sedan. Inexplicably, they became friends nearly two years ago just after the brooding genius moved to Colorado.

"How is that even possible," other students would ask.

Kevin shrugged his shoulders.

"Aren't you afraid of him?"

"No."

"A guy at MIT called him *smarter than the entire east coast*. Doesn't that scare you?"

"Not really." Then he looked over and added quizzically, "Why should that scare me?"

"Kevin, he hates everybody. He hates everything on campus. He hates teaching."

"He doesn't hate Friedman."

"Yeah, great—he hates the entire world except for two people. That's OK with you?"

"Listen, guys. I'm sorry, all right. When he arrived on campus, the Institute asked me to help him move in. We hit it off. I have no idea why. I like him, and he likes me."

They glared at him. Then he added with a twinkle, "If you want to know why he likes me, why don't you just ask him?"

Meanwhile, Craig Hunter, Kevin's best friend, knew better than to ask Weissman anything. He slumped in the back seat, carefully hidden from the mirror. His slouching was uncomfortable, but Kevin wasn't worried about him. Craig had been through worse, like sitting in a tree stand for twelve hours during a blizzard. Keeping silent for three hours wasn't easy for him either, Kevin knew, but conversation with the explosive professor was a mortal risk best avoided—unless your name was Kevin Morgan.

"Thanks again for driving us," Kevin said as they neared their destination.

Weissman shrugged. "I was coming to Denver on business anyway. When you mentioned your interview, it just made sense. I've seen your truck."

Kevin smiled. "Yeah, any trip in Dexter is an adventure." Although his battered four-wheel-drive Toyota was actually quite reliable, it looked perpetually at risk for dropping a vital part.

Conspicuously disguised by the small talk, there was mystery in the air and Kevin reached to understand it. He was, of course, pleased to be chauffeured by a world-renowned scientist. And he loved spending time with his mentor, the man he respected more than any other on earth. But Weissman did not do favors. He did not go out of his way to be polite and helpful. The great Dr. Weissman was many things, but he was *not* a chauffeur.

Craig seemed to feel it too. Kevin would occasionally shoot a quick look back, their puzzlement communicated with the glance. Weissman was acting quite normally, which in his case was weird. His serenity made them both nervous. His composure and generosity were alarming.

"I hope we didn't take you too far out of your way," Kevin said.

"In fact, my business isn't far from here. Not far at all." Then he laughed.

Kevin snuck a shocked look at Craig. Dr. Weissman never laughed. Not once. His DNA was devoid of humor.

Weissman slowed as they approached the imposing Peak Engineering International Headquarters. The Lexus turned into an elaborate entrance bracketed with beautiful stone formations. The jagged skyline of the Rockies was perfectly mirrored by the stone creation, an obvious play on the corporate name.

"I wonder if the Almighty got royalties when they copied His mountainscape?" Craig joked, breaking silence for the first time.

Weissman growled and swore something in Polish. *Or was it*

German? Kevin wondered. Craig winced.

As they neared the thirty-story building, it looked carved from a massive block of polished black onyx. It was sleek and ultramodern but also smacked of a dark, menacing juggernaut, completely blotting out the sun. Even the shadow seemed organically sinister.

The parking lot was full, but Weissman managed to find a slot near the front adjacent to executive parking. They got out, and Kevin asked Craig playfully, "My tie straight?" Craig chucked him on the back. Résumés in hand, they set out for the Foster Enterprises building. Weissman trailed behind, looking up at the commanding structure with evident disgust.

A thunderous commotion back at the main entrance made them turn in time to see a red sports car barreling into the lot. The rear of the convertible whipped around the turn, tires smoking. The Corvette shot directly at them in deafening fashion. The driver, a stunning brunette—about their age, Kevin guessed—missed them by a few feet, then screeched to a stop not twenty feet away, seemingly going from 60 to full-park in a second.

"She took the CEO spot," Kevin said, leaning toward Craig.

"Yeah, right," Craig said. "More like the mistress."

Before the engine quieted, the brunette had already exited by leaping over the door. She seemed effortlessly athletic. In no time, she was already halfway to the building.

Her passenger, a similarly fetching blonde, took a deep breath and shook her head. She leaned over and pulled the keys from the ignition, then stepped out of the car. In contrast to the intensity of the driver, blondie looked like a second-generation hippie, sun-kissed and pure. "Maggie, slow down," she said, jogging to catch up. "You almost killed us back there."

"I warned you, Summer," she said. "This always happens. The closer I get to him..."

The young women passed the gawking men without noticing. The doorman opened the plate-glass door for the pair and stepped aside. "Welcome to Foster Enterprises," he said. Maggie snarled. Summer smiled sweetly, as if to atone. Kevin, Craig, and even Weissman followed quickly behind and stood just inside the lobby to see what might happen next.

The women walked into the marbled lobby where a chunky security guard tried to flag them down. "You need to sign in," he said.

Maggie ignored him and surged past.

"Ma'am," he said, jumping up.

Maggie scowled at him and kept going.

The other guard, a thin and balding man, pulled his partner back down and whispered in his ear. The chunky guard's eyes widened.

"It's nothing personal," Summer said as she swept by, all sunshine and rainbows. An elevator appeared and the two vanished.

The doorman drew his eyes away from the scene and turned to Kevin, Craig, and Weissman. "Can I help you gentlemen?"

"Uh…" Kevin said, eyes still on the elevator doors. Craig chucked him again on the shoulder. "We're here for a job interview," Craig said with a grin.

"Check in with security," the doorman said, pointing.

"If you have a scheduled interview," the chunky guard said, "sign in here." Despite being newer to the job, he was clearly the alpha. "Then go to the twenty-seventh floor and follow the signs to Personnel."

"So who was that?" Kevin asked, still staring in the direction of the elevator. The guard glared.

"Right," Kevin said. "None of my business." He signed his name.

The thin guard leaned forward with a mischievous smile and whispered, "That, young man, was the boss's daughter."

"You mean Foster? Jeff Foster?" Kevin whispered back. "The CEO of Peak Engineering?"

"That's the one. Do yourself a favor—don't talk to her."

Kevin gave a shudder.

"If you ask me," the guard said, lowering his voice even more, "they deserve each other."

Weissman chuckled, his eyes glinting. Kevin and Craig looked at each other. It was his second laugh in the past fifteen minutes. Calculated another way, it was his second laugh in the past two years. "I'll attend to my business," he said, turning to leave, "and meet you back here around 3:00."

"Thanks again," Kevin said, but Weissman was already headed out the doors along with a sudden throng of humanity.

"What's with Weissman?" Craig asked. "I've never seen him like this."

"The weirdness is piling up," Kevin said. He tried to look into the parking lot, but the professor had already disappeared in the crowd.

They walked toward the elevators. "Did you see those two?" Kevin asked breathlessly.

"Whoa, Kev. Get a grip, man. You're a rookie—don't you think you'd better start with some sweet country girl? Those two are walking plutonium."

Kevin shivered involuntarily as the elevator door closed behind them and they lifted off.

They exited on the twenty-seventh floor and followed the signs for Personnel. After they'd finished filling out a small mountain of forms, they returned the packet to an attractive HR employee. "My name is Jamie," she said, sensibly dressed with fashionable glasses and shoulder-length blonde hair, "and I'm going to show you around. Please follow me."

The three left Personnel and Jamie began the tour. "This building is owned by Foster Enterprises. We operate our Denver office out of the top eight floors and lease out the lower twenty-two floors. We also have offices in San Francisco, Chicago, and Minneapolis."

She led them to the elevators, and they went up to the thirtieth floor. "This floor holds the office of Mr. Jeff Foster, owner and CEO of Foster Enterprises. It also has a series of conference rooms that boast some of the best views in the city."

They walked into a conference room with windows overlooking downtown Denver and, in the distance, the mountains. The conference table cost twenty thousand dollars, Jamie explained, pointing out the rosewood top, ebony center, holly inlay and mahogany edge. Around the table were sixteen supple black-leather chairs that smelled expensive. The combined effect exuded power, prestige, and intimidation.

"Mr. Foster's executive suite is in that half of the floor," Jamie said, gesturing down a long hallway. "But that's not on the tour. You'll likely never have occasion to go there. Now we'll head down to the twenty-third floor, and I'll show you Research & Development." They returned to the bank of elevators and waited.

Jamie smiled at them and asked, "Are you from arou—?" Her question was interrupted when the door to Jeff Foster's suite flew open and Maggie stormed out, Summer in tow.

"What would give him the idea that I might *want* this position?" she shouted. Summer struggled to find an answer to what, in Kevin's estimation, was clearly a rhetorical question. Jamie's countenance took on a pinched, anxious expression.

"He's got to learn that there are some things money just can't buy," Maggie continued. "A clean slate, for example. Absolution. Respect. You can dress a mobster up in a money suit, but it doesn't take the blood off his hands." She ranted her way down the hall.

"And for what? An upper management spot, condo, and a company car? What, like I need him to take care of me?"

The elevator arrived and the five of them got on.

Maggie's tirade continued. "This is the last place I'd ever want to work. Knowing what I know? Forget about it."

"Hi," the blonde said to Craig. "I'm Summer."

Craig smiled and shook her hand. "Craig."

"What brings you here?" Summer said.

"Job interview."

"—And to work for him?" Maggie continued, ignoring the social pleasantries going on two feet away. "Employees here aren't even a number. Numbers he has respect for. Here you're like a screwdriver or a hammer—use it 'til it snaps under the pressure, throw it out, and go scour the universities for fresh meat. A person would have to be brain dead to want to work here."

"Are you in school then?" Summer asked.

"Yeah," Craig replied. The irony was getting the better of him, and he was smirking. Jamie looked like she'd welcome a swift end to it all. "Colorado Institute of Mining and Technology. What about you?"

"We're visiting from California. Just here for the day." She pointed to Maggie with her eyes. "It appears we're headed back tonight."

The elevator arrived at the twenty-third floor, and Jamie led them off. Craig and Summer nodded goodbye. Maggie looked at Kevin, "If you've got any brains, you'll run for your life." Summer tried her best to suppress a snicker and then winked at Craig.

As the elevator descended down the shaft, Maggie's stream of righteous indignation receded with it.

"Well, she's got her ... theories," Jamie said in a futile effort to be diplomatic.

"She spoke to me," Kevin said in hushed breathless tones.

Craig rolled his eyes.

א א א א

The venting had done her good. Maggie felt a vague sense of control return once the elevator doors opened onto the lobby. Summer's relief was palpable.

"Let's get outta here," Maggie said and made a beeline for the exit. Summer smiled and waved at the security guards.

"Thanks again for coming along," Maggie said to Summer as they stepped out into the unseasonably warm March day. "Just, you know, to make sure I didn't kill anybody."

Summer shrugged. "I like Denver."

Walking to the convertible, Maggie saw an envelope on her seat, cream colored with gold engraving. In an elegant, flowing calligraphy it read:

Requesting the Honor of Your Presence

Jeff Foster

Maggie's first impulse was to throw it onto the asphalt and see if she could hit it on her way out, but her curiosity was piqued. She opened the envelope, read the invitation inside, then set back toward the building.

"Maggie," Summer said, "where are you going? What did that

say?"

"Give me three minutes."

Both the doorman and the guards knew better than to make eye contact this time around. Maggie jumped on an elevator and headed up. When the doors opened onto the thirtieth floor, she marched down the hall and burst into Foster's waiting room. The receptionist tried to slow her, but Maggie was having none of it. Taking hold of the brushed-chrome handle on the thick mahogany door, she ripped it open and stepped inside. Foster looked up from his computer.

"You reconsidered?" he said in a way that wasn't a question.

"Turning you in? No, still thinking about it."

A vein stood out in Foster's forehead. "What then?"

"Somebody put this on the front seat of my rental. Fan mail, I guess. Thought I'd drop it off in person."

Foster's brow furrowed, and he snatched the envelope. In a flash, Maggie was already back into the hall, hurrying to the elevator.

א א א א

Foster examined the envelope carefully for a clue, turning it side to side and end to end, handling it with the kind of caution one might use for a delivery suspected of a hazardous substance. Finally, he pushed the intercom. "Phyllis, come in here."

Ten seconds later his secretary was at his side.

"Open this for me." He handed her the envelope.

She looked suspiciously at him and took the note. "But it's already been opened," she said.

"Do I look like an idiot?" he yelled. "Just take the paper out of the envelope and give it to me." He stepped back a couple feet.

She slowly pulled the invitation out and handed it to him. He refused to touch it.

"Smell it," he said.

"Pardon?"

"Put your nose down by the paper and *smell* it."

She looked at him again, then sniffed the paper. "Seems OK to me."

"Any powder?"

"How do you mean, sir?"

"Do you see any powder on it?"

She looked at the invitation, then on her hands. "No, not really."

"Look inside the envelope. Any powder there?"

"None that I can see."

"Then give it to me." He snatched the invitation from Phyllis's hand, turned it over, and read it.

"Maggie!" he thundered. "Get back here!"

He ran to the door and into the hall, furious to find it already empty. "I could kill that girl!" He stomped back to Phyllis. "Did she say where she got this?"

"No sir."

Foster went to the window and looked down into the parking lot. Maggie jumped into the Corvette, then looked up. She smiled, waved goodbye, then rocketed out of the parking lot.

His face flushed with anger as he looked again at the flowing script.

I'll see you in hell, sir.

Chapter 2

Starry, Starry Night

KEVIN SPRINTED IN A THIN LINE OF DARKNESS BETWEEN streetlights to distance himself from the violated engineering building. The wet grass soaked his shoes and chilled his feet. Craig followed closely.

For three years, Kevin had inflicted himself on Colorado Institute of Mining and Technology. He was occasionally caught and prosecuted but never enough to be suspended. There was a great deal of ambivalence within the administration about young Mr. Morgan. On the one hand, he was the nicest guy you'd ever meet: kind, sincere, helpful to a fault. Smart too, uncommonly so, in an unpretentious manner. Everyone knew he was the brightest person in the room; everyone, that is, except Kevin. On the other hand, he gravitated toward mischief, prompting, to date, at least eight new Student Handbook rulings, such as *"Construction or firing of missiles, rockets, or pulse jet engines, propelled by solid fuel or liquid fuel, anywhere on campus (especially the Auto Shop building) requires prior CIMT administrative approval;"* or *"The no violence toward other students clause extends to possessing, using, or firing potato guns in the dormitories."*

Unfortunately, Kevin's free-wheeling creativity often exceeded the Institute's finite range of tolerance for such behavior. They seemed to forget entirely that Kevin was but a few scant years out of his teens, a time of recklessness necessitated, a priori, by the hormonal journey all passengers on the road to manhood go through. A simple problem of biochemistry and genetics, really. Somewhere in the labyrinthine network of mind and glands, a mysterious decision-making mechanism dictated that he be heavy on the gas and light on the brakes. He had not yet been weaned from danger. He was not culpable; he was twenty-two.

And Craig was no help. Tapping into an ability to use juvenile antics for self-entertainment honed to a fine point on the media-barren mission fields of Africa, Craig was a powerful catalyst for Kevin's brainstorms. Fearless himself, he pushed Kevin ever onward to dizzying heights of well-intentioned creative mischief. Having lived eighteen years "south of the Serengeti" as he said (Botswana or Ouagadougou or Djibouti or someplace like that), out there you either become a survivor or die. You might think that white people would eat off the fat of the land in Africa, due to their cultural status and superior funding. In theory that would be true, if there were any fat in the land. There wasn't. Not where Craig came from.

Despite the long odds, Craig had packed 220 pounds of rippling muscle onto a six-foot-two frame. For one thing, he ate animals. Not just cafeteria beef but *real* animals. He'd been known to trap rabbits behind the dorms and roast them over a midnight fire. When the radio played Hank Williams Jr.'s *A Country Boy Can Survive*, people thought of Craig Hunter. The guy could get it done.

Both now carried backpacks squeezed full with lasers from the lab. The heavy load bristled with sharp angles that dug into Kevin's ribs, but there was no time to readjust. They were, after all, fleeing the scene of a crime.

Patches of March snow covered the grass underfoot as they closed in on the dorms. Several mature aspens grew in the courtyard and, after reaching even the modicum of cover the trees offered, Kevin and Craig slowed their pace and snaked around back to a fire door labeled "Emergency Exit Only: Alarm Will Sound if Opened."

Kevin produced a small tool from his pocket and threaded it into the lock. He twisted it with patience and a learned subtlety. The lock clicked, and the door sprung open. No alarm. Craig glanced at his watch. "Gone in sixty seconds," he said. They ducked inside Fosbert Hall and raced up three flights of stairs. At room 315 Kevin knocked and entered.

His roommate, Wallace, sat with eyes glued to the monitor, interrupting his focus with brief flurries of typing. The glowing screen reflected back into his pasty-white face topped with jet-black bangs. Most Halloweens he was a vampire; it took too much work to be anything else.

As the door opened, Wallace turned, his blue eyes sunken into raven sockets. Kevin warned him that the days-at-a-time stints he spent in front of his laptop were the cardiovascular equivalent of living in a full-body cast, and that his odds of passing on the family name were slim if he didn't run around in the sunlight from time to time. Wallace didn't seem to care much about the family name.

"Project Black Hole," Kevin said. "You in?" Seeing Wallace's hesitation, he added, "You'll kick yourself if you miss it." He nodded almost imperceptibly. Despite his best efforts, Wallace was drawn to all things questionable. Though his mother and grandmother stacked the deck with the most straight-arrow men they could find, even this gentrified gene pool could not bring him to resist. Such a weakness would be his ruination, his mother reminded him every time they spoke.

Kevin smiled at the foregone conclusion, then barked orders and started gathering paraphernalia. Stopping for a second, he reached into a closet for his .243 target rifle. Craig's eyes widened, but Kevin shushed with a finger to the lips. "Just borrowing the scope."

He freed the scope and carried it gently in his right hand. With his left he opened the door and peeked in both directions. The trio slipped through the hall to the roof ladder. Above the top rung was a hatch bolted with a lock. Kevin possessed a key for over a year but maintenance had neglected to address the issue, essentially conceding their long-running battle with him.

The lock sprung open, the bolt pulled back, and the roof was their sovereign territory. The 2:00 a.m. sky was cloudless and star-choked as they stepped out. After taking a moment to admire the scene, Kevin and Craig unloaded their packs.

"Where'd you get that junk?" Wallace asked.

"Under the back seat of a '62 Chevy down by the river," Craig said.

"Come on," Wallace said.

"Found it in a storage closet in one of the engineering labs," Kevin said. "All boxed up in a dusty corner."

"What were you doing in a storage closet?" Wallace said.

"Looking for junk," Kevin said. "Listen Wallace, you gonna help or you gonna annoy?"

"Do you actually expect that stuff to work?" Wallace persisted. "Looks like it belonged to Galileo—right?" He snorted a cackling sound, his trademark self-congratulatory form of laughter.

Kevin picked up a fifty-foot coil of extension cord and threw it square at Wallace's chest, knocking him backward. He stumbled and bounced down at the edge of the roof.

"Come on Wallace," Craig said. "If you fall off it'll spoil our plan." He grabbed Wallace under the shoulders and lifted him effortlessly. "Do your job, man," he said, setting him down and patting him on the rear. "Big surprise coming."

"I'll let you push the button," Kevin said.

"Agreed," Wallace said with a grin. He picked up the extension cord and plugged it into the roof outlet, then connected it to a power strip. Craig set up a series of seven tripods in their proper locations. Kevin followed, placing the lasers on tripods with careful, steady hands, then using the rifle scope to sight the lasers with exacting precision.

With the lasers aimed, Kevin signaled and Wallace turned on the power strip. They waited for thirty seconds. Nothing. Five seconds later the campus went dark.

"Sweet," Wallace said. "What'd we do?"

"Last week I noticed sensing devices mounted on outside light poles," Kevin said. "Electricians installed new sensors to update the automated system that samples the ambient light every sixty seconds. It's basically a light-dependent resistor that's equipped with a time delay in the switching circuit. So when natural light reaches a pre-established low, the system flips on the outdoor lights—campus streets, walkways, courtyards. Then in the morning, after the sun comes up, the system shuts the lights off."

"So we shot lasers at the sensors," Wallace said, "the sensors read the beam as ambient light, and here we are in the dark."

"This is not dark!" Kevin said. "Look at that sky. Call that dark? We're here in God's nature. We're simply principled environmentalists. Sabotaging, even if for a few moments, this heinous light pollution."

"Right."

The CIMT blackout was broken only by dorm lights of late-night studiers and the occasional headlights piercing the darkness as cars crept around the campus loop, like motorists descending mountain roads watching for deer.

Though full of the satisfaction of a guess vindicated by experiment, there was another, smaller thought niggling at Kevin's mind. The effects of a dream, such as this majestic vision of darkness laid out before him, were different depending on one's outlook. He considered the price exacted by this little vagrancy—lights on or lights off?—and decided he'd let it stand. One of Kevin's driving forces, a conviction that mattered to him, was that people needed more adventure in their lives. Sure, these pranks were inconvenient for some but it's all a matter of perspective. *They could also thank me.*

"I think I'm having an Experience," Wallace said.

CIMT's indoctrination into the culture of experience came via the teaching of everyone's favorite English professor, Dr. Fitzsimmons, who often touted the virtues of life's great moments: receiving a standing ovation, the death of a loved one, a first crush, severe depression. Dr. Fitzsimmons stressed the importance of having capital E experiences in order to relate to the great writers and to generally become a more thoughtful person. To his more literally-minded followers, he explained that when he said great, he did not mean great, so much as he meant epic. Large. These grandiose moments were key to understanding the works of the fiction vanguard: the Tolstoys and Hemingways and Dostoyevskys. (Want to understand Dostoyevsky? Stand blindfolded before a firing squad.) If one lacked firsthand experience in the basic grit of existence, how could one hope to understand the depths of literature?

The vision of that pot-bellied, sixty-year-old chain smoker, rasping his misty-eyed way through the story of his first kiss with Elizabeth Streadley behind the swing set on their sixth-grade playground made the short list of notable experiences for most students. And of course they loved him for it. If the professorial carpe diem shtick brought him near to immortality, his second great tenet, that there was no one "right way" to do things, closed the deal. Of course, engineers knew some ways are righter than others, but they had fun playing his game.

"For me to impose a grid," he said one day, "a particular overriding and normative ideology on your young lives, would be tantamount to an art teacher telling young Vincent (you remember, young Vincent who cut off his ear?) that true artistic greatness rested in how closely he could emulate the master, Leonardo. Had he done that we would not have *Starry Night*. Good heavens, the thought of it! Some daring young nonconformists left us such bright and burning works as *On the Road*, *Generation X*, and *The Violent Bear It Away*."

Flannery O'Connor was Dr. Fitzsimmons's personal hero, if he had such a thing. Kerouac would have held that dubious honor had he not been so drunk and domesticated, so not On the Road, in the last half of his short life.

"Boys," Kevin said, drawing out a pack of venison jerky from his Army rucksack, "let's partake."

"Been into my stash again, huh?" Craig said. "I'll forgive you." He grabbed a hefty strip and tore off a chew with his teeth.

"You shot this?" Wallace asked. He wasn't the hunter type.

"Last year during bow season, over by Gunnison. Nice buck. Took a while to pack him out."

Kevin fished again in his rucksack for a two-way radio tuned to the shared frequency of maintenance and security. Sitting on the edge of the roof, the trio awaited the disaster relief forces.

Craig chomped off another bite, then turned to Kevin. "What're you thinking?"

"Guess," Kevin said.

"Me too," Craig said.

"I was wondering what she's doing right now," Kevin said.

"Well, I doubt she's sitting on a cold dormitory roof in the middle of the night eatin' jerky and staring into the blackness."

"Probably not." He thought of Maggie in glorious terms—dazzling, high-brow, aristocratic—unaware that, at this very moment, she was cleaning a drunk's blood off her hiking boots.

"Aw, Kev, forget about her," Craig said. "She's Mt. Everest and you're barefoot."

"OK Simon Cowell," Kevin said, elbowing him in the ribs. "Can't you just let me dream for a couple days?"

"Look," Craig said, "she's rich, spoiled, mean, and she's got Daddy issues. But Summer, on the other hand—"

"You don't know she's spoiled," Kevin interrupted. "She turned Jeff Foster down cold, so she can't care that much about the money. I mean, yeah, she's wealthy I guess, but that doesn't mean…" Kevin tapered off in a pensive fashion. He wasn't exactly sure where he was taking this.

"The thing I can't figure out is what was Weissman doing with a box of shells," Craig said.

"What?" Wallace said. "What are you talking about? What shells?"

Kevin glared at his friend. "Nice, Craig," he said.

"Wallace, listen up," Craig said. "I'm talking to you now. You've got to promise not to say anything."

"I promise."

"I'm serious. If I hear any rumors on campus about Weissman and ammo, I'm coming straight for you. We clear on that?"

Wallace gulped. "Sure, Craig. I won't say anything."

"I will bring you up here and throw you off. Understood?"

Wallace looked over the edge. "Understood."

"Well, I was sitting in the back seat of the Lexus on the return trip from Denver. Actually, trying to stay out of sight of Weissman. I dropped a stick of gum, and when I reached down for it, I noticed a box of shells under his seat."

"Could you tell what kind?" Kevin asked.

"9 mm."

"You sure."

"I'm sure."

"And they weren't there on the trip up?"

"Correct."

Their attention was drawn back to the mini-drama before them when the CIMT campus security roared up with the zeal of a rent-a-cop who suddenly finds something to do. He parked two wheels on the curb, two off, then stepped out of the SUV with an air of self-importance.

"Security calling maintenance," he shouted through the radio, "we've got a situation, over."

"What?" maintenance answered.

"All the campus lights are out. This is a dangerous situation that needs to be rectified. Situations are more likely to occur when darkness is upon us, and they are harder to control."

"We're on our break now, be out in fifteen minutes, over."
"But darkness—"
"Over."
"Isn't that Doyle?" Craig said with a laugh. "Got to be. Sounds just like him."

Kevin suspected he was right. Evidently Doyle, a high-strung sophomore, was security's newest recruit, looking to earn easy money during the quiet night watch.

"I guess we're about to find out if Doyle can take a joke," Kevin said as he pulled a small transmitter with an ominous-looking red button out of his backpack and handed it to Wallace.

"Push it," Kevin said.

Wallace coughed and gave him a look.

"Do it," Craig said.

Wallace's existential struggle lasted all of a millisecond. When he pushed the button, a squadron of fireworks exploded from the roof of Women's Residence Hall (WRH), the sole women's dorm on campus. Arcing high, they detonated with a thunderclap over the administration building. A few seconds later, a second volley roared heavenward, bursting into brilliant white streamers. Next came a sequence of blues and reds and greens, reminiscent of Iraqi anti-aircraft fire, flying off the roof in all directions.

"Maintenance!" screamed Doyle into the radio, "this is campus security. Code red! Code red!" No response.

"Guess maintenance turned off their radio," Craig said. "Sucks to be Doyle."

The security SUV tore off in the direction of WRH. Dorm lights clicked on across campus, windows flew open, and cheers rose from the approving student body.

"Who's on WRH?" Wallace asked.

"Better not ask," Kevin said. "Plausible deniability."

"Impeccable answer," Craig said.

With lights flashing, Doyle pulled the security SUV onto the WRH sidewalk and ran, in uniform, in the wee hours of the morning, into the only substantial concentration of eligible women for miles around.

"Wish I were Doyle right now," Wallace said.

"Maybe you should work security," Craig said.

"Not with you two miscreants out of your cages."

Their break over, a sluggish Ford maintenance van with roof racks and dangling extension cords rolled onto the scene. Two maintenance men in institutional jumpsuits piled out of the van, turned on flashlights, and began inspecting the zone of commotion.

"Maintenance calling security. We're on site. Can't find much. It's dark out here. Just a lot of ash. What's up?"

"Thanks for the help," Doyle snapped. "I'm working on catching the perpetrator now. Maintain radio silence." Searching throughout the women's dorm would delay him a bit, a serendipitous perk in the midst of an otherwise stressful night.

The maintenance men chattered as they checked this box, that breaker, this stretch of wiring. Occasional dumb luck would position one in the path of a laser and, if he lingered long enough to cut off the beam, the campus lights in that section would come back on.

"This section's back up," one called.

"What did you do?" the other would yell.

"Nothing," the first said. As he moved away, lights would darken again.

"What did you do now?"

"Still nothing. Must be a short."

Blazing flashlights came together to conference, then moved away, like stars playing hokey pokey. It reminded Kevin of minimalist theater.

"Hey Doyle," maintenance radioed, "we think it's an electrical short. Any luck tracking down the pyro?"

"When I got to the roof he was gone."

"Obviously the lighting problem and fireworks are related," maintenance said. "And we can guess who's behind it. If so, he's listening to us right now."

Kevin's cell phone vibrated in his pocket. He let it go to voice mail. Next, they heard a ring in Room 342, and Kevin knew his pursuers were waking the RA. Bert was pretty old for a young man and didn't relish getting out of bed—meaning they had about five minutes. Kevin and Craig realized they shouldn't risk going down the ladder into the hallway. Their propensity toward mischief was not accompanied by a commensurate facility in the matter of perjury. Authorities were thus best avoided immediately post-infraction.

"Time to go," Kevin said.

He removed the last item from his bag, a fifty-foot section of climbing rope. A locking carabiner secured the rope to the steel hatch, and the rappelling setup was ready.

Forgoing a climbing harness, Kevin descended old school, weaving the rope around his body like a snake and using his hands for the brake. This method involved pain but such is the price you pay—pain suffered for the sake of adventure had redeeming value in Kevin's code.

He slung his weight over the side, swinging away from the wall then back again as he dropped.

"That's got to hurt," Craig said peering over the edge. Kevin disappeared into the blackness below.

Wallace flipped off the power strip, shutting down the lasers and reigniting the campus. Next he scrambled to disassemble the lasers and tripods, placing everything under a tarp—to be returned the next evening, of course. Silently Craig followed Kevin over the wall. Once down, Wallace unlocked the carabiner and dropped the rope after them. He turned away from the edge just as Bert poked his head out onto the roof.

"Wallace, what are you doing up here?" Bert demanded. "It's 2:00 in the morning."

"Leonid shower. Meteors. It was supposed to be huge tonight, but it's been a bust." Wallace didn't share Kevin and Craig's inability to misrepresent facts. "Except for those fireworks. Did you get a load of that action? Awesome!"

"Get down off of here before I write you up. I want to get back to bed. Where's Morgan? Maintenance is after him. I couldn't find him in your room."

"No idea," Wallace said, following Bert down the ladder.

Chapter 3

Outrun, Outfight, Outsmart

Although Maggie and Summer rolled into their Palo Alto apartment at midnight, Maggie was up at 5:15 a.m., per usual, and dressed quickly. She savored her morning run and fell asleep each night anxious to wake and be off. No alarm needed. Ever.

She disdained alarms, as she disdained tiredness, fear, whining, and mediocrity. Maggie was a doer, not a sleeper. She never yawned, not once in a year. Never felt tired. When others remarked on her steel, she changed the subject—it came, unfortunately, from her father.

With no fuss, she brushed her teeth, pulled her shoulder-length brunette hair out of the way in a binder, and put on a sleek $200 pair of running shoes. Her 5'9" body was lean and tan, blessed with almost maintenance-free skin and hair. Hers was a family of lookers, smart and each successful—for one reason or another. Not respectable though. Not really.

In the still of the night, when she couldn't sleep, she often thought about them: the Fosters. She wondered if there were some sort of deep telos pulling them all to seemingly enviable positions in society. Jealous hangers-on stared at her dad's 38-foot Scarab at the house in Key West, a house that was, not coincidentally, only a couple of blocks away from Hemingway's old haunt. This had been a big selling point to Jeff who really bought into that Hemingway strong-man act.

Most people only knew of the house and trappings and didn't think any further than to be jealous. They missed the evils behind the curtain. When the spotlights flare, the Fosters are ready in all their splendor: gregarious, powerful, and charming when called for. But the Fosters are actors. *Strange that none of us went into it.*

The more fanatical onlookers see that Cindy, her mom, visits the home in the Keys more than Jeff. They see and they talk. Why does Cindy go there for months on end? Survival. Jeff's presence is like an inferno, consuming all the oxygen in a room, sending the occupants kicking down doors to get air. The word selfish comes to mind. Aggressive maybe—no, not enough. Lethal. Yes, of course, that's the word.

Maggie's thoughts occupied her down the stairs, out the door, and through the pre-running rituals. She started jogging slowly, savoring the morning and letting her body warm. The Bay Area morning was like most in early March: bracing, with an ethereal quality if you arose early enough. Fog clung low to the ground as her lithe body sliced through. Street signs and trees and buildings materialized out of the haze, then disappeared as she passed. Running in a dreamscape.

Some warned that jogging this early before sunrise might be dangerous, with muggers and rapists lurking in deep shadows. Maggie smiled at the threat. She could outrun, outfight, or outsmart any of them. Some days, she almost wished a molester would give it a try.

Within twenty minutes she had reached the Stanford campus and cruised down the Row, past the frat houses littered with the detritus of last night's debaucheries. She sped up. These were not part of Maggie's world. She raced past the Compound, her nickname for the Stanford engineering buildings and the venue of her daily conquests, climbing another rung in the slow, broken ladder women-in-a-male-world climb.

Maggie paired with Summer, her roommate and best friend, for lab assignments. Like Maggie, Summer had her reasons for avoiding men, chief among them the name she'd been given by her fertile-loined hippie parents. Still shot through with psychedelic idealism, enchanted with the myth of the beauty and goodness of peoplekind, they picked a name—Summer Skye Schaeffer—that jumps to rhyme (bummer, dumber, hummer, plumber). In the process, they tragically underestimated the cruelty of thirteen-year-old boys. Summer, selectively, had a lingering resentment. Since she was beautiful, her self-imposed chastity belt was lamented and generally regarded as quite a loss to the community, the eligible bachelors' sadness in proportion to the temptation, which was considerable.

"Listen Maggie," Summer would say, "the odds are in my favor. I can afford to be picky."

Yet, as Maggie pointed out, Summer was not looking for an actual man but for the Platonic form of a man. Cinematically brainwashed into thinking one man can be strong, good-looking, sensitive *and* intelligent, Summer forgot to factor in the artificial perfection the filming process bestows on a star, coating his flaws the same way a coat of paint glosses over the knots in a board. If an actor flubs a line he can do it over. If a voice spikes where it shouldn't, it can be edited for continuity. Witty repartee for the actor is generated by repartee specialists.

"You can't expect any one man to be that good," Maggie said, "least of all engineers. You might look for a silver-tongued devil in the English department, but then you'll have to support him. It's a tradeoff."

"Better that than these geeks who think the ability to solve quadratic equations in their heads has sex appeal," Summer said. "I almost want to tell them to save their breath, but then I wouldn't get to watch them flop around so much. It's comical."

That's about where things stood between Summer and the endless series of men coming up to her table, hunting for a smile: comical.

Despite the gender wars, or perhaps because of them, the Compound was their bright spot on campus, as day-by-day they logged small victories that added up over time in people's minds. They were bona fide engineering prodigies, the unapproachable twin goddesses of Stanford science.

The pressure to excel was on them both anyway, so they decided to make a game of it. Summer had her own reasons; Maggie's kick in the pants came from her father. Their method messed with masculine psyches. Always, always achieve the top scores. Finish labs first. Challenge wrong answers contentiously. Then leave the room discussing trivialities straight out of *National Enquirer* or *Star*. These banal discussions were a product of Maggie's reasoning that no spectacle could be more ruining to the insecure men left working, who appraised themselves so often and harshly. Yet these two women, the best and the brightest among them, wiled away extra brain cells on the kitsch of American pop culture.

Maggie finished her run with a smile and went back to shower before class.

א א א א

By late afternoon in the apartment, Maggie was deep into her studies when Summer's cell rang. Maggie followed the noise to the kitchen and looked at the screen: Corey Evans.

Well, Sunshine, this might teach you to remember your phone.

"Hello," Maggie said in her best Summer impersonation.

"Hey. This is Corey Evans." He hesitated. "Is this Summer?"

"Yes, Corey. How are you?" Maggie said sweetly.

"Uh, I'm fine. Thank you. Summer, I was wondering if you'd like to stop by O'Leary's Pub tonight. My friend's band is playing there, Blips and Bleeps."

"Who's the band again?" Maggie fired short sentences, thinking the more she kept Corey off balance and the quicker she brought this conversation to an end, the greater the odds he wouldn't grow wise.

"Blips and Bleeps."

She tried desperately to stifle her laughter—it'd be a dead giveaway. Summer's laugh was distinctive, infectious; everyone loved it. Maggie's laugh, on the other hand, often came out a sneer. She suspected that growing up in her house addled the portion of her brain responsible for genuine, cathartic, from-the-bottom-of-the-soul laughter.

Her house was like a coffeemaker: Maggie the pot, always being poured out, never replenished, the surface under her always hot, until whatever little she had left inside was charred and sticky, of no value to anyone. This emotional climate had left her snappy and reflexive, and, until a couple of years ago, unspiritual. What little acceptance she felt had been due to her brain. Success was the language spoken in the Foster house.

"Summer?"

"Oh, sorry. I'm a little tired, that's all. Sounds fun. OK, it's 5:30 now. I can finish my work and pick you up at 8:00."

"But they start at 8:00. And why are you picking me up all of a sudden?"

"You ask me out, I pick you up, that's the way it works. So, is this band headlining? We'll just miss the opener."

Corey took an uncharacteristic pause to absorb this information. "Good idea," he said, "but it won't work because there's no opener."

"All right, 7:45. I'll drive fast."

"Great. Pick me up at Campus Drive and Mayfield." The enthusiasm in Corey's voice was unmistakable, like a kid who thinks his parents don't have any Christmas money but is happily surprised when, on a long shot, he gets his new Radio Flyer anyway.

"See you soon," Maggie said. "Oh," she added. "Corey? Thanks for calling."

ℵ ℵ ℵ

"You what!" Summer gave the only sort of reaction she was capable of: visceral and unvarnished, a 50/50 mixture of anxiety and anticipation. "How did this happen?"

"Well, your phone rang, and I answered," Maggie said with a broad smile. "It's not my fault you left your cell laying around. *Again*."

"Maggie..." Summer said sternly.

"I picked up and apparently he thought it was you."

"What! You impersonated me? Maggie, I'm trying to give you the benefit of the doubt here, but, on the other hand, I just might kill you."

"Come on. It's not like I started World War III. All I did was agree to a simple date on a Friday night with a great guy who's infatuated with you. And to an Irish pub of all places."

Though Summer was her best friend, Maggie liked seeing her out on a limb. She enjoyed the genuine humanity, the drama. In Maggie's family, when people lashed out, it left a mark. Summer's tradition of hippie anger was basically toothless, a benign indignant noise rooted in the family belief in nonviolence.

"To you it's a simple date," Summer said. "You're not the one who has to go out with him."

"Summer, he's nice, he's cute, and he's the only guy within a thousand miles you kind of like. If you don't single-handedly stop the good times from rolling, you two could have a lot of fun. Tonight might be the beginning of something *beautiful.*"

"I don't want to be part of something *beautiful.*" At this point Summer was trying to scream at Maggie, realizing how funny it sounded, and laughing at herself. Maggie knew she'd won.

"Perfect. So you'll pick him up at 7:45?"

"Fine, I'll pick him up at 7:45." Summer was still trying hard to sound mad in a precedent-setting sort of way but was too overcome to pull it off. "Wait—what time is it now?" She looked at her watch. "Six thirty! Maggie, you're killing me here!"

"Relax, Sunshine. You'll be fine."

Summer headed for the shower while Maggie put away her books. She opened the refrigerator and reached for a Gatorade, then changed her mind and took the pineapple juice—an act, in itself, that reminded her just how much Summer had influenced her habits over the past three years.

In truth, Summer was the source of many changes in Maggie's life: spontaneity, sunsets, laughter, even giddiness. In contrast, the pre-Summer era of Maggie's existence had been ruled by Jeff Foster, and if the spontaneity-sunsets-laughter-giddiness quad had a sworn enemy on the planet, it would be her father.

On cue, Maggie's cell played *Taps*. She was tempted to let it ring, but after yesterday, this might be interesting.

"What?"

"Margaret, this is Jeff." He paused for a moment as if trying to remember what's supposed to come next. No one else called her Margaret, and she hated it. But it was useless to try to change his mind. Jeff's mind was prudentially immobile. Nobody changed Jeff Foster's mind but Jeff Foster. He was his own solar system.

"What do you know about the note?" he finally asked. "Where did you get it?"

"I told you—the front seat of my convertible."

"That's crazy. Who could possibly know what kind of car you were renting?"

"Apparently somebody who's done their homework." Then she added with a laugh, "Wow, that makes it sound kind of scary, huh?"

"I'm glad you find this amusing, Margaret. Well, I get death threats all the time and I sleep like a baby."

"Yeah, I've seen your liquor cabinet," she countered. "What did the cops say?"

"Who said anything about the police?" he said heatedly. "We handle these matters internally."

"Oh, I get it. Not good PR to reveal the names of ten thousand suspects who might wish you harm? That would make an interesting front page article in the *Wall Street Journal*."

"Anyone who's successful in business makes enemies, Margaret. It's a fact of life."

"Congratulations. By that measure, you've been very successful."

"It's just a juvenile prank."

"Calligraphy on an engraved invitation? I thought juveniles used spray paint and rotten eggs. And they say this generation is going down the tubes."

Jeff was twisting in the wind and he knew it. *He'll change the subject*, Maggie thought.

"How's school?" he said, a clunky segue. School, Maggie, you know—the bottom line, the family reputation, the GPA.

"The usual."

"All As? Excellent. What's your financial situation?"

"At my current rate of spending, I should have enough to last me until I'm married with eight kids."

"Has Cindy been giving you money?"

"No Jeff, you just give me lots of money and I don't spend much. It was a joke."

Pause.

"Well you're certainly not your sister. Every time I talk to her, she needs more."

"If Ana-Lese has a talent, squandering is it." Though on the surface this was a jab at her sister, Maggie was in fact directing it at Jeff. Some time back she had developed the knack of slandering a third party in a way that implied culpability on Jeff's part. He never acknowledged these circuitous allegations since she always left the shadow of a doubt as to whether or not she was directing criticism at him. He didn't want to call attention to it, just in case.

"She has taken after her mother for now, but maybe someday she'll seek the satisfaction of a real career."

Maggie said nothing, waiting to see if Jeff would keep the conversation going himself. Ana-Lese was an uncomfortable subject for him, so probably not. Understanding Jeff's mental processes as she did, she knew that the superficially caring and level-headed way he talked about Ana-Lese's train-wreck of a life was nothing more than a business habit—put a good spin on things; say nothing incriminating; protect your interests. While this held true for Ana-Lese, the same rule did not apply to Cindy. When it came to Cindy, there was no holding back.

But it was obscene, the way he talked with such detached and lifeless diction about Ana-Lese, about his own daughter, probably bombed out of her mind right now. The man was an oxymoron, a walking hedge-fund algorithm with sex organs.

Whatever. Conversations with Jeff were to be tolerated and dealt with expediently so she could get on with what comes next. Not unlike a transaction at an ATM.

"All right, Margaret. Study hard. Hold the line."

"Ah yes, the Foster way. Are we done?" Maggie asked.

"Not quite. I called one of my former classmates at MIT who runs their Advanced Degrees program. He says you could get a Ph.D. in interdepartmental studies in one year. I'd advise it Margaret. It would pad your résumé nicely—"

"Jeff," she screamed, "my résumé doesn't need padding! It's my *life* that needs padding!" She threw the cell across the room where it banged off her dresser and into a metal trash can. Then she doused it with pineapple juice.

For thirty seconds she stood in the middle of her room blowing obscenities through clenched teeth and tried to think of something else. Anything. It never worked. Not after Jeff. Finally she put on Björk, made some tea, and tried to settle back until Summer finished.

Like a black crow cawing over an imminent death, thoughts of her mother broke the fragile peace. Cindy-the-possessor. Somewhere along the line, she'd missed the cake-and-eating-it-too talk, and as a result, spent the majority of her time trying to hang on to mutually exclusive things: her money, the family name, the respect of her kids, and a second adolescence in her spare time. *I suppose she thinks she earned it, enduring a marriage to Jeff for twenty-seven years.*

Maggie wondered if Ana-Lese would figure any of this out on her own, ever have any insight into the rampant dysfunction of her parents. She knew the answer: Never. Ana-Lese's entire life was spent devising ways to drown out the sad truths that rattled around in her head. Sex, drugs, and rock-and-roll were a poor therapy, merely dulling her awareness of the ever-worsening situation without actually fixing anything.

The effects lasted only so long as the forgetfulness flowed through her veins, or for the duration of the romp, at which point she had to figure out how to get the freak out of her apartment before he steals anything. After that it was all just misery. And the methods of deadening were using her up, wearing her out. What had once passed for a mind and a personality had become sodden and featureless like a cardboard box left out in the rain.

By now, she'd ridden her size-four frame about as far as it would take her. Ana-Lese would never understand her problems on her own, and she was maybe too far gone to be able to comprehend the situation even if Maggie could present it in a lucid way. But Maggie wasn't up to that job, so Ana-Lese would hold tack until she crashed as models do, winding up at Hazelden. At least Jeff could afford her ultra-expensive, and no doubt glamorous, recovery. Way to provide for the family, Jeff.

He'd started this ball rolling by his absenteeism and emotional abuse: the more it cost him the better. Time to reap. He'd never understand it was his fault, but maybe by then she could tell him. Maybe she wouldn't need him anymore.

Summer burst out of the bathroom. "Maggie, could you clean—"

"I'll clean your car. You get dressed." Maggie laughed genuinely for the first time in days.

Twenty minutes later, Summer was preened and ready. "Sure you don't want to come? You could put in a call for yourself and we could double."

"Yeah, that'd be great. Set you up on your first date in months and then chaperone. You're just a little nervous—you'll be fine. I'm going flying."

א א א א

Maggie completed her disguise before entering O'Leary's by putting on a passable blonde wig, glasses, old jeans, T-shirt, and covering it all with a thrift-store flannel. She looked like she split time between an Alaskan fishing trawler and a Salvation Army basement—but hey, it's a disguise. Once inside, she bought a pint of Guinness at the bar and walked toward an out-of-the-way table along the far wall. The older, wealthier supper crowd trickled out while the twenty-something Blips-and-Bleeps set rolled in, a demographic tide change. Taking a pull from her Guinness, Maggie struggled to understand why she was even there. A vague sense of responsibility for this date? Feeling a little protective? Pure curiosity?

The front door opened, and Maggie heard them enter. She could see them as a couple already: the cartoonish machine gun bursts of Corey's voice followed by Summer's disarming laugh that implored people to glance over and smile. Corey loved it. He led the way to the bar and bought a coffee for himself and a Piña Colada for Summer. Together they chose a table forty feet in front of Maggie. The crowd was dense enough and the room dark enough that, as long as Maggie avoided eye contact, she had no worry of blowing her cover.

Corey appeared a respectable catch. At six feet and a wiry 160 pounds, he had the look of a Kenneth Cole model who'd wandered through a desert on his way to the shoot and managed to destroy his very expensive clothes. Buzzed black hair stood out from his tanned head like a fresh-cut lawn. Energy crackled around him, probably the result of an undiagnosed hyperactivity disorder, now mellowed, leaving behind a Type A personality without the free-floating hostility. He was an English major who made the hours of reading bearable with a lot of running. Maggie could relate.

Twenty minutes passed before Blips and Bleeps took the stage. They strapped on their instruments, and the lead singer coughed into his mic. The lights dimmed.

Silence hung for five seconds, the guitar amp let out a screech, and the band produced a rattly organized boom. The stage lights flared on, and Blips and Bleeps cranked into a set with the power of a speeding train. The guitar alternated between high cascading notes and teeth-rattling chords, the bass lines pummeled the windows, and the lead singer belted out occasionally intelligent lyrics while dancing around the stage.

Summer's head bobbed like a pigeon's to the syncopated beat, and Maggie could see her laughing at the right times. Through the odd, emotionally laxative power of their music, Maggie was starting to relax even though she'd warned herself against it coming in.

It'd been ages since she'd relaxed, and she'd forgotten how good it felt.

Four songs into the set, the glazed-over and work-weary looks disappeared from faces, and O'Leary's was doing a brisk business at the bar. Winding up "Hot Mama in a Cold Car," the singer yelled, "Everybody, thanks for coming out to hear us. This is great. Hey, I see a friend of mine and was wondering if he'd join us for a song. Come on up, Corey! Everybody, give him a hand."

Rising from the center of the curious applause, Corey bolted from the table, leaving his coffee and date, ran to the stage and jumped three feet to take his place behind the mic. After a swig of the singer's lemon water, he yelled in the mic, "All right guys, let's rock!" The bass drum throbbed, the cymbals clashed, and the Blips kicked it.

Halfway through "Your eyes are hazy and your skin is brown, but I love you anyway," an inebriated bottle sucker in the corner of the room started moving toward Summer. Maggie had noticed him earlier and pegged him as disgusting but harmless. The thick crowd forced the drunk to shove his way past tables, although those who saw him moved of their own accord. One look was enough: grungy T-shirt minus sleeves, biceps decorated with dragons, long stringy hair spilling out of an Auto Supply Store foam-and-mesh baseball cap, old grease-stained blue jeans. And this was not done in an endearing, Willie Nelson-esque way—he looked like a former Waffle House cook fired in a government sanitation crackdown.

And poor, unsuspecting Summer, eyes front and center, intoxicated by Corey—boyish but not immature, confident but not arrogant, and out of the blue he can sing. Who knew?

Perhaps here was Summer's perfect man after all.

The stranger stopped his lanky stride next to Summer and bent at the waist to talk, his hair falling perilously near her white blouse. He whispered in her ear, or the closest to a whisper he could achieve with the music playing. Summer's face changed from bliss, to puzzlement, to incredulity in a matter of three seconds. Unfazed, he yelled in her ear this time, and she looked even more put off and a little scared.

Maggie shot toward him, growing angrier with each step she took, each body she pushed out of the way, each foot she stepped on. The fact that Summer was finally out on a great date, and now this knuckle dragger was ruining it, possibly beyond repair…

The stranger turned sideways to Summer and reached his hand down, grabbing her shoulder. There was real fear in Summer's face now. Maggie stood three feet away, facing the stranger. She tapped him on the back of the neck. He turned with a look of supreme annoyance, a sneering comment no doubt brewing in his beady little brain.

Channeling years of karate lessons and pent-up rage, Maggie moved without thinking. Almost outside herself, she watched her right foot (wrapped in a sturdy brown hiking boot) enter the scene, catching the drunk on the side of his face, snapping his nose, lacerating the skin. His head whiplashed like a crash-test dummy, and he fell backward. Trying in vain to stop the room from spinning, he took deep gasping breaths, but every exhalation was laced with blood and the front of his shirt took on a red tinge.

Maggie knew she'd taken the fight out of him, but Summer was still panicked by his moaning. She dug in her purse, produced a can of mace, and gave her writhing antagonist a shower. He clawed at his face, looking like someone with a demon might.

Corey stopped singing in the middle of the second verse and jumped off the stage, in the process knocking over his mic. It made a deafening clatter as it crashed on the floor. The crowd parted for Corey—now a minor celebrity with a vested interest in what was going on—and made a place for him in their gawker's circle. The ring of spectators kept a respectful distance now that this broken man was leaking a biohazardous fluid.

When Corey got to Summer he saw the can of mace still pointing at the stranger, a single drip of mean liquid on its muzzle. "What happened? Summer, you all right? Maggie, is that you? What're you doing here?"

Summer said, "He tried to—" and before she got any further, Corey threw his coffee on the guy's exposed arm, and said, "Come on girls, let's go." As they struggled for the door, Corey yelled to the singer, "Thanks, Dave!" at which point the band launched into a jazzy rendition of "Hail to the Chief."

Maggie stopped to leave a note for the police at the bar that read, "He was harassing my friend so I kicked him in the chops. Maggie Foster 650-555-0113." They pushed through the doors into the black night air.

Outside was thirty degrees cooler, and they shivered. Maggie started chuckling, although she couldn't quite say why.

"Summer, you OK?" Corey said, unable to leave a silence. "Maggie that was awesome. You just floored him, one kick. I hate guys like that; they make me ashamed of my gender. What a tool! I'm glad you gave him a shot to the head."

Though laughing, Maggie was calm inside. To dispose of people with aplomb. Like a true Foster.

Damn you, Jeff.

Chapter 4

Tightly Coupled

THE RISING SUN STREAMED INTO DR. WEISSMAN'S MONDAY classroom creating a retreating line of shadow. He'd already been pacing for half an hour. Students trickled in, but he ignored them and continued pacing.

Two red curtains hung from the ceiling, pulled together. Every few minutes Weissman walked to the curtains, separated them with a finger, and peered inside.

He looked ghastly. His eyes were swollen and dark, his hair rumpled, as if he hadn't slept since the trip to Denver five days ago. His ancient suit was creased in the wrong places, the same outfit he wore nearly every day since he began teaching at CIMT.

Kevin and Craig walked in and quietly took their seats. As soon as Weissman was pacing in the opposite direction, Craig leaned over and whispered, "Looks like Weissman's back to normal."

Weissman was a high-profile contradiction, the kind that excited campus rumormongers. Everyone knew about his nice house in town and the expensive silver Lexus parked in the garage. Then why did he dress so carelessly for class and insist on tooling around in his old Land Cruiser? Popular opinion held that Weissman was rich but kept it hidden. "He's a Jew," some said. "Any other questions?" A more sympathetic contingent wanted to bring him groceries and do his laundry. Consensus formed easily, however, around one issue—the man was unhinged.

He sat down on the table and teased loose a strip of veneer while scowling at the clock. Precisely at 9:00 a.m., he thundered, "We've been studying the dark side of technology for two months." Every student in the room reflexively straightened, blinked, and stopped breathing. "For some of you, no doubt, it's felt like two years."

A nervous laughter—quite uncertain—rippled through the more inexperienced students, who then quickly looked around to assess what kind of peril they'd wandered into. The avoiding eyes of their peers gave them little comfort. As he spoke, Weissman stared out the window at the snowcapped mountains. "Before being unleashed on an unsuspecting public, engineers must learn the axiom of our medical colleagues 'Primum non nocere.' "

Turning to the room, he said. "Well? Anyone?" His voice quivered with disdain.

He waited, then walked again to the window and tapped his finger loudly against the pane like a water faucet dripping bullets. *Boom. Boom. Boom.*

Long after the silence had become unbearable, he said "I see." *Boom. Boom. Boom.* "Just as I thought." *Boom. Boom. Boom.* "This institution does not consider Latin essential to a proper scientific education."

A throat cleared, then a confident voice from the other side of the room said, "First, do no harm." Weissman pulled his eyes off the mountains and turned toward Kevin.

"Ah, Mr. Morgan. Yes, of course. I'd nearly forgotten you were in this class. Who said it?"

The roomful of students, now well into the background, breathed a collective sigh of relief.

"Hippocrates. The *Hippocratic Oath* I believe."

"Yes, it was Hippocrates," Weissman said, striding to Kevin's desk. "But it's not found in the *Hippocratic Oath*. Most people think so, even most physicians. The phrase comes from *Epidemics*, also written by Hippocrates."

"Why is this phrase in Latin," Kevin asked, "when Hippocrates was Greek?"

"Good for you, Kevin!" By now Weissman was smiling. He rubbed his hands together in delight. "Bravo! I doubt even my MIT students would've caught that. The phrase is widely quoted in Latin, yet Hippocrates was Greek. So, our famous 'Primum non nocere' is a translation. Well done."

Once again, Kevin had managed to relax the intense

professor, diverting the entire room from certain torment even if for a moment. To most students, Weissman was a demigod not to be toyed with, like playing chess with an opponent who sees all the possibilities on the board four moves out. Anonymity was the preferred survival strategy. Kevin, however, always seemed to run toward Weissman rather than away from him.

A cough from the back of the room returned the glare to Weissman's face.

"Yes. Enough of the classics. Back to engineering."

He stood next to Kevin's desk, considering, then gestured to the other side of the room. "Pull the window blinds," he said. Two students jumped to their feet and closed the shades, cutting off the natural light and leaving the room at the mercy of the bleak ceiling fluorescents.

Weissman walked to the red curtains and swept them open. Inside were thousands of dominoes standing upright in a complex, three-dimensional formation. The first domino was at waist height. He gave it a nudge with his index finger. The wooden pieces made small percussive noises as they toppled in quick succession. As the patterns grew more intricate and multiple lines fell simultaneously, the noise grew to a crescendo. The cascade ended in a furious storm. Then the room was suddenly silent again.

Weissman went to the wall and turned off the lights. He thumbed a remote in his hand and pointed it at the DVD player. An image flickered on the screen, the film grainy. An amateur photographer bobbled the camera as it zoomed in on the lettering *Challenger*. Then it zoomed back out, taking in the panoramic fuselage, tarmac, and blue sky.

"There's Christy in the Challenger," said an excited voice. "All set for takeoff. They're firing the engines!"

An aggressive flame and roiling smoke issued from the bottom of the shuttle as the stabilizing arm pulled away. The sensation intensified, the roar muffled by the camera's small microphone. The cameraman yelled, "There they go!" and the frame jumped as he took a step backward. He traced the space shuttle arcing skyward, proudly, securely, a moment for all humankind: for all teachers, women, astronauts, patriots.

Then, as if an atomic bomb went off inside the craft, it burst into a sickening ball of flame. Confusion and disbelief gave way to screams from the onlookers, their grief exceeding the capacity of language—seven astronauts had just been cremated before their eyes and buried at sea. Shrapnel and ash disfigured the sky. Families, friends, and dignitaries sobbed off-camera as they realized they'd just witnessed an unspeakable, hurtling funeral.

The DVD went blank for an instant, then replayed the Challenger's ill-fated final seconds in slow motion, frame-by-frame, soundless. One frame the shuttle was intact; the next it didn't exist. The students were as silent as the screen.

The room went dark again. Then a different image. The camera panned across a forest of northern pine knee deep in melting snow. A newscaster reported in lilting Norwegian as a scientist swung a Geiger counter side-to-side, the device issuing a loud radioactive staccato warning.

Then, five years later, a follow-up report. The same newsman visited the forest a second time. The Geiger counter, again registering alarm, was aimed at a crop of mushrooms. The next pictures were of reindeer gorging themselves on the mushrooms, a preferred food source. Finally, the Geiger counter was placed adjacent to reindeer scat, while Sami herdsmen stood a few feet away trying to understand.

The news-anchor continued in unintelligible Norwegian, the lone decipherable word being "Chernobyl." And, for some, "Cesium."

Weissman's remote clicked and the screen went dead. Footsteps sounded in the dark as he crossed the room and turned on the lights.

"You've got ten minutes to explain how these three things—the dominoes, the Challenger, and Chernobyl—are connected. Write the answer on a piece of paper in one sentence. Put your name at the top. I'm going for coffee." With that he closed the door behind him, throwing the room into pandemonium.

א א א א

Ten minutes later he returned, a cup of steaming coffee in hand.

"Well?" He did nothing to mitigate the awkwardness as the

silence grew more acute. After a minute, he pointed to the student located in the center of the room. "You."

"I don't know," she stammered.

"This assignment is worth ten percent of your overall grade. You just failed it. What's your name?"

"Cheryl Amdahl," she said in a quivering voice. Weissman flopped open a heavy book on his desk and made a note in red.

"You," he said, leveling a long finger at the student to Cheryl's right.

"It has something to do with complexity—"

"I don't want *it has something to do with*!" Weissman interrupted. "Everything has something to do with everything else. I'm looking for precision. What is it? What's the relationship?" He ran his fingers through his slightly graying hair, and made another note.

Weissman pointed his blood-red pen at Craig.

"The rapid cascading of complex systems," Craig said.

Weissman nodded. "Not bad. I suppose it's the best I'm going to get." He sighed heavily and continued. "What you saw were three examples of a phenomenon known as tight coupling. Tight coupling is a subset of interactive complexity. It's a condition of extreme interdependence where linkages are inseparably connected. All it takes is a small accident, some mishap, one detail that doesn't go according to plan to knock over the first link in a system. Tight coupling will take care of the rest. What happens is what you see before you," and he gestured to the fallen dominoes. "All fall down."

"Exhibit A: I pushed over one domino. Twenty-eight seconds later, 8,000 branching dominos had fallen. Tight coupling.

"Exhibit B: The Challenger was an unrivaled engineering marvel with only a small flaw in one system. Yet in seventy-three seconds, it exploded. Tight coupling.

"Exhibit C: The Soviet nuclear reactor at Chernobyl went from 7 percent power to 12,000 percent in under a minute, blowing the top off the facility and spewing radioactivity for thousands of miles. Tight coupling.

"When systems collapse out there in the world, the casualties are people. Friends. Husbands. Wives... Children. We're not talking simply about failed systems but about dead people."

Weissman turned and walked again to the window, as was his habit. He pulled back the blinds and stood silhouetted in the sunlight staring at the mountains. For sixty seconds he did not move. Then he coughed and blew his nose into a handkerchief. Did he dab his eyes? Kevin and Craig exchanged glances. Finally he continued, his back still to the class, his voice noticeably weaker.

"The most glaring example these days, known hopefully to even the dullest person in this class, is the highly-integrated world economic system. Nations are roped together at the waist, and when one falls off a cliff, the others are pulled down in rapid succession. We had three crashes in a decade: the dot.com bust of 2001, the banking crisis of 2008, and the crash of 2011. How long will it take us to realize that the dangerous mechanics of tightly-coupled systems must be fixed or we are all doomed?

"There are thousands of additional illustrations, almost all in some way benefitted by technology, and thus all related to engineering. The connections could be our spoke-and-hub airline system, internet servers, gas and oil infrastructure, the electrical power grid—the list goes on. Once the first link falls, the failsafe is gone. Systems crash and take people with them. The sheer size and complexity of systems assembled today inevitably create the byproduct of tightly-coupled instability."

He stopped again, his mind tumbling over itself, drifting from its classroom mooring. Painful memories crushed his brow. I, Anthony Weissman, teach at Colorado Institute of Mining and Technology. Why? Again he answered the question, as he did every day when the oddity of his circumstances reminded him afresh that this place was not his home. Just a temporary distraction from the pain.

Absent-mindedly he turned again toward the students. His face appeared to have aged five months in five minutes. His left eye twitched. With superhuman effort, he rerouted his train of thought back to the present. He scanned the crowd for glimmers of intelligent life, feeling, he suspected, the opposite of Carl Sagan. After years of searching galaxies, and despite all evidence to the contrary, Sagan remained optimistic that one day E.T. would phone. Weissman, for whatever intelligence may have been in this classroom, couldn't tap a bit of it, save a couple of fortunate exceptions.

"Yes, well, will anyone be so bold as to give me an example of tight coupling?" he asked, regaining control. "Please, enlighten me."

The air was heavy with silence. The only drive left in most students was geared toward passing the class by means of papers and tests. Classroom participation was too risky. Dr. Weissman—the brilliant yet unstable professor who perpetually seemed thirty seconds away from a breakdown, the kind they medicate. There were always a few souls, however, who from courage or stupidity would step up to the plate.

A brawny junior piped up from the back. "Once I was working on this project with my dad—we were building a street rod—and one breaker in the garage blew but not the other, so the overhead light went out, but the grinder he was using stayed on 'cause it was powered by the other breaker. He couldn't see, and he gashed himself in the leg, needed five stitches."

Weissman rolled his eyes upward in an unspoken plea for deliverance.

A sophomore sitting under the windows raised his hand.

"Yes?" Weissman said.

"Uh, there was a flight a while ago, I forget which airline, I saw this on TV, but it's been a while. Anyway, there was this flight where they put in a wheelchair that used batteries in the belly of the plane and didn't tie it down well. During the flight the pilots made a steep turn, and the wheelchair flipped on its side. One of the battery tops fell off, and the acid ate through the subfloor of the plane and through some cables that run the control surfaces in the rear. The pilots were only able to use the stabilizer that controls the up-and-down motion, and they had to use engine power to turn the plane from side to side."

Weissman looked at him intently, waiting for him to continue. "And?"

"They brought it down. Sort of a compromise between a landing and a crash. There were a few injuries, but no one was killed."

"Good. Your example leaves something to be desired, but I'm glad there were no fatalities," Weissman said quietly.

"Anyone else?" Again Weissman waited almost a minute

before a girl in the third row raised her hand.

"And you. What do you think?"

She flinched. When she hesitated, he asked, "What's your name?"

"Kirsten Harper."

"Yes, Kirsten Harper, please tell us all about tight coupling. And please do it now."

"One time I was riding in the car with my mom when I was a kid. We had just picked it up from the mechanic. She put the car in reverse and started to back up. But when she put her foot on the brake, the car just kept rolling, although a little slower. She ran into a parked car across the street. Later we found out that when the mechanics bled the brakes, they only did one—"

"Class," Weissman interrupted, "is this an example of tight coupling?"

When it became clear no one else was going to, Kevin spoke up. "No."

"Good Kevin," Weissman said. "Next?" He scanned the room again. He turned toward the clock, then looked back, settling on Kevin.

"Let's hear your thoughts on the matter, Kevin. No doubt you can throw me a bone, a life raft in this ocean of imbecility."

Kevin smiled, enjoying the pressure. "In 1992, a contractor was doing work on a bridge over the Chicago River. His crew was sinking wooden pilings. For their convenience, they changed the position of a new piling by a few feet and wound up driving it through a subterranean tunnel that connects to the Loop. City officials sent workers out with a barge full of mattresses and rocks that they threw into the whirlpool trying to plug the hole. It wasn't enough. As I recall, millions of gallons rushed in through the breached tunnel and flooded the Loop. The whole thing was a mess for weeks and shut down businesses. City offices had to set up headquarters on higher ground. The fiasco cost billions."

Weissman's face was aglow. "Kevin, please explain to the class why this is an example of tight coupling."

"The decision to move the piling a few feet off specification was a small one," Kevin said. "In the past it wouldn't have been a problem. But in today's world that one small decision had huge ramifications. Increasingly, everything is connected to everything else. Connectivity amplifies the potential for benefit, but it also amplifies the potential for damage." He paused.

"Are you through?" Weissman asked.

"Do you want me to be?" Kevin said.

Weissman retained the hint of a grin at the corners of his chapped mouth. "Yes," he said. "For now." For all his lauded credentials, he looked more like a rancher in an ill-fitting suit than a savvy professor with the world by the tail. His face was wrinkled and peeling from the sun, his hands callused. "We shouldn't demystify everything just yet should we?"

Kevin lit up at the word "we."

There was a murmur in the back of class.

"What did you say?" Weissman said.

"Nothing," said the hapless student.

"Tell me!"

"I just said to Mike, that guy's smart."

"Maybe it would behoove you to start taking notes when he talks." The student winced and sunk a little in his chair, wondering what he'd done to deserve this abuse.

"You're dismissed," Weissman said, turning again to face the mountains. He spent fifty percent of his class time staring up at the peaks, lecturing with his back to the students. "Every last sorry one of you."

Weissman's classes were always intense and often painful. Why people subjected themselves was a matter of rampant speculation. Maybe it was a perverse desire to see tragedy up close, a sort of academic *Faces of Death*. Or maybe daredevilry, hoping Weissman wouldn't fix his gaze on them—Russian roulette with lower stakes. Maybe the gauntlet. Whatever the motivation, they were always happy to leave.

Hurrying out the door, Kirsten said softly to a friend: "That psychopath forgot to collect our one-sentence explanations." She laughed. "What a loser." She was not the first to underestimate Weissman's acute hearing.

"Kevin," Weissman said, "would you mind staying a minute?"

ᚾ ᚾ ᚾ ᚾ

Weissman walked to his office, Kevin in tow. When the solid

wooden door opened, Kevin was greeted by the now familiar sweet smell of pipe tobacco coupled with the old-bookstore smell of collectible hardcovers. The only two sounds came from a burbling fish tank and the quiet whir of a customized desktop computer.

As first order of business, Weissman lit his pipe. "I didn't know professors could smoke in their offices," Kevin had asked months earlier. "Just me," was Weissman's answer.

In the center of the room was an ancient mahogany desk layered with scratches like a mini-lesson in archaeology. The computer, an impressive unit of Weissman's own design, occupied an edge of the desk. Angry-looking fish swam in the huge aquarium. Beside it was a small bowl of guppies.

"You got some new fish," Kevin said moving toward the tank. "What kind?"

"Oscars. Go ahead. Feed them if you want."

Kevin took the scoop and, after sloshing around a bit, caught a couple guppies and dumped them into the Oscar tank. The Oscars leapt into motion, prodded by primordial instincts. A short chase ensued, the Oscars clearly destined to win. Suddenly, for no reason Kevin could discern, they gave up the chase, twitching nonsensically and listing off in random directions. One ran into the side of the tank. The smaller guppies took shelter in the seaweed.

Kevin spun around and saw Weissman holding a small electronic device.

"What'd you do?" Kevin asked.

"I operated on these Oscars at home and installed a tiny sonic device that gives them a small charge when I push the button—like a shock collar for dogs. It took some trial and error. I killed a dozen before I got it right."

"You did this yourself? You're kidding. Are you some kind of micro-neurosurgeon on the side?"

"I've worked for decades in small-scale engineering, including nanotech and bioelectrical applications, Kevin. You know that. In comparison, these Oscars are huge."

The air between them was easy. No pretense, no pressure, no bitterness. Kevin's presence had a relaxing effect on Weissman's intensity, like David playing the harp for King Saul.

"So, if I may be permitted to get back to my story..."

"Sorry," Kevin said with neither guilt nor regret.

"Now every time I put in guppies, I let the Oscars chase. Then I give them a jolt. I'm trying to get them to associate guppies with pain. So far, I've only left the guppies in once, and the Oscars ate them while I was in class. My goal is simple: I would like the predatory species to live in peace with their prey. I would like to reprogram their instincts. They'll get all the fish flakes they want with no consequences. I would like the lion to lie down with the lamb."

"I thought that was supposed to happen through spirits, not science," Kevin said.

"Spirits, science ... what do I care?" Weissman asked rhetorically and landed with a defeatist thud in his desk chair. "I'm weary of this world." He seemed broken by a war of attrition against forces most mortals never see.

Just when someone was going to have to say something, a knock came at the door. "Yes?" Weissman said loudly. Kevin looked at the Oscars. The water was tinged red. Guppy parts swirled through the filter hose.

Dr. Michael Friedman, chairman (and sole faculty member) of the philosophy department, popped open the door. In his mid-thirties with black hair, he had eyes that could be intense or gentle at the flip of a switch and a mysterious two-inch scar that ran down his right cheek. He stood six feet with wide shoulders. Much of the time he wore a black sweater with corduroys, and the look made Kevin think of a Parisian intellectual. Among the few girls at CIMT, half of them had a thing for Friedman according to Kevin and Craig's estimates—because he was so unattainable? Kevin made a note-to-self.

Michael looked in. "I could come back later."

Weissman noticed the red in the Oscar tank behind Kevin, then glanced up.

"No. Come in Michael. Please stay a minute." With a nod, Michael stepped into the room and took a seat in front of the desk. Weissman continued: "I was preparing to discuss something with Kevin. I'd like your input." He motioned for Kevin to sit as well.

"Kevin, I have a question ... maybe a problem. I'd be

interested in your opinion. I'm a stern professor. I know that. I expect a lot from students. In my teaching at MIT I'd have twenty students like you in every class. But here... It's sad. The people sitting before me, in that class, are going to be designing the future. Building systems, configuring plans, making the world run. Sometimes I wonder if they can tie their own damn shoelaces. Frankly, I'm disgusted and feel I'm wasting my time. If there is any intelligence hiding in their ranks, I can't tap it. I'd like to hear your thoughts on the matter."

"I don't know, Dr. Weissman. Basically, you're wondering if the problem is with you or them?" He looked down at his feet and back up. "Do I get witness immunity?"

"Of course," Weissman said with an affectionate tone.

"Granted, most of my classmates are not the ripest bananas in the bunch. But they can do more than you think. Some of them are lazy, some are scared. For the lazy, that's their problem. It's hard to force someone to learn if they don't want to. But the scared—probably the majority—those you can help. They're afraid to talk unless they have the answer and they're sure of it. I don't think you'll get anywhere until there's more of a climate of intellectual freedom so they could experiment with their ideas. You could be less punishing of wrong answers."

Weissman seemed unsurprised by Kevin's candor—he expected nothing less. He looked to Michael who nodded his approval.

"I run into this problem in my philosophy classes," Michael said leaning in closer. "Not exactly, but similar. I have to teach eighteen-year olds Sartre, Camus, and Schopenhauer and keep them from sticking a gun barrel in their mouths—doesn't help alumni contributions."

"Your point?" Weissman asked.

"I find it necessary to build up a tolerance over time. Start easy with Plato. He's fun. Profound, but not too shocking. Then you can work them up to Kant, Kierkegaard, Nietzsche. You have to let them crawl before asking them to walk."

"College is not about crawling, Michael," Weissman said.

"Well, it is here. Sometimes." Michael looked at Kevin, but only received a let-me-see-you-talk-your-way-out-of-this-one grin. "I'm required to introduce students to such ideas, and—here's my point—these teachings must be paced. Students can't be expected to confront the deepest levels of philosophical thought until they're ready for it. Just as they can't confront your notion that the world's facing technological catastrophe until they're ready for it."

"Well, philosophy might have time for crawling, but engineering doesn't," Weissman countered.

"I only said you *start* with a crawl. But then you push them forward, sometimes even off a cliff. Camus wasn't thinking about crawling when he said that suicide was the central question of existential philosophy. Nor Sartre when he wrote, 'Man commits himself to his life, and thereby draws his image, beyond which there is nothing.' We are to be 'alone, without excuses ... condemned to be free.' This notion strikes a dissonant chord with students now that it's fashionable to blame neuroses on one's parents. They'd rather not believe that anything is their own fault. That they're the only ones who can do anyth—"

Michael stopped mid-sentence. Weissman looked stricken. His head was in his hands, his face hidden, his shoulders slumped.

Kevin glanced uncomfortably at Michael, but the philosopher's eyes were riveted on his colleague. No one spoke. No one moved.

"*Alone without excuses.* Is that what you said?" Weissman asked. After an uncomfortable pause, he finally whispered to himself: "*Condemned.*" Slowly he lifted his head and looked at Michael. "*Rather not believe anything is their own fault.*"

Michael did not answer.

"I happen to be on intimate terms with *alone.*" Weissman's voice remained weak, his eyes inflamed and moist, tidal pools forming behind the lower lids. A swelling tear finally breached the ridge and made its way down his right cheek. The gaze between them was fixed, so solid you could balance a sword on it. Both had forgotten Kevin.

"*Condemned ... fault ...* you don't have to teach me. I live with them. I eat with them. I lie with them every night—" Weissman stopped and lowered his head again. He took a deep breath. He pulled a crumpled handkerchief from his suit coat pocket and dried his eyes, looking at the picture of Susan and Joshua on the corner of his desk. "Camus was right—suicide is the central question."

Michael did not shrink from the obvious intent of Weissman's comment. Instead he continued looking directly at the wounded giant—it was obvious they'd visited this terrain before. Michael's eyes too were moist. He chose his words carefully.

"You know my beliefs on this Antoni. Camus and Sartre were wrong. None of us can make it on our own. And we don't have to, because we're *not* alone."

"You're not going to start preaching..."

"I'm not a preacher," Michael said. "Just a friend."

Weissman swiveled his chair around, facing the fish tank. "Understood," he said, and his body language made it clear they were through. He shocked the Oscars again for spite.

Chapter 5

Ozymandias

WEISSMAN LEFT CAMPUS EARLY, A PRIVILEGE AFFORDED THE big fish in a small pond. Short of not teaching classes, he had complete autonomy: no departmental meetings, no committee requirements, no student advisees, no grading of papers. The administrative memo regarding his arrival on campus a year-and-a-half ago was unambiguous: *Do not disturb*. The faculty resentment was socially isolating, but Weissman didn't mind in the least.

The rustic (and rusted) Land Cruiser shot east out of campus, then eight blocks later looped around and headed west toward the mountains. Although he maintained the house in town, Weissman's second residence, both preferred and clandestine, was an hour's journey from the school. The gradual 1,500 foot climb penetrated deeper into the mountains and valleys, passing aspen stands, Ponderosa pines, and mountain streams where mule deer paused for a quick glance before bounding away in the snow.

Turning right onto Gold Dust Trail, he bumped over the mile gravel road until it terminated with a left hook onto his long winding dirt driveway. The entrance was partially obscured by untrimmed brush, and a rusting mailbox lacked any identifying information. As the Cruiser rumbled into his property, two Rottweilers exploded out of the house with raised fur and bared teeth. Recognizing the truck, they jumped with excitement, wagging stumpy tails. Weissman opened the driver's door and rubbed their heads. Early in their relationship he tried throwing a ball, but they killed it.

Weissman jumped out of the vehicle and inspected the property for signs of intrusion. Every aspect of the yard was arranged in such a way that any intruder would leave a trace. Six hidden cameras surveyed overlapping swathes of land near the house, while a rotating 360-degree camera on the roof watched the horizon. A second layer of warning involved the dogs—any man or beast within two-hundred feet of the house would trip a laser motion-detection alarm, sending the Rottweilers screaming into the yard. Though the surveillance system was undetectable to the untrained eye and apparently superfluous, last October Weissman paid $37,000 for it nonetheless, and gladly.

The elaborate security grid stood guard over his paltry belongings, which, on the face of it, seemed unworthy of even rudimentary protection. All according to plan. The house provided a standing lesson that things are not always as they seem. From the road this was a decrepit mountain clapboard shack with a weathered coat of white paint. A battered roof and boarded-up window rounded out the facade. The wooden stairs to the front door were propped up by volumes A-F of the 1954 Encyclopedia Britannica tied together with twine, kept from rotting by a plastic bag.

There was no lawn, only short clipped weeds mixed with mud and snow. Behind the house stood a patchy aspen woods, the final resting place for the usual appliances and vehicles, plus a couple of dump trucks, a road grader minus the blade, and an Army field ambulance circa WWII. One '69 Chevy half-ton had a small pine growing through the bed and a bullet hole in the back window.

The air was thin at 8,200 feet, and despite his acclimatization Weissman still huffed as he walked to the door and stepped inside. The scene there was equally bleak: dishes stacked in the sink, a furrowed hardwood floor patched with putty, a refrigerator humming sickly, an ancient wooden table with one chair.

He took off his suit in the bedroom and replaced it with jeans and a flannel work shirt. Back in the kitchen he pried open a can of pork and beans and set it on the burner, stirring with a fork while talking to the dogs. After pouring a glass of milk, he removed the can with a hot pad and ate as the dogs watched hopefully.

Layering a work vest over his flannel shirt, he went out into the cool afternoon air and jumped into the truck. It lurched off, bumping over potholes in the exaggerated way old Land Cruisers do. The dirt road went from his house past the junkyard, and after a half mile reached a fenced-in mine shaft. The gate to the mine was sealed by a cable with a sign: Keep Out. Weissman unlocked the gate, grabbed his pickaxe and hard hat, and entered the mine. As he stepped inside, motion sensors flooded the tunnel with light. The dampness of the wall and mineral content of the stone yielded an impressive sparkle to the entire mine. Weissman had positioned the lamps for just such an effect, convinced it would have pleased Susan. The slope of the shaft was gradual, and ten minutes of careful walking brought him to the small line of ore he sought.

A steady rhythm with the pickaxe loosened his shoulders, his back, and his mind. His breathing quickened as the pick struck the wall over and over. The ore emerged in its time, and Weissman kneeled to collect the lode in a bucket. Susan had loved gold and silver jewelry—nothing too expensive or ostentatious but jewelry that would accent her own natural beauty, not compete with it. One of Weissman's great delights had been searching for such pieces in the fashion districts of New York or Milan or Paris, then gauging his degree of success by the look on her face as she opened the box.

But that was then. His daily trips down the tunnel now were simple, banal work—stress switching, his Boston psychiatrist called it—a distraction, something to fill the gaps in the day, gaps previously filled with the sacred duties of family. At one time he'd hoped his proximity to precious metals would bring her close, perhaps please her in some mystical way, make her face light up as it did. Instead, mining had degraded into a masochistic penance—daily labor, sweat, and dirt in an unrequited quest to atone. Containers of low-grade ore lined the walls, ignored.

His replacement family consisted of two Rottweilers, low maintenance to the point of often killing their own food. He could—as he sometimes did—put out a large water dish, disappear, and return a week later, finding them none the worse for wear. In this respect, they were a poor family, no better than he deserved.

He longed for the complications of family, remembering those events in ghostly images, memories that blurred with the passage of months and now years. At times Joshua's face was difficult to recollect; at other times his face would appear clearly, pristine before the accident. A face like Weissman's, only young and beautiful and innocent.

As the memories now came flooding back, cascading, engulfing him, he pushed against the cragged wall, eyes closed, deep groans echoing through the tunnels. He missed his wife's gentle reminders to please put his dishes in the dishwasher. He missed the way she squeezed his hand as they watched Joshua play on the beach. He missed acutely her need for intimacy, the way she looked at him. And Joshua. He missed Joshua unbearably.

Dropping the pickaxe, he slumped to the wet rock beneath his feet. Everything that meant anything was gone, the flesh and bones of his past now made one with the ground, mingled in a way that was irreversible, irretrievable, unredeemable. As a scientist, he knew their carbon atoms lived on, spread abroad for the world to share—in a bird, in an oak tree, in a child in Mongolia. But even as their elemental structures sped away to their millennial journeys, Susan and Joshua were gone.

Clawing the stone wall, he pulled himself back to his feet. Lifting his pickaxe, he slammed it sideways against the rocks. He channeled all his fury into the effort, an abstract fury at bad decisions, at the arrow of time that shot forward, forward, so there was no going back, no way to relive those fateful events and do them right. His hands numbed from the jarring vibrations of the handle. Finally, the handle fractured. He picked up the heavy steel head and threw it as far as he could down the tunnel, where it joined the others. Using the remaining handle to steady himself, exhausted in every way, he stumbled out of the mine. Sliding into the Cruiser, he drove home and collapsed on his bed like a dead man.

א א א א

Two hours later, at 8:00 p.m., he awoke with a crippling

hunger remedied with frozen meatballs warmed in the frying pan. The dogs each got two. Noticing the dishes in the sink had begun to mold, he set the frying pan on the floor where the dogs could lick it clean. Disgusted, he threw his empty beer can across the room where it clanked off a wall and added itself to the general clutter on the floor.

Of late his emotions were like a broken record, the music a melancholic minor-key dirge that came from bitter nonstop perseveration. He tried working the mine, but the only benefit was his well-deserved suffering. The dogs were a comfort at times, but on the deepest level, mattered little. Teaching was insufferable; the students hopeless.

Weissman's only relief was in science. Technology, computers, electronics, physics, mathematics: here a person could escape. He was intuitive, a natural. Since birth he was destined for greatness, his parents said, a prodigy from the bassinet. To put the best spin on his antisocial behavior, they told critics he would be a great engineer, an inventor, on the order of Edison or Fermi. Unlike most boys who rebel to differentiate themselves from their parents' expectations, Weissman followed their predictions flawlessly. Their commentaries were prophetic, almost as though they had time-traveled to inspect his future and brought back news to share with friends over wine.

In the bedroom he shed his mining clothes, hung them on a hook, and walked back into the hallway in his underwear and socks. He turned away from the kitchen and down the hall to the small room on the right. With the door ajar, he stepped into what appeared to be a general store. The perimeter of the room was piled high with utensils, food, and items of clothing. First were plates, over 200, all identical, followed by a similar number of bowls, cups, glasses, and silverware. Weissman found it easier to simply rotate new utensils than to wash the dirty. Next came forty cases of beer from the Okocim Brewery in Poland. Then hundreds of cans of beans and vegetables, followed by scores of packages of underwear, flannel shirts, jeans, and towels. Finally, a large mound of wrapped garments stacked neatly on the floor. Still in his underwear, Weissman went directly to this pile and stripped away the plastic from the top package. He unfolded a white jumpsuit, stepped into the uniform, and zipped it up. Then he slipped into white shoes with a soft comfortable lining and rubberized soles.

The only furniture in the room was a desk in the far corner, and the only object on the desk a brown phone. Weissman lifted the receiver and dialed S-1-1-7-J-3-2-0. Stepping back, he watched as a four-by-seven foot section of the floor, covered by a stiff Persian rug, lifted on a hinge. The electric motor emitted a quiet whirring as the hidden basement stairway came into view.

Weissman stepped down, hands gliding along the spotless white walls. Automated rheostats brightened the basement, triggered by the opening of the hinged door. When he reached the third step, the familiar sounds of Górecki's Third filled the room. Upon reaching the seventh step, as was his habit, he looked up to read the words: "See my works, ye mighty, and despair." Shelley's "Ozymandias," etched in a plaque, named his underground fortress.

The door above closed automatically as he reached the basement, sealing him inside Oz—his soundproof study, his global surveillance headquarters, his war room, his only stability, his one link to sanity, his only hope for future happiness, his lone chance at redemption, his *raison d'être*. The carpet was warmed by electric radiant underfloor heating. Per obsessive routine, he walked first to the three small side rooms and opened each door to glance inside: a glass-enclosed smoking room, a small sleeping room, the spotless bathroom. Next, he turned his attention to the large rectangular table in the center of Oz. It held nineteen computers, nine on each side and a master computer with large monitor at the near end. Moving from computer to computer, Weissman scanned the progress at each station. Finally he settled into the leather chair at the head of the table, pulled out the keyboard for the master computer, and worked until sunrise.

א א א

Susan and Joshua followed Weissman breathlessly through Los Angeles International Airport when an urgent announcement came over the PA: "Dr. Anthony Weissman, please pick up a blue courtesy phone for an important message."

"Susan, I should get that," Weissman said.

"Antoni," she pleaded, "We're going to miss our connection." But he'd already stopped and was looking around for a courtesy phone.

"Antoni!" she said with irritation. "They've given the last call for our flight. Can't you use your cell phone?" Seven-year-old Joshua was hanging on her arm, barely awake after their all-night flight from Hawaii.

"It's dead, and anyway, I don't know who's calling. You go ahead. This will only take a minute."

Susan turned in annoyance and rushed down the concourse towing her roller bag with one hand and Joshua with the other.

A courtesy phone connected Weissman to the information desk. "This is Dr. Weissman."

"Sir, you are to call Dr. Erwitt immediately. He said it's urgent. His number is area code 617—"

"I have the number. Thank you."

Weissman moved to a nearby bank of payphones, put in a credit card, and dialed his colleague at MIT.

"Ted," Weissman said, "I just got your page. We arrived late into L. A. and are about to board our flight home. What's up?"

"I've been trying your cell all morning," Ted said, obviously impassioned. "Your secretary gave me your itinerary so I called LAX—"

"Ted, slow down," Weissman said with a laugh, knowing his colleague's tendency toward excitement.

"No, no. Anthony, you don't get it!" Ted yelled. "I've got great news. Your name is in the final group for the Nobel. There are five names in physics: three Americans, one German, and one Japanese. The decision is in two weeks."

"That's incredible! Are you sure?" Weissman said. "How'd you find out?"

"A friend of mine, Rolf Gunterson. He's very close to the committee," Ted said. "He called today."

"I know Dr. Gunterson. Not personally, but I know who he is. Listen, Ted, please contact me if you hear anything else. My cell's dead but we should be home in about six hours."

"Will do," Ted said. "And Anthony, congratulations are in order."

"Thank you, Ted. I really don't know what to say. This is a

huge honor. Thank you."

He hung up and dreamt for an instant what life would be like if he won. His parents would have been so proud! And Susan—

Suddenly remembering his flight, he jolted and almost dropped his briefcase. He raced toward the gate. As he knifed through the swarms of people, he saw Susan at the end of the concourse waving, Joshua at her side.

"Antoni, hurry," she yelled. "They're shutting the door!"

"Wait!" he shouted. "Susan—hold up." He ran as fast as any time in the past twenty years and was completely winded, more from excitement than exhaustion.

His face was beaming. He closed now to within ten feet. "Susan!" he gasped. "I'm on the list for the Nobel Prize—that was Dr. Erwitt. He just found out. Isn't that unbelievable?"

"That's wonderful Antoni!" She dropped the roller bag and threw her arms around his neck in the middle of the concourse, kissing him on the lips. "I'm so proud of you," she whispered with a huge smile.

"Folks—listen. Are you going on this flight or not?" said the gate agent. "We're already late thanks to you. I'm closing this flight out in thirty seconds, so make up your mind."

"Get on" Weissman told Susan, motioning her toward the plane. "Go ahead. I'll be right behind." Susan grabbed Joshua by the hand and disappeared down the jetway.

Weissman fumbled through his pockets, unsuccessfully, for his boarding pass. The gate agent spotted it sticking out of the side of his briefcase, grabbed it and tore off the stub. "Oh, yes, sorry," Weissman said, taking the stub and rushing through the door. The aircraft hatch was just starting to close when he dove into the plane and passed a harried flight attendant.

Since two of their first class seats had already been reassigned, Susan took Joshua to sit in the only row available at the back of the plane. She bumped the roller bag through the narrow coach aisle, enduring impatient glares from passengers worried about tight connections. Still, she couldn't help but smile.

"Pardon me," Weissman said generically to the First Class compartment, throwing his briefcase onto seat 4D and stepping across the adjacent passenger. As he fastened his seatbelt, the ground crew retracted the jet bridge. Out his window, he saw a worker loading the final two suitcases—his matching black leather Guccis. Another worker walked behind the plane with orange wands.

The plane did a slight lurch as the pushback tractor engaged. Once the plane was backed out of the gate, they unhooked the tractor, and the pilots began the slow journey to their assigned runway.

Weissman was almost giddy thinking of the honor that would come his way, not even so much for himself, but for Susan, for Joshua, for his departed mother and father. What joy Susan and he would share tonight over a bottle of champagne after Joshua dozed off. As soon as they were airborne he'd go back and fill in the details. Surely someone would switch for his first class seat so he could sit with his family.

The lumbering Airbus 319 rolled down a taxiway for several minutes, then turned to cross a perpendicular runway. Gazing out the window, Weissman noticed the morning mist drifting in and thought, above the mist is...

Suddenly, a massive Boeing 737 dropped straight out of the fog. A deafening roar filled the cabin. Passengers screamed, clenching their armrests. Mothers threw both arms tightly around lap infants.

It was a hundred yards out ... a mere second...

The Airbus pilot gunned its engines, slamming passengers against their seats. A desperate attempt to sprint the runway.

Then everything exploded. The fuselage lurched violently to the side with a thunderous detonation. The head-splitting convulsion was accompanied by a sickly grinding and tearing as the jet spilled its contents across the tarmac—a horrifying mixture of fuel, baggage, and humanity.

Weissman's body jarred with the impact, swinging hard to the side, his arms flapping like a rag doll in a dog's mouth. The left side of his head struck the shoulder of the businessman sitting next to him, then snapped back, wrenching his neck.

Engines howled over pitiful screams, and he could smell a nauseating electric-metallic smoke. A strong wind rushed in from the back of the plane.

Susan! Joshua! Tearing off his seatbelt, he scrambled over the unconscious man beside him. Spinning toward the rear of the plane, he tried to look through the smoke. People were pushing around and jostling into the aisles. He stood, then bent and strained to get a view.

Then he screamed a grief-stricken wail and slumped unconscious onto the aisle.

The aft of the plane was a gaping, smoking hole.

אאא

He awoke in Oz, head down on the keyboard. A puddle of blood had collected over the center keys. Cursing, he leaned back in his chair facing the ceiling, handkerchief pinching his nose. He looked at the clock: 5:45 a.m.

Despite the pressure, blood kept coming from both sides. Finally, he took a facial tissue, rolled it tightly and jammed it in his right nostril. The same for the left. They stuck out like two cigarettes but seemed to do the trick.

He arose unsteadily, unplugged the keyboard, and carried it to the bathroom. Cleaning it was awkward, but Weissman took his time and used several damp cloths. He carried it back to his station along with a large white towel. He worked for another twenty minutes, then the nose pack began dripping again. He grabbed the towel just in time to spit up a large clot from the back of his throat.

Chapter 6

But Is He Right?

KEVIN WALKED OUT OF A TUESDAY AFTERNOON FITZSIMMONS class full of distracting factoids on the life of Percy Shelley. He had just read "Ozymandias" for the first time, a work so superior that it didn't just usher in a new paradigm but a whole new level of being. His mind wandered over the length of the poem as he descended the hill to The Circuit, the campus coffee shop equivalent that was no more equivalent to a real coffee shop than saccharine was to sugar. Its virtue was proximity, nothing else, a monopoly on convenience.

He ordered a large coffee in a mug, then found a sequestered window overlooking the campus. Outside a gray amoebic cloud blocked the sun and the hill fell into shadow. The wind whipped through skeletal aspens—unearthly tall stick figures, anorexic and albino. He sipped quietly, taking up space, the senior wondering what will become of him post-college and how much say he really had in the matter. Do we make our own way, or do those gentrified few on the nosebleed top of the socio-economic ladder just hand down rulings that reshuffle us like pawns until everyone's properly stratified? Poetry made his mind nomadic.

The bell above the door kept a steady rhythm as students and faculty alike dropped by for a pick-me-up. A herd of sophomores exited loudly while Dr. Friedman held the door. Kevin didn't feel much like talking, but Michael was precisely the person he needed to see.

After paying for his coffee, Michael scanned the room. His eye swept over a table of freshmen girls who looked away red-faced. Kevin waved him over.

"C3 pounding down your office door yet?" Kevin asked.

"Sorry?" Michael said, sliding into a chair.

"Charles Weatherspoon *the Third*. I was passing your classroom the other day and heard him railing against the supernatural. He was pretty testy. You handled him well."

"He doesn't like to lose an argument so I'm sure we'll have Round Two. I tried to warn him, but he didn't catch it. Not a philosopher I guess." Michael shrugged his shoulders. "You and Craig ready for spring break?"

"Yeah. Well, Craig is anyway. Camping down by the New Mexico border is probably a bit more than I can handle, but he promised to pack me out if I die." Kevin laughed. "He wants to hunt prairie dogs and coyotes and says he needs me along to cook 'em." He smiled again and shook his head. "How about you? Got any plans?"

"I'll spend it at the cabin. There's six feet of snow up there, but I'll bring my snowshoes, a shovel, and lots of books." Michael lit up in anticipation. "I can hardly wait. It's an annual pilgrimage for me. I'll read, rest up, soak in the beauty, and spend some time with the Almighty."

"Think I'll switch plans and come with you."

"Actually, I've been meaning to have you and Craig come up there sometime. You'd love it."

Kevin sipped at his coffee. "Not to change the topic, but can I ask you a question?"

"Of course. I thought you had something on your mind besides spring break."

"In Fitzsimmon's class today we discussed 'Ozymandias.' Know it?"

"*Round the decay of that colossal wreck, boundless and bare the lone and level sand stretches far away.* Yeah. It's always been a favorite. As a matter of fact, that poem is part of the reason I decided to teach philosophy. There're enough people teaching kids how to make money and reach for power. They don't realize that the pen is mightier than the sword. And the dollar. That poem helped me realize it. So I decided to take the high road, to teach kids altruism and virtue. Every idea comes back 'round again and has its day in the sun; why not this one?" Michael rubbed his hands together slowly as he spoke.

"I've always liked the idea of a philosopher king," he said, "but in democratic society, numbers are what count. I realized that we need philosopher businessmen, philosopher plumbers, philosopher surgeons—and yes, philosopher engineers. The seat of power in society is with the people, and when the people live right, the government doesn't need to be iron fisted. Thus my mission—to change the world one brain at a time."

"You've changed me," Kevin said. "I guess this is a good time to say thanks. Not just for your classes, but especially—you and Craig both—for helping me find my way after my dad died." He shifted in his seat and then looked out the window at the aspens. Michael waited patiently. Kevin turned again and stared into his coffee. "So, anyway, God used you two. I can't imagine where I'd be without you guys."

"I remember those days well," Michael finally said. "Midnight often seems the darkest hour. And the longest. But Jesus specializes in hopelessness." He looked directly at Kevin. "It was an honor to walk you through that night. A high honor." Now it was his turn to glance over at the aspens. "Years ago—in my university days—a friend did the same for me. So, perhaps now it's your turn."

"When you talk about midnight it makes me think of Weissman," Kevin said. "I wanted to ask you about him. You seem to know him better than anyone. I realize the provost is his brother-in-law, but they don't seem close."

Michael replied with caution. "It would be safe to say Anthony is closer to me than to Provost Reed."

"You and Weissman are easily the most complex profs here. You two have got the others lapped."

Michael looked amused. "Thanks, I think."

"My question deals with Weissman's psychological makeup. Naturally, I thought of you." Kevin hesitated.

"So what's the question?" Michael asked. "The suspense is killing me."

"It's about Weissman."

"You said that."

"I just feel reticent to ask."

"Reticent? Kevin Morgan? Now that's interesting. I don't know whether to be excited or disconcerted."

Kevin shrugged. "It's just a question. In three parts. First, Weissman is the best engineer I know. I suspect he may be one of the brightest in the world." Kevin rolled his head around on his neck like a prizefighter getting ready for a bout.

"Second, I want to be an engineer. That's what I enjoy doing, it's what I will do. And I want some idea of what to expect from my future.

"Third, Weissman is both the smartest and the gloomiest person I've ever met. My question to you: why are those two things so strongly associated in him? He's all death, destruction, and despair when talking about the future. Why? Other engineers are optimistic about the promises of technology: nanotech, gene therapy, a supercomputer in every pocket. When Weissman talks about these things, it's as though he visibly sinks into depression. Why? My question boils down to this—many people accuse Weissman of being a chronic pessimist, a prophet of gloom, and, if you'll excuse the phrase, maybe even a bit over the edge. But is he right? That'd have major implications for my future. Goodbye 2.5 kids, suburbia, golden retriever, white picket fence."

He cupped his hands around the coffee and took a deep sigh. "Hello Armageddon."

He leaned back against his chair and glanced out the window at the emaciated aspens superimposed over craggy peaks. "His ideas violate the whole reason I went into engineering. I like building things and working with computers and machines. It's fun. I don't think I could handle a depressing career."

Michael looked into his cup as though trying to divine the grounds. "I don't know if you'll understand this yet, but sometimes you don't pick your career—it picks you. That's a pretty loaded idea… But for now, let's focus on the reasons for Anthony's gloom, since that's obviously what's on your mind." He paused for a sip.

"Is he accurate to be so bleak? Top academics across the world have been asking that question since Anthony started talking this way. When a thinker of his caliber levels a judgment this serious, we must work it through with an appropriate gravity.

"My intuition is that Anthony's spot on. It's chilling, even morbid, and initially I wanted to avoid it. But I can't shake the elegant logic of his position.

"The heart of the question is whether Anthony is a pessimist or just a realist who arrives at terrifying conclusions. Generally speaking, he's dealing with the same phenomena as everyone else: the inexorable proliferation of technology. Some predictions suggest the next hundred years will experience twenty-thousand years of progress. Most of us really don't understand what that means. Anthony does.

"Many futurists look at similar variables yet arrive at vastly different conclusions. Some are unapologetic technological optimists. Anthony camps out on the opposite end of the spectrum. He believes the phenomenon of tight coupling will inevitably cascade the world system toward what he calls a threshold of lethality. By my reckoning, those who don't agree with him usually haven't followed the math out far enough."

"So you agree with him?" Kevin asked.

"Well, I'm neither an engineer nor a mathematician, but when Anthony and I discuss this stuff, invariably I come away convinced of his perspective."

"That's scary."

"There's just no escaping it—but don't you see? That's why we need people like you. Enjoy the bounties of progress and technology, but don't pour gas on the fire. Instead, be a watchman on the wall."

"Great. I can make business cards: 'KEVIN MORGAN - Talking the world down from the ledge for twenty years.'"

Michael wrote his phone number on a piece of paper. "Here's my number at home—call whenever you want. Just don't give it out."

"Thanks," Kevin said as he folded the paper into his pocket. "I had it already, but it's nice to have permission."

"How? It's unlisted."

Kevin smiled.

They talked for another ten minutes as they finished their coffee, then rose to put on their coats. As they left the coffee shop, a cold wind assaulted them. Leaning into the blast, Michael shouted: "Let me leave you with reflections from two of the smartest people in history. Solomon wrote, 'He who increases knowledge increases sorrow.' And Einstein, two days before his death, said 'Those who know the most are the gloomiest about the future.'"

Down the hill, a mighty gust of wind snapped a pine mid-trunk and it crashed to the ground.

אאאא

It was four o'clock when he entered his room, time to begin his daily pre-dinner routine. First, check the snakes. Dorm pets were forbidden, but Kevin had nevertheless stashed two boas in a giant loop of four-inch clear tubing that circumnavigated mid-level around the room, all under the sleepy eye of Bert. The three-foot snakes were fed live mice every few days, a spectacle that never failed to attract a crowd.

Second, check his New Zealand stocks. On the wall above his bed was a electronic banner scrolling quotes from the NZSX 50. At 4:00 p.m. in Colorado it was next-day noon in Wellington and the market was in full swing, up 5.97 to 3221.8. Every day he recalculated his financial position, hoping his micro investments in gold, timber, and oil would soon buy him a cup of coffee.

Third, check his blog **epicengineeringbreakdown.com** for feedback. He averaged a hundred hits a day from eight countries celebrating bizarre engineering accomplishments, disincentive stories, notable technological malfunctions, and the occasional serious reflection.

Fourth, nap. At precisely 4:30 p.m. the single-use digital clock mounted on the ceiling alongside the smoke alarm played a mellow "Tears in Heaven." On cue, Kevin dropped into bed, closed his eyes, and drifted off.

אאאא

During his solitary walk back from dinner, Kevin ruminated on the day. Was melancholia synonymous with choice? Was he free? Was anyone?

Freedom was his blessing and his curse, a lesson learned between the lines of college life. Four years ago he'd been enamored with it all, this glamorous new world of the university. Entire days passed playing ping pong, pool, and swimming. In those heady days he'd go on weekend rock-climbing trips, took one serious bender and decided it wasn't for him, played video games, and studied to get by.

And then one day he saw it. The underbelly. He discovered that with labor he could go in one direction, a direction that may or may not be the right one. He realized every free decision propelled him in a direction, say, toward being an engineer. And time spent engineering is time *not* spent on a thousand other things. What if I want to have more than one focus? More than one identity? Be a renaissance man?

He'd always hoped to one day be in a band, for example. Yes, play guitar in a band, get famous, make exorbitant money, never grow up. But every programming language he learned was one riff he didn't. Every step toward the computer was a step away from the guitar. It was the first he'd seen time as his enemy.

Or, take the decision to come to CIMT. This means I'll never have an Ivy League education. Will that be important when I'm forty-five? Maybe this charming and comfortable school will one day seem parochial and inadequate. As Sartre said, we're condemned to freedom without the criteria at hand to make good choices. Is Sartre right, or was Auden, that the distresses of choice are our chance to be blessed?

Climbing the dorm steps, Kevin headed for his room, then changed his mind and stopped by Craig's on the second floor. He knocked twice and entered. "Hey," he said, dropping into Craig's full-size dorm couch, a rarity attracting its fair share of loiterers.

"What's up, bro?" Craig asked. His faintly African inflections were hard to pin down, and all the more noticeable juxtaposed against the Western/nowhere accent of Colorado. "You look like you just lost your best friend, but that's me and I'm right here."

"Been thinking about Weissman. Wondering if he's right."

"You mean about the world circling the drain?"

"What if he's on to something? I don't want to spend my life chasing a dead end."

Craig shrugged, then pulled a chair over by the sofa and crossed his legs. "And what's a guy like him doing in a place like this?"

"Yeah, that too," Kevin said. "Well, the provost is his brother-in-law—that's got to have something to do with it."

"He's our best prof," Craig said.

"By far. He could teach anywhere: Cal Tech, Stanford, MIT."

"Why wouldn't he go to one of those? Those places are the World Series of professoring."

"Maybe he didn't want the pressure."

"What pressure?"

"You know ... pressure to excel, to publish, do research, make discoveries, that sort of thing. All they care about here is if you can teach. Judging by Dr. Grazic maybe they don't even care about that."

Dr. Grazic was a recent immigrant from the Baltic hinterland with an excellent understanding of physics but bad stutter-stop English. He would get hung up on words like capacitor or attenuation or vector, and mutter to himself, "what is word? what is word?" and in rare desperate cases would resort to drawing the object on the board spurring a round of impromptu Pictionary, except that in Pictionary the drawer knows the answer. Finally they got him a TA and a better Russian-English dictionary.

"Why would Weissman not want pressure?" Craig asked. "He's as smart as anyone in the world. What I don't understand is why does he even want to teach? I don't think he likes people. Especially not students. Except you."

"Did you know he was nominated for a Nobel Prize in physics a couple years back? Michael just told me."

"Nobel Prize! That's awesome," Craig said. "Weissman might be weird, but he's wicked smart and we're lucky to have him. I've only got a couple months left on campus and I can tell you this—I'm not missing any of his classes. Not often do you get to sit ten feet away from a certifiable Einstein. I just hope we can keep him at CIMT."

"I just hope we can keep him alive."

Chapter 7

Taking Flight

Maggie swung open the door to the Engineering library and walked through the security scanners. She scouted the floor for friendly faces to avoid. Her objective was strictly business, her goal solitude. Not unlike her life.

She set out in search of a barren corner, keeping her head down to avoid eye contact. The precautions proved insufficient, as a shuffling motion to the left indicated her presence had been detected—Dave was moving in her direction. It was widely known that Dave Emerson "carried a torch for her" as her grandmother liked to say. Encountering him was a known hazard of coming here.

Since a meeting was now all but inevitable, she stopped and pretended to look at the new books. His footsteps fell heavily as he pushed some chairs aside and jogged around others. Dave was pathologically enthusiastic, which Maggie found off-putting.

"Hey Maggie," he said as he jogged up and chucked her on the shoulder. She waited for him to continue. "What's up?"

"I'm looking for cockroaches to freeze in liquid nitrogen and drop on hard surfaces while I videotape them shattering into a million pieces, which I will slow down and put on the web to sell to some band trying to make a video, and that way I'll get my name in the credits. Then, if I can keep producing raw and vulgar vignettes of life ending catastrophically, I thought maybe I could augment my modest income as an aerospace engineer. What're you doing?"

"Uh... Studying. Want to study together?"

"Not unless you're a cockroach."

Dave's face went blank.

"See ya," she said as she walked away. Finding a quiet cubicle, she pulled out the chair and nuzzled in. The assignment was for advanced circuit analysis class with application in avionics controls. She grew quickly immersed. Oh, to be free of all thoughts but mathematics and physics. The answers were finite, objectifiable, measurable. There was a comfort in knowable answers, so opposite her personal life. In engineering, ambiguities were only ambiguous for lack of information or lack of understanding the science. These things were discoverable with work.

This property made engineering different from the inner workings of her family. Probing the tangled depths of her kin revealed only inexcusable dysfunction. Jeff, for example, once boasted he'd fired three employees with decades of faithful service simply because he needed a scapegoat. Peak Engineering's stock had experienced a momentary downturn, and, at about the same time, these men had made a slight, non-culpable error on a project only tangentially related to the stock problem. The stock problem was, after all, a reflection of their public image, and their project had not even been made public yet, so it could be argued that their screw-up had nothing to do with it. Yet, after decades of service, Allan Jones, Bill Alveri and Ted Maxwell received pink slips and became the stars of technically accurate but fundamentally misleading media sound bites.

Jeff had announced the event at dinner by way of how-was-your-day talk, just a little oil to lubricate the conversation. Maggie nearly stabbed her tonsils with a fork, the impaled piece of chicken falling off and sliding down her throat sideways. She had run to the bathroom to give herself the Heimlich maneuver on the countertop while Jeff and Ana-Lese chewed contentedly, gazing out the picture windows of their dining room at the setting sun, smug that Jeff had kept the family fortune intact yet another day.

Maggie clenched her pencil, clamping her jaw until her molars ached. A sudden tap on her shoulder sent her mood over the edge as she spun around to send Dave Emerson off once and for all.

It was Corey.

"Corey," she said, lowering her eyes. "What're you doing in the engineering library?"

"Looking for you, as a matter of fact. You OK? This a bad time? I could always come back, it's not really important I guess, I just had a question to ask you, but it doesn't have to be right now…"

Maggie looked at Corey, trying to decide which phrase to respond to.

"Do you want to talk about it?" he said. "I've got a little while, I think, before I have to be anywhere, let me check…" He pulled out a tattered green and white tablet, spiral bound and opened to a dog-eared page. "I've got an hour and forty-seven minutes. That should be as long as it takes," he looked at her again, "…or not."

"Corey, breathe man." Maggie spoke deliberately, incredulous anyone could talk that fast. She rolled her head from side to side, stretching out her cramping neck muscles and scanning the room in the process. Much to her dismay, her eyes landed on Dave, who was drinking from the fountain like a bull elk at a mountain stream. He came up from his guzzle, water dripping from his snout, panting, engaging her with a look, his enthusiasm having taken a right turn toward desire. When he spotted Corey, his eyes darkened. She turned quickly away, in a mock attempt to pretend their eyes had not met, a small gesture to induce a seed of doubt in Dave. *Did she really see me looking at her? Is this situation as awkward as it seems, or is it just me?*

"Corey, my neck's killing me. I've got a big knot on the right side. Would you mind rubbing it for me?"

"OK, but I'll need some information in return," he said, pressing his thumb against the base of her neck.

"Deal."

"I can trust you, right? This is important."

"Of course." Maggie cocked her head and looked out the corner of her eye at Dave, who was striving, incognito, to exit the building when the alarm went off.

"Excuse me," said the gray-haired lady at the desk. "Excuse me, young man. I believe you have an unchecked item."

Dave, sorry-eyed and with his tail between his legs, turned and shuffled back to the desk. The humiliation was more than Maggie could bear to watch, odd in that Maggie had a high tolerance for humiliation.

"What do you want to know?" she asked Corey.

"Two things, and you can't tell Summer we had this conversation, because, well you just can't. Deal?"

"Cross my heart, hope to die."

"Is that a yes?"

"Corey, did you have a childhood? Yes, that's a yes. Ouch."

"Too hard?"

"No, it's good. Pain is weakness leaving the body."

"What did Summer say? You know, what's the girl talk? I know this puts you in a tough situation, but give me whatever you can."

Maggie pondered the question, striving in vain to balance her desires: A) to give Corey information, but of course B) not to betray Summer's confidence in their discussions, and filtering all this through her desire C) that Cory and Summer get together, divided by her belief D) that people should not manipulate each other. She flipped a mental coin, and let it fly.

"After we left O'Leary's, Summer and I stopped at The Blackest Bean to debrief. We sat outside in the cool air. The night was dark, the stars immense. You could look down and see all the city lights, and it just puts things in perspective somehow. A bit like flying. Anyway, Summer had a great time with you. She likes your personality. She says you're effervescent, which is good, if you're into that. Not my thing, but she seems to like it. I find the disembodied trait of effervescence vexatious, but you don't bother me. Consider that an oblique compliment."

"People who aren't English majors must have trouble talking to you."

"Everyone has trouble talking to me, but non-English majors get it coming and going. First they have to look up the word, then they're offended."

"You know what I think it is?" Corey asked, then didn't wait for a response. "I think it's some twisted psychological mechanism by which you subconsciously insult people but avoid conflict at the same time."

"It's not subconscious."

Corey shook his head.

She paused while Corey kneaded next to her spinal cord, which felt luxurious. She was tempted to just leave it at this, but the truth was that Summer had said more—that while Corey's effervescence was winsome, it seemed not so much directed at *her* per se as just something he was unable to turn off. A personality trait, and a good one, but not a validation of true affection.

"Do you like Summer?" Maggie asked. "I mean, want to go out with her again?"

"Of course," he said with emphasis. "Why do you think I tracked you down? My behavior is not that of a man uncaring." He hesitated. "Is there a problem?" Corey's speech was oddly slow and cadenced, like he didn't want to ask this question but knew he had to.

"I wouldn't call it a problem. A misunderstanding perhaps. Summer enjoyed your general happiness, but she felt it to be directionless. I tried to talk sense into her, but you know… Let me put it this way. She didn't feel so much that you were happy *with her*, just that you were happy *in general*. She enjoyed the song though. So did I. Didn't know you had it in you, honestly."

Corey ignored the compliment, giving instead an intense focus on resolving this misperception. "Maggie, help me out here! What should I do?"

"I wish you hadn't asked that question, and I'm not going to answer it. I never seem to get these things right. Follow your intuition. Don't men have intuition? That's what I'll tell you."

"Do you know her parents?"

"What's that got to do with anything?"

"Just, do you know them?"

"I've met them. Of course, Summer talks about them."

"Tell me about them."

"Why?"

"Don't you think knowing someone's parents is an important component for knowing who that person is?"

"Her parents are incredibly resolute hippies who live in the Waipio Valley in Hawaii. The Big Island. Berkeley dropouts—that's where she gets her science. Anyway, they still believe in the hippie vision, you know, peace, love, conservation, music, drugs—although they've quit everything except the occasional ganja. They're gushy. It's weird. That's all I'm going to say.

Anything else, talk to Summer."

"Fair enough. You're a good friend to her."

"Thanks, now be gone. I've got work to do. Then I'm going flying."

Corey dragged himself off with a somewhat hopeful yet apprehensive look on his face. Consonant with his odds, thought Maggie.

Finally alone, she breezed through her studies, a solid feeling of accomplishment followed shortly by emptiness, followed by a sharp drive to do something else, the bane of the unsocialized workaholic. She wished there was a monitor to access—go to My Brain, Control Panel, Add/Remove Programs and weed through her personality. Alas, her mind stood impenetrable. She wondered if it would have been possible for her to be a Deadhead, or a Phish-head, to wear tie-dye clothes, grow leg hair, to follow the band in a decrepit VW minibus, selling woven bracelets, making enough money to eat ramen and organic apples and get hooked up with low quality Mexican weed. She suspected not.

Exiting the library, she walked briskly across campus to her red Volkswagen, the thirty-five-thousand-dollar antithesis of the hippie mobile, got in, and cranked the engine. She had opted for the CC with the V6 and 4motion: expensive, plush, and very, very fast.

The car leapt forward. She took a quick right to clear the curb, then floored it. She loved the liberation, the momentary fix that a solid burst of acceleration gave her.

א א א א

Within twenty minutes she arrived at the Palo Alto airport, bordered by a golf course on one side and a wildlife sanctuary on the other. *What kind of ecologist would put a wildlife sanctuary at the end of a runway?* The airport consisted of a dozen buildings and a few hundred planes sitting out, tied and chocked on the tarmac. Her need to fly was strong, making her tense and edgy, twitchy, like a smoker stepping out of church.

Maggie entered the security fence. Derek, one of the mechanics and self-appointed watchman over her plane, was sitting on a lawn chair outside a hangar reading a back issue of *Plane and Pilot*. He kept himself tidy and even had a uniform of sorts printed up—*A & P, Palo Alto Airport*—in big block letters like a Federal ATF agent.

He spotted Maggie over the top of his magazine. "Going up?"

"Once you get accustomed to two hundred mph, it's hard to settle for less."

"You know Maggie, they broke the mold when they made you. I went out with this girl last night, Krista, I think it was. She took a call in the middle of dinner about rescheduling a hair appointment and then could talk about nothing else. Bet that doesn't happen to you."

"Not really," Maggie said. "How's that Cessna 150 of yours?"

"Reliable. It's wings and it's paid for, which is more than most people can say."

"Guess you got something there."

"And I do my own work on it, so that makes flying affordable, will wonders never cease."

"There are two ways to make flying affordable. The other is to make more money."

"Your bird would be fun. I'd have one too if I were independently wealthy."

"A common misconception. Actually, I'm dependently wealthy. Not that I blame you for resenting it—I resent it myself."

"Can I go up with you sometime? I'd love to sit in that seat when you punch it up to three grand, with the Hartzell three blade out front..." He had dreamy eyes, like Summer when she talked of chocolate.

"Actually, I don't run it up to three grand. Maximum horsepower available for takeoff occurs at twenty-five hundred and seventy-five RPMs, so that's what I run it at. Sometimes twenty-six."

"Whatever, Maggie."

"Whatever doesn't get you too far in aerospace engineering. Probably not the best attitude for my mechanic either."

"Come on, you know what I mean."

"I never presume to know what anybody means. First you think you've got somebody figured out, then they turn out to be some backstabbing prick. No thank you."

"Whatever."

"Before you work on making your fortune, I'd spice up your rebuttals." She turned away, tired of the conversation. Conversations between Maggie and Derek had a way of going south within five minutes.

She walked to her plane, a sporty four-seater Piper Arrow with a two-hundred-horsepower turbocharged Continental, three-blade prop, and retractable gear. It was painted yellow with subtle nose art of a tiger making a killing swipe, and underneath it read, La Tigre, using the feminine pronoun in front of the masculine noun, the ensuing disjunct being fully intentional.

After her preflight walk-around, she hopped in and cranked it up. It started with a sputter but quickly smoothed out. Taxiing adjacent to the runway, she did the magneto check and tested her radio. That done, she rolled onto the runway, firewalled it as she turned the corner, the plane spinning out sharply, straightening, smooth down the runway, faster, slipping into the sky. She felt herself not a caveat to the law of gravity, a mechanically enabled exception, but rather a defiant spirit, acknowledging the law and beating it. Once she recognized the cogency of this observation she latched onto it as a metaphor for life.

The Arrow pulled upward, gaining 900 feet per minute, until she leveled out at 2,000. It was low enough to see the world, high enough to stay out of trouble.

Her flight plan cleared with air traffic control, she turned north past San Fran to swing by Alcatraz, the old fortress, the bulwark of secrets long forgotten, of isolation and brutality. Flying over it had become something of a loose routine. The Pelican (Alcatraz was Spanish for the big-jowled bird) held an obscure importance for her. The thought of the prisoners, existing on and on in the darkness, smoking and playing cards in dank and moldering buildings, suspended forever over the water, stuck in the concrete pouch of the great fisherbird.

But now the Pelican was dead. The tin roofs were rusty, the windows broken. People come only for an afternoon thrill, to stand on the concrete walked by murderers, bank robbers, and gangsters, then go off to some trendy restaurant in Chinatown for Ginger Asparagus Shrimp.

Sailboats left tiny white Vs in the water as they sliced through. After circling Alcatraz, watching the tourists march in and out like ants, she pointed her nose toward the Golden Gate Bridge, wagging the wings side to side as she flew over. She leveled out and headed south along the coast, then east to Palo Alto. In twenty minutes she was back on the ground.

Chapter 8

You Can Never Go Home Again

As Weissman approached the Logan Airport baggage claim he was greeted by a uniformed limo driver. "Hello, Dr. Weissman. My name is Roger and I'll be your chauffeur today. I doubt you will remember, but I used to drive you quite a bit. It's a pleasure to see you again, sir."

"Yes, Roger," Weissman said slowly. "I remember you." Social pleasantries were always difficult for him, yet he genuinely recalled having a fondness for this round little man with a kind heart. It was such a rare emotion that he wasn't quite sure what should come next. Finally he said, "It has been a while."

"Indeed, it has. Here, let me help you with your bag if I might, sir. It's this one here, isn't it? I recognize the tags. Good. Now, please follow me—it's not far."

After walking thirty feet, Roger slowed and then stopped. When he turned, his eyes were moist and he was having trouble controlling his feelings. "If you will permit me to say so, sir, I am so very sorry for your loss." He took a handkerchief and dabbed his eyes. "Perhaps I shouldn't be bringing this up, sir, but Mrs. Weissman and your little boy, your little Joshua, they were always my favorites. Not a week goes by but that I mourn them." By this time tears were streaming down his face. He did his best to wipe them, and then, of necessity, to blow his nose as well. "I'm sorry, sir. I didn't mean for this to happen. I mean, not like this. I'm sorry, please forgive me." He wiped his eyes again, and then folded his saturated handkerchief.

"You were very kind to them both," Weissman said, quite taken aback. "I remember that." It came to him that Roger always refused a tip when Susan and Joshua were in the limo, insisting that the pleasure of driving them was enough. They had developed a warm friendship over time and it was Susan who learned that Roger was married when younger but now had been a widower for thirty years. When his story was discovered, Susan took to giving him baking or boxes of candy nearly every trip. Once Joshua asked about his birthday, and Susan, listening carefully as was her way, then remembered the occasion with a beautiful watch. That was three weeks before the crash.

With great effort, Weissman stopped his thoughts dead in their tracks. The chauffeur's unexpected display of love for Susan and Joshua overpowered him, like someone trapped two years in a cave suddenly exposed to bright sunlight. He was ill-prepared for an emotional meltdown. To travel any further down this road would lead to a cliff. He had been there before and didn't have the strength to survive it again.

ℵ ℵ ℵ ℵ

Sitting on a wooden stool, elbows splayed out on his kitchen island, Weissman gazed over the top of his Viking range and out to sea. In the kitchen, the only light was from a pair of candles whose flames were duplicated in the picture window, flickering like memories of those departed. Their faint light spilled onto the veranda and, Weissman imagined, continued toward the stars. He drank 1993 Napa Valley Merlot from an MIT coffee mug and tried to determine why it was he decided to come to Boston for the ten-day spring break instead of remaining in Oz.

Susan and he had purchased this seaside home nine years ago, and it was here that Weissman spent the happiest years of his life. Located on Second Cliff in Scituate, it was close enough for an MIT commute but far enough out for privacy. The house enjoyed a stunning ocean view to the east, and the sweeping veranda was the center of many family evenings. This had been such a wondrous place for them. But now...

Encouraged by half the bottle, he padded silently in his slippers across wooden floors to a Steinway baby grand. Setting the mug on the polished black piano, he fumbled in the bench for his music. Choosing Vivaldi's *Four Seasons*, he sat down and started with "Winter."

His hands played flawlessly until the middle of the third page when the transmission lines from eyes-to-mind-to-fingers became garbled, and the music coming out of the Steinway no longer matched the music in his head. Sixteenth notes in F minor are buggers to play after a few mugs of wine. When the music died, Weissman again needed something to occupy the lifeless air—air unfit for human use due to an intangible sort of deficiency. Probably the stagnant quality it took on with no happy voices to push it around. Life in a vacuum.

Abandoning the piano, he opened his attaché and took out the account ledger. Even though it was a week early, he wrote the April check to the World Jewish Relief for their Ukrainian orphanages. Sealing the $10,000 gift in the envelope always provided the satisfaction that, once again this month, against all odds, he found compassion in his embittered soul. He wanted to care for those less fortunate, but from a distance. No pictures of starving kids. No sob stories. No swimming in their wounds.

He dug once more into the attaché and took out a Cohiba, clipped the end, and went to the veranda. There was no one in the house now to fuss, but still he couldn't bring himself to smoke inside. He sat in his favorite deck chair, pads covering the wood out of deference to his fifty-four years. It was unseasonably warm for the end of March, and a lap blanket allowed him to remain outside longer. Roger had reported that a storm was coming, but, for tonight, it was fifty-eight degrees with little wind. He lit the Cohiba, then lay back and listened to the steady rhythm of the Atlantic breaking on the shore below him. Nature's music, spare and comforting.

When his cigar was nearly done, he rose stiffly, walked to the edge of the veranda and stroked the oak branch growing over the railing. Though every year the branch's intrusion increased, Weissman didn't have the heart to prune it—it connected to the tree Joshua climbed when Susan wasn't looking, she being of the school that boys his age were fragile. Weissman, of a different school, allowed the climbing as their little secret.

A thousand memories lingered: by comparison the present was a yawing void. After extinguishing his cigar on the railing, he went inside and turned up the stereo on the soprano's Polish

Lament:

Synku miy i wybrany,
Rozdziel z matk swoje raný
A wszakom ci, synku miy, w swem sercu nosia,
A takie tobie wiernie suya.
Przemow k matce, bych si ucieszya,
Bo ju jidziesz ode mnie, moja nadzieja mia.

My son, my chosen and beloved, share your wounds with your mother
And because, dear son, I have always carried you in my heart,
And always served you faithfully
Speak to your mother, to make her happy,
Although you are already leaving me, my cherished hope.

The music of Górecki's Third looped and the hours passed. Finally, exhausted, Weissman crawled to the sofa for the night. Sleeping in their bed was unbearable. Even walking past the master bedroom was impossibly painful. And Joshua's room? A single glance destroyed him. His last thought, while still in control of his mind before the vagaries of the subconscious took command, was a wish for the dreamless sleep of the dead.

א א א א

Early Monday, Roger drove him to Boston where he stopped at *Riles & Sons,* a violin shop in Back Bay. There, under glass, lay a violin made by Nicolo Gagliano of Naples at the close of the eighteenth century. It would be sold with the certificate of J & A Beare, a long-standing and trustworthy institution in London. The instrument bore a striking resemblance to his first, the Weissman family violin his father taught him on after the war. In the same tradition, Weissman taught Joshua, who learned quickly and showed great promise. With an act mistaken for immense generosity, Weissman had given the violin away, no longer able to bear its proximity. Had the old violin now come back to haunt him? The grain of the wood, the way the neck rested in his hand, the manner it squared with his chin—all felt too familiar. Holding it out before him as a doctor might a newborn, he looked over its markings until finding a difference. He was relieved.

Roger tried to convince Weissman to play the violin in the limo, but he declined, saying he'd be willing to play once they returned home. And so it was that Roger, after all these years, finally saw the beautiful home and walked the wooden floors where Susan and Joshua had lived. As they sipped coffee together on the veranda while looking out to sea, Roger again warned that the storm, a nor'easter racing up the eastern seaboard, would hit the next evening. "It's going to be severe, sir, so best be ready," he said, and then he noticed the oak. He jumped up, arms outstretched. "This must be the tree that young Mr. Joshua always talked about. Oh, how he loved this tree!" He petted it as one would a favorite horse. Weissman was pleased to share the stories with someone who understood.

They moved back inside where he took up the new violin and, as promised, played three songs: a favorite of Susan, a favorite of Joshua, and then his own personal favorite, Mendelssohn's Violin Concerto in E Minor. When he finished, the little round man with the full heart and leaky eyes did his best to collect himself and then, handkerchief in hand, bid goodbye. "Thank you, sir, for your kind hospitality. This has been one of the best days of my life."

The house was once again vacant and echoing and lonely. Weissman filled the air with the violin, playing nearly continuously until 3:00 a.m. Despite a two-year hiatus from the instrument, his fingers took to the strings with minimal coaxing. The violin was elegant and the notes that sounded from the F-holes were sonorous and resonant, the wood having three centuries to age to perfection. The music itself was a comfort, better by far than his therapist. He especially loved playing Wagner backwards in rejection of the bigoted German's music.

א א א א

The next afternoon Roger dropped Weissman at the airport. The fast-approaching storm would trap him inside for three or four days, so instead, on impulse he bought a same-day $7,640 first-class one-way British Airways ticket Boston-to-London-to-

Warsaw to hear Górecki in Poland, where he should be heard.

Three days later, despite the aesthetic richness of the trip, he yearned again for the tortured memories of home. He returned in an expensive, drunken, first-class stupor.

Truth be told, Weissman was tortured by memories on either side of the Atlantic, trapped between nie wieder, *never again* and nie vergessen, *never forget*. It was a life-defining entrapment, the one constant of existence, the thread that coursed from past-to-present-to-future-to-death. But not beyond death, of that Weissman was certain.

"May the worms choke on it."

אאאא

Weissman staggered off the plane, hungover and exhausted from the long flight. Roger stood waiting at baggage claim, looking, if possible, even worse than Weissman. His eyes were swollen, his countenance broken.

The storm had been ruthless as advertised. No snow, but six inches of rain. And the winds—forty mph sustained, with gusts up to seventy-four. Joshua's oak had blown down, the roots ripped out of the ground. Half the veranda was crushed. Thankfully the house only sustained minor damage.

Knowing how important the tree was to the Weissman family, Roger rose in the middle of the night and drove to Second Cliff during the worst of the deluge, only to discover that the tree was already down and there was nothing he could do. He surveyed the outside of the house to make sure there were no broken windows or water damage and then waited in his car until morning light to check once again.

"I'm very sorry, sir. I know what that tree meant to little Joshua. It breaks my heart to have to tell you."

Weissman collapsed in the nearest chair, stricken. He put his head in his hands and sobbed beyond measure.

אאאא

The night was difficult. Darkness did not mute the pain of the still-collapsed oak across the shattered veranda. Alcohol permitted fits of sleep, but no rest. He dreamed of running over two baby ducklings on the pond road. In the middle of the road, he sat clutching their bloody bodies to his chest with one hand and pounding the asphalt with the other. As blood splattered his shirt and face, the mother duck attacked him again and again. His wailing awakened hollowed-eyed spirits that flew up and down darkened corridors, taunting him with woeful images.

Saturday came, and Saturday went. Weissman mostly lay on the couch listening to Górecki's Third. It was good he was so weak. Strength he might not have survived.

Sunday morning, Roger arrived at 9:00 in time to get Weissman to Logan for his Denver flight. Weissman apologized for dragging him out on a Sunday morning, but Roger would have none of it. "That's all right, sir. Really. As a rule I don't schedule myself on Sundays, I try to keep it a day of rest and, well, I'm a churchgoing man, sir. But in your case, I'm happy to do it. Being with you brings me wonderful memories. Your wife loved you very much, and I know she'd want me to be your chauffeur."

The rest of the trip was quiet, solemn. Roger parked at the curb and helped Weissman check his bags with the skycap. Then they returned to the limo together. Weissman offered his hand, and Roger, surprised, grasped it with a smile. The shake was warm and firm. When Roger started to move to the driver's door Weissman said, "A word with you, Roger."

Roger turned back around with a smile. "Yes, sir. What can I do for you?"

"I have a special favor to ask."

"Anything. Ask me anything at all. It will be my pleasure." His smile increased.

"I need you to take this." He held out a small envelope.

"What is this?"

"Something for you to remember us by."

Roger glanced at the envelope with a measure of alarm. "No, sir, I can't take that. No, no. Really, I can't." Then, looking at Weissman, a radiant smile came across his face. "You see, sir, I don't need anything to remember you by. The memories are in here." He patted his hand over his heart. "They never go away."

His eyes glistened. "Yes, I mourn, but I also rejoice. Since my wife passed—did you know her name was Susan too? but she spelled it S-u-z-a-n-n-e—since she died in childbirth along with our little baby boy, well, for many years I had a wound that wouldn't heal. And then one day God sent me to pick up your family. Something remarkable happened that day: my pain went away. My wound was healed. Your family was a gift to me. I guess you could say a gift of love."

Weissman looked at him, completely unsure what might be said after such a report.

"Roger, please do this one thing for me. *Please* take it. It is a small gesture from our family. It is very important." Again he handed over the envelope.

Roger looked him in the eye, unusual behavior for Roger with any of his clients. But, then, this was an unusual moment.

"Please," Weissman said. "I know it would make Susan very happy."

Though hesitant, Roger said, "Well then, it must be done." He took the envelope and put it in his coat pocket. "Thank you, sir. I wish you wouldn't have, but, I guess ... well, thank you."

"Wait until you get home," Weissman said, and he stuck out his hand again. They shook hands one final time, both with a tight grip looking at each other man-to-man. With that, Weissman turned and disappeared into the terminal.

א א א א

That evening Roger sat down and placed the envelope on his small table. The front said *Roger* in beautiful calligraphy. He opened the envelope and took out a small note card that read: "See Abraham Jonas of Alcock, Berner, and Fleigle Tuesday morning at 11:00. He is expecting you."

א א א א

A plush downtown law office? Roger had driven rich clients, but he'd never had *personal* business in lofty places. He was a simple man with simple tastes who believed in simple things. He lived in a small flat and worked only enough to pay his bills. His colleagues could have the stress if they wanted it. Roger just wanted to help people. He drove in order to be of service.

Mr. Jonas was very pleasant and got right to the point. He pulled out a file labeled "Antoni Weissman/Roger," opened it, and spread it on the desk for both to see.

The first document was the deed to Weissman's house on Second Cliff in Scituate. "It is currently appraised at $2.8 million dollars but of course market values change frequently," Jonas explained matter-of-factly.

The second document stipulated that ownership of all the items in the house were transferred to Roger. Each piece was listed with the appraised value, the total coming to $1.34 million. "The artwork and antiques make up the majority of that amount," Jonas said. "Dr. Weissman made it clear that any of these materials could be sold if needed to pay for expenses on the house, such as taxes, upkeep, and so on. The property taxes for this last year, for example, were $18,356. You are simply to contact me if you need funds and I will be at your service to sell any art or antiques as you wish. In such circumstances I can usually get the money to you within one or two weeks."

The third document was the title and also the keys for Weissman's Lexus sedan in the garage. "He has one like it in Colorado and said that he has no need for a second."

The fourth document was a signed agreement with a florist near the cemetery where Roger's wife and infant son were buried, stipulating that two fresh roses would be at the gravesite continuously for the next forty years. "Dr. Weissman explained to me that since each of you lost your wife and son in a tragedy, you shared a bond. His Susan and Joshua, well, perhaps you knew, but there was a horrible fire at the airport and nothing was recovered. What I am saying is that there were not even ashes. Nothing. He was never able to put them in a grave." Mr. Jonas's eyes were very sympathetic as he continued. "And this part he did not tell me, but I know it is true. He lost many relatives in the gas chambers and furnaces of Auschwitz... Let's just say that I know him well, and he is *honored* to be able to place roses on the grave of your wife and son."

They both took a moment to collect themselves. "And lastly," said Jonas, "Dr. Weissman wishes you to have this letter." He handed across a sealed envelope. "I am not aware of the contents. Please," he gestured. "Open it and read it, in case there are any questions that I need to answer."

The letter said: "Two weeks ago I wondered why I was making this trip to Boston. Now I know—it was to meet you. Our home in Scituate is filled with wonderful memories but also insufferable pain. I can no longer bear it. When the tree fell, I made the decision to destroy the house. Then I thought 'What would Susan want?' The answer was clear. You are helping me with a very difficult problem. Thank you. Your friend, Anthony."

Chapter 9

The Assignment

Rolling over, Kevin stared at the GE alarm that stared right back at him, screeching. He hit it and the noise stopped. The first morning after break was always tough. Four minutes later it wailed again: *Jeet! Jeet! Jeet!* He slapped it off, then looked at Wallace who slept like a corpse. Falling out of bed, he stumbled to the sink where he tried to rub the red out of his eyes. Wallace snored.

As Kevin went through his morning routine, he periodically threw things in Wallace's direction in a futile attempt to rouse him. Finally, after pulling on tan cords and a white T-shirt, he shouted, "Wallace, get up! You're going to miss breakfast."

For his trouble Kevin received only a vague, uncomprehending gaze.

"Wallace—I'm going now. I woke you up, so if you go back to sleep it's your own fault."

Wallace nodded imperceptibly and pushed to a sitting position as Kevin bolted out the door.

The cafeteria was known as "death on a stick" for their Tuesday afternoon corn dogs that, of late, were declined even by the ravenous. It seems a few months ago, uneaten corn dogs were thrown out in the dumpster and the next-day breakfast contingent witnessed the gruesome spectacle of three lifeless squirrels, each hunched in a final death convulsion.

Breakfasters were a rare breed but Kevin was a regular. Cafeteria food was the cheapest option for massive calories on a fixed budget. Monica, immersed in her supermarket romance *Desire in the Lilacs*, swiped his card and gave it back without lifting her eyes. He started down the line: two bagels with cream cheese, bacon, sausage, eggs, biscuits and gravy, cantaloupe, yogurt, milk, coffee and apple juice. Stepping into the main room, he scanned the tables until he saw Craig sitting with a couple of guys by a window.

"Hey," he said, walking over. "You guys prepping for Weissman's class?"

Craig looked up. "Wouldn't miss it. I'm a sucker for academic carnage."

Kevin sat down and bowed his head, habitually thankful even on a Monday morning. Once his reverent silence ended, he inhaled an entire sausage and joined the agitated conversation.

"Kev," Ryan said, "What do you think's going to happen?" Ryan, a third-year electrical engineering major, had more reason to fear Weissman than most due to a painful encounter four weeks ago. Not waiting for Kevin to finish his bagel, Ryan continued: "He warned us the assignment would 'destroy our innocence once and for all.'"

"I'm curious about his *gird up your loins* comment," Craig said smiling.

Kevin tried unsuccessfully to chuckle and swallow coffee at the same time.

"Yeah, laugh it up, Morgan," Ryan said.

"Sorry guys," Kevin said, as he shoveled in a mouthful of eggs. "Personally, I think we should just wait and see. Worry is a waste of time and energy."

They stared are him. Their futures were balancing on a knife's edge, and the best Morgan could do is lead them in a round of "Don't Worry, Be Happy."

"Worry is its own infinite loop," Kevin continued. "Only one sort of worry is permissible—to worry because one worries." They looked at him as if he were speaking Portuguese. "Hasidic proverb."

Ryan just shook his head.

Craig burst into a laugh and pointed at Ryan. "You're brain's so fried, Weissman's gonna eat you alive!"

"You Jewish or something?" Dylan asked Kevin. "Is that why Weissman likes you so much?"

Kevin looked at Craig who was laughing so hard he almost

spit out his mouthful of coffee.

"No, I'm not," Kevin said with a smile. "And what's that got to do with anything? Look, I'm just saying that worry is senseless." He paused. "How about this: 'Pray and let God worry.' Martin Luther."

"You a worry therapist?" Dylan asked.

"I'm not Jewish, I'm not Lutheran, and I'm not a therapist."

"What if I don't believe in God?" Ryan said.

"Well, now would be a good time to correct that deficiency," Craig said. "Prayer might be your only hope."

Together they watched the clock tick down to 8:52, and then they made their move. "Dead men walking," Ryan said as they left the cafeteria. Then he decided to keep saying it, all the way to class.

The classroom was full, only five seats remaining. A few new faces occupied the desks that were normally vacant. This was, of course, the ultimate compliment to a professor—unscheduled students coming to observe—but Weissman seemed almost to resent the attention. Kevin, Craig and the others scattered into the remaining chairs. Another group entered and started the floor seating. Word was out—this was the hottest ticket on campus.

Weissman sat on a metal stool gazing off into mountain peaks. When the clock struck 9:00, it was as if an alarm sounded in his head. He sprang from the stool, closed the door hanging a DO NOT DISTURB on the outside. The newbies laughed. Weissman shot them a stern look, silencing them for the rest of the hour.

"For three months we have examined complexity as a specific entity of concern," he began, pacing across the front. "Progress leads axiomatically to technological complexity; technological complexity leads axiomatically to tight coupling; tight coupling leads axiomatically to catastrophe. Catastrophe, therefore, is your inevitable future." At this, he stopped and stared at the students. "I repeat: *Catastrophe, therefore, is your inevitable future.* Unless you move to stop tight coupling before it destroys you. Clear diagnostics and forceful intentionality are required. Ignorance might be bliss, but it will not grant you a functional exception from the ruinous consequences of tight coupling.

"For those of you in a cerebral coma this past semester—and we all know who you are—let me be uncharacteristically kind. I will offer you a final illustration of the dangers of tight coupling in the remote hope it might fire up a few of your stuporous synapses. This example concerns global economic integration.

"Electronic money flies around the globe at the speed of light and huge amounts of hot currency can be invested or withdrawn in the blink of an eye. The resultant level of volatility is custom-made for crisis. This global economic integration—which has been a stated goal of several White House administrations—leads to tightly-coupled economic systems. And, as we have learned, tight coupling can lead to falling dominoes. Experts have lost the ability to predict when seizures will pass through world markets. This year's economic miracle turns into next year's economic debacle—and nobody knows exactly why. The truly frightening part is how often these changes are not even considered in the realm of plausibility.

"In 1997, Thailand's economy tanked and the Thai baht collapsed. No one cared. Officially, it was written off as a nonissue. Then, in order, it shattered the government in Bangkok, toppled the thirty-year-old Suharto government in Indonesia, devastated the Malaysian ringgit, popped the prosperity bubble in South Korea, sank Japan even deeper into economic turmoil, collapsed Moscow's stock market, and threatened China's stability. Millions were impoverished, governments were overturned, ethnic Chinese in Jakarta were brutalized, and Boris Yeltzin personally drained all the vodka in Moscow.

"The convulsion, however, wasn't exhausted. It jumped the Pacific, devaluing Brazil's currency. Next the contagion infected Ecuador. Ecuador was forced to close many of its banks, destroying overnight people's entire life savings. This in turn led to massive labor unrest and finally resulted in the fatal shooting of an Ecuadorian legislator and his bodyguard on the steps of the capital.

"So maybe the Thai baht is insignificant. But you should tell that to the children in Quito who now mourn their dead fathers. All compliments of tight coupling."

Weissman moved to his laptop and projected the dreaded final on the screen.

"For your final exam," he said, "your assignment is explained on this screen. It's worth fifty percent of your semester grade."

> **Using the principles of complexity and tight coupling, create a scenario in which a small group of people with significant resources in power and money can bring about one of the following consequences:**
>
> **A. Destroy a trillion dollars from world equity markets**
> **B. Begin a regional war**
> **C. Collapse the internet**
> **D. Cause an ecocatastrophe**

"Grading will be based on both the credibility and severity of the scenario. Extra credit will be awarded if you solve two separate scenarios, or if you can find a credible way to accomplish your goal through a single isolated individual rather than a group. You have two weeks to complete the assignment.

"Any questions?"

The room was silent. A girl behind Kevin lapsed into a coughing spell. Many shifted in their seats, no doubt scanning the insides of their expensive craniums for some way to orient the task.

Craig raised his hand.

"Yes?"

"The slide says 'Create a scenario in which a small group of people with significant resources...' What size group of people and what amount of resources?"

"No more than thirty people. As for resources, I will grant wide latitude. Any other questions?"

After a ten second pause, another tentative hand lifted. "Isn't this a socially irresponsible assignment?" Kirsten asked, the rather bold environmental engineering major who always seemed to provoke Dr. Weissman.

Weissman erupted. "The only socially irresponsible approach is *not* confronting this inevitability." He ran down the aisle and was yelling directly in Kristen's face. "Military war colleges work continuously on such scenarios. So should engineering colleges. It's only a matter of time until some small group has enough concentrated money and power to cause catastrophic global damage." His countenance was beet-red, stroke-like. By now, he was screaming at the entire class.

"The only *responsible* option is to recognize such threats as early as possible and make strategic plans to neutralize them. The only *responsible* option is to ignore the naïve who spew pacifistic nonsense about the basic goodness of the peoples and technologies of the world. The only *responsible* option is to ignore the cretins who believe somehow that optimism and the power of positive thinking can avert the inevitable and entirely predictable destruction of the human race at the hands of unbridled technological progress. The only *responsible* option is to ignore the half-wits who were surprised when Chernobyl melted down, the Challenger and Columbia exploded and the World Trade Towers collapsed. *Mit der Dummheit kämpfen Götter selbst vergebens.*"

Weissman rolled his eyes and turned his shoulder. "Any other asinine questions?"

"Very well," he said. "Forty years ago, Bertrand Russell reflected on technology gone awry and concluded that the problem is educated man himself. 'He has survived, thitherto, through ignorance. Can he continue to survive now that the useful degree of ignorance is lost? We are now asking a narrower question than can man survive? We are now asking can scientific man survive?'

"This," Weissman said, "is the larger question we are asking: *Can scientific man survive now that our useful degree of ignorance is gone?*" He turned to face the class and glared at Ryan. "You're dismissed. Have fun scripting Armageddon." Ryan squirmed.

The class rose as one and exited into the hall, anxious to flee the room. Kevin was the lone exception. After putting his laptop into his backpack, he shouldered the load and took a step forward. Turning around, Weissman was surprised to see anyone still there.

"Only the brave remain."

"I noticed you referenced God," Kevin said.

"You speak German?"

"Enough to get your meaning."

"Schiller. *With stupidity, God himself fights in vain.* I didn't think anyone would understand it, but it seems I frequently underestimate you."

"Would you still have said it if you knew I'd understand?"

"Of course. Your question?"

"You believe in God, then?"

"Why do you ask?"

"Just curious."

"Inquisitive," Weissman said. "I like that about you. What other way is there to be? You remind me of myself, minus the years and the miles."

"I'm flattered," Kevin said. "So?"

"My parents were reformed Jews and that's how I was raised. But for me, God died in the Holocaust. It would be glib to say that time healed that wound, yet I was getting to a place where I was ready to consider again..."

He stopped mid-sentence, turned and walked to the corner of the room where he could look at the mountains from the shadows.

After a long pause, he said with finality, "No, Kevin. I do not believe there is a God."

Kevin wanted to keep the discussion going, but something held him back. Weissman took advantage of the dead air, "What did you think of the assignment? Can you do it?"

"Piece of cake."

Chapter 10

Collateral Damage

WEISSMAN'S STUDENTS WALKED OUT CONFUSED, ANGRY, wobbly, the very ground under their feet pitching and rolling. American soil, the soil of Colorado, had always seemed firm and stable. Today it felt neither.

Some students complained about the destructiveness of the assignment; others the impossibility of designing such epic scenarios; others blasted the unfairness of deriving fifty percent of the semester grade from one absurd project—the lunatic professor obviously intended to flunk the entire class.

For Kevin, it wasn't the assignment that bothered him—he actually looked forward to the challenge. What bothered him was the essential validity of Weissman's thesis. We *are* in trouble. This isn't theoretical; it's our future. Perhaps alone in the entire class, Kevin got it. He saw it, understood it, believed it.

Craig waited outside and together they walked over to Kevin's truck, Dexter. After unlocking the decrepit 4WD Toyota with a screwdriver, they headed for the mountains. No better place to ponder the mysteries of the universe than dangling from a rope in the middle of a hundred-foot cliff.

Other students rendezvoused at The Circuit and started serious discussions over coffee. Most felt they were staring down the barrel of an impossible assignment, especially in such a short timeframe, and were brainstorming about how to salvage any kind of grade from the class. The visitors to the class, unencumbered by GPA concerns, were free to ponder the larger issues of national security, world sustainability, and technological culpability—conversations that generated more heat than light.

Some fiery thinkers, led by Kirsten, took a stab at elucidation and missed widely, but that didn't deter them from firing off electronic missives to the four corners of the globe, spreading the confusion. The first two hours saw at least twenty email permutations on the assignment, and it devolved exponentially from there. The blogs picked it up, and overnight, derivations of the deranged professor's assignment to destroy civilization reached the desks of both Reuters and CNN.

א א א א

When Weissman arrived the next morning, he found a note from the Office of the Provost on his door: "See me immediately. Bob."

Weissman set down his briefcase and struck out for Bowman Hall. On the quad he bumped into Michael who mumbled, "Good luck," as he passed.

"Long way from the philosophy department," Weissman said without breaking stride. A running joke between them, the entire humanities department at CIMT—consisting of nine offices—was relegated to the distal edge of campus.

Michael turned to rebuttal. "I'm no stranger to engineering you know. Circuits and such. Soldered a new switch in my blender just last week."

Weissman shook his head without slowing pace. It was a beautiful spring day, 68 sunny degrees, and he felt strangely ebullient. As he closed in on the administration offices, students stole furtive glances in his direction. Aside from Michael, he received no greeting nor gave any.

He entered the building and took the elevator to the third floor, then down the hall to Bob's ornate corner suite. Roberta, Provost Reed's secretary of nine years, did not offer any personal greeting but instead picked up the intercom phone and announced: "Dr. Weissman has arrived—Should I send him in?"

Turning to Weissman, she said: "Please go in, sir." He walked to the door and opened it without knocking. Roberta shook her head and exhaled softly.

Bob was pouring a cup of coffee from a four-cup coffeemaker he kept on his desk despite Roberta's protests. "Hello Anthony.

Thanks for coming. Can I get you some coffee?"

"No thank you," Weissman said as he settled into the overstuffed chair Bob kept for visitors. Bob sat back in his chair and cradled his mug while gathering his thoughts.

"I suppose you know why I've called you in," Bob said. He stopped, straightened a silver pen on his desk, took a deep breath, and shook his head. "I'm sorry Anthony, I sound like a high school principal. Please excuse me. We're both adults here."

He took another short break, tapping his desk with the silver pen, and then continued. "I can see that your finals assignment is going to be a political nightmare for me."

"I suspect it might." Weissman was not a patient man, and he had little tolerance for verbal foreplay, but Bob was family, and some nagging hook inside would not let him jettison Bob from the increasingly short list of people he gave a damn about.

"Did you have to do this?" Bob asked. "I mean, is there no other way to accomplish your goals—whatever those might be—without causing the uproar that's going to take place right across this desk?"

"No, Bob, there isn't."

On the surface, Weissman retained his composure but inside bristled at the accusations. If Bob led the way, permission would be granted to every other member of this jealous groupthink faculty to openly malign Weissman's motives, methods, and sanity. Not that Weissman cared about their opinions. What bothered him was being surrounded by swarms of small-minded people—it bothered him like flies bother a buffalo.

"The assignment reflects the topic precisely," Weissman said. "The assignment is grisly and disturbing because the topic is grisly and disturbing. And true, absolutely, inevitably true. Look, do you want to prepare these kids for a fairy tale world in which everything ends well, where people marry, produce and educate their progeny, own pets and hike, on and on for thousands of generations until the sun burns up, or do you want to prepare them for the world that's coming?"

"So far we've established two things," Bob said with obvious irritation. "You have an apocalyptic bias, and you're stubborn." He stopped himself and settled back into his chair, taking a moment to cool down. It didn't work. "Anthony, please at least try to appreciate my dilemma. I have to guard the reputation of this school. I have to ensure that future generations of students will come here, and I can tell you that despite your alleged veracity, all discussion about your topic has degenerated into alarmist rhetoric. People are being told we're an indoctrination center for a right-wing militia group or something. That's not just a political nightmare—it's unsalvageable. It'll be a black spot on the reputation of this school for the next thirty years. And all this for your precious, nebulous goals. I hope it's worth it."

Weissman closed his eyes and lowered his head. "You're right about the risk. I measured it before giving the assignment." He paused, considering whether to proceed. "But you must understand. All of this—" spreading his hands in a gesture that encompassed the school, "is collateral damage." Bob responded with a look of disbelief. "The world must be warned," Weissman continued. "It's my duty, and I must carry it out no matter the consequences to you, to me, or to this school. I owe your sister that much."

Both flinched at the mention of Susan. Weissman crossed his arms.

"As terrible as the possibilities of tight coupling are right now," he continued, "they'll grow exponentially. This generation—these students—it will fall on them to find safety for their families in a world of near infinite power. Yes, yes, yes, this power will be accessible for the purposes of good. Of *course* it will. I understand that. But this power will equally be available for the purposes of evil. People who don't comprehend this don't take the trends out far enough, they don't do the math, and they don't do the integration. As a matter of fact, the problems are so advanced that it might already be too late. I don't even know if future safety is achievable for these students. But I can guarantee you that it won't be if I'm unable to teach them. I don't want their blood on my hands."

He paused, jaw set firmly. When he spoke again, after an uncomfortable silence, his words held the conviction of a man whose people had stood at the receiving end of a shattering, unimaginable violence. "I will not stop. I cannot stop."

"Anthony," Bob said, nearly in a whisper, "you and I, we both know that education does not solve everything. That's the dirty secret of every hall of learning, isn't it? I don't need to remind you that Germany was the most educated country in the history of the world at that time. And it did not prevent them from being given over to evil."

Weissman glared furiously at him. "You will not reduce education to quantity solely! If students do not learn the right things from the right people, it's worthless. It's less than worthless. It's not about facts. It's not about information. It's not about science. It's about wisdom. About understanding. The academy must be about understanding. *Though it cost all you have, get understanding.* I'm ashamed to be instructing the head of this institution in a three-thousand-year-old teaching."

Bob stiffened at the insult. He stood abruptly and marched over to the corner window. With his back still to the desk, he said in a stern tone, "I'll get back to you."

Weissman stormed out of the room and slammed the door.

א א א א

Michael was waiting in the hall. Suspecting Weissman might need a friend, he had changed his plans and parked himself outside the provost's office. Weissman gave him a quick sideways glance. They walked briskly through the corridor, down the stairs, and out into the quad.

As they neared the middle of the campus, Michael broke the silence. "Well?"

"He's a fool." Weissman talked fast and walked faster.

"What about the assignment?"

Weissman stopped and faced him. "How did you know about the assignment?"

"A little white rat in the laboratory told me. Look Antoni, everyone on campus knows about The Assignment."

"He wants me to rescind the final. He thinks I'm going to destroy the school."

"What did you say?"

"A whip for the horse, a bit for the ass, and a rod for the back of the foolish."

"You said that to him?"

"No, I didn't *say* it to him. I *glared* it to him."

"Isn't that in the Old Testament?"

Weissman stopped again. "Yes, it's in the Old Testament." His countenance softened. "You and Kevin... I can't seem to slip anything over your heads. I'm accustomed to flinging my references randomly and with impunity and in any language—skewering people without them realizing it. But you two..."

They continued, now at a slower pace, to the Doane Science building. Taking the stairs to the second floor they entered Weissman's office in tandem. Weissman dropped loudly into his chair, put his hands behind his head and leaned back. Seconds later, he jumped up and marched over to the fish tank. With an unsteady hand, he scooped guppies out of their tank and fed them to the Oscars, not bothering to shock the predators.

"He would have us send lambs to the slaughter. Is that what the university has come to?"

Without hesitation, the Oscars followed their instincts. Soon the guppies were shredded, small parts loose in the tank, blood in the water. Both men were unable to take their eyes off the deaths. When there was nothing more to see, Weissman fetched his keys from the desk drawer, picked up his briefcase, and walked out.

א א א א

Driving the Land Cruiser was a small but reliable joy. With the warming weather of early April, Weissman had removed the doors, and the wind flowed past his face and across his body. Halfheartedly he attempted to conjure a sense of wonder at nature, to contrive some sort of primeval connection with the land to free his besieged spirit. But rather than seeing the beauty of the forest—the aspens flexing and swaying with the wind, not breaking but bending, and just enough—his eyes saw instead the bare patches on the forest floor, the brown pine-beetled trees, and a dead porcupine bisected by a Goodyear. A crow was plucking an eye out, tearing the little marble ball connected to the skull by a pink spaghetti strand. As the Cruiser drew closer, the crow took flight, eyeball in beak, breaking the strand.

Forget solace.

He sped into the mountains. He made a sharp turn into his driveway, then locked brakes and shuttered to a stop in front of his alpine shack. He sprung from his seat and headed inside. Caring nothing for food, he ground coffee beans and started a pot, his sole nutrition for the next twelve hours.

א א א א

The familiar sounds of Górecki signaled the nightly sealing of Oz. Weissman walked around the massive central table, stopping at each station where his presence triggered the screen and awakened it out of hibernation. Scrolling data greeted him, all compiled, compared, analyzed, weighted, and integrated by HAL-T, his tentacled computer network.

He worked through another exhausting night, taking a break every few hours to smoke a Cohiba in his smoking lounge. Then back to work. He was the earth's self-appointed everything expert, the only person who understood, the sole link between the world system and eventual annihilation. There was much at stake.

Just before drifting away for his two hours of sleep, he thought, "I hope inviting Kevin wasn't a mistake."

Chapter 11

This Will End in Tears

Kevin walked through the front doors of the convention site and let them close softly behind. The scene was like some *Discover* magazine's Engineering All-Star Team after a photo shoot. He abandoned the idea of recognizing anyone since he was a thousand miles from home and his only acquaintance was ensconced in the speaker's ready-room preparing for the keynote.

While helping himself to a donut and coffee, the corner of his eye caught sight of a shapely calf and elegant ankle adorned by red heels, a welcome relief among this otherwise stilted textile forest. He turned quickly but the leg's owner had already passed. He tried to follow her through the thick crowd, having some success by watching heads turn—the same procedure as tracking a wandering mouse at a Mary Kay convention minus the screaming. He finally spotted her bouncing brown hair just as she walked around a corner and disappeared.

Hmmm.

Glad for something to occupy him until Weissman's upcoming talk, he gave discreet pursuit. When he arrived at the corner, she'd already vanished into the crowded lecture hall. He opted for the middle doors where he was handed a program titled: *Global Implications of Future Technology*. Inside was a vast room, the seats of red velvet, the aisles carpeted. The stage was adorned with all the simplicity money could buy: a tasteful wood podium in the middle, four high-backed wood chairs off to the side, also upholstered in red.

Kevin continued scanning the audience as he made his way

down the middle section and picked a seat in the eighth row. The area around him filled in more than he'd hoped, capped off by a fat man in a blue suit who crashed into the seat next to him, shaking their whole row and bathing the area in a smell of overworked Old Spice. He looked at Kevin, smiled diplomatically, and said, "Sorry 'bout that," with a measured nonchalance, as though for years his sitting had been the occasion of minor seismic events.

Kevin twisted in his chair to glance at the clock mounted on the rear sound booth—8:55—five minutes to go—and then he saw her, walking down the aisle to his left, parting the crowd as she came. The first glimpse of her face—

He jumped up from his seat and turned in her direction. His shocked expression caused twenty others to turn in unison. They, too, continued to stare.

When he'd seen her in the lobby, he'd assumed people stepped aside out of knee-jerk chivalry brought on by her radiant beauty, as surefire as a rubber hammer to the patella. But as he saw Maggie's face again, he realized that she was indeed as stunning as he remembered. She was also something more. She was fearsome. There was an unmistakable dark intensity on her tan features. *What's she doing at an engineering conference?* Then it dawned on him. *She's an engineer? Unbelievable!* He wanted to text Craig immediately but wasn't about to distract himself from her entrance.

The sensible part of him wondered what damage he may suffer at her hands if he dared attempt contact. In that, Craig was probably correct. Kevin didn't fare well with the ladies even under optimal conditions, and she was certainly formidable.

"But she's so..." he whispered under his breath, in hushed tones like a paleontologist finding a completely new species of dinosaur. Among so many archetypal engineers, she is the archetype woman, Eve in all her glory, freshly clad in fig leaves after the Fall, and wearing a scowl of determination to find out how to reverse this curse laid upon her bones. The imposing look of one who will not ever resign herself to her fate as a woman, because she does not *have* a fate as a woman, damn it.

As she walked, his heart ignored the brain's dual policy of caution and reasonable pace, and he felt the start of what looked to be a fatal attraction. Emotionally hazardous, with a good chance for bodily harm to boot. Realizing the insanity of this kamikaze love instinct, he clutched for his heart, trying desperately to entangle it with reason, to wrest it back to the realities of her utter magnificence contrasted with his shabby curb appeal, but it struggled through his grip.

He smacked his forehead with his palm, in an effort to recalibrate his thoughts, to pull the stars into alignment—most importantly, to remind himself that she was *way* out of his league.

Five thick, sweaty phalanges clutched at his right hand. He looked over with a glance that swerved instantly to shock. The friendly giant was holding his hand with a fevered grip.

"Kid, I can see what you're thinking. And let me tell you..." He paused to catch his rasping breath, then whispered. "Life's too short to compromise in things like this. Take it from me."

The man mountain reached into his back pocket and pulled out his wallet. Kevin braced himself. Flipping his wallet open, the man came out with pictures of a blonde in her mid-forties. She was hot, if you could say that about someone old enough to be your mother.

"Let me guess—the one that got away," Kevin said uncharitably, not happy about the distraction.

The big guy continued, unflapped. "Actually, this is my wife, Barb."

Kevin's eyes narrowed. I'm confused enough already. I don't need this right now.

"I know what you're thinking," the fat man said. "But I've got more pictures to prove it." He dug deeper in his wallet, producing pictures of a man that looked like him minus significant girth, with a lady that looked like the aforementioned Barb. In chronological succession, he showed five pictures in which the man got heavier and the woman aged attractively. He grinned, with a sheepish hint of a blush on his bearded cheeks. "She's a good cook," he said, patting his ample midsection good-naturedly.

"I'm Thor, by the way. You know, the Norwegian thunder god? Big hammer? Barb's sense of humor, but it stuck."

He pointed toward the front of the auditorium in the direction she'd gone. "About the girl," Thor whispered in Kevin's ear, and curiously, Kevin didn't feel it to be an invasion of his personal space. "I know she looks invincible, like a great stone fortress. If you go about it like most men your age, fools throwing up ladders and climbing walls, you'll only get a hot oil bath for your trouble. But somewhere, somewhere…" he said this slowly, like a magician building up to a trick, "there's a key, something that will open it all up for you. Good luck, here's my card. Email me if you have any problems." He handed Kevin his card, gave him a good thump on the back, and with that replaced his wallet and sat heavily on it. He buried his nose in the program, grunting softly every ten seconds.

Kevin closed his eyes, sure that when he opened them he'd be in bed, staring up at the stuccoed ceiling, hearing Wallace snore, wiping crusted drool from the corner of his mouth. But with his eyes closed his ears were still open, and he heard a voice, close, that could only be hers.

"Excuse me," she said, as though it were a command.

He looked up to see her selecting a seat three rows in front of him, her seductive figure, the strong slope of her shoulders, her arms lean and tan, every bit of her curvaceous in just the right way. It was too much. Turning again in his seat, he looked back at the clock—9:00—in big red digits. I've just experienced two weeks' worth of life in five minutes, he thought. If this is what it's going to be like I can't take it.

Thor looked at him, his face concerned. "Buck up, kid, it'll be all right," he said. He paused. "I never caught your name."

"Kevin."

"Kevin. Right. Good name." Thor looked back at his program.

"Thor, are you an engineer or a love counselor?"

"Bit of both, I suppose." He laughed. "Engineering's the part I get paid for."

"Right."

א א א א

The lights dimmed, all eyes went forward, and the dean of the Stanford School of Engineering took the stage. He introduced Dr. Antoni Weissman: graduate of Harvard at twenty with dual degrees in physics and engineering; Ph.D. in physics from MIT; holder of thirty-eight patents; Director of R&D for Martin Marietta; Lead Project Researcher for the Department of Defense; Professor of Engineering, MIT; Nominated for the Nobel Prize in Physics for his groundbreaking work in DNA nanotechnology and molecular self-assembly.

"It is our privilege," continued the dean, "to have Dr. Weissman open our Fourteenth Annual Conference on Global Implications of Future Technology with his presentation: 'Tight Coupling and the End of Life as We Know It.' Please welcome Dr. Antoni Weissman."

Weissman walked briskly to the podium and started speaking. He did not wait for the polite applause to end. He did not say *Good morning—It's nice to be here—Thank you for the honor*. Instead, he burst through the gate as if a stallion held back too long.

"The world of the twenty-first century is flush with more. More and more, faster and faster is the mantra of our age, driven by the fury of progress. Technology is the preeminent engine in this irreversible drive toward profusion, and technology always amplifies whatever it touches: more information, more communication, more mobility, more speed, more weaponry, more power, more money, more complexity. As a result, technology and profusion are growing hand in hand in a historically unprecedented manner. The math involved is exponential in the extreme."

He did not look at his scant notes. His cadence was rapid, his pronunciation crisp, his demeanor authoritative, even authoritarian. "To be sure, none of us is surprised by this state of affairs. Indeed many here are immensely pleased by it, even proud, for we brought it about. A reason to celebrate. But is it? We must now be more careful." People were being confronted and they sensed it.

"Technology amplifies everything, yet that includes not only our successes but also our failures; not only our strengths but also our vulnerabilities. Our interwoven, convoluted, highly-complex systems have become an inherent part of high-tech societies and increasingly these systems are dangerously tightly coupled.

"It can be stated that progress leads necessarily to technological complexity; technological complexity leads necessarily to tight coupling; and tight coupling leads necessarily to catastrophe. Everything depends on everything else: a shudder here becomes a seizure there. Systems thinking and design redundancies—as valuable as they are—will not save us.

"These tightly-coupled complexities I speak of are not evil, and we should not reject them on false grounds. But too often they are inflexible, unmanageable, and autonomous. Their sheer size and complexity bring them beyond the scope of anyone's possible control. Inexorably, we are threatened with heightened vulnerability."

Kevin felt adrenaline surging both in pride and fear. He pulled back long enough to glance around the auditorium and observed looks running the gamut from shock to awe to jealousy to anger.

"Tightly-coupled systems inevitably lead to unanticipated consequences. In the past, such consequences were small scale and manageable. In the future, however, such consequences will be large scale, rapidly developing, and catastrophic in scope."

Weissman spoke even more quickly now, never looking down. "In any discussion of tight coupling, size and speed deserve special mention. We revere size and worship giantism. Progress begets growth; growth leads to bigness; bigness leads to complexity; and complexity leads to vulnerability. The inherent complexity of size has a way of removing the issues from our understanding or influence. A colossus is able to usurp power unto itself and perpetuate its own existence simply because of the intimidation of size. Bailouts are not so much a matter of justice or even mercy as they are a function of survival for all the others that would be affected should a collapse occur. The complexity of size threatens us with ultimatums and chain reactions if we do not yield."

Making no pretense of academic detachment, his words came from deep within. He asserted that ever-escalating speed, power, and complexity were suicidal, yet the vast majority of attendees *craved* speed, power, and complexity. A fight was in the offing, and everyone in the room felt it.

"We also worship speed. We not only want bigger, we want faster. Technology has been accommodating. Our current situation is like a bullet train, exploding out of the station and careening at breakneck speed. But soon it will run out of track, for we have navigated ourselves off the map. Under continuously accelerating conditions, experts have lost the ability to predict. Situations change from undetectable to overwhelming in the blink of an eye. Neither science nor intuition is sufficient to warn us under such exponential explosiveness.

"For the technological optimists, I admit that the positive benefits of technology are increasing rapidly. Very rapidly. This is a laudatory result of our life's work.

"Yet, never forget, the negatives are also increasing rapidly. Unanticipated consequences are real, persistent, and universal. Both natural evil and moral evil lurk at the fringes of each new development, exploiting each new opportunity for malicious intent.

"Even though the positive benefits grow faster than the negative damage, this does not mean we are safe. The positive and the negative must be accounted separately. For, regardless of the positive, once the quantum of negative reaches a critical mass—a threshold of lethality—it will prove fatal for the system involved. At that point, no amount of accumulated benefit can prevent the lethality."

From the corner of his eye, Kevin again noticed Maggie, the smoldering woman in her red dress. She flitted her head sideways and he tried to gauge her reaction to Weissman but was unable to catch more than a passing glimpse.

"Let me illustrate," Weissman said. "The most complicated piece of machinery ever built at the time, the Challenger space shuttle had a million components. If each individual piece of technology was examined separately, there were a million flawlessly constructed parts. A marvel of human engineering. Yet in seventy-three seconds it blew up. Therefore, it was not a marvel; it was a disaster. The disaster, however, is only understood when the faulty O-rings are factored in with the other 99.9999 percent of perfectly functioning parts. The disaster only becomes apparent when analysis integrates all the technology together to discover how one flaw doomed the entire project in a tragic fireball. Seven astronauts were murdered by tight coupling.

"In Paris, a sixteen-inch metal strip falls off a taxiing Continental DC-10, and five minutes later the metallic debris punctures the front tire of a following Air France Concorde. Tire fragments rip into an underwing fuel tank, plunging the supersonic jet into flames and killing 113 people. Only tight coupling could use small shards of metal to turn the world's safest airline into the world's deadliest airline in three minutes, ultimately dooming the entire Concorde enterprise.

"Tight coupling affects the energy industry as well. Elevators in Madison, Wisconsin, came to an abrupt halt. Throughout 3,000 buildings, including the entire University of Wisconsin campus, clocks froze at 12:05. Computer screens went blank, frying pans went cold, pop machines wouldn't dispense, and bowling alleys had to close. A lightning bolt? Student vandalism? It was a little red squirrel who ate his way through a power switch at an electrical station. The fact that one rodent can bring an entire city to its knees is a tribute to tight coupling.

"At Chernobyl, the reactor went from five percent rated power to one-hundred-twenty times normal power, a 600 fold increase, in four seconds. Thousands died. Again, tight coupling.

"Transportation and energy are connected intimately with manufacturing and jobs. A Midwestern corn farmer discovers that his fortunes rise and fall with the Eurasian climate. A factory worker is laid off because his product is interdependent with another plant on strike. A manufacturer discovers the distribution network has become so complex that a breakdown anywhere in the pipeline affects thousands of workers in otherwise unrelated occupations. This national and global interrelatedness is tightly coupled and increasingly precarious."

Weissman gripped the sides of the podium like an evangelist. Beads of perspiration formed on his brow.

"Take the Great Recession of 2007-2009, the worst economic downturn since the 1930s. Nobody saw it coming, no one knew how deeply, quickly, and unpredictably it would strike, or how long it would last. *Forty percent of the world's wealth was destroyed in five quarters.* Job loss was devastating and persistent. Volatility in all sectors was extraordinary. Russian markets shut down five times. Britain experienced the first run on a bank in 150 years. Belgium's government collapsed. Iceland was sold on eBay." His one attempt at levity came and went silently, Kevin noticed.

"U.S. housing prices fell faster than in the Great Depression—even though Greenspan said it was impossible.

Goldman Sachs lost a packet of money for something their computers said would happen once every 100 millennia. Citigroup spiraled downward, striking fear in the hearts of those who said, should it collapse, it could easily take the entire world financial system with it. The S&P 500 dropped like a stone until it finally bounced, perhaps appropriately, at 666. In essence, the economy fell off a cliff and was mere hours away from total collapse. How could this happen? Greed? Stupidity? Deregulation? Yes, of course. But also because of *tightly-coupled systems with insufficient circuit breakers.*

"Multiply the magnitude and gravity of each of the above illustrations by a million. Then multiply that result again by a million. You may think me sensationalistic, but I remind you that the math is exponential. Change is happening at breakneck pace, and if there is any potential for miscalculation in our thinking it will come from underestimating rather than overestimating the magnitude of this dilemma. Can anyone seriously believe we are exempt from danger?"

Weissman had been building his case for over forty-five minutes, though to Kevin it seemed like seconds.

In his argument, Weissman ranged far beyond engineering, showing a breadth that stunned Kevin. There was a profundity and a depth to his eclecticism, integration, and passion that CIMT students never experienced. He invoked not only principles of engineering, math, and physics but also of history, philosophy, theology, economics, law, military science, ecology, and futurology. He explained how progress worked by differentiation and proliferation, then applied this to limits adaptability and systems theory. He discussed, in turn, computer speed, the internet, software glitches, hackers, terrorism, information technology, communication, transportation, power grids, nuclear accidents, chemical plants, and pollution.

He demonstrated how electronic money, global economic integration, and tight coupling could combine to cause a global chain of defaults through software glitches, or how the world's banks could be shut down by a software bug, or how a banking panic at the right time could cause a depression, which in turn could cause a war, which in turn could trigger a nuclear exchange.

He detailed how, as complexity escalates, systems require

subsystems for monitoring and control, which then require additional subsystems, and subassemblies upon subassemblies, in a downward array of connected systems growing more inflexible in proportion to the size, and all dependent on each other.

He pled with the audience, but mostly he badgered them. At times he raged. For a few seconds, he lapsed into Polish. Another time, German. Then, catching himself, he stopped, his face contorting, his eyes blinking rapidly.

The darkest moments of his talk were reserved for a ten-minute discussion of potential uses of tight coupling by people with hostile intentions. If tight coupling was a serious problem even without factoring in human evil, how much more damage would be caused by the intentional manipulation of tight coupling by terrorists, criminals, narco-traffickers, and other nefarious human agents. What kind of annihilation lay in wait for the world systems when guided by the hands of evil genius?

"In summary, this thesis is about trends and thresholds. Most people are not trend perceptive and therefore, do not comprehend the full implications of current patterns. Such ignorance, however, will not exempt anyone from the inevitable consequences of tight coupling. For as these trends advance, relentlessly and irreversibly, they place us all on a collision course with the threshold of lethality.

"The six degrees of separation principle is perhaps truer than our worst imaginations. What if there are only six degrees of separation between technological optimism and technological disaster: only six quick, tightly-coupled steps between utopia and Armageddon? I fear, if we are not careful, this will end in tears."

He did not smile, he did not bow, he did not linger. He did not wait to receive applause. Abandoning his papers on the podium, Dr. Weissman walked across the back of the platform, down the steps, and out the door before most in the auditorium hardly realized he was finished.

א א א א

Kevin watched as Maggie stood up and walked out. He tried to gauge her reaction and noted, incredibly, that her icy countenance had thawed. Rising from his seat and sardining his way through a tight maze, he tried to follow but lost her in the dense crowd.

After a short break, the conference divided into workshops. Attempting to guess which elective she might select, Kevin narrowed the choices down to five possibilities:

1. Bioengineering and the Feeding of the Developing World, Dr. James Dube
2. Nanotechnology and the Third Wave, Dr. Michal Gordov
3. The Coming Revolution in Hydrogen-Powered Cars, Dr. Sylvia Kline
4. The Jolly Roger of the Twenty-First Century—High Crime upon the Seas of Cyberspace, Dr. Steven Godden
5. Slippery Jets and Friction Coefficients, Dr. Henry Wold

Judging she had a liberal's tragic eyes, Kevin figured it was either the Feeding the Third World or Hydrogen-Powered Cars. And since the hydrogen car seminar was taught by the lone female presenter, it had to be the one. He headed resolutely in that direction. Suddenly and without warning, a starving child infomercial flashed in his brain. He took it as a sign—feeding the poor.

Dr. Dube's lecture was near the main auditorium, and Kevin merged into a steady stream entering the room. He took up a standing position in the back where the whole assemblage spread panoramically before him. There were hundreds in the room, and the percentage of females was now much higher. At least on that score, he'd guessed correctly. He scanned the room repeatedly but could not see her. She was not here, at least not yet. Stragglers continued to make their way in, giving him hope.

At the stroke of 11:00, Dube closed the door. Kevin felt entombed. Standing in the back meant he would have to squeeze past a hundred tightly-packed bodies to make his escape. Leaving now was no more possible than opening a can of peaches with his bare hands.

Valiantly he tried to pay attention as the presenter droned on about the pros and cons of genetically-engineered food. The body heat in the place made it feel like a barn.

After what seemed hours, Dr. Dube issued his closing edict to a smattering of applause. Finally released from the professor's grip, the crowd spilt into the hall and, like maze-trained mice, followed the arrows to the dining area.

Kevin continued to seek the object of his affection as the crowd streamed past. Being an instinctual mathematician, he walked counter the flow to geometrically increase his odds. As he neared the distal end of the workshop area, the needs of his bladder exceeded those of his stomach, and he diverted in the direction of the restrooms. Walking backward so he could still examine the milling crowds, he pushed on the bathroom door when it slammed back at him. Turning to apologize, the door opened.

Maggie!

His brain frantically searched for some sort of appeal or precedent but found none. He looked up, panic-stricken, noticed her smirk, as she pointed to the blue universal sign with a female figure etched in white.

"Hi, I was just..." say something! "looking for a place to be alone for a minute. What better place than the ladies room at an engineering convention?" He gave a weak smile.

She grabbed his arm and pointed him toward the men's. Her grip was strong.

"Thanks..."

"Glad to help," she said and walked away. He disappeared into the men's room, dignity in tatters.

א א א א

Kevin picked out his food in a daze and sought an empty table where he could collect his thoughts and formulate Plan B. Suicide perhaps? A lone table in the back corner—the only one in the room—became his castaway island.

Putting one leg over the bench, he sat down sideways and lowered his tray unceremoniously to the table, where it thumped, rocked slightly and shuddered to a stop. He spilled his apple juice, and it filled his tray just shy of the gunwales. What of it? He grabbed the fork and stabbed his lasagna, cycling bites plate-to-mouth-to-plate-to-mouth, chewing without tasting, trying to recover.

Detached from his surroundings, staring at the back wall, he ate mechanically when a voice near him broke through his consciousness.

"...since you happen to be sitting adjacent to the only unoccupied piece of real estate in this cafeteria, I thought I would follow the traditional North American custom and ask permission to sit here. So, would you mind? Of course, we both realize this is just for form's sake, since I'll sit here anyway."

He sat up, straightened his tray, and looked at her with the slightest smile. "Well, if you're going to sit here one way or the other, you may as well sit here with my consent. In fact, you have my blessing." Much better, he thought, pulling his other leg over the bench so they could sit side by side. She sat across the table.

She made a drum roll with her hands. "Let the small talk begin. You go to Stanford? You look like one of Dr. Wold's little minions."

"Never heard of him."

"What? You mean you skipped the aviation workshop on Slippery Jets and Friction Coefficients? It was riveting. No pun intended."

"Actually, I don't think you can say that."

"Say what?"

"No pun intended. You made a pun—at least on a subconscious level. It wanted to express itself and it did so by interrupting the seamlessness of your caustic banter, catching you off guard. Fascinating. Maybe that says something about you, but then what do I know—I don't go to Stanford."

"Caustic?" She said. "Play the amateur psychologist much? That was the worst stab at psychobabble I've heard in all my years of therapy."

"Ah hah, I'm on to something, and now you're trying to cauterize the wound with sarcasm. Clever. But I digress—you wanted to make small talk."

Kevin heard a roaring laugh and turned his head. Thor shook mightily four tables away, stamping his foot on the ground. *I can see why Barb calls him the thunder god.*

"You go first," she said. "I don't like talking to strangers. I make them cry."

"A lady of such impeccable manners?" Kevin fought sarcasm

with sarcasm. Not that he intended to, as usually he eschewed it—in most cases it's a rather transparent defense mechanism. But in these situations you do what you must. "That's hard to believe. I gather you go to Stanford?"

"Yes, as a matter of fact, I do. I have Dr. Wold this semester, which is why I went to his lecture. Not too bad actually."

"And so your major is..."

"Aerospace engineering. And yours?"

"Major in astrology, minor in numerology."

She rolled her eyes and waited.

"Electrical engineering and computer science. Minor in philosophy."

"Ooh, an egghead. Impressive."

"You know, we've met before. That's how I know your name is Maggie. But you probably don't remember. Peak Engineering in Denver," Kevin said. "On the elevator. I was getting the tour along with my roommate, Craig."

Maggie stabbed her pasta with her fork, twirling it absently. "Ah yes, I remember. Well, I don't remember you, but I do remember the elevator."

"You were kind of on a rant."

"It was a well-deserved rant. My father is a malignant ass, and I tend to call it like I see it."

Kevin raised an eyebrow inquiringly.

"Let's just say he's got a lot of skeletons in the closet."

Kevin pondered this. "Doesn't every rich person?"

Maggie smiled and met Kevin's eyes, staring him down. "I wasn't being metaphorical."

Kevin withered under her gaze. Desperate, he decided to change strategy. Time for the Hail Mary—let it fly, all-or-nothing. "Dr. Weissman is my mentor," he said, carefully gauging her reaction.

She stopped eating and stared at him. "You know Weissman?"

Kevin smiled, seeing the tables had turned. "We're like this," he said, knotting his fingers together.

"Could I meet him?" Her sarcasm had disappeared.

"I can take you to see him, but you'll need to be careful what you say. He's touchy."

"I promise to be good."

Kevin looked skeptically at her then pulled a cell phone out of a shirt pocket and flipped it open. He pressed 1, then noted the look on her face that Weissman was on speed dial.

"Hi, Dr. Weissman, this is Kevin. I ran into someone who wants to meet you." Pause. "I don't know, I'll ask." He turned to her. "Do you agree with his thesis, or are you ignorant?" He spoke back into the phone. "She's in agreement." Pause. "What do I think? She's a bit pompous—" Maggie grabbed his little finger and bent it back "—but she is quite convincing." He turned to her again. "He wants to know a good place, so he doesn't run into a bunch of dim people who'll waste his time."

She thought for a second. "Junger's Emporium. It's not far."

"Give him directions." He handed her the phone and shook his bruised finger. *Ouch.* She bobbled the cell, a hint of nervousness creeping into her eyes. Then she spoke carefully, respectfully, and handed it back to Kevin. She jumped up and started for the door, leaving her barely touched dinner on the table.

He put the phone back in his pocket and ran after her. It was difficult keeping up until he took on a sort of loose-limbed power walk.

"By the way I'm—"

"Kevin, I know." He looked surprised, then remembered using his name with Weissman.

"So, Maggie, does your family live around here?"

"Let's leave them out of it."

What was this, strike four now?

"OK, so how did you decide to go into aerospace engineering? Not a career for a girl is it?" Kevin said, tongue firmly in cheek.

"No, it's not a career for a girl, which is why it's a damn good thing I'm a woman." Maggie sounded defensive. They walked a couple blocks in silence.

"Is that the place?" Kevin asked as he peered up the street toward the flashing neon lights signaling to everyone, including all manner of aerial traffic up four thousand feet, that here, larger than life or even the movies, was Junger's Emporium, home to 62 flavors of ice cream. For the benefit of those slow on the draw, the sign boasted that this was twice as many as Baskin Robbins. "Well, it's discrete if nothing else."

אאאא

Kevin and Maggie lingered inside Junger's until Weissman arrived twenty minutes later. He looked like a freshly-released POW standing in an entire store dedicated to health and beauty—needful, but slightly disapproving.

"Dr. Weissman, this is Maggie. Maggie, Dr. Weissman." She reached out her hand with, it seemed, a touch of reverence. Like Moses taking the stone tablets from the hand of God.

Kevin watched carefully to see if there were any recognition between them from the lobby scene at Peak Engineering Headquarters. Finding none, he was relieved. He didn't want Weissman dismissing Maggie outright as a diva—which she was, of course. But the next hour should play out on its own terms, and who knows where it might take him?

Maggie took a steering role in the conversation. "Let's get some ice cream." To Kevin's shock, she sounded bubbly. Fun. Weissman didn't give any sign of caring about fun, so she got down to business.

At the counter she said, "I'll take a double moose tracks on a waffle cone." Ed, the man in the striped shirt and apron, started digging.

Maggie turned her head and said, "What do you think about the possibility of artificial intelligence with the capacity for free abstract thought?"

Muffled slightly by the glass shield between customers and ice cream, Ed said, "I don't think we'll ever be able to come up with a device having the capacity for free thought, for to do so we would need to be able to come up with a truly random number, which is the starting point for a mechanical device being able to supersede its programming."

"I wasn't talking to you," Maggie said.

"Sorry," Ed said. "Just making conversation."

"I'll take Ed's answer," Weissman said. "Thank you, Ed. I'd rather have you in my classes than most of my students, Kevin here being an exception. And I'll take a single scoop vanilla on a waffle cone." *Weissman playing the peacemaker?* Kevin thought.

Ed dished Weissman an extra scoop, gratis.

Kevin ordered a double mint chocolate chip on a sugar cone and a glass of milk. Maggie paid. "That's more like it," Kevin said, and she kicked him in the shin, raising a welt. They made their way to a booth in the back and sat, Kevin and Maggie on one side, Weissman on the other.

"You wanted to see me?" Weissman nibbled on his cone.

"Yes, well, let me say I loved your keynote. Absolutely profound." She was animated and found it difficult to sit still. "The most fascinating lecture I've ever heard. You analyzed issues I've wondered about for a long time. I've always been suspicions of unrestrained technology, but I didn't anticipate all the implications you exposed."

"I wish I had that kind of support from my institution."

"You don't? Why not?"

"Politics," he said, making no attempt to hide his disgust.

"Well," she said. "This topic should be required curriculum for all engineering majors."

Maggie worked on her moose tracks, the wheels turning into her next question. Kevin sat watching her, trying not to stare. He pondered what twists of fate had brought them to this place, but calculating predictive probabilities would've been less reliable than forecasting the weather a month out.

Here he was, sitting round a table at Junger's Emporium with the most intelligent man and the most beautiful woman in the world, and he, Kevin Morgan, who was definitely above average. Yes, certainly above average.

The air at Junger's was filled to overflowing with a sort of 1950s optimism, the Great War safely in the past, the economy booming, suburbia being born, God blessing America. The staff here had gone to great lengths to put up a useable shrine to a decade of happiness, the "good ol' days" including a yellow '52 Ford pickup.

Kevin was snapped out of his trance when he heard Maggie ask, "So, given your—or should I say Ed's—answer about artificial intelligence, does that negate the possibility of a post-human species? Take the Matrix for a worst case scenario."

Weissman scratched his chin and downed the rest of his cone. "The possibilities for a post-human species are very real. It'll be a few years... We don't need to have truly free AI to have enough

AI to get the job done. You're familiar, no doubt, with the philosophical argument known as determinism, which is also known as fatalism in pop culture, or as compatibilism among philosophers splitting hairs. This argument says that there is no such thing as a truly free thought because our brains are finite, albeit very complex, physical organs. So every thought that makes its way into our heads will be, at the root, a mixture of previous thoughts we've had, memories we have, current sensory input, and so on. In other words, the information in your brain is all you have to work with, nothing else.

"Where the contested free will comes in is with the arrangement and organization of the seemingly original thoughts we have. Free will advocates argue that the immaterial portion of persons—the mind—is a generator of true original thoughts. These are combinations and extrapolations from data previously in our heads, but it's the way the thought is composed and expressed that makes it new.

"Conversely, if the brain is material only, then it functions along strict causal paths, and therefore no thoughts are truly free. I'm not saying I subscribe to this theory of persons, I'm just saying that it would apply to robots. The causal chain that results in a 'thought' would be so labyrinthine that it would appear free, though that would never be the case.

"Given that, it may be the case that there's no such thing as truly free thought, even in humans. Seems to me all we'd need for a post-human species is something with a very complex understanding and an ability to learn. Computers, as you know, already have the ability to learn by working from the known to the unknown in the way set out for them by their programming. There are some technical obstacles here when we start talking about a being that will function better than a human, but they are not insurmountable. It's a matter of time."

"I knew it!" Maggie exclaimed with righteous indignation. "Some of my friends are poorly informed on this topic."

"Do you think the human brain will be replaced entirely by a computer or will the computer simply augment the brain?" Kevin asked.

"The barriers to fusing brain and machine are quite substantial though not prohibitive," Weissman said. "In fact, many of the medical technologies in use now will be adapted toward that end."

Maggie had been pinching the top of her nose like she was trying to remember something, and finally came out with it. "You mentioned medical devices... I've been trying to figure out what sort of latitude our genes afford us. In my case, I'm hoping they allow me quite a bit. This goes back to your comment on determinism. Brilliant parents often have brilliant children, but I wonder about the types of intelligence. For instance, might a brilliant mathematician have a child that turns out to be a poet like Allen Ginsberg? Is intellectual capacity genetic in degree only, in kind, or in both? Since you're brilliant, I thought maybe you'd have an opinion, even personal experience." Maggie was entranced. Weissman's face had gone sour a couple sentences back, but she hadn't seen it.

Without waiting for Weissman's consent, Maggie, who had noticed his wedding ring, pushed on. "I was wondering if you have any kids? And, you know, how they're turning out."

Weissman clutched the right side of his face. Kevin could see the veins in his hand, and it looked thick and weathered and tired, like a steel worker's. The muscles clenched, relaxed, and clenched again, as though he were trying to pop his skull like a balloon. He pushed back his chair, stood up without looking at them, and walked out the door.

Chapter 12

The Relentless Wound

WEISSMAN'S BONES FELT LIKE LEAD. HIS HEAD WAS A subwoofer pounding the rhythm of his heart. He inspected the half-empty bottle of Absolut on the dresser and tried to remember anything after Junger's Emporium. With stiff, wooden motions, he pulled himself out of bed. Then he slowly dressed, tucking in only half his shirt, brushed his teeth, and packed his bags.

Kevin met him in the lobby. They exchanged a dozen words in the cab to the airport. Body language to be sure, and long, heavy silences, like two people with something terrible to talk about, though neither wants to.

They traveled first class back to Denver, Weissman giving Kevin the window seat, a peace gesture. A fine theory except it wasn't paired with any peace. When the flight attendant offered Weissman a lunch tray, he didn't respond. No acknowledgement even of her presence. He stared straight ahead, eyes red, mouth partly open, until finally lapsing into a fitful sleep. A slight drool escaped from the side of his mouth as the mountain turbulence bounced him up and down.

א א א א

Kevin stole quick glances in Weissman's direction while trying to eat his turkey wrap. Finally, he set it down. He managed only half his ice cream. Computer games didn't work, so he flipped through the in-flight magazine. He refused all beverages for fear he'd have to climb over Weissman to go to the bathroom.

As they sliced through the thin air over the Rockies, he finally found solace in the mountains. They reminded him of God. Unchanging. Anchored in sheer permanence. Unlike his father. Unlike Weissman. He wondered where Weissman would be in a year. His father had disabused him of the notion that living people tend to stay that way.

At least God wasn't going anywhere.

The 757 produced a small cloud of smoke as its tires smacked the Denver tarmac. Kevin woke with a jolt and leaned forward. He reached into his pocket and removed a piece of paper with two email addresses—one for Thor, the other Maggie—written in pencil on the back of Thor's business card. Yes, real, not an apparition.

The stiff silence continued, hovering over the two-hour limo trip home.

א א א א

Weissman instructed the driver to let Kevin off first then drive to his residence. Alone in the back seat, the pressure in his head began to ease.

As the black Lincoln turned onto Princeton Avenue and pulled up to Weissman's yellow two-story house, the driver looked with surprise, straining to see if he was at the right location.

"I'm sorry sir. Is this the correct address?"

"Yes," Weissman said, glaring at the swastika painted on the garage door. "I've lived in the same place my entire life."

He gave the driver $300, not waiting for change. This was expediency, not generosity.

The driver removed the bag from the trunk and handed it to Weissman who was looking at his Land Cruiser. All four tires were slit.

"There's some real rednecks 'round here," the driver said with disgust. "Want me to call the police?"

Weissman took the bag. "You'll do nothing of the sort." He hauled the bag into the house and locked the door behind him.

As the limo backed out of the driveway, Weissman collapsed onto the couch. The bag fell to the floor beside him, never to be unpacked.

Weissman lay face down, arm hanging off the side, trying not to move, occasionally trying not to breathe. Annoyed by the mottled light, he mustered enough strength to walk across the room and close the shades. The act felt monumental, exhausting, like ten hours of manual labor.

When he awoke, the room was pitch black. Not just the faintly yellow compromise of shades battling back the sun; this was the black of night.

He stumbled to the liquor cabinet and poured himself a glass of vodka. Then three more.

Chapter 13

Deep Greens and Blues

Kevin walked into his dorm room and booted up his laptop before unpacking. Force of habit. Wallace and Craig were both gone and he was in no mood to hang with the others.

Forty-two new messages, including, in his very own inbox, a communication from the one he could not put out of his mind, perhaps the only one who could capture his bruised mood and restore it to buoyancy.

> From: Maggie Foster
> Subject: *What's with the good doctor?*

He stared at it for thirty seconds, almost afraid to click it open, trembling in a high-school-junior-prom sort of way.

> Kevin,
> Maggie here. How's Dr. Weissman? I didn't want to be responsible for him redecorating his kitchen red-on-white in the style of Jackson Pollock using a shotgun and the human body, if you take my meaning.
>
> Make yourself useful and get him some Prozac. And tell him I'm sorry for whatever I said, or something like that. Ad lib, make it sound good.
>
> I hope you're doing better than he is.

Cheers, or not.
Maggie

So, we're emailing now, are we? As his hands reached the keyboard, a dread welled up. *In my fingers I hold the seed of this relationship. Plant it in loamy soil, Kev.*

> Maggie,
> Weissman just dropped me off. While I wouldn't say he's chipper, I don't think he's contemplating offing himself. Well, maybe...
>
> As far as his reaction, he tends toward melancholy. He's sort of your archetypal tragic hero, although I don't know all the details. Talk of family is out-of-bounds, as you discovered. Yet he thrives on discussing the end of the world. Go figure.
>
> If you see him again, confine the conversation to something safe—like the globe exploding in a fireball—and you'll do fine.
>
> Deep greens and blues are the colors I choose,
> Kevin.
> (I'll check on the Prozac.)

א א א א

> Kevin,
> Glad to see you caught my Jackson Pollock reference and therefore are not a full-on cretin when it comes to the art world.
>
> Keep me posted on Weissman. I find myself thinking of him frequently.

Good mountains in your section of Colorado? You a climber? Snowboarder? Don't tell me you're a skier. I loathe skiers.

Maggie

א א א א

Hey Maggie,
About the art world—I attended a two-part exhibit last month with the rooms like lobes of a brain: Degas on one side and Duchamp on the other. Artists are a strange lot...

He didn't talk the entire trip home—taxi, flight, limo. Six hours. But I'm used to it. He's like my dad that way. I'm not complaining. He paid for my trip.

Yes, we have sweet mountains. I board and climb. Climbing's good now. That's how I unwind.

I'm graduating next month. You?
Kevin

א א א א

Kevin,
I keep thinking about Dr. Weissman. He's mesmerizing, like a campfire winding down. Or an apartment building burning up. He's the sort of person who'll be idealized three generations downstream from us, whose life will be retold as a cautionary tale about the vindictive gods and what they do to people who know too much. They're crushed: Job, Socrates, Galileo.

I'm graduating too—twenty-nine days, baby. And with that, I'll be extricated from my dad Jeff's posh security blanket—that I did not ask to be wrapped with in the first place.

I sometimes wonder if there's a great cosmic reason we get the families we do. I doubt it. Whoever put me in my family deserves to die—but I digress.

I'm coming to Denver after graduation to cut the paternal umbilical cord. Maybe we could talk again about Weissman, without him there. Just so we're clear—him not being there would be for his protection, not mine.

What're you doing after graduation? NSA beatin' down your door?

If your climbing rope's more than five years old, buy a new one.

Divining my future from goat entrails,
Maggie

א א א א

Hey Maggie,
Your dad sounds scary.

I'd like to get together when you come to Denver. Before or after you cut your dad off?

I agree with your assessment of Weissman. He *is* like Job—good call. Job, who had the first existential crisis in recorded history. But the book ends well, and I pray the same for Weissman.

I think Sartre actually ripped off Job, plus the trappings of Parisian left bank culture circa the 1940s. Sitting on bony-butt wooden benches in Les Deux Magots. IMHO.

Regarding my post-graduatory-employmentary prospects, I've got a few leads on regional jobs. Electrical engineering plus network troubleshooting.

Any post-grad plans for you?

Maybe we could go climbing. Need a ride from the airport?

One more thing: What about your mom?

Do you have one?
Kevin

ℵ ℵ ℵ ℵ

Kevin,
If you want to know the truth, TV's my dad. Jeff's the guy who knocked up my mom. It's best not to confuse the two.

I liked the Job thing.

I do have a mom—Cindy. She and Jeff are permanently separated. Jeff tried to divorce her once until she blackmailed him. He looked at the threat, examined the dirt, did the math, and figured it'd be more cost effective to keep stringing her out on monthly installments. She tried out for *Survivor*, but they said she was too mean. Don't get me started.

She lives in Key West, in the arty district. After Jeff sold the Scarab, she bought a sailboat on which she hosts three-day drunks at sea for pretentious artists or anyone who can fake it passably. She's all about being entertained.

Then there's my sister, Ana-Lese. She was coked out of her mind a few years back, so I doubt she's got two functioning synapses to rub together. Lives with my Mom sometimes, when she's not in NYC modeling or being schlepped by someone in a promising local band. Her way of supporting the arts.

Jeff's an arrogant blister on a maggot's ass who doesn't care about anybody. Mom's a spineless money grubber who's distant. Ana-Lese is weak and in denial. I've written them off.

What about your family?

Climbing sounds good. I'll bring my stuff. I lead 5.9s. You?

I won't be needing a ride. Fosters don't *need* things. Got it?

And, lastly, my immediate post-graduation plan is to be an itinerant, following the example of the man in my life, namely, Cat.
Maggie

Chapter 14

The Genius Is off His Meds

Monday and Tuesday came and went without Weissman coming or going. He had no scheduled classes. Few, except for the watchful, noticed his absence.

Upon his arrival on Wednesday morning, another note awaited him from the Office of the Provost, tucked into a colored envelope and written on personal stationery with the heading *Congratulations from Bob Reed*. The message was not typed by the secretary but scribed in Bob's own hand.

Welcome back Anthony. Congratulations on your keynote. When you have an opportunity, please stop by my office.
Thanks.
Bob

Weissman read the note and threw it in the wastebasket. He went to his desk and picked up the picture of Susan and Joshua from the desktop. After examining it, he kissed it and gently placed it in his briefcase. Next he pulled opened the right top drawer and removed an aging black-and-white photo in an antique gold frame. This, too, he examined tenderly, then placed it beside the other picture. Finally, he retrieved from the drawer a leather-bound album crammed with family keepsakes. After laying it on top of the two pictures, he locked the briefcase. Walking to the door, he switched off the light, stepped into the hall, and left his office without even saying goodbye to the fish.

The cross-campus walk to Bob's office had a different feel from the previous week. Weissman's eyes were sunken, he blinked often, and passersby stared. Despite the mild spring day, he seemed afraid of the sun and placed his right hand above his eyes as if to shield himself from glare, unusual only because there was no glare.

As he entered the provost's office, Roberta was alarmed by the change: hair uncombed, five days of stubble, one button undone, mud on his shoes. His fashion sense was famously haphazard, but today marked a new low.

Roberta picked up the phone to signal his arrival, then turned and announced, "You may go in, Dr. Weissman."

Weissman just stood next to her desk, showing no response. The air smelled lightly of alcohol. After an awkward minute, Bob opened the door.

"Anthony, thanks for coming," he said with a smile. "Please come in."

Weissman followed Bob back into the office. It was left to Roberta to get up from her desk and close the door.

"Please Anthony, have a seat," the provost said, motioning toward the overstuffed chair Weissman always favored.

"No," Weissman replied.

Bob looked worried. Weissman's breathing was irregular with occasional long gulps. His reddened eyes could not stay anchored but flitted back and forth like a mother bird watching an approaching bobcat.

"How was the trip to Stanford?" Bob asked. "It's an honor for CIMT to have you headline in such an important engineering conference. I'm sorry I couldn't attend."

Weissman ignored Bob's words.

"Look, Anthony," Bob said. "Perhaps this isn't the best time to bring this up, but we need to talk again about your assignment. We've both had opportunity to think about it, and, as you know, school ends in three weeks."

Weissman was unresponsive.

"Any thoughts?"

"No, Bob," Weissman said, voice dripping with contempt. "No thoughts."

"Well, I can see this isn't going to be easy," Bob said, "so we might as well just put it all on the table." He sat down behind his expensive wooden desk, an oft-used fortified wall between provost and adversary.

"You need to void the assignment. There's no choice in the matter, really. I've been hearing from students, who are either up in arms or making jokes. The faculty won't give me a moment's rest. Parents are shocked—one sent a poem "The Charge of the Fright Brigade"—want to hear it? It's quite clever. Here, take a look." He slid the poem across the desk in the direction of Weissman. "It's gotten completely out of control."

"The worst," Bob continued, shaking his head, "are the trustees." His eyes conveyed genuine fear.

"They're on my back about this, Anthony. They demand not only that the assignment be voided but that you issue an apology. The chairman of the board, Randolph Harper, is enraged. You have his daughter in your class, Kirsten Harper. Recognize the name? Anthony, did you really call her a cretin in front of the class? Did you really need to do that?" He jumped up and paced in front of the windows.

"I bring you into CIMT and pay you a nice salary—far more than any professor in the history of the institution—and talk you up to the board. And pretty little Kirsten, with tears in her eyes, says you're a rude, intimidating, insulting, condescending chauvinist. Basically, the worst teacher in the universe."

Weissman was seething, his face twitching with anger.

"I'm sure you see my position," Bob continued. "We have no choice. Retract the assignment and offer a substitute. I don't care about grades—hell, give 'em all As." He looked up at the sky, his default position whenever office negotiations became tense. "This will all settle down in a couple of weeks—"

"I'll not retract the assignment," Weissman blurted, his face contorting.

"OK, I can see we're through here. I'll come to your class this afternoon and tell the students myself. This is not optional. The board left no room for negotiation. Listen to me for once. Would you please just *listen* to me, Anthony? We're talking about my job, about the school. Forget your pride, you arrogant—" He caught himself and didn't finish the sentence.

Weissman exploded, his face crimson. "You're just using me, Bob," he said. "You always have. You want my reputation. My money. You're nothing but a parasite." He turned, furious, and thundered toward the door. "You're a bloodsucker, Bob," he shouted over his shoulder. He opened the door and turned. "That's what you are, Bob. A bloodsucking parasite. Always have been." He stormed past Roberta. Before entering the hall, he turned and screamed at her: "*Nie pogrywaj ze mna.*"

Weissman left the building, rampaged across the campus terrorizing bystanders, jumped into his Land Cruiser and accelerated toward the mountains.

א א א א

Provost Reed, standing next to Roberta's desk, said in a low voice: "Get me Dr. Joseph Billingham, Massachusetts General Hospital, Department of Psychiatry. Tell him it's urgent. His psychotic genius is off his meds."

Chapter 15

Goodwill to Cats

KEVIN,
Sorry it's been a while since the last email. I've been busy GRADUATING. In case you were wondering, the people who masquerade as my family came, and I resisted the urge to do them bodily harm. Cat came too.

I'll be in Denver over the weekend. If you're free (and even if you're not), I'll call you Sunday and tell you where and when to meet me.

Peace on earth, goodwill to Cats,
Maggie

א א א א

Maggie,
Yeah, I've been busy with the cap-and-gown stuff too. It's nice to be on the matriculated side.

I wanted to take some time off, like you, but landed a good job at Peak and they wanted me to start right away. I told them I knew the boss's daughter, so we worked out a compromise on the start date and got it moved back until June 19. They also hired my best friend, Craig, so we'll be rooming together. We just moved into our new apartment in Denver.

It'll be good to be a breadwinner and since I'll only be a breadwinner for myself I don't need a lot of bread but since I'm winning kind of a lot of bread I have more bread than I need and, let me tell you, it's been a long time.

I have some bad news to report. Dr. Weissman left campus four weeks ago and no one's heard from him. I didn't want to tell you. I was waiting, hoping we'd hear something. Also, his house burned down. Cause still undetermined. Forensics didn't put anybody inside. The whole thing's a mess. A black cloud over graduation.

Call me Sunday. It'd be great to see you.
Kev

P.S. Who's Cat?

Chapter 16

Hardball

Kevin and Craig slid their new sofa into its corner just as Maggie's call came through.

"Hi Kevin. I just finished with Jeff and need some caffeine. You free?"

"You bet."

"Children of a Greater Bean isn't far from my hotel," Maggie said. "I'll meet you there in half an hour."

With no more warning than that, Kevin was thrust again into the great escapade that was Maggie. Sometimes a season of love must also be a season of bravery. A life decision ball would start rolling tonight and be directed. They, man-and-woman, water-and-oil, fire-and-ice, would play games with his posterity.

Kevin ran out the door after dressing as urbanely as possible given what he had to work with, wanting to arrive in time to pay for her coffee. She probably wouldn't allow it, but he could at least attempt to start this off on a traditional leg. Show her where he stands.

The evening was chilly by May standards, the sky full of threatening rain. He fired up the sluggish-when-awakened Dexter, generally moody, even melancholic, but tonight the Toyota was a runner, a swirling storm of pistons, rocketing Kevin down the uncrowded side streets. He hoped he didn't see any cats 'cause he wasn't slowing for anything less than a dog.

He parked in a lot and looked at his watch. Twenty-three minutes—perfect. As he crept near the coffee shop window, he peeked in, there was Maggie, a mere fifteen feet away, and she again took his breath away—slim, tanned, beautiful as anyone he'd ever seen—but sitting at a table with two drinks. To make matters worse, across from her was a pushed-back chair with a coat draped over it. Just then, the first drop of water fell out of the threatening sky and struck him on the head. He looked up to commune with the darkness.

I was a fool not to see it. She was too good to be true. Right from the start I've been a fool. He turned up his collar against the drizzle. *What a mess.*

After a half hour of mortal anguish—or ten seconds—Maggie looked out the window and saw Kevin standing with a James Dean pout. She furrowed her forehead and motioned him in.

א א א א

"Why were you standing in the rain?"

"Trying to figure out your companion."

"Oh, that. I didn't want people bothering me. Happens a lot."

"It almost worked."

"Maybe you should stop jumping to conclusions." She gave him a coy smile.

"Could you please stop smiling like that?"

Maggie grinned wider. Kevin twisted her ear playfully. She chopped his forearm.

"I took the liberty of getting you a coffee. A double latte. Hope you don't mind."

"Good choice. How did you know what coffee I like?"

"I'm good at telling people what they like."

"Then how did you know when I'd arrive? This latte could have been cold by now, and cold coffee is a heck of a way to start things off."

"That would've been your fault for arriving late."

"Hardball, huh?" *Love is a many splendored thing,* he thought. He lifted the mug and took a long sip. "So how'd it go with Daddy dear?"

"Jeff needed to be straightened out. I'm an adult and will be treated that way. With him, however, that can be a dangerous thing."

"As in trench coats at 3:00 a.m.?"

"Dealing with Jeff is like detonating a nuclear bomb. You

don't know the full extent of the damage until the final cancer tallies come in from the perimeter of the blast zone. But I wasn't killed in the initial drop. So far, so good. I may catch some fallout, but that'll be later. No use worrying about it now. At present I'm free as a feeling in the wind. I've got time on my hands, my Volkswagen, my plane, my jeep in Alaska, and no student loans. Life is good. I am woman, hear me roar."

"You have a plane and a Jeep? You've been holding out on me."

"You've no idea. Anyway, we're not in that kind of relationship. I'm not even sure I'd call this a relationship."

Kevin smiled weakly. "Tell me about the plane and Jeep."

"1982 Piper Arrow turbo, low-wing, 200 horsepower Continental. It's a beautiful thing. The Jeep is a '97 Wrangler I keep at Salmon Ella's. Cat drives it when I'm not there."

Kevin dreaded this moment but knew it'd be coming. He hesitated, looked at the fire crackling in the fireplace, then asked, "Who's Cat?" He quickly added, as a distraction, "And what's Salmon Ella's?"

Maggie's face warmed.

"Cat. How to explain Cat?"

She rested her chin in her hand. "Well, I care for him. A lot. I think it would be safe to say that he has schooled me in the ways of love. He's the man in my life."

The words were uttered as though they were only tiny markers, regrettable for their insufficiency: they didn't shed light fully on what she was feeling, in the same way a lighthouse doesn't illuminate a craggy island for the passing sailor. It simply says, "I'm here."

Kevin had trouble discerning his tangled emotions at Maggie's latest bomb. Disappointed. Sad. Possibly furious at Maggie for leading him on. Or was she leading him on? Was that just his imagination? Was this the way men and women were friends? It struck him unlikely. Inside he was getting up to go, yet his body was unable to move. Finally she rescued him.

"Cat's sixty-two-years old," she explained. "I guess he's my honorary dad."

Shaking his head, Kevin wondered if he had the right to be angry, or if this was just something men and women do to each other. Unable to attain even the smallest semblance of clarity in his swirling emotions, he decided to keep listening and process it later.

"I met him at Salmon Ella's fishing camp. He lives there. Jeff sponsored a business trip five years ago and brought me along—I think to give the drunken fisherman something to gawk at when they were back in camp. If this strikes you a bit strange, you're starting to get the picture." She shook her head in disgust.

"Anyway, like always, Jeff was a Nazi about the fishing and made everything a big contest. So I told him to grow up and went fishing with Cat instead. Cat's kind of a squatter at the camp. He helps out around the place and cleans the customer's fish. In exchange he gets a tiny cabin to live in. It contains all his worldly possessions: cot, sleeping bag, table, two chairs, fishing rods, guitar, typewriter, three or four sets of clothes, the usual cooking stuff, maybe fifty books, and a half share in my jeep—my birthday present to him last year. That's it. He's happy. If you want to understand him, think of the opposite of Jeff and that's Cat. He's a lover, a poet, makes eight thousand dollars on a good year, spends most of his time fishing, and a bit of time fixing things. I love him."

Kevin was one-part interested in Cat, and nine-parts relieved he was old enough for AARP.

Maggie turned her attention to Kevin. "Enough about me," she said and seemed to soften a bit. "How about you? You know—your family, hometown, transportation, batting average, GPA, net worth, love life—whatever."

"I have a truck named Dexter—my transportation that doubles as my love life. He's an old, sturdy Toyota pickup featuring lots of authentic mountain scars. And a 1947 Triumph Speed Twin, still in pieces. Haven't ridden it yet."

"A Triumph?" Maggie said with a smile. "Where'd you get that?"

"It's a bitter story. I got it from my dad."

"I don't understand. A dad gives his son a motorcycle: where's the bitter?"

Kevin sighed, and looked away. He put his right hand on his forehead and scratched at his hairline. "He didn't give it to me, as such. I just got it. It's complicated." He sighed again.

"We've got time," Maggie said. Kevin searched her eyes for sympathy.

"Maybe," he said. "I'm going to refill my coffee. Want some more?"

"No thanks. I'm good."

He slid his chair back a little too quickly, took his mug, and walked to the counter.

The barista refilled the coffee. Kevin paid his dollar and returned to the table slowly.

"Thought it best if I started with a fresh cup," he said. Maggie nodded, waiting. "You sure you want to hear this?" She nodded again.

"I've only told a very few..."

She locked eyes and offered a soft smile. "It's all right."

"About five years ago, my father, Kevin Sr., just started talking less. Stayed in his room a lot. Cried about small things. None of that was normal. If there was a problem at work, he'd come home and brood—you couldn't talk to him. We didn't know why.

"This is when I went off to college. It wasn't easy going away, but you can't put your life on hold to help your dad who won't accept your help. That's what my Mom said."

"You can't help people if they don't want it," Maggie agreed, as though it were a law of the universe, no more negotiable than gravity.

"Yeah." He rubbed his eyes. "During that school year, my freshman year of college, my sister got pregnant. She was seventeen. She did it on purpose I think, to get my dad's attention. She wouldn't say that, but you could read between the lines. Anyway, it didn't have the desired effect, whatever that was. Dad blew up. He also moved out of the bedroom, slept on the couch downstairs. And when I say blew up... Wow."

He shook his head and turned away from Maggie for a few seconds. When he turned back, his eyes glistened. "She had the baby, by the way," he continued. "Named Andrew. Cute kid."

"Do you have pictures?" Maggie asked. Kevin sensed she was trying to give him a break.

"Let's finish this first. I don't want to have to start up again. I still can't believe it's real sometimes. My mom threatened divorce.

She didn't mean it, just trying to scare him into getting help. Pretty retarded strategy, considering the precedent set by my sister..." Kevin tapered off, unable, as always, to make any sense of this story.

"One night he left home and took the old car, a little tin can he used for commuting. It was ancient. We didn't hear anything till the next day. When we did, it was from the police. They're the ones who found him." Kevin's voice was husky, threatening to give out.

"Went too fast around a curve. Rainy night, hard to see—the headlights weren't the best. Slid into a bridge abutment. He wasn't wearing a seatbelt, and his head hit the windshield. It happened on a back road, so no one came by for a while. He bled to death."

"So, that's the story of my bike," he said, choking out a little laugh. "It was my dad's. It wasn't running when he got it. An eBay special—he drove to Kansas for it and planned in some nebulous way to fix it up. That's how I met Craig. I mentioned to a mutual friend at CIMT I had this bike that needed work. Craig volunteered, and he knows his way around a bike. I took him home on weekends so we could work on it together. Must've been horrible for him ... being at my house, I mean. My mom crying all the time, my sister pregnant and running around. It was about a month after the accident."

"Ouch," Maggie said, and shook her head.

"We were never sure what happened. There's a dark spectrum between suicide and a legitimate accident. The life insurance company gave us the benefit of the doubt and paid up. But I don't believe it: I think he killed himself. No use now casting about for blame, but it's hard ... to sit around the table and eat, the three of us, we look at each other and..."

After a moment's pause, Kevin wiped his eyes. "Anything else you want to know? I guarantee the worst is over."

"Let's see those pictures."

"Right." Kevin dug in his wallet and found pictures of a beautiful baby boy. He had three photos in one-year increments.

"Good-looking kid," Maggie said.

"What do you mean? He's a *great*-looking kid! Takes after his Uncle Kev." He smiled in delight at the three pictures spread out on the table.

"Just what I said, *great*-looking kid."

"He learned to say Java even before he learned Mama. Awesome. My sister was bummed until I pointed out he'd make her a million before he was twenty." Kevin picked them up and put them back in his wallet. "Speaking of geniuses," he continued, "you want to talk about Weissman?"

"Definitely," Maggie said. "But after Jeff and Kevin Sr., I need a break." She seemed remarkably at ease and took a sip from her coffee while looking slowly around the room. *She's so beautiful it hurts*, Kevin thought. He wondered if she was doing this to him intentionally. If so, he didn't object.

She reached across and touched him briefly on the top of the hand. "What else you got for me? The night's young."

Kevin blinked, then gulped, hoping it didn't show.

"OK," he said, trying to regain his bearings. "Let me tell you about Michael. He's my Cat-equivalent you might say. My second mentor, after Weissman. And he knows Weissman well."

"Shoot," Maggie said. "Since Cat coaxed me away from the edge of the abyss I've developed an interest in the role-model-mentor-superhero type. I hate to think where I'd be if it weren't for him."

"Michael teaches philosophy. Great teacher. A genius but too self-effacing to admit it. Ask him anything in the entire tradition of Western philosophical thought, and he'll know it. When he speaks, he sounds like a book—but in a good way. And he makes philosophy practical. That's not hard with Machiavelli. But it's a challenge if you're talking about Wittgenstein or Descartes."

"You're really into this philosophy and metaphysics, huh?"

"I think we all are—but not everybody realizes it. Take you for example. What do you think is ultimately true? What is the really real? What's the most basic stuff of the universe, do you think there's a God, and so on."

Not missing a beat, Maggie said, "One is truth. Two is the way of falsehood. You come to realize this through meditation. Meditation, however, is only a means to the end, and not the end itself."

"No offense, but you sound like a record. So you're Buddhist."

"Or Hindu. I didn't tell you yet."

"I'm guessing Buddhist."

"OK, you're right, but the point is, don't assume you know things about me. You may be surprised."

"Right. I understand your need to preserve the 'feminine mystique.' I'll give it to you."

"Oh, you will. How charitable of you to give me my feminine mystique. Here's something mysterious about me you didn't know."

She leaned further across the table, put her lips next to Kevin's ear, and lowered her voice ten decibels. "Did you know I almost killed somebody?"

She looked down and her speech became very slow and deliberate.

"He walked in the door to our house about midnight. It was unlocked. Jeff and I were the only ones home: Cindy was in Key West, and Ana-Lese hadn't been heard from in days. I was in the kitchen, and I saw this stranger coming. I reached into a drawer and pulled out a seven-inch serrated steak knife. The front hallway light was off, and I just had a small light in the kitchen. I didn't want to lose the element of surprise. As soon as he stepped in, he started looking around, trying to figure his way around the house without turning any lights on. He was wearing a long, black trench coat, and suddenly he reached in the coat to pull something out.

"That's when I rushed him. I jumped him silently and stabbed him in his big meaty chest. He was bleeding all over on his jacket. I got a good look at his face and thought maybe I'd seen him before. Once he got over the shock, he starts screaming like you've never heard. Jeff came running downstairs, and you should've seen the look in his eyes. Turns out this guy was coming to do business with Jeff. At midnight! And is there any family briefing about this? No. So who gets blamed? Me. Turns out I *had* seen this guy, from a picture on Jeff's desk earlier that day. Someone coming over to the house on business is rare, especially at midnight. In the dark. It was probably some cloak-and-dagger operation they didn't want anyone to know about."

She smiled in disbelief at the memory. "Anyway, loooong story short, it cost two hundred thousand in lawyer's fees to get me cleared. So I'll preserve my mystique, because it's not a put on. There are just some things I'll be keeping from you, and that's that."

Kevin eyes were riveted on the blanched knuckles of his thumbs.

"Sorry," he said, with what he hoped was sufficient conviction.

"Not your fault. That was eight years ago. While it never really goes away, time does at least scab the wounds over. I should be all right, with an occasional sleeping pill."

She stretched her arms out wide, making a Y shape, as though she were letting go a bird. It seemed she was trying, psychosomatically, to release herself of this. She smiled again, tired now.

Kevin opened and closed his mouth a couple times like a fish breathing, steadying himself to speak. "It was your choice to bring that up, you know."

Cutting him off, she said, "Shut up, we're past that. Tell me about Craig."

They talked about Craig, then Summer and Corey, then baseball, fishing, NASA, epistemology, blackjack, and finished by coming back to Craig's missionary family.

Maggie frowned. "Our family's experiences with Christians have been pretty nasty. They're always condemning us for having money, or for our heathen lifestyle, or workaholism, whatever. All of which is true, in a sense, I guess. I mean, even *I* condemn my family for those things. But it just leaves a bad taste."

"Don't prejudge Craig. He's a great guy. As a matter of fact, I'm a bit fearful of introducing you two. He tends to have an intoxicating effect on vulnerable women."

Maggie slapped his hands. "So I'm a vulnerable woman now?"

"I never said that. Quit acting so vulnerable."

She glared at him, and then broke out laughing. "OK. If he's so intoxicating, I won't prejudge the Jesus freak."

"You didn't judge me—and faith is important to me."

"I never suspected it."

"I don't know whether to feel complimented or embarrassed," Kevin said.

"Neither," Maggie said. "You just seem different."

"I don't know whether to feel complimented or embarrassed."

"Stop repeating repeating yourself."

"Is this some kind of infinite feedback loop?"

"You won't know 'til you catch up with yourself in a rear-end collision."

"Roger that," Kevin said.

"Anyway," Maggie laughed, "do you ever talk philosophy or religion with Weissman?"

"Yes. I'd love to again," Kevin said. "Can't find him. He's vanished."

"Any way to find out what's happening with him?"

"I've tried calling his cell. He's never answered, and he's never called me back. Maybe Michael has talked to him—he's the only faculty Weissman would trust."

"When can we talk to Michael?"

"Right now if you want." Kevin pulled his cell phone from a jacket pocket and speed-dialed the call. Michael picked up with the third ring.

"Hey. This is Kevin ... Doing well, thanks. Craig and I moved into our apartment in Denver ... Yeah, I'll start my job in about a month."

Kevin laughed, then steered the conversation toward Weissman.

"Actually, I was wondering if you've heard from Dr. Weissman? I'm with a friend from California who heard him speak at Stanford. We're both worried. I still haven't been able to reach him." Pause. "OK. Thanks anyway. Let me know if you find out anything."

Kevin hung up and looked over at Maggie. "Michael has talked to Weissman's brother-in-law, Provost Reed. He said not to worry. Weissman gets like this sometimes, but he always comes out of it. His emotions are cyclical, according to the provost, like the seasons in Fairbanks. They have four seasons, but winter is longer than you'd expect. Just between you and me, the provost is a piece of work." He took a sip of coffee. "Anyway, Michael's going to keep trying to reach him."

Maggie appeared both upset and perplexed.

"What do you think?" he asked her.

"I don't think we have much choice. Weissman's one-of-a-kind. I don't think we can, in good conscience, sit back and hope he'll be OK."

"I agree. Weissman's given the provost massive headaches, and I don't think Reed's very committed to helping the man. But I also don't know if us attempting to contact him will be helpful. I just don't know."

"Well I do," Maggie said. "We need to see him somehow. At least *I* need to see him even if you don't. I want to make sure he's OK. You never know, it might mean a lot to him. And I definitely feel responsible."

"What're we going to do, be his therapists?"

"I don't know. But tomorrow we try to find him. Glad to know you're with me on this."

"Yeah, right," he said, still trying to sort it out, including what he'd just agreed to.

"Good. We have an early morning ahead of us. You'd better go so I can get back to my hotel and get some sleep."

Kevin felt lost.

Maggie stood up. "Well, goodnight then."

Kevin stood slowly. "Goodnight, Maggie."

As he said this, she came alongside and gave him a quick hug. He didn't want to leave, but she pushed him out the door. Then she went to refill her coffee.

ℵ ℵ ℵ ℵ

Kevin drove slowly through the night, signaling turns a block too soon, seeing a steak knife slashing through a trench coat and coming out red. He wondered if he should frisk her next time they met, then he wondered why he wondered, then he wondered what frisking her might be like.

The apartment was empty, Craig gone for the evening. Kevin's laptop had one new message. From Maggie Foster, at the coffee shop.

This should be interesting.

"Kevin, JK. Never stabbed anybody. Had you going though."

Chapter 17

The Smell of Death

THE 7:15 A.M. ALARM SOUNDED AND KEVIN JUMPED OUT OF BED in the direction of the coffee maker. The night had been fitful, disturbed by persistent amorous feelings competing against a bloody dagger. True, Maggie's email helped calm his fears. But in the middle of REM sleep, even nonexistent daggers drip real blood.

And that she could concoct such a story on the spur of the moment!

The grinder screamed against the quiet of the morning as the beans were martyred for the cause. After making quick work of a big breakfast, he sat at the kitchen table in his pajama pants and sipped rainforest blend. Steam rose from the mug and dissipated in curls. The morning was delicate, perfect right now. The sun was rearing its sleepy head, the Denver smog softening its edges. Out his third-story window, he could see the commuting Highlanders and Explorers, status tools of choice for the class of suburbanites who have great imaginary adventures. Or, at least, if a great adventure came up, they would be ready. Chrome lettering on their tailgate says so.

Last night Kevin suspected life might change indelibly; today he was sure of it. He sat silently, pondering. As he tried to rope in the possibilities running through his mind, they scattered like wild horses on the plains, each going its own way and each vying for attention. Maggie will be here in fifteen minutes. Where is she leading me? What's happened to Weissman? Each question led to another in the confounding way that matters of the mind resist simplification.

Though reluctant to break the morning's spell, he put the remaining coffee in a travel mug and returned to his bedroom to dress. Opting for cargo shorts, a U2 shirt, sunglasses, and hiking boots, he was ready in three minutes. Craig still showed no signs of life when Maggie buzzed.

Kevin went down to intercept her at the entry, avoiding the possibility she would meet Craig just yet. Six feet plus of solid muscle, rugged charm, an exotic accent, a permanent deep tan? I need to sink my hooks in a bit deeper before introducing those two.

"Top o' the mornin' to ya," Maggie said as Kevin stepped out the door.

"And a bloody fine morning it is," he said in a poor Australian accent.

"I see my bloody knife has already affected your speech patterns," Maggie said, pinching him in the ribs.

"That story took six months off my life."

"You probably should keep this then," she said, handing him a seven-inch knife pulled from her purse.

"No thanks. When the police pull us over I don't want my fingerprints on anything that belongs to you."

"Most guys would love to have their fingerprints on things that belong to me."

Kevin knew checkmate when he saw it. He decided to yield. Maggie, with a mischievous twinkle, held her gaze on his face. He met it with a grin, then realized his mistake and looked away, terrified she'd notice his reddening face.

"Your face is red," she said. "Why's that?"

"Which car is yours?" Kevin asked, in a foolishly transparent attempt to change topics. "You want to drive?"

She poked him in the ribs again. "One, nothin'," she said.

Kevin tried to ignore her, all the while realizing his blush told the true story. She poked him again, enjoying her advantage.

"Say it," she insisted, "I got you—one to nothin'. Say it or we'll stand here all day."

After fifteen seconds of silence and another poke, Kevin responded. "OK, I'll say it. Maggie ... you were right. I should've taken the knife." He held out his hand.

Maggie threw back her head and laughed.

Kevin extended his hand further. "Give it to me."

"You want it?" Maggie asked.

"Or else we'll stand here all day."

"If you insist," and before he had the slightest idea what was happening, Maggie stepped forward, causing her breast to briefly rest in his outstretched hand. She quickly stepped back, turned, and faced the parking lot. "Oh yes, the car. It's the black Navigator over there, the one with *Foster Enterprises* plastered on the door. But if it's all the same to you, I'd like to take your truck. More fun. This Navigator has no soul."

Kevin's knees were weak. His blood pressure had gone either fifty points up or fifty points down in the past five seconds—he wasn't sure. Same difference. He leaned against the nearest car, a Camry, attempting to stabilize himself.

"Dexter—" It came out an octave too high. He cleared his throat. "I mean, Dexter accepts your compliment and wishes you to know that he does indeed have soul. But he developed a back problem last night and needs to visit his chiropractor."

He leaned more heavily on the Camry, triggering its alarm.

"Let's get out of here," Maggie said, grabbing his hand and half-dragging him to the Lincoln SUV.

א א א א

As they slipped past the Denver suburbs, the air cleared to a lively blue, washed clean by the pine and aspens blanketing the hills. There was so much to talk about that starting anywhere seemed arbitrary. Instead they rolled on in a contented, if slightly uncomfortable, silence.

Kevin secreted a glance at Maggie now and then: she seemed to be enjoying herself. At peace perhaps? She certainly was a different person than the one he'd seen raging in the Foster building.

When the urban yielded to the rural, Maggie spotted a mule deer and pointed it out. Then she looked at Kevin. "You're quiet this morning," she said.

"I'm a little afraid of opening my mouth lest it become two-nothin'," he said with a smile.

"That happened half an hour ago. Now it's three-nothin'."

"See what I mean?"

"And," she said, "I can run up the score to four to nothin' in, oh, about thirty seconds." She looked over at Kevin with a devilish smile and Kevin half-feared, half-hoped she might attempt to prove it.

"But we have a job to do," she said, "so you should stop distracting me."

"I'll do my best," Kevin said, mopping his forehead.

"Actually, I was thinking how much Cat would love it here. Landscapes affect him deeply. He writes poetry about the effect of the land on a person's spirituality. I think he would find this semi-arid terrain fascinating."

"Do you know any of his poems?"

"You mean memorized?"

"Yeah. I'd like to hear one."

She cleared her throat.

Redwood taller than the sky
Moss thicker than my eye
This rock more weighty than my home
Here when my bones lie white in the ground
When my spirit's free, I'll see you
Old one with your mossy beard
Do not forget me
When we walk the ancient paths

Poetry, once again, served as a conversation killer. Neither was willing to break the moment until the essence had disseminated enough that they could speak without danger of seeming trite.

"What're your plans, now that you're freed the shackles of academia?" Kevin asked. "Besides flying around in your private plane offering your services to bipolar sages, I mean. Sounds so glamorous, doesn't it?"

"I don't believe in glamour," Maggie said. "It's just a moneymaking tool of the advertising industry. I have a 'glamorous' sister and all that glamour has made her totally incapable of making any normal human decisions. If it's glamorous, she does it; if it's not, she doesn't. No truth, no virtue, no nobility, no humanity, just tedious, brainless glamour." She hit the accelerator and pushed it to 76 mph.

"And you might be surprised what a hard calculation 'glamour' is. You've got to be very up on what's very in. If you're in front of the trend by a shade, that's the best. Then your act will still be in the collective memory when the trend comes into vogue, and you'll be touted as forward thinking. Of course, if you're too far in front, you'll be misunderstood. That's the terrain of suffering artists—no glamour there, just unpaid bills. Bonus points if you can associate yourself with charitable causes, you know, starving kids, clean water..." She passed a lumbering semi, then dropped back to 70 mph.

"About your question—I'm taking six months off to travel, be free, and—get ready for the cliché—find myself. Normally, I suppose, I'd plunge into a job, but Cat advised me to take some time off. He wants me to think through my family heritage and decide what kind of person I'm going to be."

"And you decided to be the kind of person who strokes out young men in the prime of their lives," Kevin said.

"Poor Kevin." She petted his knee.

א א א א

The CIMT campus was a relative ghost town, and Michael's office was locked up tight. The administration building was Kevin's second choice, and, sure enough, Roberta was at her station.

"Can I help you?" she deadpanned.

"Hopefully. My name is Kevin Mor—"

"I know who you are Mr. Morgan," she interrupted. "You are—or *were*—discussed quite frequently in this office." She eyed Maggie suspiciously, then looked back at Kevin. "What can I do for you?"

"We would like to inquire about Dr. Weissman. I haven't been able to contact him. Do you know where I can find him?"

"I can't give you that information," she said. "Confidentiality."

"Could I talk to Provost Reed?"

"I'm afraid the provost is out of the country and will not be back until the middle of July."

"Oh," Kevin said. "I'm sorry to hear that. Can you give us

anything at all?"

"No, I cannot," she said. "Actually, I don't have any information myself. But if I did, I still couldn't give it to you." Her eyes went back to the papers on her desk. Then she set down her pencil and looked at them again.

"Look. Dr. Weissman hurt this institution immensely. First, as you well know, Mr. Morgan, he gave that horrible assignment. Media all over the world have been running stories on the Colorado Institute of *Militia* and *Terrorism*. Several major donors have withdrawn their support, and twenty-three incoming freshman have changed their minds about enrolling here. The faculty are in open revolt. Frankly, it's the worst crisis this school has ever faced.

"No one has seen or heard from Dr. Weissman since he left this office five weeks ago. He walked out that door and disappeared," she said, pointing. "He didn't finish teaching his classes; he didn't turn in grades; his phone's disconnected; his house burned down. He disappeared."

She huffed loudly. "Speaking for myself, good riddance. I hope we've seen the last of him."

Kevin leaned over her desk. "I realize it's been a difficult time for you." He wrote on a card and handed it to her. "Here's my number. If you hear anything—anything at all—please give me a call. I'm concerned about him." He looked directly at her and said with gentleness, "Thanks for your time."

Just as Kevin and Maggie were closing the door on their way out, Roberta called them back.

"Is anyone in the hall?" she asked.

Kevin looked in both directions. "No. Just us."

"Come back in then and close the door. I shouldn't tell you this, but Provost Reed had a conversation with Dr. Weissman's psychiatrist. There was concern that he'd gone off his medications. It seemed a big deal. The doctor calls me twice a week from Massachusetts to see if I've heard anything." It was hard to tell from the look on her face whether she was disgusted or angry or sad. "That's it."

"Thanks," Kevin said, glad to finally have some information even if the data was disturbing. "I appreciate it."

א א א א

As they descended the steps onto the quad, Maggie shook her head. "Wow."

"Menopause."

"What?" Maggie said, looking at him. "Are you kidding?"

"I just know things," Kevin said with a shrug as he headed for Weissman's office. They were relieved to find the building open but seemingly unoccupied. Weissman's door, locked tight, was covered with taped notes.

Kevin looked both ways to be sure no one was around. He walked down the hall, into the bathrooms, and listened at the stairwells. Nothing. Returning to Weissman's office, he pulled a small packet of wires from his back pocket.

"What're you doing?" Maggie asked.

"Maggie, there are certain things you just shouldn't ask me about," Kevin said, looking her in the eye. "But this isn't one of them. I'm breaking into the office."

"You're what?"

"Shhhh."

Kevin picked the lock in twenty seconds. As he cracked opened the door, the odor was overwhelming, spilling into the hall. They looked at each other in alarm.

"Come on," he said. "We need to get inside so we can lock the door and turn on the light."

"I'm not going in there!" Maggie yelled. "There's a dead body in there. I can't do this, Kevin."

He grabbed her wrist and dragged her into the room before she could dig in her heels.

Chapter 18

Nice Doggie

Kevin quickly shut the door and locked it. Then he flipped on the lights. Maggie, eyes closed, was trying to scream, but Kevin had his hand over her mouth. She retched from the smell.

"Maggie," he whispered. "It's OK." He tried to straighten her up. "Look, I'm going to take my hand off your mouth now, OK? Don't scream."

He slowly released his hand. "Maggie, open your eyes." He shook her lightly. "Take a look."

She slowly opened her eyes. "What's that smell?" she said. "I think I'm going to throw up."

"I don't know. But I don't see a body."

Weissman's body was, in fact, not in the room. The air hung putrid and rank, but there was no evidence of a suicide. No signs of violence. Except for the smell, everything appeared in order.

Kevin turned to the fish tank. Oscars and guppies were floating upside down, bloated and festering.

"Thank God," he said. He pointed at the tank. "There's the smell."

They clutched each other with relief. Despite the dramatic moment, it was not lost on Kevin that their bodies were pressed together. He lingered.

"Can we do something about those fish?" Maggie asked, breaking away. "They *reek*."

"In a minute," Kevin said. He ignored the stench and looked quickly around the room. He examined the shelves, then the desk. Except for the right upper desk drawer—which was empty—everything seemed in order.

Then, with some trepidation, he switched on the desktop computer.

"Kevin!" Maggie said. "What're you doing? You know they can trace the date and time of any computer activity."

"Hold on. Let me check something."

His fingers flew as he checked files and directories and documents. Two minutes later, he said: "Maggie, take a look at this. This subdirectory is labeled aurum. Recognize that?"

"Should I?"

"How about *Au*."

"The chemical symbol for gold," Maggie said. "Is that where *Au* comes from, Aurum?"

"Right. It's Latin for gold. And under that subdirectory is a shipping document to Anthony Weissman on Gold Dust Trail!"

"Where's that?"

"No idea," Kevin said, switching off the computer. "But it's a start."

He went to the fish tank, scooped out the dead fish and threw them into trash can liners. Knotting the bags, he tucked them under his arm, grabbed Maggie by the wrist and said, "Let's go. I'll explain everything after we're out of here."

א א א א

Using library computers, Kevin located Gold Dust Trail and within twenty minutes they were back on the road headed into the mountains.

"OK, I'm waiting," Maggie said, looking over at Kevin. "We've got an hour's drive, and you promised to 'explain everything.'"

"What do you want to know?"

"How did you get into the room?"

"I broke in. You saw that."

"How did you do it?"

"Easily."

"OK, genius, how'd you manage to get into his computer? I'm sure everything was password protected."

"Over the past year I've spent a lot of time in his office,"

Kevin said. "Sometimes just the two of us, sometimes with Michael, sometimes by myself."

"Wait. How are you hanging out in Dr. Weissman's office by yourself?"

"I'd be working on projects. He'd set me up on his computer and then sometimes disappeared for an hour. He gave me his passwords."

"Just like that?"

"Just like that," Kevin said. "I didn't even ask for them. He just gave them to me. I'll admit it seemed strange."

"Remarkable," Maggie said.

"I can't explain it; I just have this effect on people."

Maggie looked over and caught his grin. "OK. Third question: How did you know about Aurum? I mean, how did you suspect anything with gold?"

"Exhibit A: Weissman drives two vehicles: a late-model Lexus and an '84 Land Cruiser. When he drives the Cruiser, it's always covered with dirt and dust. That didn't make any sense if he keeps it inside his garage. Exhibit B: Once I spotted a pile of new pickaxes in the back of the Cruiser. Exhibit C: He always used two small ingots of gold on his desk for paperweights. Exhibit D: His hands were always rough—not professor-like, more like a miner's."

"Impressive, Sherlock."

"Maggie, this school is called Colorado Institute of *Mining* and Technology."

After a pause, he continued: "There's another item I should tell you about. The shipping document on his computer was for dynamite."

ℵ ℵ ℵ ℵ

As they climbed deeper into the mountains, the air became thin but deliciously pure, laced with fresh pine scent. The roads were increasingly pocked, almost as though you could see the tax dollars shrinking. After an hour, with Kevin navigating, they found Gold Dust Trail. Turning right onto the road, Maggie again picked up speed. She took a short, steep hill too fast and the front tires lifted off the gravel as they crested the top. The

Navigator slammed back down with a thud. Kevin hit his head on the roof. "You should wear your seat belt," she said.

Only five driveways opened onto Gold Dust Trail. The first four were clustered close to the main highway with labeled mailboxes—Erickson, Ebert, Hampton, Willoughby. At the end of the Trail, the final driveway lacked any identifying markings. It looked obscured, foreboding, and distinctly uninviting.

"Doesn't look like the entry to any property Weissman would own," Kevin said. "But it appears to be the only choice."

"Let's stop at the other houses and see if they know where he lives," Maggie suggested. She turned the vehicle around and stopped first at the Ebert home and then the Hamptons, the only houses visible from the road. Neither occupant recognized the name of Anthony Weissman, but then "folks out here pretty much keep to themselves." The edge in their voice suggested Maggie should do the same.

"I guess we might as well give that last place a try," Kevin said. "It's possible this trip was a wild goose chase."

Maggie drove back to the unmarked driveway and slowly turned into the ominous entrance. After fifteen feet, the path took a left turn where they encountered a large yellow sign—Danger: Beware of Dogs. They crept past the sign, the vehicle scraping against thick untrimmed brush. After another fifty feet, the driveway again turned, this time to the right where it finally broke into a clearing. Two hundred feet straight ahead stood a ramshackle white house. Hulks of old pickups, immobile cars, and appliances cluttered the backyard.

Maggie pulled off the driveway behind a tree that'd blown over in a windstorm, its serpentine root structure sticking six feet into the air. They both stepped quietly out of the SUV, leaving the doors ajar. After a quick survey of the property, Kevin turned to Maggie.

"See any dogs?" he whispered.

"No," she said, then added with a shiver, "I *hate* dogs."

"Watch my back," Kevin said as he started toward the house.

After taking ten steps, a sound echoed from the rear of the cabin like a door opening then slamming shut. It was immediately followed by a crescendo of barking and snarling. Kevin turned and ran as fast as he could for the Navigator, the sun now blinding his eyes. He looked back over his shoulder and saw two massive Rottweilers foaming as they streaked around the house. The gap was narrowing quickly.

"Hurry Kevin!" Maggie screamed. "Run!"

Suddenly both dogs slammed on the brakes and stopped, growling ferociously. When Kevin reached the vehicle, he and Maggie jumped inside and locked the doors.

"That was close," Kevin said, panting. He was sweating profusely.

Just then, Weissman stepped out the front door, his skin pale from lack of sun, with a large bruise on his forehead. His beard had gone wild, his hair twice its normal length and uncombed. He had lost weight, maybe ten pounds. He squinted into the sun, trying to see the intruders. The dogs, growling and barking, paced back and forth along an invisible line.

"Hey!" he screamed, "Get off my land! Who's out there? Get off my land! I'll let these dogs go, I swear I'll do it." He reached down and picked up a rock, throwing it violently in their direction. It missed by fifty feet, but the intention was clear.

From inside the vehicle Kevin stared at Weissman, stricken with shock at this man he'd known as unassailably strong. To see him so reclusive and unsightly was a real blow.

Maggie grabbed Kevin's shoulder. "See that remote in his hand? Those dogs are wearing shock collars. That's why they stopped. There's an invisible fence."

"I knew engineers were good for something," Kevin said.

Weissman pushed the button on the controller and released the dogs. In horror, Maggie started the Navigator and pulled a quick U-turn. The crazed growling dogs ran alongside barking with a primeval fury. They violently jumped against both doors, their thick claws making loud, horrible screeching noises as they etched jagged lines in the paint. They bit at the tires and scratched at the fenders. One leapt onto the hood, its open mouth gaping and drooling against the windshield. Its monstrous fangs scratched against the glass, and Maggie panicked wondering if the animal might actually be strong enough to break through. His clawing feet dislodged the wiper and the dog immediately, in a rage, dropped his head and snapped it in half. The broken, jagged wiper blade lacerated his gums and blood streamed out mixing with slobber and coating the windshield. The presence of blood made him even more deranged. His bark was deafening. Maggie screamed, hit the gas and then slammed on the brakes. The beast finally slid off. She sped past it, and finally they broke onto Gold Dust Trail.

Maggie gunned it and outdistanced the pursuing dogs. Stunned and speechless, she sped away, Kevin hitting his head on the roof again. Maggie slid through the stop sign, spun around the turn, then floored it, kicking up a small twister of dust and gravel. Both shivered as they raced from the scene.

"What happened back there?" Maggie asked.

"That was close," Kevin said, gasping, still trying to get his breath.

"What should we do?"

"Just drive. I'm thinking."

"Good idea." She was trembling.

Five minutes later Kevin broke the silence. "You've got your plane in Denver?"

"So."

"Let's use that."

"To what end?"

"It might give us a different perspective," Kevin said.

"I love flying and don't need any excuse to go up," Maggie said, still shaking. "But I don't see how doing a fly-by is going to tell us anything more than what we already know, namely that our boy needs some serious help ASAP, as in the men with straitjackets and the little white truck. We need to get inside his head, not fly over his house."

"Listen Maggie. Either we try to help Weissman, or we don't. If we don't, he's going to end up institutionalized. You saw him!" He paused and bit his lower lip for just a second. "So, yes, maybe it won't make any difference. Maybe there's nothing new to discover. But what can it hurt? We certainly didn't see much today."

"I saw enough. Let's get him a social worker and go home."

"Come on Maggie, you know what I mean. OK, I agree—he's psychotic. But we still know virtually nothing about his situation there."

"So whose problem is he? The family's. Maybe the school's."

"He has no family. None. And the school is finished with him. Listen Maggie. I lost my father. I'm not going to let it happen again." His eyes moistened just a bit. "And you, well, you flipped a dark switch at Stanford by asking about his children. We've both got something at stake here, and I think we both want to make a difference."

Maggie was quiet.

"Let me put it this way. What would your dad do?"

She looked over at him. "Nothing."

"How about your glamorous sister?"

"Nothing."

"And your mom?"

Chapter 19

A Hole in the Wing Is Worth Two in the Heart

AT 8:30 THE NEXT MORNING THEY ROLLED DOWN THE RUNWAY, Maggie completed her preflight checklist and obtained clearance from the tower. Kevin listened in awe through a headset.

"Training wheels," Maggie said, flicking his headset with her finger.

"More like a baby seat. You won't even let me touch the yoke."

"You've touched enough for this week." She looked over with a smile. She gunned it and lifted off.

Kevin had never been in a plane this intimate before. The sheer proximity of everything was both magnificent and a bit frightening. Here they were, in this marvelous machine, climbing over the trees, through the sparse clouds, the engine beating out a perfect rhythm.

"I can see why you like it up here."

"It's even better when you're the one flying," and with that she banked hard right and dropped the nose, as though falling out of the sky. Just when Kevin's stomach began to adjust, she leveled out and did the inverse maneuver, this time banking to the left and climbing. Kevin refused to protest, and soon he was beaming like a rookie riding a Harley who'd just swallowed his first sixty-mile-an-hour moth.

"Tough as nails," Maggie said, clapping him on the back.

"Glorious," Kevin said.

"It's spiritual for me."

Kevin nodded. He looked for a way to understand the experience, then he found it. "...*slipped the surly bonds of earth ... touched the Face of God.* I heard it somewhere."

"I love that poem. *I have slipped the surly bonds of earth ... Put out my hand and touched the Face of God.* Reagan quoted it after the Challenger accident. Know where it's from?"

"Where?"

"It was written at 30,000 feet by an Allied World War II pilot," Maggie said. "Died when he was nineteen."

They flew silently along the front range, then turned into Weissman's valley. Mountains came and went, falling behind as road signs behind a car. Kevin switched on his GPS, programmed the day before to pinpoint Weissman's house.

They spotted Weissman's cabin, and Maggie flew straight over as though she were making a bombing run. "What are you doing?" Kevin asked. "You're supposed to bank so we can see."

"Don't worry. I'll give you a good view." She turned to the right and began a wide circle, dipping the wing low. Kevin snapped pictures as fast as the camera permitted.

Weissman's old Land Cruiser was parked outside the door, and the Rottweilers patrolled the compound.

"This place looks as depressing from the air as it did from the ground," Kevin said. "Actually, I think it looks even more depressing."

"I'm not seeing much. I'm afraid this isn't going to help."

"One more circle. This time a little lower. I saw something catch the light behind the house." Kevin pointed in the direction of junked vehicles, and began taking more pictures.

"Anything?"

"Solar panels I think. In the bed of that rusted truck and on top of that old refrigerator."

"Look out," Maggie said. "Here comes our favorite stone thrower."

Weissman came out the front door and looked up. He followed the plane for thirty seconds, then dashed back into the house.

"OK," Kevin said. "Coast's clear. He went back inside."

"I'll just fly away for a bit and give you a chance to study the pictures. I can come back if we need more."

She followed the dirt road behind the house while Kevin zoomed on selected pictures with the LCD viewer. He spotted sections of at least six solar panels, one taking up the entire bed of a dump truck.

"Look," Maggie said, pointing. "This jeep road goes to that old mine shaft. Do you think Weissman owns that?"

"Not sure. Let me get some pictures." After spending a few minutes circling the mine, Kevin said, "Let's take one more swing over the house before we go. I want to see what kind of power lines he's got connected."

"Why?"

"Because of the solar panels. I just don't understand why he needs all those panels. The guy's got enough money to afford normal electricity. It just doesn't make any sense. If he's an environmentalist, fine. But why try to hide it?"

They circled back, Kevin continuing to photograph anything of interest. With the zoom he was able to spot power poles and lines running up to Weissman's house.

"Maggie, we better split. He just came outside again."

א א א א

Weissman stood in the kitchen waiting for his coffee to finish brewing when he first heard the plane. The dogs started barking and ran outside. A small plane was not unusual, but this sounded close. He stepped out for a better look just as it made a lazy circle over his house. His bloodshot eyes burned with the bright mid-morning sun as he followed the plane carving through the sky.

It kept circling.

"Black," he called to one of his Rottweilers, "what're they doing?" He bent over and picked up an old spark plug. "Get out of here." He winged the plug into the sky.

He ran back inside, through the kitchen, down the hall and into the storeroom. Picking up the phone, he entered the password. The floor section lifted and he jumped down the stairs two at a time. Sitting at his surveillance computer, he repositioned the camera on the roof top until it picked up the plane. "Piper Arrow," he muttered. Enhancing the resolution revealed the tail number. After a quick computer search, he tracked the ownership of the plane to Foster Enterprises.

"Foster! Two days in a row."

His hands shook with rage as he ran up the stairs and burst into his bedroom. Opening the closet, he pulled out a 30-30, pocketed some shells, and ran back into the yard.

ℵ ℵ ℵ ℵ

"Kevin, I think he's got a gun! Look! He's got a rifle!"

Kevin put down the camera. "What are you talking about?"

"Kevin! He just shot at us! I saw smoke come out the barrel."

"Get out of here! Come on, Maggie. Hurry!"

Maggie banked hard right, pointing the nose out of the valley.

"Look out!" Kevin said. "Another shot!"

"We're hit! He just shot a hole in my wing!"

"Really?" Kevin looked past Maggie to the left wing. "Any damage?"

"I don't know. I don't see any fuel coming out. But I can't see very well. Hang on—I'm going low." She dove straight down until they hugged the trees, then leveled off.

"What do you think?" Kevin asked. "Is it safe to fly?"

"I think so—not like we have a choice." She kept looking over at the wing. "Let's follow the road in case I need to land."

Kevin's eyes stayed on the wing searching for signs of trouble. And there it was—a thin stream of avgas coming out the hole.

"Maggie, we've got a problem." He pointed. The flow increased as she banked the plane slightly to the left. "It's coming faster now."

Maggie looked over at the spray. "This is not good. The right tank's empty from the trip up, and now the left's got a hole in it. The fuel level is dropping pretty fast. I don't know how much time we have. We better look for a place to set her down."

Both scoured the ground for a place to land. The canyon had steep rocky banks, and the floor was covered with Ponderosa pines large enough to rip the fuselage apart if hit at seventy miles an hour, the slowest an Arrow could land without danger of stalling.

"You thinking what I'm thinking?" Kevin asked.

"No choice but the road."

"Sure we can't make it somewhere safer?"

"The fuel is dropping too fast."

The road was a bumpy, pocked surface clinging to the side of the mountain. "Doesn't look too promising," Kevin said. "Ever land on a curvy runway before?"

"I don't think it's possible," Maggie said. "I hope it'll straighten out once we get further down the canyon—if our fuel holds that long."

Kevin understood that following the road down the canyon was, quite literally, a do-or-die proposition. If they didn't find a couple thousand feet of straight road, their options went from bad to worse. Landing in the creek bed would be suicide. Look for a hundred feet of grass and land, gear up, hoping the plane would skid to a stop before hitting a tree?

As they descended further the road finally straightened and was relatively level. "That's it," Maggie yelled. "That's our spot."

"Probably as good as it's going to get," Kevin said.

This plane that earlier had seemed a marvel of flight, now struck him as a flying death trap. All thanks to a single, well-placed .30-30 round. Shot down by his hero, the great Dr. Anthony Weissman? Hard to fathom.

"I'm going to fly over once to get the lay of things, then circle back," Maggie said. She came in low, 200 feet over the treetops, looking for rocks or huge holes in the road. "I've never landed on anything like this before, but that's our best shot. OK, I'm going to circle back around. If you're the praying type, now would be a good time."

"I am, and I've been." Though the raw terror hadn't dissipated, he felt a remarkable calm. "I think we'll make it. God's helping us."

She looked over at him like he was daft, then banked the plane and doubled back to make an approach. She lowered the landing gear and fully extended the flaps. The winds were gusting, the plane quaking. "I wish I shared your confidence."

Maggie bit her lip as she turned and lined up with the road. Her descent nearly brushed the treetops before they came to the straight portion of the improvised runway. She feathered the throttle, deftly manipulating the plane and keeping it just above stall speed. They touched the ground at 65 miles per hour.

The plane popped back up in the air, then came down hard, kicking dust and gravel. Maggie cut the throttle and put the brakes on full. The Piper careened toward the left, and she corrected the steering. They went back right, then straightened out again. The left wheel dropped into a deep pothole at 30 mph, jarring them and the plane.

Finally, mercifully, they skidded to a stop.

Maggie took a deep breath and peeled her hands off the yoke. "Any other brilliant ideas that might result in death?"

But Kevin had thrown open his door and spilled his breakfast on the wing. He wiped his mouth with the back of his hand, coughed, and settled back into his seat to catch his breath. "What did you say?"

Maggie rolled her eyes. "That happens a lot when people fly with me."

Kevin smiled grimly.

Now that the danger was over, the realization of what had just happened was setting in. "This is what I get for getting involved," she said. "We could have been killed."

"But we weren't. We're alive," Kevin said. "Don't you see? Didn't I tell you we'd make it? You had help, Maggie. I'm sure of it. I mean you've never made a landing anything like this before and you nailed it."

"So maybe I'm a great pilot."

"Oh, you're a great pilot all right. But I'm telling you, there's more to it."

"Well, whatever the reason, we're safe. Let's get out, I need to look this over."

The Arrow had one door, located on Kevin's side of the cockpit. He unbuckled himself and stepped onto the wing. The nonslip surface was slick with vomit so he had to be careful on the way down.

"Hang on," he said. "Let me clean this up before you come out. Sorry about blowing chum on your plane, by the way."

"The least of our worries."

Chapter 20

Want a Pickle?

KEVIN AND MAGGIE STOOD BACK AND TOOK A DEEP BREATH. "OK, we crashed," Kevin said. "We have a plane down. You know, Maggie, this is something I've never run across before. Congratulations on that."

"Hold on a minute. We didn't crash—we made a forced landing," Maggie said. "I just saved your life. I'd like you to acknowledge that."

Kevin considered for a minute. "Absolutely, you saved my life ... in a crashy-sort of way ... with help from the Lord God Almighty Himself."

Maggie chucked him in the arm. "Well, how about that. I never saved anyone's life before. Usually I'm on the other side."

"You hurt?"

"A little bruised from the seatbelt. How 'bout you?"

"Whacked my head when we hit the bump. Stomach feels like it's full of salsa and gasoline. I'll survive."

She stepped over and put a finger in the bullet hole. "Look what you did!"

"What *I* did? I'm not the one with—"

"Your idea to get involved. This is the price I pay—shot down behind enemy lines on a dirt rut in Nowhere, Colorado."

"Please," Kevin said. "We're not in the middle of nowhere. We get reception here." He pulled out his phone. No bars. "OK, so we're too deep in the canyon. I'll just climb up that mountain a ways and make the call."

"Make what call? Call who?" Maggie said. "I have insurance. Just call a flatbed to truck it out."

"Whoa. Wait a second," Kevin said with alarm. "You file an accident report and it'll get in the news. We don't want that. 'World famous lunatic genius, Dr. Anthony Weissman, AWOL from Colorado Institute of Mining and Technology, discovered living in a squalid shack with two killer Rottweilers, shoots down plane with favorite student inside.'"

"So what's your idea? Something tells me I'm going to regret asking."

Kevin scratched his chin. "OK, how about this. If I can get this thing fixed, can you fly it out? It might be the only way to do this under the radar."

"How do you propose to do that?"

"I'll call my people. They can be here in a couple of hours. They'll bring a truckload of tools and plenty of avgas."

"Wait a minute," Maggie said. "You've got *people*? What's that supposed to mean? And why should I trust them with my plane? I can't believe I'm even considering this."

"Listen, Maggie. We have at least ten guys at CIMT that fly. Probably more. Two or three have their own planes. Jim Adams just graduated with me and he's worked on planes for eight or nine years. He has his A&P license." Kevin didn't know if he could convince her, but it wouldn't be for lack of trying. "Let me see if I can reach them. Jim is working at the local airport with his dad—not far from here. Maybe a couple hours." He looked at her and his eyes lit up. "Once we took apart a Cessna and reassembled it on the roof of the Dining Hall."

Maggie stared at him. "That's supposed to convince me?"

"Good," he said with an exaggerated smile. "You look over the plane for any structural damage. While you're doing that, I'll check if my friends can come. After they get here, if you don't trust them, we'll go with Plan B." He cocked his head sideways. "Deal?"

"I suppose if my plane checks out, we could just shut down the left tank and fill the right. It might work. If anyone asks, say we ran out of gas. Which, technically, is correct." Then she glared at him. "You, Kevin Morgan, are a dangerous man."

"Thank you. That's the nicest thing you've said to me in, well, I guess in my lifetime."

"Make the call. I'll check the plane and pace out the distance to see if we've enough runway."

א א א א

Kevin called in the cavalry and got three takers. By the time two trucks showed up a few hours later the number had swollen to five. CIMTers stick together, and besides, everyone knew Kevin's propensity for exotic adventure. Translated: this might be the highlight of the summer.

It didn't hurt when Kevin mentioned rescuing a damsel in distress—a very beautiful damsel at that. As the average CIMT guy was romantically challenged, even the hint of a pretty skirt was enough to bring them out *en masse*.

Fortunately, Craig was off hiking the mountains. Kevin was still trying to keep the two apart.

Maggie didn't see any structural problems with the left wing or the landing gear and Jim Adams concurred. "No prop strike," Jim said. "Good job landing, Maggie. I'm impressed."

They shut off the left tank and plugged the holes, then put twenty-five gallons of aviation fuel in the right side.

Though Maggie thought she had enough distance to take off and clear the forty foot trees, Jim Adams and Mike Wolcott—both experienced pilots themselves—thought the plan smelled risky. Wallace, mostly along for the ride, suggested they tow the plane down the road to where it was paved, wider, and straighter.

Maggie looked at Jim. "Should be OK," he said, "as long as you go slow."

"Brilliant," said Kevin, patting Wallace on the back.

א א א א

It took an hour to tow the plane to a good stretch of road. "Well, it's not perfect, but it's better than rural Afghanistan," Kevin said.

He shook hands around. "I owe you one," he said. Maggie swept in and gave hugs. After squeezing Wallace, she kissed him on the cheek. The team looked shocked, mouths open.

Kevin seemed defensive. "She's just playing with you guys."

He turned to Maggie. "You better give them all a kiss now, Maggie. You owe them that, don't you think?"

"Maybe next time," she said as she climbed aboard. She turned and blew them a kiss instead.

"Sorry guys," Kevin said. He whispered to Jim, "Now you know what I have to deal with."

"You complaining?" he said.

א א א א

By 5:00 p.m., the Arrow had once again slipped the surly bonds of earth.

As they glided through the mountain air, Maggie kept a watchful eye on the wounded wing but felt increasingly confident they'd make it to Denver.

Kevin did what he could to review the photos on the camera. "Can't see much," he finally said. "We need a bigger screen."

Setting the camera aside, he turned to Maggie. "Any thoughts?"

"Other than grateful-to-be-alive?"

"I guess. Why did he shoot at us?"

"Maybe he was pissed you broke into his office."

"Or maybe he couldn't stomach a tiger-decorated airplane stalking his compound."

"Seriously, Kevin, I've been thinking. Perhaps we deserved this. Maybe we should just let him alone. It's a free country. I've always been pretty laissez-faire when it comes to intervening in people's lives."

Kevin didn't argue.

"On the other hand," she continued, "if he's going to wind up hurting somebody—or himself—I suppose we should do something."

"Unfortunately we just don't have enough information to make a decision," Kevin said. "We need to watch him or listen to him or get inside his head or get inside his house or hack his computer or ... something."

"Have you discussed this with Craig or—who's your philosopher friend?"

"Michael."

"Have you discussed this with Craig or Michael?"

"Craig's up to speed—we talk about everything. I haven't talked to Michael since the coffee shop."

"Time to consult. I mean, I'm just struck by the weirdness of the situation: it seems like we need to do something, but for the life of me I can't figure out what. I have conflicting moral intuitions about the whole enterprise. The right to privacy, the right to be peculiar and not be harassed, counterbalanced by the simple concern for one's fellow human. I don't know. We need help—and sadly, Cat's not here."

"Beep beep, back it up," Kevin said. "We don't need more people—we just need more information."

"Kevin, this is getting into dangerous territory with the possibility of crimes being committed—his and ours. If you have friends whose judgment you trust, they should be consulted."

Maggie was making sense and Kevin knew it. "All right, I admit it. You're right. Craig's the guy for the job. He's intelligent and perceptive, with a clear moral vision. Plus he's really strong. He's perfect. And I'll try to reach Michael again."

א א א א

As they landed in Denver and taxied to her spot, Maggie said, "Let's go back to your place and look at the pictures."

"Maggie—the first time, *I* need to invite *you*. So, Maggie, why don't we go to my place and look at these pictures?"

She feigned a swoon. "Love to."

As they pulled into the parking lot Kevin hoped Craig wouldn't be walking around in his skivvies. In fact, it was worse.

The apartment, predictably, was a mess. Kevin's Triumph engine sat on a pile of newspapers on their coffee table, looking vaguely indecent with the heads off and the pistons removed. Bolts and wrenches lay scattered.

Craig had just returned from a workout at the YMCA and wore baggy black shorts and a white T-shirt cut off at the sleeves revealing his giant python biceps. He walked past them into the kitchen.

On the face of it, Maggie took it all in stride. Kevin glanced down at his own biceps, then away.

"Craig," Kevin said, "come out here. There's somebody you should meet."

"I'm making tea. You two want any?"

"No and no."

Craig came out after setting the water to boil.

"Tea after a workout?" Maggie said. "A little strange."

Craig looked her in the eye. "Who died and made you my personal trainer?"

The tone of Maggie's face changed from joking to competitive and defensive. "Want to arm-wrestle?" she asked.

"You serious?" Craig looked over at Kevin, then back at Maggie.

"Always. Spot me a forty-five degree angle."

Craig gave her a "this has gone far enough" look, but she held his eyes with intensity.

"All right," he said shrugging his shoulders.

The two sat at the kitchen table and locked hands. Craig yielded forty-five degrees, and Kevin said, "Ready—Set—*Go.*" Maggie's muscles tensed. Craig got off to a slow start, not taking her seriously. It was a miscalculation that didn't last long.

"By the way, Maggie, this is Craig. Craig, Maggie."

Both grunted.

"No way to treat a lady," Maggie said.

"Your idea."

In the course of the next four seconds Craig tackled the project with earnestness and beat Maggie soundly. She did not look frustrated or wounded or angry, or any of the manifold emotions felt in loss. Instead she stared at Craig until it became uncomfortable for both men, a fact she understood but did not acknowledge. She then looked Craig up and down like a horse at auction, and finally said, "He'll do."

Kevin doubled-over laughing.

"Thank you, Captain Obvious," Craig shot back to Maggie. "Of course I'll do. The question is, do what? The question is, do I *want* to?" He looked over at Kevin. "*Kevin...*"

"We're on a mission."

"What've you got?"

"In the mountains," Kevin said fancifully, "lives one with knowledge unsurpassed among mortal men. About his presence is a shrouded and rarified air. He faces trials, many of which spring from a source within. In his land are many troubles, more every day. He is accompanied only by two lesser creatures, with evident musculature, both of ferocious temperament. We fear his cup of wrath will overflow, rendering our spherical blue-green abode unfit for man and beast, so great is his power."

Craig frowned gravely, so gravely that he pulled a jar of pickles from the fridge and, dipping them in peanut butter, ate loudly.

"You two are freaks," Maggie said.

"Want a pickle?" Craig asked. Dip, crunch.

Kevin continued, "There was a reason we were so consumed with vagrancy in our college years. We'll need every bit we can muster: surveillance, breaking and entering, drugging Rottweilers, hacking, taking the law in our own hands, and whatever comes after that."

"Nice to hear there's an upside."

"Freaks." Maggie spun around and sat impatiently on the table. "Kevin, would you quit playing games and explain to this Neanderthal what he's getting himself into?"

Both men gave her puzzled looks.

"I already did."

"He already did," Craig agreed.

"Oh, really. Tell me Craig, what's going on here?"

"Weissman, of knowledge unsurpassed among mortal men, is living a tormented existence in the mountains, with no human companionship, hence the rarified and shrouded air, so there is no one there to moderate him, and his fears are running wild. He is besieged by what's running through his mind, and given what we know about him from his classes, he is thinking about euthanizing the world. In his remote state, full of sadness, this would seem to him to be a better option, a more humane option, than letting events progress unfettered. You two feel a moral responsibility to stop him but felt the scope of the project was becoming too large for two people, so you're asking for my help. You want to watch his cabin, break and enter, gather whatever information is available, and make policy after reviewing the data."

Maggie recovered quickly from her shock. "We'll need you to drug the dogs."

"I know."

Maggie opened her mouth, but Kevin interrupted, "You two—it's so adorable—you're like instant family, you know that? Get you together and you fight like you've been doing it for twenty years." Making a show of wiping his eyes, he added, "It's absolutely beautiful." He scrambled for a tissue and dabbed his tears. Then he dropped the tissue, picked up a pickle, and said to Craig, "Let's hook up to the TV."

Craig adapted his laptop to their large screen TV and within minutes they were analyzing the fly-over photos. Craig was shocked at the level of Weissman's squalor. Picture by picture they sought clues. The man was wealthy, so why would he choose to live in such run-down conditions? Why all the solar panels, especially for such a post-Flintstone clapboard house that already had accessible power lines? And was that a satellite dish hiding behind the road grader? Why was he disguising it? What did the old mine have to do with anything? Why would he shoot at an airplane?

"What about just talking to him?" Craig said.

"We tried," Maggie said. "Not an option. First, we can't make it past the Rottweilers." Kevin winked at Craig. "And second, he obviously doesn't want to talk."

"Kev," Craig said, "you and Michael are perhaps his only friends. Don't you think he'd talk if he knew it was you?"

"Can't take that chance. He's so unhinged he might shoot me."

"OK. I'm in," Craig said. "What's the plan?"

"The first order of business is a stakeout," Kevin said. "We need to establish his patterns in-and-out, and what he's got for security. Someone with his money, technical ability, and paranoia, he's got to have a security system."

Maggie looked at Kevin, "I thought people installed security systems when they had something valuable to protect. Jewels, expensive cars, bank safes—you put up surveillance and alarms. Smarmy decrepit shack? It doesn't fit."

"We can't go too much on appearances," Craig said. "Weissman's the smartest man you'll ever meet in this lifetime. Don't underestimate him. Certainly he has computers in that house. And whatever he has on those computers will be valuable to him. Plus he just might have gold or cash or the deed to his mansion in Bermuda. Or the Ark of the Covenant filled with 280 pounds of antimatter."

"Freaks."

"We must begin with the operating assumption that he's got security beyond the Rottweilers," Kevin said. "But let's not belabor it. A stakeout—agreed?"

Finding no dissenters, they settled in to examine more photos on the big screen. Maggie sat between the guys on the new sofa but leaned toward Kevin. Craig took notice with an approving smile.

Most photos showed the old cabin and environs, with a second set of pictures following the gravel road to the mine. They looked at the power lines and attempted to spot any obvious security apparatus without success. Finally, they looked for possible stakeout locations and decided on a ridge well off the road and two hundred yards to the south of the cabin.

As the evening wore on, Kevin offered that Maggie could stay the night—she could use their bedroom, the guys sleeping in the living room.

"I haven't peeked in your bedroom yet, but something tells me I'd rather stakeout for a week in thirty below temperatures and fight Rottweilers for the last bite of food than sleep in one of your beds."

Craig looked at Kevin, "You told her about that?"

"About what?" Maggie asked.

Craig and Kevin laughed.

"Cretins." She marched to the door and slammed it on her way out.

א א א א

The next day was spent on preparations, and at 5:00 p.m. they piled into Dexter for the three-hour journey. Kevin tried to persuade Maggie to sit between them but she insisted on the jump-seat. As they entered the target area, Kevin avoided Gold Dust Trail and instead pulled off the main paved road and into the brush. The mile hike into Weissman's property was made in the dimming light with guidance from the GPS and blue-filtered flashlights.

Kevin led recklessly fast, not difficult because the underbrush was sparse. When they came to a small embankment, they regrouped and everyone checked in OK. "Let's not talk unless necessary," Craig said. "The wilderness has ears." Kevin scampered up the mound, then tumbled back when a sapling pulled out. He scratched his face on the branch and fell into Maggie who plummeted into Craig. Craig caught them both. "Thanks," she said, then added, "Don't get used to it."

"Chattering doesn't cook the rice," Craig said, grabbing some moss off a nearby rock to disinfect Kevin's wound and stop the bleeding.

"I think this one might turn into a nice scar," Kevin whispered to Craig. Maggie offered an opinion about Y chromosomes and retardation. When Craig threw a dirt clod, she tried to whack him on the shin with a branch, but he caught it with a quick motion that broke the stick in half.

"What's the matter with you two?" Kevin hissed. "We're on a stakeout." They headed over the embankment again.

They reached their destination on the ridge just as the full moon crested the horizon. It was a glorious night for late May. From their position they were able to look down on Weissman's house. The lights were on but without any signs of activity.

Their position was an old Jeep trail that afforded them a spot wide enough for three sleeping bags. They established a rotating surveillance schedule, keeping a notebook updated every fifteen minutes.

The dogs being Craig's responsibility, he took mental pictures of their territory and habits, looking for specific favored places where he could neutralize them. They never strayed outside a fifty-yard radius from the cabin—not even to chase chipmunks. With binoculars he could pick out the electronic receivers around their necks. He noted precisely where they stopped their chasing, and he mapped out the border for the electric fence. "I could simply stand at the perimeter when Weissman's gone, they'll run up to me and I'll tranquilize them."

Night and day they watched. Kevin's cut infected nicely, not too much, and he thought it showed promise, an opinion Craig supported.

Weissman left only twice during this forty-eight hours, both times with the Cruiser, and both times in the direction of the mine. He returned, dirty and sweaty, three hours later, always between four and five o'clock. The lights in the house were never turned off, not in daylight nor night, not when he was home or gone. Yet they also almost never noticed any movement behind the windows.

For two days they kept vigil, then broke camp and retraced their steps back to the truck.

"We know more than we did," Kevin said, "but still not enough."

"He's not acting weird," Maggie said. "Or at least not dangerous."

"We just can't tell," Kevin said. "I wouldn't exactly sign off on that place as a normal wholesome environment. He's ten standard deviations off the mean."

"Well, I'm not lying in the dirt with you two for another stakeout."

"Video surveillance," Craig said.

"Could you do it?" Kevin asked.

"Otherwise it would've been a wasted education."

"Settled," Kevin said. "Now, I could stand a hot meal and shower."

"Finally, a point we can all agree on," Maggie said.

"Showers are for wimps," Craig said.

Chapter 21

The Break-In

That night Maggie decided to sleep on Kevin and Craig's sofa, since they promised to be good and all. "Right," she said. "I'm a scientist who draws conclusions based on available evidence—and you expect me to buy that?" But the hotel was a hundred bucks a night and it was time to begin her frugality crusade.

The goal of these six months was to find herself, and it was a bit perturbing to be thinking about money. How ironic, how unbohemian, that it takes money to find yourself. Or is it just me? What about Kerouac—hopping trains, working odd jobs, getting by on apple pie, ice cream and coffee, with no more possessions than his clothes and pack? And Cat? The man lives in poverty but is the most contented person I've ever met.

Maggie, of late, was given to reverie. For once in her life, she had something important to do. Sure, the banter was nonstop and there was the mess of sleeping next to the disembodied engine of a '47 Triumph. But underneath, there was peace in the house and nobility in their purpose. In a few short days, the three had become bonded by common cause and an easy affection, so natural it was unnatural.

This brought about a sensation she'd only experienced rarely and for which she had no specific name—something akin to rest. Whatever it was, the Foster household knew it not. In time she hoped to understand the feeling better, but for now, it was enough to settle in and begin her journey in a good place.

אאאא

The next morning the trio made a quick return to Weissman's to set up a battery-powered surveillance unit Craig cobbled together, mostly borrowed from CIMT, as in "we'll-return-it-in-a-week-and-they'll-never-miss-it-in-the-summertime-and-this-has-to-do-with-CIMT-doesn't-it?" borrowed. It was based around a Sony 168 hour real-time VCR that the college wasn't using any more and supplemented by $200 of Maggie's money. First he mounted a camera forty feet deep into the brush from the perimeter of the yard. It had a clear line on the front door. Then he ran a twin coax cable a hundred feet further into the woods and there positioned the VCR unit and battery pack. Everything was weather proofed, then camouflaged to Craig's impossibly high standards.

Each morning before dawn, he made the long journey back to the site to switch out the batteries and retrieve the twenty-four-hour tape. He had the option of recording for seven days, but the battery needed more frequent replacement, and the group—driven by Maggie—was anxious to move the project along.

So, for the next several days, they took turns watching Weissman's activities from the comfort of their couch.

Maggie went jogging twice a day for her conditioning and sanity. Craig did pushups and lifted weights. Kevin, feigning intellectual superiority, refused to be intimidated by their "sweaty, bronzed one-upmanship." Craig boxed his ears.

Weissman, for his part, kept to the previously observed pattern of leaving for the mine every afternoon between 1:00 and 2:00 and returning precisely three hours later. The only exception to the blandness of the digital stakeout was Weissman's unexpected appearance on his front porch at 10:30 a.m. on the third day. He walked two-hundred feet to the south of his cabin, directly toward their video camera, then turned to one side and reached up into a tree working with his hands.

"Hey, guys!" Craig yelled. "Come take a look at this: I think we've got something here."

Kevin and Maggie ran out of the kitchen as Craig rewound the tape.

"He's not pickin' apples," Craig said.

"We just found the first surveillance camera," Kevin said.

"How do you know there're more?" Maggie asked.

"Because it's Weissman," Craig said.

"Let's check that spot next visit," Kevin said.

"Which would be...?"

"Tomorrow," Kevin and Craig said in unison.

א א א

They arose before dawn. By 9:30 a.m. they were reoccupying the same ridge as five days earlier. Beneath them, Weissman's house looked as bleak as a Dickens novel. Maggie felt a triple impulse: melancholy, pity, and fear. And, yet, there was a sense of excitement too. And camaraderie. This "finding yourself" is a bizarre journey, she thought.

Craig was the first to leave the nest, descending to recover CIMT's "borrowed" spying equipment. While Craig was gone, Kevin scoured the area with binoculars looking for any additional surveillance cameras. Upon Craig's return, he slipped down to circle the property for a closer look.

He returned an hour later. "I spotted four," Kevin said. "He probably has others, but I think I marked the important ones. There are two cameras that cover the front porch. We need to disable those two. That will allow us freedom of movement in that quadrant. Then we can approach the house from that direction."

"How will you disable the cameras?" Maggie asked.

"Ever heard of lasers?" Kevin said.

"Ever heard of manslaughter?" Maggie said, holding up a clenched fist.

"We'll set up a laser and aim it at the camera aperture. When we turn the laser on, presto. The camera goes blind."

"That's crazy," Maggie said. "You guys aren't sleuths. You're hicks. You need to be within the camera's range to sight the laser, which means Weissman will see you. And, secondly, when the laser burns out the camera, he'll suspect saboteurs."

"Maggie," Kevin said. "Trust us. We have what you might call experience in this technique. It has always served us perfectly."

"Actually, Maggie's right," Craig said. They both looked at him. "Remember the first couple times, Kev?"

"Long sublimated synapses are reemerging from the depths of my neocortex and they remind me, that, yes, Maggie has a point—"

"And..." Maggie said. She waited, then hit Kevin in the ribs. "And..."

"OK," Kevin finally said. "I admit we fried a camera or two. But if you remember, Craig, the cameras were replaced and shortly after, the technique was perfected. We were young. Not schooled in the ways of precision."

Craig turned to Maggie. "What he means is that a rheostat fixed the problem." Craig opened his backpack to reveal rheostats and batteries, while Kevin unpacked three lasers, all borrowed from CIMT, plus the scope from his rifle.

"I can't believe you two," Maggie said. "Just how many surveillance cameras have you installed? It makes me want to electronically sweep the shower tonight before stepping in."

"Accuse us of whatever you wish but we never used cameras for *that*," Kevin said.

"Never," Craig said, perhaps a bit too quickly.

"We don't do that kind of breaking and entering," Kevin added.

Craig heard a noise below and turned his attention to the cabin.

Maggie snuggled up next to Kevin. "Who said anything about *breaking*," she whispered. "There's such a thing as entering without breaking." She blew in Kevin's ear and unbuttoned the top button of her blouse. This was not propositioning, only tormenting. Both realized it. Maggie enjoyed power games and knew how to use her full arsenal.

"Maggie—"

Just then Weissman stepped out on the porch.

"Heads down," Craig said.

Weissman glanced up in the direction of the ridge, then scanned the hillside for ten or fifteen seconds.

"Did he see us?" Maggie asked.

"Not a chance."

Weissman walked slowly around to the back of the house. The dogs wandered the yard, playing with each other, digging holes, fighting over a stick. After five minutes, they all retreated inside.

"He looks rough," Craig said. "That hair and beard..."
"That's why we're here," Kevin said.

א א א א

They waited thirty minutes, and then Kevin and Craig descended to set up the lasers. Weissman's break with precedent two days in a row was unnerving. They proceeded with caution. Not only were they wary of Weissman making another unexpected appearance, but—just as Maggie had pointed out—they also needed to be sure the targeted cameras did not detect their presence.

The second concern was foremost in their minds. Both remembered Weissman's rifle and his obvious willingness to use it. If Weissman was looking at his monitors just now, they could all be dead within minutes. If not from his rifle, then from his dogs.

Craig volunteered for the close work, and Kevin did not question the choice. While in Africa, Craig had developed the ability to move quickly and quietly through any terrain. He now demonstrated that ability to perfection, sliding through the brush until he found a shallow depression just large enough to hide in. Peeking his head up, he could see both cameras. He felt confident that neither could see him. The first camera was the one they'd spotted by videotape the day before. The second was thirty yards to the west. Both were focused on the front porch. Once Craig had the lasers mounted, he sighted them with Kevin's scope. Then he unpacked the batteries and rheostats. The setup was ready.

Kevin and Craig climbed slowly back to Maggie. They shared a sandwich and rested until Weissman's departure for the mine.

א א א א

At 1:35, Weissman came out of the house, climbed into the Cruiser, and drove toward the mine. The dogs were nowhere to be seen.

"OK, guys," Kevin said, feeling no need to whisper. "This is it. You ready?"

Craig nodded. Maggie just looked at them.

"OK. Well, let's review the plan. First, we'll all go down the hill to our laser setup. When we get about thirty feet away, we'll need to descend very carefully so Weissman's cameras don't spot us. OK, Maggie? Then once we're there, Craig will flip the switches on our lasers while I recheck the positioning with my scope. If it works, Weissman's surveillance will go blind." Craig gave him a thumbs up.

"Second, the dog fence. The buried one—the electronic one. The dogs always stop at that line. We'll use that fence to our advantage, Craig—" he looked at Craig "—when you shoot them." Another nod from Craig.

"Third, Weissman's laser fence that triggers the dogs inside the house. I've marked it on the map here, where the transmitters and receivers are located. Also the mirror system that directs the beam around the house. This beam runs about 20 or 25 feet *inside* the buried dog fence. It's about a foot off the ground." He looked at both of them. "Got it? 20 or 25 feet *inside* the underground electronic dog fence."

"Concentric circles are not a conceptual problem, Tarzan," Maggie said. "The problem is how you're going to get past that beam. Step over it?"

"I'm going to walk directly into it," Kevin said.

"What?" Maggie said. "Are you insane?"

Kevin grabbed her hand. "It'll be fine. I'll start at the dog fence. I know exactly where that is. Then I'll walk slowly until I hit the laser. Once I cross the laser, the dogs will come out. They'll chase me and I'll lead them to Craig. He'll be hiding behind a bush. I'll be sure to give him a good shot with his darts."

"You're crazy," Maggie said. "That's like knocking on the front door of the bank just before you rob it. Besides, if you're so out in the open, won't Weissman's surveillance pick you up somehow?"

"We better hope not. Weissman's two front-door cameras should be dead at that point. As long as we confine our movement to within that quadrant we should be fine."

"Look, Maggie," Craig said. "The dogs trigger that system all the time when they're in the yard. So do deer and small animals. With the cameras disabled, Weissman won't be able to differentiate." Kevin nodded agreement, and both looked at Maggie. "Besides," Craig added. "It's the best way to get the dogs. The dogs are really our biggest concern."

"OK," Kevin said. "All agreed?" Craig nodded.

Maggie looked first at Craig, then Kevin. "Freaks," she said.

"Good," Kevin said. "All agreed."

אאאא

The trio descended the hill, slowing to a crawl as they neared the bottom. Craig snaked his way to the laser setup. He looked over at Kevin. Kevin first held up one finger, then two, then three. Craig toggled the switches. Kevin double-checked the position of the beams with his scope.

"Perfect," Kevin said. "Those cameras should be blind as bats."

Kevin stood and walked the rest of the way down the hill and into the yard without fear. He was now on level ground and about 200 feet in front of the porch. He walked forward to the point where the dog fence was buried. Then he stopped. He looked back, allowing Craig to get into position behind a mound of brush. When Craig gave him the sign, Kevin moved forward one step. Then he waited.

Nothing.

Another step. Nothing.

Another step. Nothing.

After the seventh step, the result he'd been hoping for—an explosion of barking inside the house. The back door swung open and shut, followed by the dogs rounding the house exactly as when they chased Kevin the week before.

He turned and quickly took ten steps back. Then he waited. The Rottweilers were closing fast, about fifty feet out. Kevin took a few more steps back through an abundance of caution— actually, raw fear. He was betting his life that Weissman had not deactivated the dog fence. But stop they did, barking and growling and clawing the ground in fury. They never even saw Craig as he shot them silently with his blowgun.

א א א א

It took fifteen minutes for the dogs to go down. At least the fight had gone out of them, enough for Kevin and Maggie to slip past.

"You have a couple of hours," Craig said. "I'll watch these critters." He poked them gently with his blowgun. No response. "Keep your radio on."

Maggie fidgeted on the front porch as Kevin picked the lock. Finally the door swung open. Kevin reminded Maggie to put on her gloves, and they went in.

The mess was epic. Tendrils of smell had wriggled through the door while Kevin was working the lock, but it didn't prepare them for the situation inside. As they'd assumed, the furnishings were spartan and utilitarian, the walls a monotonous off-white except for the occasional stain. The air felt as though it hadn't been circulated in a month.

"The dog smell is intense," Maggie said, gagging. Physical evidence of the two brutes was everywhere: corners torn off a couch, dirty paw marks on the walls, wood floor full of scratches, short black and brown hair clinging to every surface, dry food pellets on the kitchen floor like an abandoned game of marbles.

Kevin worked his way through the kitchen with difficulty and felt profoundly sorry for Weissman, that he'd been married and well cared for and now slipped to this.

"Everything's decades old," he said. "I don't see anything that looks newer than the 70s."

Next they went into the living room and bathroom. Nothing, except the same smelly mess. It was hard to believe anyone could actually live here.

"Remember that satellite dish in the backyard? So far I don't see any TV or computer," Maggie said.

Maggie opened the door to Weissman's bedroom. "Kevin," she called, "come here. Look at this."

He followed her in. The chaos of the other rooms was absent. The dogs had been kept out, and the room was clean and tidy. Everything was in its place. The bed was made up in military style with white sheets and a green wool blanket. Everything in the room—bed, dresser, bookshelves—was old but in good condition. Hooks on the wall held Weissman's crumpled suit and white shirt.

Opening the closet, Kevin found the rifle propped against the corner. "Take a look at this." He picked up the gun. "This is a hunting rifle Maggie, a 30-30. I'll wager it's the same one that almost knocked us out of the sky." He examined the chamber. "It's loaded. He keeps it loaded."

Maggie shuddered.

Kevin put the rifle back and knelt down next to some boxes on the closet floor. "These boxes are full of ammunition. He's got enough ammo here to fight an army. Hundreds of rounds. Maybe thousands. Why would he need so much?"

Maggie crossed the room to a vintage cordless phone on the nightstand next to Weissman's bed. She picked it up. "No dial tone. Looks like it's been a while since our friend paid his bill."

"I don't get it," Kevin said. "The rest of the house is a mess. Yet this room is pretty normal—certainly cleaner than mine."

"What's your point?"

"If he's as derailed as he looks, how does he keep this so clean? Cleaning requires a certain amount of health. You know, some attention to detail. It doesn't fit."

"Clean except for the dust," Maggie said, running her finger across the top of an old trunk. "This looks like it came across the prairie in a covered wagon."

"Maggie!" Kevin yelled. "What're you doing?"

"Oh, I'm sorry! That was really stupid. I'm really sorry." She slapped herself on the arm. "Can we put the dust back?"

"No, we can't put dust back," Kevin said sarcastically. He stopped and scratched his temple. "Actually, that might work. I'll get some dust from under the bed where he won't notice. Maybe we can distribute it across the trunk. See if you can find a piece of paper."

Kevin got down on his knees and looked under the bed. Unexpectedly, he found a violin case and Weissman's briefcase. Carefully, he slid them both out. The violin was covered with a thin layer of dust. He lightly brushed it off onto a piece of paper and then transferred this to the trunk, titrating the dust fall with engineering precision. Gentle blowing completed the makeover.

"What do you think?" he asked.

"Looks good to me," Maggie said. "Thanks." She was genuinely grateful. And relieved. Kevin meant adventure, to be sure. But he also gave her a sense of security. Never before in her combative life had she deigned to accept security from the presence of another.

He knelt again to slide the violin and briefcase back under the bed.

"What's in the briefcase?" Maggie asked.

"Actually, I was wondering the same thing. It's the same one he brought to campus every day." He sat down on the floor, laid the briefcase across his legs, and opened it. "A couple of framed pictures and an old album."

Maggie dropped down beside him, and together they examined the picture of Susan and Joshua smiling on a deck next to an oak tree.

"His wife and son," Kevin said. "This picture was on his desk at CIMT. I saw it there but never asked about it. Figured it'd be best if he brought it up himself. He never did."

"A beautiful lady."

The second picture was a black-and-white with a very sober-looking man and woman. "I bet this is of his mother and father. Probably just before the war."

Next Kevin lifted the album and willed himself to open it. Breaking into the house didn't bother him, but this seemed like a sacred violation. Inside the front cover was an old black-and-white of a teenage boy and girl that Kevin surmised were Weissman's parents. The man bore a resemblance—the eyes, the chin. It had to be.

On the next page were more individual pictures of Weissman's father and mother, beginning with their childhoods. Each looked reasonably happy, a brisk glow of intelligence in their young eyes. The following page jumped perhaps fifteen years, both now in their twenties, clinging to each other, their eyes full of dread.

Later, following their wartime despair, came a new life, a baby boy. Weissman's childhood was thoroughly captured. He was like a tiny daisy growing through the cracks in a New York City sidewalk. In his maturing visage was written the story of a child's natural optimism being trained out—choked by smog and deprived of light by the skyscrapers of bitterness and pain that towered over him.

In his eyes was the same bright flash of perception that had always been his mark, but along with it a burden, a weariness so thoroughgoing it was palpable even in these aged images.

"What a load of bad karma," Maggie said.

Craig's voice crackled over the radio. "OK guys, it's been an hour. You have twenty or thirty minutes, no more."

"10-4. Thanks Craig." Kevin carefully placed the album and framed pictures back in the briefcase and slid it under the bed with the violin. As they got up from the floor, Maggie said, "This bed doesn't look like it's used much."

"What do you mean?" Kevin asked.

"I don't think he would make it up this nicely every day. It's not consistent with the rest of the house. And look up here..." She pointed out a small patch of white sheet exposed near the top of the pillow. "See this? It's got dust on it. A person sleeping here every night would have brushed against this dust. You know, with his hand, or his pillow. Or head."

Kevin bent to look more closely. "You're right. But if he doesn't sleep here, where does he sleep?"

"There's one more room. Let's take a look."

As they went down the hall, Maggie grabbed Kevin's arm. "Look," she said pointing to the wall at the end. "That must be where the dogs get out when the alarm goes off."

They went to inspect it. "A pet door on hinges," Kevin said. "The alarm sounds and the door unlocks."

"Then the Rottweilers kill you," Maggie said.

"Tell me about it."

They went back to the last remaining room and tried the door. Locked.

"Strange," Kevin said. "Why would Weissman bother to lock an inside room? We might have something here Maggie." He kneeled to examine the doorknob and the small keypad just beneath. He thought for a moment and then entered 1-1-7-3-2-0. There was an audible click and doorknob turned.

"You're scary," Maggie said in a whisper.

"Remember when Weissman gave me his passwords? One of the office passwords was 1-1-7-3-2-0. I searched the web for the birthdays of his wife and son. His wife, Susan, her birthday was January 17. That's where the 1-1-7 comes from. And his son, Joshua, he was born on March 20. That's the 3-2-0. It's the oldest password gimmick in the book. Weissman knows that, but he did it anyway. And now we're in."

They pushed opened the door and entered the room. "Interesting," Kevin said. They both looked at the copious merchandise stacked along the walls. "I guess he doesn't like shopping in town so he has his beer shipped in by semi."

"What's with all these white uniforms," Maggie asked, pointing to the stack. "Have you ever seen him in one of these?"

"Never," Kevin said. "It sure doesn't match the rest of the house."

They did a mental inventory of everything in the room, including the two cases of vodka and one case of champagne sitting on the rug in the middle of the room.

Craig called again. "Ten more minutes, guys. Better wrap it up."

"OK," Kevin said. "Almost done."

"We still don't know where he sleeps," Maggie said. "But it's not in here. Let's get going."

"One more thing, Maggie. Let's spend a few minutes searching for every electrical device in the house. Maybe he's got a couple appliances or pieces of electronics that we're missing—electric heaters or something. We need to account for the solar panels. Weissman may be a little wacked right now, but he wouldn't have all this solar power without a reason. Besides, what's the security system for? There's nothing of value here—no safe, not even a computer. Nothing."

The search left them bewildered. Everything was fueled by propane: furnace, fridge, hot water heater.

"What's electric?" Kevin asked.

Maggie shook her head. "The only things I can find are the lights, two phones that don't work, and an electric clock."

"This just doesn't add up," Kevin said. "He's not one to sit on his hands, but there's no evidence of work. We've been watching this place for almost a week. He goes to the mine every afternoon, but aside from that, he's inside this house with the lights on twenty-four hours a day. What's he doing? And where is he doing it? And where does he sleep? He's got to have computers. Where—"

The radio broke his thought. "Time's up," Craig said. "I want you two out, or else I'll send the dogs in after you."

Kevin and Maggie walked directly back into the kitchen and out the front door, Kevin pausing briefly to lock it.

Craig was kneeling by the dozing Rottweilers. "Not so tough when they're sleeping. Kind of cute, actually," he said, grinning. "You two head up to base camp. I want to be sure these jackals are up and around before Weissman returns."

Just as Craig predicted, the dogs started to rouse twenty minutes later. They walked like puppies at first, trying to get their muscles to wake from the fog of sedative. In another fifteen minutes they were tearing around the property, chasing every noise. When Weissman pulled up in the Land Cruiser they almost knocked him over with their jumping. He scratched their ears.

"So far, so good," Craig whispered returning to the ridge. Weissman disappeared into the house. All three held their breath knowing there was nothing to do now but hope the break-in would remain undetected.

They waited an hour without incident and then quietly repacked their gear. Soon dusk rolled in, and they began the trek back to Dexter. The hike out was calming. The woods felt benign and soothing compared to Weissman's house.

"What've we got?" Craig asked when they arrived at the truck.

"Not much," Kevin said.

"He has precisely three things that run on electricity," Maggie said. "Lights, phones with no dial tone, and an alarm clock."

"Don't forget about the electronic dog fence and his laser setup," Craig said.

"The surveillance cameras too," Kevin added. "But it still doesn't add up."

"No computers?" Craig asked.

"None we could find," Maggie said.

"Not even a microwave?" Craig asked in disbelief.

"It's primitive in there," Kevin said. "The main living area is a disaster zone, even by our standards. But his bedroom is different. Except for a layer of dust, it's clean. It looks undisturbed. Looks like he hadn't been in there for months."

"Where does he sleep?" Craig asked.

"No idea," Kevin said. "But we don't think it's in that bed."

"We did find his briefcase and violin under the bed though," Maggie said. "And there was another room that looked like a mini Wal-Mart."

"What?" Craig said.

"Yeah," Kevin said. "He had tons of stuff in there. Clothes, food. He had Polish beer and vodka and even a case of French champagne."

"You're kidding," Craig said. "I thought Weissman hated the French."

"Well, Weissman hates most of Europe, I think," Kevin said. "But he sure loves their booze."

"What did you learn, then?" Craig asked. "I mean, did you find out anything about what he's doing or why?"

"Not really," Kevin said. "We might even know less now than we did before."

"We need your philosopher friend," Maggie said.

"Michael," Kevin and Craig said in unison.

"Yeah," Maggie said. "That's him. We need the archangel."

Chapter 22

May the Mountains Bring Peace

Dr. Friedman's summer place was a log cabin high in the mountains twenty miles north of Weissman's. Neither Kevin nor Craig knew its location, but after reaching him by phone they were able to arrive in time for dinner.

As they neared, Craig pointed out a massive dog running through the pines chasing a marmot. The marmot ran out of gas, and the dog caught him playfully, sniffing, even venturing a lick.

Kevin's Toyota bumped into the gravel driveway. The dog looked up, then barked loudly and raced down the hill. His canine guard duties seemed a simple matter of making noise until Michael came out.

"Reminds me of the Rottweilers," Maggie said.

Craig laughed. "That little guy? I'll bet he's sweet as sugar and soft as butter."

Michael poked his head out the door just as the Toyota parked. Three passengers exited with his approval, so the dog dropped any pretense of guarding in favor of greeting. He stood at the truck and wagged his tail.

Craig kneeled down and wrapped his arms around its neck, scratching behind the ears. "Hey there little fella. How're you?" The animal slobbered Craig's face.

"Hi Michael," Kevin said. "Who's this big guy?" The dog came over and licked his hand, then rubbed against his legs, knocking him sideways.

"Lacan. He's a Greater Swiss Mountain Dog."

"What's his name again?"

"Lacan. When I got him at the Humane Society he wasn't

neutered. I thought it best to have the procedure done so he went under the knife. The historic personage, Lacan, was a French psychoanalyst in the Freudian tradition who held that everyone is castrated, metaphorically speaking, by the way we use language. Perhaps you see a connection—this would tie Lacan in with humankind and lessen the alienation he must feel since separated from his manly parts. Of course, there are very real physiological aspects of castration, and those I can do nothing about, but I'm trying to make his inner life as comfortable as possible."

"You're nothing if not altruistic," Kevin said, laughing.

"Getting a bit deep," Maggie said.

"Oh, sorry. Maggie, this is Michael. Michael, Maggie."

"I've heard so much about you," Maggie said, with a coy smile that was to die for. "Kevin's your biggest fan."

Michael laid his hand on Kevin's shoulder. "If everyone on the earth died in a nuclear accident except for two people, and I was one, Kevin would be on my short list of people I'd like to be marooned with. That is if we might divorce this theoretical exercise from the more pragmatic concern of repopulating the earth."

"Weissman would suggest your 'theoretical exercise' is more imminent than we think," Kevin said.

"Antoni. Yes. That's why you're here," Michael said. "Well, let's go inside. I've got some steaks thawed and dinner will be ready in half-an-hour. Anybody care for a strawberry lemonade while we wait?"

"Love one," Maggie said. She turned to say something to Kevin, but he'd wandered off to follow Craig, who'd wandered off to follow Lacan, who'd wandered off to find the marmot last seen by the beaver pond.

"Boys will be boys," Maggie said.

"You've noticed," Michael said. "Please, come in." He opened the rough-hewn door and stepped aside. "Make yourself at home." He went to the fridge and poured two glasses of strawberry lemonade, handing one to Maggie.

"Thanks. Great place." She was fascinated by the inside of the cabin where every piece of furniture was handmade from pine logs. "I can see why you like it here."

"It's small but that suits me. Not fancy. That suits me too. I find it very comfortable. And personally, I find it inspirational." He led Maggie over to a picture window looking on the mountain ridge.

"Awesome view," she said.

"May the mountains bring peace to the people, and the hills bring righteousness," Michael said. He spoke with reverence. Maggie looked over at him. "Amen," he whispered.

"Amen," Maggie repeated, not knowing why, or what it meant. Still, somehow it felt good to say it.

Michael went back to the kitchen counter. "Solomon wrote that three thousand years ago," he said and began working on dinner.

"Can I help you?"

"No need," Michael said. "But I appreciate the offer." He pointed to a bar stool a few feet from where he was chopping together a salad. "If you don't mind, have a seat over here. We can get acquainted while those guys work up an appetite."

"Well, if I can't help, would you mind if I pick your brain while you work? I've got some personal questions, and Kevin says you're the guy to talk to."

"Be gentle when you pick."

Maggie laughed. "I wouldn't be rough with you, Dr. Friedman."

"Please, call me Michael. This isn't the university—just a cabin in the mountains. We're all friends here."

"Thanks." She sat down and looked out the window for another minute before proceeding. How strange, she thought. To be pouring out her personal story to a handsome philosophy professor she'd just met in an oversized gazebo at nine-thousand feet while her immediate support system was off chasing a giant castrated Swiss dog across the mountaintops. It'd been quite a day...

Well, I guess it can't hurt. "Maybe Kevin has told you some of this..." She paused, shaking her head again, incredulous at this improbable confessional/counseling/cooking session. "OK. My dad's a workaholic, my mom's constantly in denial, my sister's a fashion model with the addictions that make it all bearable. In summary: the Foster family is a mess. Much as I hate to admit it, I follow after my dad's propensity toward workaholism. But I'm taking six months off postgraduation to process all this, and I'm hoping the taste of freedom will balance me out."

She took a drink of lemonade. "Here's my question. It seems that the reason workaholics strive so endlessly is that they're after something: money or success or respect. Or power. Maybe it's happiness. Contentment. I'm not sure. Something. Maybe they're just addicted to it, I don't know. Listen, I've got nothing against work—I'm kind of driven myself. Actually, I love working and maybe that's why I'm afraid of it. I'm just not sure that work or money can produce happiness. My dad's been down that road and he's one miserable slab of humanity."

She looked Michael directly in the eyes. "If happiness is not a fish we catch through working, how do we get there?"

Michael put down the salad and leaned over the kitchen island. "Great question. I suppose this extends even to Anthony's situation, doesn't it? He has wealth and has always worked hard. But he's not a happy person.

"How should I put this? Any material want or need can be bought or sold: heat, food, drink, sex, cars, yachts. But immaterial things, such as states of the soul, are an entirely different matter. They're *affected* by physical things. But they're not *determined* by them.

"Many of our contemporary values emphasize the material and coax us down that road; get a bigger house, a larger paycheck and you're on the road to utopia. Yet surveys consistently demonstrate that the desire for material acquisition acts as a happiness suppressant. Surprisingly, the happiest countries are not the richest countries. And depression is increasing in industrialized nations, a finding not observed in developing countries. So how do we explain this?"

Michael, it seemed to Maggie, could not help talking like a philosopher. Philosophy was not something he *did* but who he *was*. And his passion was evident even at 9,000 feet in the middle of a salad. He walked around the island and took a seat next to Maggie. He was speaking to her soul.

"The deficit, Maggie, is a deficit of meaning. One must have meaning in life, and I'm talking about something far deeper than work or money. I'm talking here about transcendence. I'd suggest a serious exploration of the spiritual life and see where it takes you. Jesus once asked what it would benefit us if we gained the whole world but lost our soul. It's of course true that we all live in that world, so work, money, and possessions play a role. But don't neglect the things that matter most. And included in that category are your relationships—to yourself, to others, and to God."

"I watch how Kevin is so concerned about Weissman," Maggie said. "I think I'm learning from him. My father only values utilitarian relationships. But Kevin is willing to pursue Weissman even at his own peril. It's quite remarkable, really."

"That's because he's a remarkable young man," Michael said. "By the way, how're you and Kevin getting along?"

She paused. "We're kind of in that netherworld between nothing and something."

"Been there myself."

"If you promise not to tell him—I agree with you. I mean, about him being remarkable. I can't say exactly what it is, but he's certainly different from any guy I've ever met." She laughed. "Did you know that he blushes? Stanford guys don't blush. And Kevin never takes advantage of me. Instead he turns red. I love it."

"That sounds closer to something than nothing," Michael said with a smile.

Maggie had started down this road and now, surprisingly, she didn't want to stop. "I've never felt this way about a guy. Truthfully, I don't think I'm prepared for it. Kevin and I barely know each other. Yet..." She got up and went to the window. This was foreign territory—she'd never spoken about her feelings like this. Not even to Summer. Certainly not to a stranger.

"Before Kevin, all men seemed the same to me. There were two categories. Either loud, stupid and obnoxious, or else wimpy, geeky, and sniveling." She looked up at Michael, afraid he'd be insulted. Amused, he waved for her to continue.

"Kevin doesn't fit either mold. He's different. His nearness doesn't feel like a nuisance or a threat."

When she didn't continue, Michael said cautiously, "More like a completion?"

She looked at him, surprised he would say such a thing. Then she nodded.

Michael started to say something more, but then he jumped up. "Hey. There you guys are. Just in time."

Maggie turned, startled. Kevin, Craig, and Lacan were piling through the door.

Michael glanced at her and winked. He pulled her over and whispered in her ear, "He didn't hear us."

Maggie looked relieved, then quickly recovered her bearings. "Watch this,' she said to Michael.

She walked up to Kevin and gave him a hug too nice for the public eye, causing Craig to turn away. Michael, however, looked for the red face. Sure enough. He winked at Maggie.

"Men are mountains, and women the levers that move them," Craig said to Michael.

Maggie let the weak-kneed Kevin go. "Dr. Friedman told me to," she said.

"Well, not exactly," Michael defended himself.

"Michael, we really wanted to ask about Weissman," Kevin said, again trying the change-the-conversation defense. "We're worried."

"I am too," Michael said. He motioned for them to have a seat, then continued. "I've emailed him. I've tried calling dozens of times. At first he didn't answer his phone and now it's disconnected. I tried writing. Nothing. It's frustrating not to know if you're getting through."

He looked at Maggie. "As you know, his house burned down." He looked back at Kevin. "I just talked to the police today. They think it was arson but can't be sure. Weissman's made no move to collect the insurance money, even though it's over $400,000."

"What do you think happened to him?" Craig asked.

"I have no idea. I'm mystified. After the fiasco at the school, he just disappeared. To be honest, I fear for him. This total disconnect has me worried."

"I can't divulge sources," Kevin said, "but it appears he's gone off his meds and his psychiatrist from the east coast has repeatedly tried to contact him. Think that's serious?"

Michael dropped his head and covered his face with his hands. After a minute, he let out an involuntary sigh. Finally looking up, he made no attempt to hide his tears. "Extremely," he said.

The four talked until late. The company, the food, the view—

all were outstanding. Yet the evening was blanketed by a gathering sense that Weissman was sinking into the abyss. None of them, not even Craig, could finish the meal. Before they departed, they joined hands around a circle—including Maggie—while Michael prayed for their tormented friend.

א א א

Miraculously, Dexter ran quietly all the way home. The trio, too, was quiet. Partly from exhaustion, mostly from Weissman.

Maggie spent the trip looking out the rear window. The stars were impossibly bright, but her thoughts were much closer to home. *I wish Michael would've included me in his prayer. Kevin is not going to understand why I'm leaving tomorrow.*

Chapter 23

Follow Your Heart

"WHAT DO YOU MEAN?" KEVIN SAT UP AND LOOKED AT THE clock. "Maggie—it's *six o'clock*. Go back to bed and we'll talk in the morning."

"It is morning. I need to go. There are some things I've got to do."

She bent down and gave him a peck on the cheek. "I'll call you in a day or two." And with that, she was out the door.

Kevin sat on the edge of his bed and rubbed his eyes. "I can't believe it."

Craig rolled over and slowly opened one eye. "What's the matter? Bad dream?"

Kevin flopped back into bed.

א א א א

Maggie touched down at the Palo Alto airport just after 6:00 p.m. She jumped into her Volkswagen and drove to her apartment.

"Hey Summer," she said coming through the door.

"Maggie!" Summer ran out of the bathroom where she'd been working on her hair. "Where have you been? Why didn't you call?"

"Long story. I'm on assignment and not supposed to talk about it."

"What? On assignment for who?"

"NSA."

"What's that?"

"Summer, Summer, Summer. You're so innocent it makes my hair hurt. Speaking of hair, what's up with yours?"

"Hot date with Corey tonight," she said, walking back into the bathroom. "Come in here and tell me everything."

"Glad to see the good times are rolling even in my absence. Didn't I tell you? You fill me in on Corey first, and maybe I'll loosen my tongue. I just might have a Corey of my own."

"Maggie!" Summer said, jumping up and down.

א א א א

The next morning Maggie arrived back at the airport at 7:00 a.m. She walked through the gate and bumped into Derek.

"Hi Maggie. Haven't seen you in weeks. Where've you been?"

"Gone." Maggie marched past him. "Help me prep my plane and maybe I'll talk to you next time."

"I see you've done some work on your left wing. What happened?"

"Ah, perceptive. Well, if you must know, I inadvertently flew through a war zone and people shot at me."

"Come on, Maggie. Hit a bird?"

She filed a flight plan, fueled up the Arrow, did a preflight check, and lifted off. Heading: due north. Fifteen hours later, at 11:05 p.m., just as the late-May sun was setting, she touched down in Port Alsworth, Alaska.

א א א א

Maggie rose to a grand sunrise that she treated as the treasure it was, then went on a long hike with Cat. The air was clean and cool. An eagle flew overhead and cut a simple dark silhouette against a placid sky. It seemed the ground was a constraint and that earthbound creatures were forced to walk a less-real existence. She thought of Dr. Friedman's advice to delve into the spiritual. No better place than Alaska.

Cat was in the middle of a new batch of poetry, fueled by a "geyser of poetic creativity" as he called it, the principal inspiration being a collection of caribou skulls he'd found over the years. He was a sporadic poet. For a month he would write nothing and then the muse would strike. In three days, he'd have the drafts of ten new poems. He would revise and refine these for a week or so, then lapse back into inactivity.

"Did you ever consider putting in a few hours each day on your poems?" Maggie asked. "You know, since it's what you're leaving behind, your legacy."

They walked a few minutes while he considered his answer, and finally he said, "Maggie, poetry just happens. I can't make it happen. All I can do is listen and write it down when it comes. I'm not really a poet. More like someone that poetry gives itself to."

"Any new ones for me?"

They stopped and faced each other. "The context here is caribou skulls I found in the woods." He cleared his throat.

On your sharp nose, I cut my finger.
Blood runs red, dries on your white skull,
Pink - the color of little girls.

An old hippie and a dead bull,
A resolute lover, a fighter to the end.

Is this what girls are made of?
A question for the ages.

"It's nice," she said. She gave him a squeeze around the neck and a platonic peck on the cheek. "Why don't you come in a twenty-five-year-old version?"

This was a running joke between them. "I'm my own demographic, kiddo."

They walked beside a mountain river, along a minimalist path Cat had carved. "What makes this place so special is that people haven't ruined it yet," he liked to say.

Cat's philosophy was a tonic to her soul. She'd long ago wearied of the ultra-modernism pushed upon her as a child. Cindy made certain that every couch and TV, every pot and pan were there on a trial basis, and the minute something better came out, the Fosters owned it. The house was like a revolving door for high-end furniture, all items continuously weeded out for the better and best. It was a disorienting phenomenon. Never was there a stain on a couch or a rug she could show a friend and say, "I made that." It gave the place more the feel of a five-star hotel than a home.

"How's Ella?" Maggie asked.

"She's been into the grayling and rainbows for a week now, so the fishermen are happy. Dolly Vardens are hitting, too. Mid-June the salmon will start. You know how crazy that gets. But she likes this season—it's time to earn some money." He chuckled. "Couple days ago, a drunk businessman from Boston proposed to her. She doesn't mind. When they sober up, they're embarrassed and always give bigger tips." He roared with delight.

Maggie contemplated her life as Ella. One of her enduring metaphors was that of a *Choose Your Own Adventure* book, the future hanging out in front of you, open-ended, waiting for you to make a decision, to pick a page, and make that ending real. From today forward, Maggie had thousands of life decisions to make, and a certain combination of them might turn her into someone like Ella. Which wouldn't be so bad.

But there was another more recent choose-your-own-adventure that turned in the direction of Kevin Morgan, and that wouldn't be so bad either. It surprised her to be thinking this way, to think of a man, Kevin Morgan, as a good person—someone who meant her well, not harm.

They continued to walk along the river for another three miles. Cat didn't wear a watch but instead kept an eye on the sun and around eleven o'clock, he reached into his canvas backpack for a small telescoping spinning rod. He drew it out to its five-foot length and tied on a silver-and-blue Little Cleo.

"Hungry, child?"

Maggie nodded. He called her child when feeling paternal. From anyone else she would've railed against it, waxing angry about the phallocentrism of language. But these things didn't apply to Cat who didn't have a malicious bone in his body. Angry words had no place here, like violence has no place in the soft world of babies.

Cat carried the rod deftly through thick brush until coming upon a promising eddy. He handed Maggie the pole and coached her patiently. "There you go, child, stand over there. Cast upstream of that eddy and reel it slowly through. Give it a little tug so he'll think it's alive."

Maggie did as instructed, but her cast fell too close to the eddy. They saw a small, sleek form dart upstream. Cat laughed softly, not at Maggie, but at the vagaries of fishing that make it so loveable.

Twenty yards further they found a promising undercut bank. Maggie cast perfectly, and the spoon drifted through. A tug came on the other end of the line, and Maggie pulled the rod back to set the hook. The grayling started upstream, stripping line from the reel. Maggie fought it well and inside of five minutes, the fifteen-inch grayling slid up the bank by Maggie's feet. Cat grabbed it by the gill and struck its head against a rock. While Maggie gathered dry wood, he cleaned the fish, and within twenty minutes they dined at nature's table.

Maggie lay down in the patch of grass, looked up at the blue sky, and smelled a sublime mixture of the campfire, cooked fish, and trees. She felt close to comprehending the circular nature of things, of the made-up-word history, the endless karmic cycles, rebirth, rebirth, rebirth, and maybe escape, but the deeper understanding eluded her as always. One is the way of truth. Two is the way of falsehood. She wondered if she was just thinking too much and not meditating enough. She looked at Cat cooking the fish with absolute contentment, and just for an instant she seemed to feel it, or see it, the precious enlightenment, then, just as quickly, it was gone. Which begs the question, did I make it up? Can I manipulate myself into this?

"What's wrong Maggie?"

"It's that obvious?" She shook her head. "It's about the first noble truth."

"Suffering?"

"Yes—that life is suffering. It doesn't ring true. Sure, sometimes that's the way of it, I'm not one to deny that suffering exists; I've had my share... But it doesn't seem to me, at least not right now, that you can just say that about the world, and say that it's true all the time, as a maxim. I'm not suffering now. I'm enjoying life. So now I could say life is enjoyment. But that's not true all the time either. Sometimes life is boredom. Sometimes it's suffering, sometimes it's anger, sometimes it's beauty. Life is life. The only way I can define it is to refer back to itself, which means you must have experience to put content into the words.

"This brings me to what I don't like. The only means the Dharma has of making things right is not to save the world but to extinguish it. After all, Nirvana means extinction, or snapped relationship. But this place, life here, is not all bad. Not all life deserves extinguishing. Wouldn't it be better to save what's good and get rid of what's bad and we could live in a glorious world without the suffering?"

"Maggie, remember who you're talking to. I'm a hippie, not a monk or guru or theologian. I don't know how much I can help you. But I *am* a spiritually-minded person, and we're dealing with a spiritual reality. It operates on its own terms, and it's not in a realm we can manipulate. You're a scientist, your job is to figure out how to make physical objects do extraordinary things. Take a gigantic hunk of metal and make it fly a hundred people across the country in three hours. But that's not the way this works. We have to take the terms we're given. We have to confine ourselves to what is metaphysically possible."

"Remember when I first came here with Jeff?" Maggie said.

"Of course."

"He called you a rank old hippie, drowning in idealism, aimless, a drain on the economy. Then he took off in the boat by himself and left us behind."

"How could I forget?"

"Remember what you said while he was trying to start the motor?"

"I'm not aimless—my aims are just different from yours."

"Then you bowed. I was shocked. He didn't bother you! You just laughed and then we went fishing together." She reached over and gave him a hug. "That day changed my life. I began to see there could be a different way."

She lay back down again, looking into the clouds. "I grew up around a man driven by ruthless aggression. First, it seemed all about business. Then it was all about money. Now I think it's all about conquest. He's a warrior all the time, whether there's a war on or not. If there's no controversy he'll create some. I hated him."

Maggie sat back up—it's hard to relax and talk about Jeff at the same time. "And most of the guys I grew up around were testosterone monsters, football players, they were just like him. I hated them too. They couldn't decide what to think about me. They were baffled by the thought I wasn't attracted to them. And so they wanted me, because they couldn't have me. See? It's conquest again. When I saw that, I hated them all the more. Just a downward spiral.

"When I met you, you were different. You were masculine but also disarming. You were strong but in such a different way. In a quiet way. I don't know—you were just right."

"That's a bit overdone," Cat said with a laugh.

"Once I found out you were for real, not a game, not a front, not Ella's token rugged outdoorsman to lend an air of authenticity to the camp—well, I thought I wanted to be like you. You're the most balanced, centered human I've ever met. All of this to say that you may not be a theologian, but your advice is worth more than anything I got at the university."

Cat walked toward Maggie and took her small, smooth hand delicately in his rough paw. "Thank you, child. That was beautiful." They stayed like this for a moment, and Maggie found in him all the comforts she never found at home. Through their singular connection she struggled to make up for the lifetime she'd spent scraping by on emotional leftovers and occasional feel-good movies.

They ambled down by the river. Maggie leaned against a tree, while Cat settled down on a large flat rock. "Mind if I smoke my pipe?" he asked.

"I love the smell of your pipe. You know that. "

From his shirt pocket he dug out a pipe whittled from a single piece of wood. He packed it, touched a flame to the bowl, took a couple puffs, tamped, and relit.

"I suppose," Cat said, "many people are attracted to an idea or philosophy because someone attracts them to it, not just on the merits of the metaphysical system. But you know, people say a lot of things: some are true, some aren't. You can't believe something just because the Joe who said it was a nice guy. You've got to make your own decisions. That's where you're at. You're on a journey of discovery. It's a precious journey. Leave your father's contamination—for that matter, your whole family—leave it in the past. Just drop it on the side of the road. No need to bring it on the journey. Follow your heart."

Maggie nodded. "Kevin and Craig—these two I told you about—they're like us. They're our kind of people. They're healthy, they make sense. But the trouble is, they're Christians. I really didn't think that was possible. I suppose too many years of Flanders had colored my thinking. It's jarring to meet someone who's not accurately satirized on the Simpsons."

"Who's Flanders?"

"Never mind. Not important."

"Don't label people, Maggie." He looked up at her. "Port Alsworth is a tiny town, and most of the people here are Christians." He shrugged his shoulders. "They're my friends."

"You're right of course. I guess I just need to take a closer look at what these religions are saying and see which is more likely to be true."

"I think you found your answer." After a pause, he continued. "This is a good thing you're doing with Kevin and Craig. I know you're doing it to help the professor. But I want to hear from you why you're doing it. A fire in the heart can create smoke in the mind."

Maggie shifted her position against the tree. She broke off a small green branch and fashioned a toothpick. "I feel an affinity for Weissman. He's a misunderstood, maladjusted genius, and it's sad. But what we're doing is risky. Actually, it's dangerous. He's really deranged. We flew my plane over his house and he shot at us. Obviously he's not rational right now."

Picking up a dry stick, she started breaking it into pieces, six inches at a time, tossing them into the river. "Maybe I'm trying to work off some karmic-curse savior complex."

As Cat waited for Maggie to continue, he poked the coals of the dying fire.

"We can't go to the authorities because they'd lock him up and that could be disastrous," she continued. "I'm not optimistic. The man's both depressed and psychotic. Hard to know what might put him over the edge."

"But he hasn't done anything yet?"

"Not aside from shooting at my plane. At least, nothing we

know of."

"Help an old man up, child." Cat said this though he didn't need it. He wrapped Maggie up in his hulking frame, his flannel shirt enveloping her like a giant warm blanket.

He pulled back and looked down on her lovely face. "I'll be here if you need me."

"I know that," she said. "I think I've always known that." And she hugged him as if she would never let go.

Chapter 24

Salmon Ella's

AT 5:00 A.M. MAGGIE'S BRAIN JUMPED AWAY FROM ITS DISTANT slumber. She sat up and shook her head, trying to separate REM from reality. Life had taken on a surreal glow since reality became consistently stranger than her dreams.

She pulled on a set of bona fide army cargo pants and a white T-shirt, accessorized by a Leatherman and cell phone. Then she sat at the table sipping coffee and pondering the past month.

What, after all, have we accomplished? Prudence dictates laying low to avoid muddying the situation and perhaps ending up with a criminal record to boot. But prudent people rarely make history.

With effort, Maggie arrested this line of questioning. If there ever were a time for exercises in futility, this was not it. This was a time of need, and she was a woman of action. The only clear course was to make the call.

א א א

"Hello." Kevin's muffled voice spoke half into his pillow.
"Wake up."
"Who is it?"
"What do you mean *who is it?*"
"Maggie?"
"Do you have other women calling you this time of morning? Yes, it's Maggie. Now wake up."
"What time it is?"
"7:30 a.m. Mountain Time. 10:30 p.m. Tokyo Time. Stop

whining—"

"Tokyo Time? Maggie, where are you?"

"We need to talk about Weissman."

Kevin's voice took on a serious tone. "You still in?" He propped himself up on one elbow.

"Always have been," Maggie said. "This is part of my life now. Sometimes I wish I could roll back the clock, but then I realize that life exists for such moments. Like I said, we need to talk."

"I've got a couple hours before church. Want to talk now?"

"Needs to be face-to-face."

Kevin's heart jumped.

"When and where?"

"Today. Alaska."

"Alaska? Maggie, why Alaska?"

"Because that's where I am, and I want to take you fishing."

"Fishing? I thought you wanted to talk."

"We'll do both. At Salmon Ella's."

"Where's that?"

"Here."

"How am I supposed to get to Alaska? A same-day ticket for Alaska would cost a fortune. I hate to break it to you, but money's one thing in short supp—"

"Get yourself to the airport by noon and go to the Peak Air desk. A ticket will be waiting with your name on it."

"Maggie, you can't be buying me tickets."

"My dad owns half the airline."

"What do I bring? How long will I be gone? Who's going to feed and water Craig?"

Maggie laughed. "Just bring your toothbrush."

"What happens when I get to Anchorage?"

"Kevin. Trust me. Just come. I need to see you." She hung up.

א א א א

Kevin exited the plane at Anchorage International Airport and made his way down the concourse to the baggage claim area. He seemed a bit unsure what to do or say.

Maggie stepped up and gave him a quick hug, a bit tentative herself.

"Any bags?"

"One," Kevin said with a smile. "Replacement toothbrushes."

"How was the flight?"

"Great. I got a much needed nap," he said pinching her cheek. "But the snack—you've got to talk to your father. I've had more food stuck between my teeth."

They stopped for sweet-and-sour chicken and two egg rolls which Kevin consumed at a gluttonous pace. As he told Maggie, "If you eat fast, you can fit more in."

They picked up his bag and headed out the door. "Where'd you park?" he asked.

"We're flying."

Maggie hailed a cab for the short ride to Merrill Field. She went into the terminal and allowed Kevin to pay the cabbie, who sized up the two of them and drove away with a smile.

As they reached the plane, Maggie opened the side door and brought out a new rod and reel. "We're going to catch northern pike. A good-sized fish would break many rods in half. Use this—it's yours." She handed Kevin a six-foot Shimano rod with a perfectly balanced spinning reel spooled with twenty-pound-test line, selected specifically for him.

"I don't know what to say," Kevin said. "Thank you, Maggie."

"Don't mention it."

They climbed into the Arrow, taxied out to the runway, and lifted into the west. The sun hovered on the horizon just behind the mountains, and Kevin said he felt like they were flying into an orange peel turned inside out.

They flew southwest down the Cook Inlet and then hung a right into the mountains through Lake Clark Pass. The pass was clear.

"This part is dangerous in low visibility," Maggie said. The sharp-sloped mountains seemed near enough for Kevin to touch. Winds bobbed the plane up-and-down like a cork on an ocean without water.

Kevin's feelings were overwhelming: going to bed last night thinking Maggie was lost and the quest to rescue Weissman's sanity much harder; now being in Alaska of all places, flying into indescribably beautiful scenery next to the irresistibly beautiful Maggie who had just given him a specially-chosen gift and asked him—of all the men in America—to join her for a fishing trip. He was befuddled.

As they slipped through the pass, a thirty-five-mile-long, deep azure-blue lake came into view, rimmed in its entirety by snow-capped mountains. Kevin leaned forward, wide-eyed. "Maggie, this is gorgeous!"

"Lake Clark National Park. I've been all over the world—the Andes, the Rockies, the Alps, even the Himalayas. But for my money, I've never seen anything more beautiful than this spot."

"You've been to all those places?"

"The chance to travel was the only real benefit of being in Jeff's family."

"Did your family vacation here?"

Maggie laughed disgustedly. "Yeah, right. Remember when I told you about Jeff bringing me on a fishing trip? This was it. Eight depraved business associates and one teenage girl. These guys had nothing on their minds but fishing, beer, and sex. Well, there was plenty of fishing and they shipped in plenty of beer. Then Daddy dear brought me as eye candy. He even offered me $1,000 if I wore my bikini all week." Her face bore an almost explosive rage. "If any of them would've touched me, I'd have killed 'em. But they violated me with their eyes and with their jokes. Cat finally got me out. Jeff hated him for it. That day Cat became my father."

Silence hung in the cockpit for a minute.

"As furious as I was with Jeff, that trip allowed me to discover this place. The beauty, the people, the serenity ... and of course Cat lives here."

"They meant it for evil but God meant it for good."

"What?"

"It's from the Bible, in the Old Testament. About Joseph."

"This really is a spiritual place Kevin, and I wanted you to see it."

Maggie flew halfway down the lake, then turned across Hardenberg Bay and made a flawless landing. She taxied in, spinning the plane around into its parking pad. They tied the tail with a rope, and Maggie chocked it.

Kevin saw a Jeep Wrangler behind the plane sporting a one-word bumper sticker that said *Question*. "That the Jeep you told me about?"

"The one and only." Maggie clicked her key chain, eliciting a half-hearted response from one of the turn signals.

"Since when does Rent-a-Ticking-Time-Bomb put esoteric bumper stickers on their fleet?"

"It was a rental out of Anchorage. In my maiden voyage I hit a moose. The moose ran away. After a new radiator I was able to drive the Jeep from the shop. Rather than pay damages, I bought it. A sledgehammer pounded out the dents and now I keep it here. Cat drives it when I'm gone."

"You're an odd duck, Maggie. Who buys totaled rentals?"

"This vehicle helped me survive against a bull moose, and I'm loyal to my friends."

They jumped in the Jeep, and Maggie stuck her key in the ignition and turned. Nothing. The dash lights came on, but the motor was unresponsive.

"The heart of a champion," Kevin said, deadpan.

"Get out and push you lazy duffer." Maggie stuck it in neutral and got ready to push on the driver's side, one hand on the steering wheel, one hand on the door, while Kevin went around the back. For some reason, it made him think of bobsledding.

"Push," Maggie yelled. They both leaned into the task and soon the Jeep was rolling down the runway at seven or eight miles an hour.

Maggie jumped in, popped the clutch, and took off like a shot, leaving Kevin face-down in the gravel inhaling the Jeep's oily belch. She drove fifty yards and promptly killed it. Kevin shook his head in disbelief. To his chagrin, Maggie cranked it right back up and drove over to him.

"Oops, guess I didn't turn the key far enough the first time. These old vehicles can be quirky." She smiled, and Kevin knew this little exercise had been intentional on Maggie's part and for her entertainment.

"Are you always like this, or just on your good days?" He climbed in, but any retaliation was disarmed by the view of the cliffs, the water breaking white on the rocks, the snow-capped craggy mountains on the horizon, and a blue sky to set records.

Maggie's 80-grit behavior didn't fool Kevin. She had as much a sense of the beauty of things as the next person. He suspected that for Maggie it went deeper, a sense of the unspeakable majesty of the cosmos. But it was no good trying to talk about it, for it only scarred the moment with human bungling, another lesson in the limitations of language.

Maggie swerved around potholes, churned up dust, and within minutes they reached a crude wooden sign with a painted weather-beaten King Salmon announcing *Salmon Ella's*. An arrow pointed left down a two-rut trail.

Maggie slowed to pass a small frontier-style general store and an aptly-named mess hall. A sign in front of the general store declared, "If one of these is open the other isn't."

Maggie turned between two spruce trees and pulled up in front of a small log cabin stained dark brown. It seemed a part of the woods as though it had just grown itself without human involvement. She whanged the door open with a squarely placed kick and entered.

"Who's staying here?"

"We are."

"You booked us in the same cabin?"

"Separate rooms," she said. "The camp is full and I was lucky to get this. What is it with you, anyway?"

"Just surprised. I guessed you were a little disgruntled when you left so abruptly last week."

"You guessed wrong."

He went into his room and stretched out on the bed, checking for firmness and bugs, and found it to be with and without. As he lay there processing the rapid and remarkable events of the day, he heard another arrival, then Maggie giggling. Kevin leapt out of bed to investigate.

In the living room Maggie stood happily in the grasp of an older man with long, gray hair pulled back in a pony tail, sunglasses, silver earring and slight paunch. He looked like a cross between a rock star, a biker, John Muir, and a sea captain. With his deep leathery tan, green and black flannel shirt, Carhartt overalls, and old school leather walking boots, he could do a cameo on the X-Files without makeup. Kevin could hear his smooth voice, resonant, filling the room like an acoustic guitar with new strings, a voice too good for radio.

"Kevin, this is Cat. Cat, Kevin."

"Kevin, good to have you. Nice to get some young blood 'round here. I sure get tired of seeing old people all the time. Most that can afford to come here are in their forties and up. You know the kind—rich business types, whiny, no fun. If it rains, they think it's my fault. No fish—it's Ella's fault. Anyway, now you're here, and any friend of Maggie's is a friend of mine. Welcome home."

Cat swatted Kevin playfully on the shoulder. Kevin neglected to reply in light of the more urgent matter of making sure his bones were still intact. With that, Cat took two steps and out the door. "See you two later," he yelled over his shoulder with a hand lifted up.

"He's as advertised," Kevin said, still rubbing his shoulder.

"Pretty fit for an old hippie, huh? Still just a beatnik. Back in the sixties he didn't fit in, so, like the bohemian he is, he took to the road. He wanted to get as far away as possible from people who would box him in. My best guess is that he just started rambling, looking for open-mindedness. When he got to Salmon Ella's he found it. He told me the reason he ended up in Port Alsworth is because you can't go any further."

א א א א

Kevin awoke the next morning to a 6:30 alarm. Through brushing his teeth and eating breakfast, there was no sign of Maggie. He grabbed his new fishing rod and started down to the boat when it occurred to him that he hadn't the foggiest idea how to fish for pike. Actually, fishing in general was a bit fuzzy. He decided to follow standard procedure and compensate for ignorance by enthusiasm.

It was a beautiful day, unseasonably warm. The sun had risen into a clear sky. He followed the path to the lake and crested the top of the hill overlooking the bay. The lake was unpolluted and unpopulated, and he could see down into the water, under the deep end of the dock where someone had thrown a fish carcass the previous evening. Whitefish were nibbling at the flaps of skin that hung loose in the water.

Kevin walked onto the dock to find their boat—Maggie said Lund #4—just as Maggie and Cat came over the top of the hill.

Cat wore gray Woolrich pants that looked like they had seen fifteen years of hard use and a blue T-shirt with a crude drawing of a chainsaw. His hair was ponytailed back and clenched firmly in his teeth was an old-sea-captain-style pipe.

Maggie was a striking picture as she walked down the slopes, unnaturally cheery, bursting with the glow of health and youth, looking even peaceful. There was something incongruous about this serenity on the face of such a seething crucible of womanhood. She wore a white V-neck T-shirt with jeans and an open black jacket.

When they came within earshot, she said, "Cat's joining us," and without taking a breath, "Beautiful day, isn't it?"

"Great," Kevin replied, with a semi-forced smile.

Kevin stepped into the boat and Maggie set her things on the back seat. Cat came out of the boathouse with a yellow rain slicker, a broomstick-sized fishing rod with bait casting reel, and a five-gallon plastic bucket with notches cut in the side. As he came thumping down the dock, Kevin could see the points of hooks hanging in each notch and judged the lures to be massive.

Maggie stepped to the rear of the boat while Cat untied and pushed out from the dock.

"You let her drive?" Kevin asked Cat.

"Don't have much say in the matter!" he roared, reinjuring Kevin's shoulder with a hearty slap.

The Lund floated peacefully backward until Maggie pulled the cord churning the Evinrude to life. Backing the boat up until it pointed in the direction of the outlet of the bay, she chopped it into forward and twisted the handle until the motor thrummed, efficient and well muffled.

The boat planed easily, even with 215-pound Cat in the front, and skimmed over the surface. Looking down, the lake was so clear it seemed as though they weren't on water at all. Weeds and rocks and fish zipped by beneath them.

They motored for fifteen minutes before Maggie began to slow. The sensation of being on such an open body of translucent water was miniaturizing, like flying over a city. It seemed as if the sky and lake were competing to swallow them whole, to disappear their Lund without a trace.

Slowing to half throttle, they ran parallel to the shore on the left while Cat tied a steel leader to his line, then did the same for Kevin. As much as Kevin envied the affection Maggie lavished on Cat, it was impossible not to like him.

"Heey, Kevin," Cat inflected with his hipster voice, "this daredevil is a great spoon in this bay. You must cast this spoon with great bombast and reel it in fast so it don't get stuck in the weeds."

Maggie turned into Chulitna Bay and cut the engine. She slipped off her jacket, picked up her rod, and made a long, arching cast that landed close to shore. Her yellow lure, almost a foot long, had a spinning blade and a hair tail. She retrieved quickly, just under the surface of the water.

Kevin watched Maggie make several casts and resolved to copy her exactly. He opened the bail of his new spinning reel, pulled back on the rod, heaved it forward and released the line just as Maggie had. His lure went straight for the heavens, then dropped and landed with the sound of a rifle shot. He reeled the spoon through the clear water, over and between the weeds back to the side of the boat. He cast again, flattening the trajectory and started reeling as soon as it hit the water. Suddenly, a long, green fish hit the lure with a huge splash. Kevin cranked back on his rod but the lure flew out of the water and shot right back at them, missing his ear by a foot before landing on the back side of the boat.

Cat bent over with laugher.

"Kevin, could you be serious here," Maggie said. "I'm trying to fish."

Maggie resumed casting and hooked a northern, the line screaming off her reel. In a few minutes, the weakened fish was pulled near the boat and as it swam by Kevin, suddenly, explosively, it dove for the bottom of the lake splashing him in the face.

"How big is he, Cat?" Maggie asked.

"Eight or ten pounds. Nice fish."

Cat gently pushed Kevin aside and reached in the lake for the resurfaced fish. It sat exhausted, gilling, at the side of the boat. He picked it up just behind the gills and in one smooth motion lifted it out of the water. With his Leatherman he removed the hooks and gently laid the fish back into the lake. For a minute it sat suspended trying to recover. Then, in a flash, it took off for the deep weeds and disappeared.

Cat sighed contentedly, pulled out his pipe and stuffed it with tobacco.

"Let's cut to the chase," Cat said, with a grin. "You two in love?"

Maggie nearly dropped her rod in the water. "Cat, I can't believe you—"

Cat put up a meaty hand, signaling an abrupt end to the indignant diatribe poised to fly off Maggie's tongue. To Kevin's amazement, Maggie stopped.

"Maggie, I might be old but I ain't dumb. All the signs are there. You're awkward around each other. You steal glances when the other's looking away—"

"Honestly, this is ridiculous. I'm leaving."

She set her rod down, kicked off her shoes, and dove overboard shallow and long, like an Olympic swimmer. With a few graceful strokes, she was to shore. She pulled herself out of the frigid water, took a small metal container of waterproof matches from her pocket, and quickly gathered driftwood to build a fire. Within minutes, she sat before it to dry herself off, completely ignoring them.

Neither Kevin nor Cat said anything. Kevin was too stunned. Cat just puffed contentedly on his pipe, stuck in the middle of a broad smile. When he spoke, it surprised Kevin. "As happens so often, truth is stranger than fiction. We may as well keep fishing. It'll be a while before she's ready to get back in the boat."

Walking to the stern, Cat took a seat by the motor. He fired up the Evinrude, moved fifty yards down the shore, and started casting. Kevin spotted a massive submerged rock and cast in its direction even as he kept looking back at Maggie, shivering, huddled around the tiny but growing fire, her wet top drawing his embarrassed attention. He looked back at his lure in the air, then back again at Maggie. His spoon hit, and the water exploded like a hand grenade. Cat gave a shout as Kevin pulled back hard on the rod. The fish flew out of the water, then ran for the shore.

"Keep him out of the weeds," Cat yelled. "He's a big one."

Kevin worked at turning the fish only to have it tangle the line in a submerged tree.

"Pull back hard and see if you can free the line," Cat said.

Kevin yanked on the rod, the line slashing back and forth in the water, beating it to a froth.

"I'll motor over," Cat said. "Reel in the line as we go so it doesn't get caught in the prop."

Kevin did as instructed until the front of the boat bumped against the offending tree. The northern sat beneath the boat, sullen. Kevin could see the hook in its maw, only one point of the treble holding to a thin strip by the mouth. Just then, the northern gave a furious shake of his head and was free, splashing Kevin in the process.

Cat laughed. "That's the breaks, kid. Let's go check on Maggie. By the way, you in love with her? Because if you are, I'm OK with that. I'm a good judge of character."

Kevin looked confused, prompting Cat to take another shot at it. "I'm acting in place of her dad. That's the way she wants it. Just so you know. Anyway, not that you would, but if you did, ever, you know, want to get married, I'm your man. Not that I'm saying you would have to. I never did, and I've been with my share of women. But then I suppose parents are more careful with their kids than they were with themselves. Just so you know."

Kevin searched frantically for the right words. Finding none, he settled on "OK."

"Glad we got that over with."

"Me too," Kevin grunted reflectively. "You'd make a great father-in-law, you know. For whomever the lucky guy is. It's a bit early to be assuming anything. Since we haven't kissed yet. Or held hands for that matter. Actually, affectionate words have been pretty sparse, come to think of it."

"Believe me, I know how she can be. I can only imagine what it'd feel like to be in your shoes. I just want to hand her off, via marriage or simple couplehood, to somebody I can trust, and I get the feeling I could trust you. Maggie says so."

"She does?" Kevin said.

"Well, in her way." Not prepared to go any further on that topic, Cat changed directions. "You smoke a pipe? I brought an extra one in case."

Kevin reached over and took the pipe. "Never tried a pipe."

"Stuff it with this tobacco. That's right. Then pack it tight with your little finger. Fill it up to a quarter inch below the top. Now put that Black and Gold in your shirt pocket and don't lose it. I have to order that stuff over the internet."

Kevin shot him a sideways glance.

"Well, actually, Maggie orders it and has it sent to me," Cat admitted. "Now, just make a little igloo with your hand over the bowl to keep the flame from going out. That's right." Kevin got it lit, but in ten seconds it was out again.

"You've got to keep after it steady for the first bit," Cat said. "Then it'll go on its own."

"Thanks." Kevin did as instructed. The pipe complied, supplying him with little puffs of sweet-smelling smoke.

It was five minutes before either of them noticed the boat had drifted well out from shore, and Maggie was beckoning them to return with smoke signals. Cat started the motor and went in to pick her up.

"About time," Maggie said.

"You're the one that jumped out of the boat," Cat said.

Maggie caught the nose of the boat as Cat eased it between two rocks. "I'm hungry," she said. "Kevin, go down the shore and catch us something to eat. Cat and I have some talking to do."

Kevin wandered along the shore, while Maggie began chewing out Cat good naturedly. After ten casts Kevin hooked a smaller fish. Dragging it onto land, he grabbed it around the middle with both hands, holding it horizontally the best he could while tucking the rod under his arm, and returned to the others.

"The mighty hunter returns to rescue me," Cat said, with a smile.

The northern slipped out of Kevin's grasp. "They're slimier than they look," he said.

Cat pinned it underfoot, conked it expertly on the head with a rock, and soon they were enjoying hot fillets over an open fire.

א א א א

That night Kevin couldn't fall asleep. Not exactly insomnia. Just that he couldn't stop wondering what tomorrow might be like.

He woke in the morning to the smell of blueberry muffins baking, coffee perking and the sound of an acoustic guitar playing the blues. Pretty well, actually.

Cat's boomtown tenor came in flawlessly, "Well your eyes are hazy and your skin is brown, but I love you anyway." Maggie shot out of her room.

"What did you sing?" she asked, with an urgency that surprised Kevin.

"Your eyes are hazy and your skin is brown, but I love you anyway. Why?"

"I've heard that before."

"Blips and Bleeps?"

"How'd you know that?"

"I started that band in the seventies."

"What do you mean I started that band in the seventies."

"I started that band in the seventies."

"You're kidding! Why didn't you ever tell me about that?"

"You never asked."

"Cat, I swear, you're impossible."

"I think my muffins are done."

Chapter 25

Must Be Love

IN THE COURSE OF HIS REMAINING DAYS, KEVIN'S FISHING skills increased appreciably. What surprised him was not that he liked fishing but how *much* he liked it. It became, in one sense, a new way of seeing. When the three of them were on the lake, the dichotomy between man and nature was diminished: Man seemed simply another step in the chain of being. Amidst the ancient carpet of green surrounding the pristine lake he stumbled into a wordless understanding of the oneness of physical things.

But the picture was not so simple. He had another insight, nearly opposite, and was frustrated because he found both compelling. In the high plains where spirits moved without walking, the inverse was true. Even though Maggie and Cat would resist his conclusion, being in the presence of two such extraordinary people gave Kevin a sort of visceral confirmation, a clear understanding, that the difference between humans and nature at large is a difference that cannot be accounted for by simple gradations. It is a difference of kind: oil and water.

The week was the most exhilarating of Kevin's young life and passed too quickly—fishing, hiking, overnight river rafting from Upper to Lower Tazimna. But mostly, talking. With darkness almost nonexistent this time of year, the three spent long hours stoking campfires, sipping coffee, smoking pipes, and contemplating the bubbling, yeasty caldron of existence. They swirled and milked the muses on technology, terrorism, politics, Buddhism, Christianity, Alaska, oil, the wilderness, grizzlies (one came into town to kill chickens, passing not far from them), love, the future. And they talked about Weissman.

"I wish you could meet him, Cat," Maggie said. "He's one-of-a-kind. Like you, except completely different."

"He's brilliant, intense, and opinionated," Kevin said. "Yet, somehow, I've always gotten along well with him. I'm not sure why he liked me so much, but we spent a lot of time together."

"Is he evil?" Cat asked bluntly.

"No! Definitely not." Kevin said. "He's just wounded. This is what happens when intense people are deeply wounded. He's besieged by demons, but he definitely isn't evil. He's opposed to everything evil represents. I'd stake my life on it."

"I would too," Maggie said. Kevin looked at her, surprised she'd go so far. "I've been around evil people—Jeff and his friends, for example. Weissman's not like them."

Cat finally said: "Clearly, he's worth saving. Your quest is noble." Listening to himself, he laughed. "I sound like the Dalai Lama." As he rose to leave, he extended an offer. "Let me know if there's any way I can help. I mean that," and for emphasis, he wagged his finger at them both. "Now it's time to put these old bones to bed and leave you two lovebirds alone."

He stretched to standing, turned to Kevin and laid a hand on his shoulder.

"You've got a good head and a good heart. Welcome to the family." He grabbed both of Kevin's hands, pulled him to standing, and enveloped him in a bear hug. Kevin tried to hug back but his arms were pinned in a vice.

Cat dropped the hug, turned quickly, and disappeared over the hill.

Kevin and Maggie appreciated the opportunity to be alone. After seven days of joy and clarity, the week was drawing down in a way neither wished to see.

"Kev, it's time."

"I know. It's going to be hard to leave. I can see why you love it here."

"I'll fly you into Anchorage in the morning. We should leave around nine. Weather is supposed to be good for the pass."

The air was intensely full of meaning, as if the rest of their lives would be determined in the next five minutes. Each hesitated to speak.

"What're your plans?" Kevin finally asked, laden with dread.

Why would she leave this? He couldn't ask her to return to Denver—what was in Denver that could compare to this? Sleeping on a sofa belonging to two sloppy guys with no money, in the same city as her creepy father, pursuing illegal maneuvers to rescue a psychotic recluse.

"I'll stay here," Maggie said, and Kevin's heart sunk. "—until Friday. Then I'm coming back to help you with Weissman."

"You're coming back? To Denver?"

"Of course."

"What happened?"

"Cat gave his approval."

"Approval of what?"

"Both of you."

"Both of whom?"

"You and Weissman."

"What happens after Weissman?" Kevin asked, surprising himself.

Maggie reached over and squeezed his hand. "That will just leave you."

She pivoted onto his lap, put her arms around his neck and kissed him.

א א א א

After the baggage claim coughed up his bag, Kevin walked to the curb looking for Craig. Already influenced by Cat, he separated himself from the frenzied shoving crowd and instead sat on a bench and cocked an ear. Still two hundred yards away Kevin heard Dexter's distinctive exhaust, the muffler with a small hole. He stepped into the street as Craig neared, threw his bag in the bed of the truck, and off they went without coming to a complete stop.

"Nice pickup," Kevin said.

"How was the trip?" Craig asked.

"Ausgezeichnet!"

"What?"

"Outstanding. Absolutely incredible. Best week of my life."

"And..."

"You almost need to go there to understand."

"Come on—you can do better than that."

"Lake Clark is beyond beautiful. It's like all the artists and landscape architects in heaven collaborated and then dropped their creation in an isolated mountain range hoping it wouldn't attract too much attention."

"So, Alaska is beautiful. Wow, breaking news." Craig hit Kevin in the shoulder. "Come on—I want a Maggie report."

"I think I'm in love."

"Tell me something I don't know. Like is Maggie in love?"

"Cupid hit us both."

"How do you know?"

"I just know." He shrugged. His face turned red.

"Kev, that's awesome! That's awesome. Sure you're ready for such a filly? She's a handful."

"That she is."

"I saw your grin," Craig said as he kept one eye on the road and one eye on Kevin's face.

"What can I say?" Kevin smiled as recent images flashed across his mind. "You'll have to bear with me buddy 'cause it might be a while before I come back to earth."

Craig kept slapping the steering wheel in excitement.

"And you're not going to believe this beatnik guy—never met anybody like him. He's a 60s hippie who works part-time maintenance at the fishing camp. He writes poetry. Pretty much functions as Maggie's dad."

"Maggie's surrogate father is a part-time maintenance beatnik poet from Alaska?"

"And a good fisherman to boot. We caught tons of fish and Cat—"

"That's Cat?" Craig asked incredulously.

"Yup. He caught the biggest fish, an eighteen-pounder. The man is suave. Seriously, you've got to meet him."

א א א א

Following a quick supper of hot dogs, Kevin and Craig moved to the living room and lingered over coffee, contemplating the events of the past month.

"Sometimes I don't know if I'm coming or going," Kevin said.

"My biorhythms are fried. My brain's a jumble."

"I think they call that love."

"Feels like existential whiplash."

"Yup, that's love," Craig said. "Fitzsimmons would be proud. Fitzsimmons would definitely be proud."

"Is this what happens after college? I always expected life would become more predictable, that we'd be forced into some 9-to-5 mold. Remember how we swore we'd never turn into the people who get poured into a funnel, swirling downward into an ever narrowing vortex, and in the end they all come out the same place, the same way?"

"Squeezed out by the Great Machine into tiny cloned turds," Craig said.

"And then we're recycled, as Maggie would say," Kevin added.

"Well, we always wanted a ticket out of the vast social Coriolis effect. I'm just not sure if this is an answer to our prayers or the opposite," Craig said.

"Are we swirling water around the drain or is this just what freedom feels like?"

"What're you going to do?"

"Gird up my loins and fight."

"Personally, I'd say it a bit differently: buckle your seatbelt and hang on for dear life. Maggie and Weissman, both at the same time? What were you thinking?"

"Must be love."

א א א א

The next morning Kevin began crossing off days on the calendar with a red marker.

"What're you doing?" Craig asked.

"Marking off the days until Maggie comes."

"Isn't that Friday?"

"Yup."

"Dude, that's only three days from now. Can't you do that in your head?"

"Get your own girlfriend." Kevin dove into Craig's midsection, knocking him into the couch. They tussled good-naturedly for a few minutes, Craig finally pinning Kevin to the floor and threatening to keep him there until the Best Man job was guaranteed.

Working on the Triumph occupied the better part of their morning, after which they headed to the gym. Craig knew it well, having visited almost daily since their recent arrival to Denver. "We men are like soup," he kept repeating, "better to be beefy and thick." Kevin's interest in fitness, on the other hand, was completely newfound, related directly to Maggie's proximity. Her disciplined workout schedule was coercively inspiring.

To Kevin, the locker room smelled like a hockey bag. He made an intentioned effort not to be dramatic about it since he already stuck out among the veteran members of the club and had no desire to advertise his presence beyond breathing.

After exerting a decent minimum on the treadmill, exercise bike, and weight machine, Kevin felt there was precious little to show for it. He coveted a quicker return on his investment but knew that muscles, like mutual funds, take time. It occurred to him that if impressing the ladies was the goal, buying a Porsche might be easier, never mind that being equally impossible.

Craig meanwhile lowered the bar to his chest. As soon as it touched, he pushed the 225 pounds back up, breathing out with an eerie calm. He repeated the cycle, again and again, like a piston. Kevin lost track at ten and eventually Craig stopped. He then walked off for a drink of water, barely sweating. Invincible was the only word Kevin could think of, glad they were on the same side.

א א א א

The next morning, on Wednesday, they drove to CIMT. Kevin needed to recheck Weissman's computer. Finding what he was after, they walked over to pay Roberta a visit.

"Good morning," Kevin said as he opened the door to the provost's office and stuck his head in. Roberta did not look up, so they entered. "My name is Kevin Morgan? I visited a couple of weeks ago. This is Craig Hunter, another recent graduate."

No response from Roberta, who was typing on her computer with a stern look. They waited for her to glance up, which finally she did. Her facial appearance did not soften, nor did she offer a greeting. She just looked at Kevin with angry eyes. Prompted by awkwardness, Kevin continued.

"We're wondering if you've heard anything about Dr. Weissman?"

"No."

"I realize this is somewhat privileged information but, has his psychiatrist heard anything? Is he still calling your office?"

Roberta stared at them silently.

Kevin continued the one-sided conversation. "Is the provost still out of the country? Any way I could talk with him?"

"The provost will not be coming back," she said as if this news were somehow Kevin's fault. "The board released him from his position."

"He's been fired?" Kevin was stunned. "Why? You mean because of Dr. Weissman?" Roberta scowled. She was an unhappy woman and Kevin felt it best to cut his losses and get out of the room. "I'm sorry to hear that. I'll leave you to your work then. Thanks for your time."

Craig opened the door and they both fled the office.

אאאא

The two worked through the night on the Triumph, finally falling into bed at 6:00 a.m. Craig woke at noon and went to the gym without waiting for Kevin.

An hour later, Kevin was awakened by persistent knocking on their door. Dressing hurriedly in a T-shirt and shorts, he opened the door.

"Maggie?"

He blinked to be sure it wasn't a dream. She pushed past him, dropped her backpack on the floor, and wrapped him in her arms. He lost his balance and nearly fell over, but Maggie grasped him tighter and they stood there together, neither willing to let go. Thinking he'd have to propose if they stood intertwined much longer, Kevin reluctantly pulled back.

"I think Weissman needs another definition for tightly coupled," Kevin said trying to catch his breath. "I thought you were coming on Friday?"

"Disappointed?"

"You kidding?" He grabbed her again to make the point. "What made you decide to come today?"

"Changed my mind. Women do that."

Kevin took her hand and led her into the living room, still a greasy shambles from the motorcycle repairs. "Come into my chambers."

"You guys have been busy," she said looking around. "Wasted no time redecorating the place as a service garage." She ran her hand across the Triumph. "Sweet."

"Looks good doesn't it?"

"Can't wait for a ride. Oh, that reminds me, Cat's in the car."

"Cat's here?"

"He came along for moral support. And to feed me Triscuits while I flew."

"Why's he in the car? Let's go get him."

"Kevin, you're not the one who asked him to stay outside."

"You do think of everything."

"That's one of the definitions for woman—the one who thinks of everything."

She turned and walked down the stairs. Kevin took his keys and followed.

"How did you get in the building?" he asked.

"I followed a guy. Told him that if he didn't let me in I'd tear his ear off. I think he believed me."

"Simple but effective."

They walked across the parking lot toward Maggie's Trailblazer rental.

"No more Foster Enterprises vehicles?" Kevin asked.

"I'm done with him."

Reaching the red Chevy they found Cat snoozing in the front seat.

"Cat!" Kevin said, awakening him with a start. "Great to see you." They latched onto each other in a hug.

"Thanks Kevin. Maggie here was missing you horribly—"

"Cat! You weren't supposed to say that. Just shut—"

"What did I do?" He winked at Kevin. "Anyway, we decided to push up the schedule a bit. Hope it didn't surprise you too much."

"Almost died. Other than that, no objection. Come on in."

"We've been flying the better part of twenty-four hours," Maggie said. "Both a bit sleepy."

"I brought a sleeping bag," Cat said. "Just give me six feet of floor space and I'm out of your hair."

Kevin brought them up, and Cat went instantly to the motorcycle and whistled. "Nice Triumph!"

"Know anything about them?"

"Had one in the 70s. Great bike."

"Haven't had it running yet, but it's close. We can talk about that later. You need to sleep."

He brought Cat into the bedroom and insisted he use Craig's bed.

"Nope," he said laying the sleeping bag on the floor. "This will work fine."

"Sure?"

"Class A accommodations."

When Kevin returned to the living room, Maggie was sitting on the couch. She was jittery, frazzled by the trip. "You look tired," he said. "Want me to fix you a place to sleep?"

"I can't sleep just yet. Let's talk."

Twenty minutes later, Maggie was slurring words.

"We've got a sleepy girl on our hands," Kevin said. "I let you stay up past your bedtime."

"Right." She slumped into his shoulder.

"Cat's sleeping on the bedroom floor. You can have my bed or the sofa."

"If I sleep on the sofa, what'll you do?"

"Sit here and watch you sleep."

"I'll take the bedroom."

"Need something to sleep in?"

"No," she said, kicking her bag, "brought my own." Maggie eyed her bag full of clothes and then said, "On second thought, let me see what you've got."

The prospect of her wearing his clothes to bed made him tremble. Trying to stay calm, he rummaged around in his dresser, Cat snoring on the floor. He decided on a well-worn gray CIMT T-shirt and blue athletic shorts. He offered them with excited hands and no words.

After remarking how precipitously her standards were

plummeting, she walked into the bathroom to change, locking the door loudly. Five minutes later she slipped quietly from the bathroom into the bedroom. Then, opening the door a crack, she whispered in a seductive voice, "Good night, Kevin."

א א א א

Eight hours later Maggie woke just as the sun was setting. She came out of the bedroom and walked down the hall to the kitchen. Craig and Cat, already fast friends, had disappeared into town. Kevin was ostensibly reading a repair manual for the Triumph, but after Maggie opened the door, further pretense was essentially useless. He watched her turn down the hall and open the refrigerator. High-mindedness and spiritual integrity were important to him and he kept telling his eyes to behave themselves, that they should only go so far. But despite his best efforts, he was unable to think about anything except her wearing his blue shorts. Her legs were long and lithe, brown, muscled and powerful in the most attractive way possible. She had neglected to wear a bra under the gray shirt, which was starting to wear thin.

Maggie walked toward him with a giant glass of orange juice in her hand. "Do you miss Salmon Ella's?" she asked. She slithered up to him and sat on his lap.

"You have no idea."

"Oh, I think I do."

As she took a drink, Kevin tried to shift his weight. He slipped and doused them both with OJ.

Chapter 26

Bomb!

DESPERATE FOR SOMETHING OTHER THAN HOT DOGS AND chocolate ice cream, Maggie took Cat in search of alternatives. The Trailblazer pulled into the first grocery store they came to, a monstrosity advertising 40,000 products. They walked through sliding doors into a store "bigger than Port Alsworth" by Cat's glum assessment.

He lingered at the fish counter while Maggie was sorting through the vegetables. Just as she was weighing some tomatoes, her cell phone rang.

"Hi Kevin."

"Have you seen the news?" he yelled.

"What news? What's the matter? You still at the airport?"

"Listen, Maggie. It's horrible." He was breathless. "At 3:30 a bomb threat was called in to the Chicago Airport Commission. It was for Terminal 3 at O'Hare. Very specific. And the timing was peak flow for the airport. The bomber was obviously planning for maximum disruption. Security evacuated everybody. They'd just started their search when a siren went off. A very loud siren. It was inside the terminal. The bomb squad finally tracked it down and disabled it. There was some kind of warning written on the box. Sounds like some kind of crazy, or joke, right? But no harm, no foul, right?"

"I'm glad it—" Maggie started to say.

"Wait, Maggie. I'm not finished." Kevin was still yelling into the phone. "An hour later a bomb actually *exploded* in Terminal 3. Did you hear me? It *actually exploded* Maggie. And get this—it was right next to the Peak Air counter. Apparently hidden in an empty luggage cart. Maybe a pipe bomb, I'm not sure. A whistle went off seconds before the bomb blew. The terminal was still evacuated but there were a few people in the area. When they heard the whistle, they started running as fast as they could. The bomb did some damage but nobody was injured because of the whistle. Now they've shut down the whole airport. All the terminals. People screaming. Hundreds of flights cancelled. Air traffic backed up all over the country."

"Kevin, that's horrible."

"That's not all."

"What?"

"It gets worse. A lot worse. Someone just called in a bomb threat here."

"Denver? At the airport? Are you still at the airport?"

"Yes."

"You're not inside—?"

"No. No. Everybody's outside. They evacuated everybody. It's packed out here. Nobody has any idea what to do. They won't let anybody go home."

"Had Friedman's flight landed yet?"

"It was diverted to Colorado Springs. I haven't been able to reach him. I'm hoping he can rent a car."

"Do they know who's behind this?"

"They won't tell us anything."

Kevin's voice sounded very agitated.

"Kevin? What is it?"

She heard Kevin take a deep breath to calm himself, then he lowered his voice. "Maggie, this is the scenario I wrote up in my paper. Almost exactly." Maggie listened closely: he was silent for a moment and she could hear the caution in his voice when he came back on. "I don't want to say much on the phone. The only difference is that in my paper, I focused on the Atlanta and Dallas airports—this was the Chicago and Denver airports. Everything else is the same. The times of day, everything."

"What are you talking about? I thought that assignment was cancelled."

"It was. But I wrote it up anyway, out of respect for Weissman. I mailed it to his home with a note thanking him for the Stanford trip. Then his house burned down, and I was never sure he got it."

"You're imagining—"

"No Maggie, I'm not! This is real. Listen, previously we were dealing with a *potential* situation. Now everything is—"

Maggie heard a deafening blast through the phone, followed by a hail of glass falling to the ground and people screaming. With a background of wailing car alarms, any possibility of rational conversation was drowned out.

"*A bomb!*" Kevin yelled. "Maggie! A bomb just went off. My ears are ringing. It's bad here. I'm OK, but I gotta go. The guy next to me is bleeding. Call you later."

The line went dead.

א א א א

Maggie stared at her phone, then dropped it in the shopping cart. She leaned against the cart and covered her face with her hands. "Please, please, please, please…"

Cat walked around the end of the aisle with a big smile on his face, carrying an overpriced package of salmon fillets wrapped in Styrofoam and plastic.

"Hey Maggie! Look what they're charging for these tiny—"

He saw Maggie slumped over the cart, moaning. He ran up to her and wrapped his arms around her trembling body.

"What's the matter, child?"

She was unable to talk. She shielded her eyes with her hand, then buried her face in Cat's shoulder.

"I don't understand, Maggie. What happened?"

Phones rang all throughout the store.

א א א א

Kevin tore off the sleeve of his best white shirt and tied it around the bleeding man's forehead. Even in the midst of his distress, the man had the presence of mind to insist Kevin take a fifty dollar bill for the shirt, a bill Kevin then gave to a Skycap employee from Africa in a small effort to make the world right. It wasn't much, but he felt better.

Traffic leaving the airport was gridlocked, a slowly-moving, exhaust-filled parking lot. After thousands of ten-foot increments—and three hours—Kevin finally walked in the apartment and fell into Maggie's arms. Craig and Cat huddled close.

They listened to his report, and Craig insisted on checking him over to be sure he was OK. Maggie asked, "You think it's him? Weissman? I guess your reasoning makes sense, but there's a big part of me that doesn't want to believe it. Like you said, if he's involved it'd change everything."

"It's always possible this could be somebody else," Kevin said. "But I really doubt it. I mean, what're the odds? This is exactly my paper, straight from theory to application."

"But he can't be two places at once. Not Denver and Chicago at the same time," Maggie said. "Are you saying he might have an accomplice?"

"In my paper I left that option open. But I also achieved the same effect using remote cell phone triggering devices. So this could still be a one-man operation."

"You going to the police?" she asked.

"No!" he nearly shouted. "Wait. Not yet." He stood up from the sofa and walked across the room, then quickly back again. He was exhausted and hyper at the same time. "Listen guys—we gotta be very careful here."

Each was silent. Kevin kept looking at Maggie causing the others to as well.

"Maggie?"

Finally she managed a weak "OK."

"That was thinner than the shadow of a photon."

"What do you expect?" she shot back. "This isn't easy."

Cat put his hand on her shoulder. "Everything will be OK. We have each other and that counts for a lot in my book. I think Kevin's right. This will work out."

"Let's see if there're any new developments on TV," Craig said in an attempt to reunite their focus. He unmuted the television and switched across the cable news outlets. Most coverage ran interviews from the two airports mixed with pictures of bloody victims and emergency vehicles. Police offered little in the way of forensic details and had no clues as to the identity of the bombers. No fatalities. The injuries, for the most part, were cuts and bruises.

"Hey," Kevin said pointing at the screen, "that's my shirt sleeve! That's my bleeding neighbor. He's wearing my sleeve." In a completely incongruous way, they laughed at Kevin's suboptimal medical bandage.

Without warning, all stations interrupted coverage with breaking news.

"FBI headquarters in Washington, DC has just released a message sent by today's bombers. They have requested this message be shown in its entirety. You will now see the message as scrolling text:

> The bigger the system grows, the more disastrous the results of its breakdown will be. The network of causes and effects is far too complex to be untangled and understood. Autonomy becomes less and less possible as local communities become more enmeshed with and dependent on large-scale systems. Also operating against autonomy is the fact that technology applied in one location often affects people at other locations far away. Not only do people become dependent as individuals on a new item of technology, but, even more, the system as a whole becomes dependent on it. During the next several decades the industrial-technological system will be undergoing severe stresses. If the system breaks down there may be a period of chaos, a "time of troubles." It is impossible to predict what would emerge from such a time of troubles. If the machines are permitted to make all their own decisions, we can't make any conjectures as to the results, because it is impossible to guess how such machines might behave. We only point out that the fate of the human race would be at the mercy of the machines. As society and the problems that face it become more and more complex eventually a stage may be reached at which the decisions necessary to keep the system running will be so complex that human beings will be incapable of making them intelligently. With regard to revolutionary strategy, the only points on which we absolutely insist are that the single overriding goal must be the elimination of modern technology.

"This message has been identified by FBI counterterrorism agents as pieced-together excerpts from the 1997 Unabomber's *Manifesto*. The FBI is now in the process of questioning the Unabomber in his Colorado prison to see if he has any information about today's bombings."

"I can't believe it! This sucks," Kevin said.

"What's the matter?" Maggie asked.

"Kev, you better lie down," Craig said. "You don't look good."

Kevin sat back in the chair, closed his eyes, and took several deep breaths. The color drained from his face and he started to perspire.

"Get me a cold washcloth," he asked Craig. In seconds, Craig was back with the cloth and laid it on his forehead. Maggie helped him lay down on the couch.

"Tough day," she said.

He opened one eye and looked at her. "Ya think?" Then he closed it again.

They gave him a couple minutes to revive, and finally he said, "I'm feeling a little better."

Cat brought him a glass of water.

"What's the problem?" Craig said.

Kevin took a drink, then put the cloth back over his forehead and closed his eyes again. He spoke slowly and deliberately. "Weissman and I talked about the Unabomber on the flight to Stanford. I asked what he thought about Kaczynski. I assumed he'd brush it off. He said: 'Two things I can tell you about the Unabomber. One, he's crazy. Two, he's right.'"

"This clinches it," Maggie said. "We call the authorities."

"What're you going to do?" Craig asked Kevin.

"Hate to say it, but we've got to go back to Weissman's. Break in again and sweep it top to bottom. We missed something important. I'm sure of it. We still have no access to his computers. He must have computers. We just haven't found them."

"Come on Kevin," Maggie said. "Been there and done that. There's nothing there. Just a trash pit."

"I've got an idea," Kevin said.

"This is getting dangerous," Maggie said. "I think we should call the police or FBI."

"I understand why you think that Maggie," Kevin said, propping himself up on an elbow. His color was returning, and he was acting more like himself although still talking slowly. "But Weissman is like family to me. Right now he's really sick. If we send in the police, I'm afraid what would happen. Someone might die. I hate to say it, but I have this feeling—I think someone would die. Either Weissman would die, or whoever tries to arrest him would die. And if Weissman survives, they'd lock him up for the rest of his life."

He'd never put it in such fatalistic terms before.

"So you want us to die instead of the police?" Maggie asked.

"When do we go?" Craig asked.

"Tonight. We should go tonight to see if anything's different." By now, he was sitting up. "This will be quick: no break-in, just surveillance. With all that's happened today, if Weissman was involved, we'll notice something different. Some variation of his routine. Maybe he'll be gone. Anything. Craig, you and I go. We'll leave Maggie and Cat back here to monitor the news and be our phone contact."

"I'm going," Maggie insisted.

Kevin looked at her, then at Cat.

"Don't ask me," Cat said, putting up his hands.

"All right," Kevin said. "Within the hour." Then he added, "Craig, you drive."

"This is crazy," Maggie said. "I hope your faith protects us."

"I hope so too. But either way, I'm good."

"Don't mess with me like that," Maggie snapped. "Just don't get yourself killed. A limb blown off I could deal with. Just don't get yourself killed."

"We'll be careful."

"Right. You and Craig. Careful is the first word that comes to mind."

א א א א

They parked off the main road and walked through the woods, finally reaching the ridge at 11:00 p.m. The dogs were sleeping outside on the front porch, breathing loudly, occasionally having the fitful rabbit-chasing dreams dogs have. The trio unrolled their sleeping bags quietly and lay down without a sound. House lights were on, as always, with seemingly no activity in the main room or kitchen. Everything status quo.

Craig fell asleep around 2:00 a.m. but Kevin and Maggie sipped coffee for warmth and caffeine. Thankful for the stakeout, neither could have slept anyway. Visions of the airport were looping through Kevin's head: the man bleeding, car alarms, people screaming. He felt like a war reporter.

"Did you notice that both airport blasts—both Chicago and Denver—happened by the Peak Air ticket counters?" Kevin asked in a whisper.

"Yeah. Think it's significant?"

"No idea. But—"

Suddenly floodlights flashed on below them, drenching the compound with halogen brilliance. Kevin nudged Craig awake. A raccoon had waddled onto the property. The dogs snarled into a frenzy of barking, then ran and caught the intruder within a few feet of the electronic fence. A great frenzy ensued, the dogs lunging and ripping, the raccoon squalling as they tore it limb from limb. One of the dogs picked up the limbless carcass and shook it back and forth in its jaws like a rag doll. Blood spattered everywhere.

Weissman stumbled onto the porch to check on the commotion.

Maggie caught her breath. "He looks ghastly."

Weissman tripped across the stoop, appearing either sleep deprived or drunk. He was wearing a white jumpsuit.

"Looks like he's shaved since we saw him last," Kevin whispered. "And Maggie, look. He's wearing one of those white outfits."

"Why would he dress in white?" Maggie said. "It doesn't make any sense. The place is a compost heap."

Weissman started to walk into the yard but then changed his mind. "Black, Brown," he yelled. "Come." They obeyed immediately and all three went inside for the night. After five minutes, the floodlights went dark.

The rest of the night and morning was quiet. At 1:15 p.m.,

Weissman reappeared and drove off toward the mine. He returned three hours later. Except that he was shaven, there was no deviation from the previously established pattern. The spies pulled together their gear and headed home.

"We'll be back," Kevin said. "Soon."

Chapter 27

Terrain Denial

THE MALL OF AMERICA WAS ALWAYS DIFFICULT. MARSHA Williams ripped her children away from the acres of consumer orgy for the tenth time. Temptation everywhere. Around each corner something Sam Jr. or Lily couldn't resist: dolls, scooters, remote-control cars, alien brain-suckers. They'd just finished lunch and she needed only one more item...

Sam Jr. darted into a store and grabbed a demonstration doll whose main selling point was the ability to soil diapers. He squeezed its tummy and tore open the diaper.

"Ah, just wet," he said. When a pungent odor suddenly struck his nose, he changed his mind. "But the smell part's good!" he shouted.

"Wow," Lily squealed, holding her nose in delight, "it really works." She was too young to understand sisters aren't supposed to encourage crass behavior.

Marsha ran into the store in a desperate attempt to salvage dignity. By now a fetid smell filled the room, an all-powerful rapidly increasing stench. "I'm really sorry," she said to the frowning clerk, grabbing the kids and escaping out the door.

But, outside the store, the putrid stink was even worse. It triggered a human stampede. The crowd, gasping and retching, raced for the elevators and escalators, pushing baby carts beyond their speed ratings, knocking shopping bags against their knees. The ghastliness of the smell overruled whatever bumps they might sustain in the rush. Several older shoppers fell beneath the advancing phalanx of panicked feet.

This time Marsha didn't need to beg her children to follow.

They merged into the violent, swirling human river and sprinted for the door.

א א א א

After a gagging drive home and arduous showers that only partially ridded them of the clinging odor, Marsha abandoned the effort and watched the news. On location at the mall, the reporter regaled the nation with the tale of this strange new plague, himself writhing in agony whenever doors opened and the malevolent odor singed his nose.

Back in the cable newsroom, Lauren, the afternoon anchor, began a satellite interview with a specialist in nonlethal weapons.

"We have reports that the military has been developing, literally, stink bombs," she said in her best can-you-believe-that-darn-military voice. "Can you confirm this?"

"Absolutely. We call them terrain-denial devices. When deployed, anybody in the vicinity is unable to remain. The smell is so noxious that it's literally impossible for a person to endure even if leaving the area is dangerous in itself. The intended application is to flush the enemy out of occupied areas: caves, buildings, things of that nature."

"Do you think the device deployed today at the Mall of America was one of these terrain-denial devices?"

"Sounds like it to me. Fits the description."

"Do you think it was civilian or military in origin?" Lauren asked.

"Of course the investigation has just begun but, in my opinion, the magnitude and intensity of odor generated would suggest a military device."

Lauren abruptly terminated the interview. "Sorry to cut you off sir, but we have another breaking development. This just in— the one who deployed the terrain-denial device at the Mall of America sent the following message to the FBI: 'To him who has ears to hear ... nothing beside remains. Round the decay of that colossal wreck.'"

"Truly a very cryptic and frightening message," Lauren said in a redundant effort to reinforce the newsworthiness of the event. "At this point, we have no word from authorities as to what this message might mean. We do know that the Bloomington Police Department and National Guard are taking this very seriously. There is a bomb squad combing the mall grounds. We'll make details available to you as they are forthcoming."

Someone off camera handed Lauren another message. She scanned the headline before continuing.

"Another breaking story ... this one from Denver. We don't have a news team at this site yet, but we have aerial coverage from a local traffic helicopter. Some type of sonic blast has occurred in an office park in a Denver suburb. Actually, I'm not sure if *blast* is the right word. The reports indicate that this does *not* appear to be a bomb. At least no bomb explosion has been reported. Apparently, the sheer noise has incapacitated workers at an office complex. The Denver Police Department is en route. Our traffic copter is in position now."

The screen switched to show the targeted office building. A Dodge sedan with its windows blown out was parked one hundred feet in front of the Peak Total Communications building and was obviously the source of the noise.

"Lauren, we've just arrived on the scene and we're hovering above this truly bizarre situation," the traffic reporter said. "People apparently are trapped inside this office building. It seems they're having great difficulty trying to get out. Those we can see are having trouble walking, trouble with their balance. Some are crawling around. Others are vomiting and for obvious reasons we're not going to give any close-up shots of those victims. It's very difficult to move around under the assault of this noise."

The picture showed a small number of sick-looking workers crawling near the front entrance of the building, dizzy, disoriented, staggering, most attempting to reenter the building. Each was holding his ears against the hideous sonic weapon.

"There are other doors to the side and back of the building, but no one seems to be leaving. I'm guessing the other workers have been advised to remain inside."

The camera turned toward an arriving ambulance.

"Here comes an emergency response vehicle arriving at the scene."

Just as the ambulance driver entered the parking lot his windows shattered. The vehicle veered out of control and collided with a parked car.

Two squad cars hot on the heels of the ambulance pulled up alongside. The policemen wore bulky ear protection but still struggled to get out their pistols. They fired at the offending Dodge sedan, the clang of bullets punctuating the roar emitting from the car. For a brief moment the deafening noise stopped, then resumed.

The two officers from one squad kept shooting while the other squad opened their trunk and emerged with sleek, black shotguns. They knelt, anchoring the guns into their shoulders, then blasted the Dodge with buckshot. Strips of metal exploded off the car like string cheese. After five shots, a new quiet hung in the air like the pall of a funeral when everyone has finished saying what there is to say and there's nothing left but the burying.

Some office workers attempted to get up now that the malevolent assault on their inner ears had ended. They would stand, then fall, stand, then fall, like forty-year-old toddlers. Finally, most gave up and dragged themselves to the grass where they splayed out waiting for help.

א א א א

Craig and Cat, inseparable of late, raced into the apartment and scrambled to the television.

"Guys, you'd better get in here right away," Craig shouted.

Kevin and Maggie were packing the last of the food for tonight's stakeout. Craig's urgency was convincing and they dropped the apples on the counter.

"Check this out," Craig said pointing at the TV. "Terrorism hits the Twin Cities and Denver."

"What happened?" Kevin asked.

"We were listening to the car radio and heard this just before we got home," Craig said. "It all happened in the last few hours."

Craig, speaking over the reporter's voice, summarized about the stink bomb and the sonic weapon. Then he muted the TV and turned to Maggie.

"This sonic weapon was positioned outside a company named

Peak Total Communications. Does that have anything to do with Peak Air or Peak Engineering?"

"Jeff owns them all."

"What does this have to do with Jeff?" Kevin asked.

"No idea," Maggie said. "But he's also an investor in the Mall of America."

"What's going on?" Kevin said. "Yesterday it was Peak Air. Today this. Somebody's after Jeff."

Cat whistled. "That's sure gotta be freakin' out your ol' man."

"If that's all I had to worry about, I'd be celebrating," Maggie said. "But this..." She shook her head.

Craig turned to Kevin. "Do you think Weissman had anything to do with this?"

"Not his MO," Kevin said.

Another news alert hit the TV screen. Conversation ceased and they turned up the volume.

"—located the stink bomb inside a ventilation shaft at the Mall of America. It was indeed a military device. But the frightening thing is that they found a canister of cyanide sitting next to it in the ventilation system. The stink bomb was detonated but the adjacent cyanide canister was not detonated." She paused for listeners to consider the consequences. "This could have killed hundreds of people. Maybe thousands."

"I hate to say it," Kevin said, "but now this is starting to sound like Weissman again. First, at the Stanford conference they mentioned he had been a lead project researcher for the Department of Defense, which means he might have worked on nonlethal weapons development. Second, I used terrain-denial devices in my apocalypse paper."

"They've got the FBI involved now," Maggie said. "Maybe they'll nab him before he hurts anyone, and we can just stay out of it."

Without meaning to, Kevin sighed. "Either we turn him in based on what we know right now, or we wait. Come to think of it, he didn't really hurt anyone, did he?"

There was a moment of silence, then Maggie launched a rebuttal. "What about the people working at Peak Total Communications? They were knocked off their feet and throwing up."

"But Maggie, that's my point. No one was seriously hurt. Not at the mall. And probably not at Jeff's company. The workers were exposed to a loud noise and dizziness. Probably no permanent injury."

Maggie considered Kevin's theory. "What about the cyanide?"

"The bomber wanted exactly the reaction you gave. Shock. Horror for what could have been. It had the potential to be 9/11 all over again. It might have gone down as one of the biggest terrorist events in history. But he didn't do it. See?"

"It's probably just a matter of time," Maggie countered.

"We don't know that. What if there isn't a next time? Maybe he just wants people to learn about tight coupling by demonstrating it. They won't let him teach it in the halls of academia, so he's trying to show what it might look like in real life. Or maybe he hates your dad for some reason."

"Yeah, well, stand in line," Maggie said. "There are thousands who'd love to nail Jeff's hide to the wall. Myself included."

"Or," Kevin continued, "maybe he's just gone completely off the rails."

"Or maybe it isn't him at all," Cat said. "Heaven knows I've been accused of stuff I never did."

"We leave tonight," Kevin said. "The break-in will be either tomorrow or Wednesday depending on what we observe. He's got computers—I'm sure of it. I want one more chance to hack them."

Maggie pointed at the television. "Look at that headline: *The Benign Bomber.*"

A cable newsman turned to the expert-of-the-hour, a product-development manager for a security company. "What's so perplexing about these attacks is what motivated them," the expert said. "It's obvious that the saboteur had more lethal means at his disposal than what was deployed. Theories run the gamut from a massively destructive but nonlethal practical joke, all the way up to a botched attempt at mass murder. My thought is that whoever's responsible did not mean to kill anyone. For example, the triggering device on the cyanide canister was apparently perfectly functional.

"The best clue to the motives of this saboteur—or saboteurs—is that they left a stink bomb along with the cyanide canister yet only deployed the stink bomb. Had they meant to kill as many as possible, the stink bomb was a counterproductive measure. Cyanide released into the air would not have been detected until it compromised a large number of people. The stink bomb, or, terrain denial device, was simply a warning. But a warning about what? That's the big question."

"They're looking for answers," Craig said. "Maybe we can help."

"Or maybe," Maggie said looking at Craig, "we can be dead." She looked at Kevin. "Or maybe we can be maimed by dogs." Back to Craig. "Or maybe we can be put in federal prison for a decade." Back to Kevin. "Or maybe we—"

"OK, Maggie, you've made your point," Kevin said. "If we find evidence, we call the FBI."

Chapter 28

The Nineteenth Icon

"WHAT'S THE PLAN?" MAGGIE ASKED AS THEY DEPARTED Denver city limits.

"Same as before," Kevin said. "You and I go in. Craig keeps sentry."

"Works for me," Craig said.

"Strictly business. Keep radio chatter to a minimum," Kevin said. "We've got to find his computers. He's got a network in there—this is Dr. Anthony Weissman we're talking about. He must have some kind of basement."

"What about the mine?" Maggie asked. "Could he have computers there?"

"Not likely," Craig said. "He's only there three hours, and he comes back filthy."

"If we don't find a basement," Kevin said, "we'll check the mine later."

Maggie's rental Trailblazer first drove to the darkened CIMT campus where Kevin re-borrowed a duffel of lasers and batteries, fully intending, of course, to return them later, also under cover of darkness. Leaving campus, they ripped through the mountain highway. In what seemed like no time, their vehicle was parked off-road, and they were deep into the woods making their way to the ridge.

Maggie looked down on the moonlit shack. "If I were Catholic, I'd say this place looks like purgatory."

They unrolled the sleeping bags on the ridge and Craig used binoculars to scan the cabin. Lights on, per usual. Weissman nowhere to be seen, per usual. Land Cruiser parked in front of the house, per usual.

"The dogs are out," he reported. "We'll have to be careful."

Nothing to do but wait. Craig took first shift. Kevin and Maggie lay on their sleeping bags looking straight up into the aspens. The sky was alive—big sky with brilliant, dazzling stars and a half moon that shone more than whole. Kevin's senses were the sharpest he could ever remember. He saw and felt everything: the tiny root in the middle of his back, the leaves shaking above with each micro-tremor of wind, the bat darting invisibly ten feet from where he lay. Even perhaps Maggie's heart beating. Yes, he was sure of it.

Maggie reached over and took his hand, and they lay there very much in love. But it was not as simple as that. He was regretful for what was about to happen. Even ashamed. His future was open and promising. Weissman had no future. His time was short; things were ending badly. Kevin felt guilty being in love this close to judgment day.

He looked over at Maggie. Her eyes were closed, and she was smiling. He let it be—she'd spent so little of her life smiling.

ℵ ℵ ℵ ℵ

The night slipped by like a river, continuously changing yet appearing unchanged. There was no sign of Weissman throughout the night and into the next day. At 1:00 p.m. they anticipated his arrival on the porch. By 3:00 Kevin turned to Craig: "If he was responsible for yesterday's events, that'd explain why his routine is off. This doesn't look good."

Just before dusk, a grey Lexus entered the property. The dogs alarmed as it angled through the brushy drive, but recognition quieted their clamor. Weissman parked next to the Cruiser.

"That's his other car," Kevin whispered to Maggie. "He must park it in that outbuilding by the mine."

The dogs surrounded the vehicle, tails wagging, tempted to jump but disciplined to refrain. Weissman opened the door and threw dog treats over their heads. Then he stood and looked around the property. His beard was trimmed and his hair combed. He wore khaki pants and a dark blue shirt, covered with a lightweight black jacket. Despite his fashion improvements, he appeared spent and moody.

Maggie, Kevin, and Craig peeked over the embankment. Weissman's gaze lingered when he looked at the ridge. Although two hundred yards away, they held their breath and lowered themselves flat on the ground.

Weissman called the dogs and fastened heavy chains to their collars, then clasped the chains to an eye bolt anchored into the house. With binoculars, Maggie could see the chains and eye bolt were connected by means of a pull pin, like farmers use to connect tractors and trailers.

Suddenly the dogs went wild, straining at the tethers, their muscles rippling, the chains tight. The bloodlust was unlike any noise Maggie had ever heard. She chilled to think Craig would be required to deal with these beasts.

"What in the world?" Craig whispered.

From the trunk of the Lexus, Weissman removed a rabbit cage. The dog's feverish noises increased. Maggie tried to avert her eyes from what came next, but she couldn't.

Weissman set the cage down and released the rabbit. It sprinted for the woods. Weissman waited, then pulled the pin restraining the dogs. Their legs blurred as they ran, dragging chains, bawling like hounds on the moor. One of the chains wrapped around a root, tightened abruptly, and stopped the dog short, standing him up straight. Given the momentary advantage, the other dog was on the rabbit. The rabbit managed a single, shrill cry of absolute terror before the dog crushed its neck. The first dog pulled free, dragging a section of root along with its chain, and both laid into the rabbit, ripping and tearing. The sound of bones crunching was audible even on the ridge. Weissman looked again at the woods and ridge, then went back inside, the dogs still devouring their prey.

"Reminds me of lions," Craig said.

"Reminds me of the Foster house."

"Sure you've got enough drug on those darts?" Kevin asked Craig.

"I'll be OK." He dug in his pack and took out a Glock 9mm.

"Wait just a minute," Maggie said. She looked at Kevin. "Did you know about the gun?"

"We're not planning to use it."

"Just one problem," she said. "This is no longer breaking and entering, it's—I don't know—*armed* breaking and entering or something."

"We'll just leave the gun outside," Craig said. "And we'll just not get caught."

"Besides, Weissman wouldn't press charges," Kevin said, looking slightly unsure.

"Would you rather get shredded by those beasts?" Craig asked.

Maggie yielded but let her anger hover in the air. She'd never admit it, but she found the gun comforting herself. If given the chance, the dogs could kill them all. Even Craig.

The evening settled down as the Rottweilers wandered back to the porch and slept.

א א א א

Just after noon the next day, Weissman came out dressed in work clothes.

"Welcome back, chief," Craig whispered under his breath. "About time."

Ignoring the Lexus, Weissman took the Cruiser and rumbled toward the mine. It had the distinctive growl of an old, abused truck, easy to hear if he came back early.

"Go time," Craig said.

"Agreed," Maggie said.

"Let's do it."

They waited five minutes, then moved slowly down the hill while keeping a close eye on the dogs—Craig with his 9mm and blowgun, and Kevin with the duffel of lasers, batteries, and scope. Their first priority was blinding the surveillance cameras. The laser positions from the first break-in were too close to the yard, positions that were safe enough when the dogs were inside the house but risky now that they were roaming. Kevin and Craig descended only as far as necessary, then set up the first laser.

The second camera required a lower angle, closer to the dogs. They inched themselves slowly down using brush as cover. When still twenty feet from where they needed to be, Craig whispered, "I'll throw a rock across the yard." From his knees, he threw over the house and into the trees on the far side of the compound. The dogs jumped from the shade of the porch and raced to the noise, barking loudly. Kevin and Craig quickly crawled the remaining distance and positioned the laser. Then Kevin returned to the first laser and, counting 1-2-3 with his fingers, they flipped the switches simultaneously.

Craig crawled to a junked car at the perimeter of the yard. Kevin threw a stick into some bushes beyond Craig's position. As the dogs came back to investigate, they passed broadside twenty yards away. Catching his scent they pulled up and snorted the air in a primal gesture that gave Maggie shivers.

Craig appeared calm as he blew the dart. It landed in the muscled hind leg of the first dog. The shot betrayed his general position and they came toward him. He blew another dart that struck the second animal square in the chest.

Craig held his position behind the car, protected by the underground fence. Within ten minutes both dogs descended into an uneasy sleep. Craig unscrewed his blowgun and stashed it in his backpack.

With pistol drawn, he slowly approached the dogs. Ten feet away, the second dog dug deep into its reserves and wobbled to its feet. Craig stopped dead in his tracks. He did not move. The dog shook its massive head in a drugged slow-motion. Then it looked straight at Craig. It took a few seconds to focus. It showed its teeth and tried to growl with little result. Craig continued to stand like a statue and didn't breathe. The dog shook its head again. With no more warning that that, it lunged for Craig, teeth bared. Craig sidestepped just in time, and as the brute stumbled by, he brought the pistol down viciously on its head. The dog dropped and didn't move.

Kevin and Maggie watched from the hill. They were squeezing each other's hands. When the dog fell, Kevin started toward the house and pulled a reluctant Maggie with him. Craig concealed himself once more behind the junked car, gun in one hand, radio in the other.

Kevin picked the porch lock and opened the door. The place had continued its entropic trajectory, all shab and clutter.

Following his hunch, he walked through the kitchen and down the hall to the room at the end. Maggie followed closely. Kevin bent to work the keypad, and within ten seconds they were in the storeroom. He ignored the merchandise ringing the room and walked directly to the boxes of vodka and champagne on the Persian carpet. Sliding them off to one side, he knelt and attempted to move the carpet.

"Just as I suspected," he said.

"What?" Maggie asked.

"This carpet is glued. I think we've just found the basement."

He went to the small desk in the far corner and picked up the phone.

Nothing.

He entered the same six digits as the keypad, then waited.

Still nothing.

He entered another sequence, then another. On the fourth try, a whirring noise rose from beneath the floor. The carpet began lifting.

Maggie stepped behind Kevin. "How did you do that?" she whispered nervously.

"First, I tried the same sequence as the keypad—his wife and son's birthdays. When that didn't work, I tried his other passwords. The magic happened when I included an S for Susan and a J for Joshua."

They fell silent as the basement entrance slowly opened.

"I can't see a thing," Maggie whispered. As soon as she said it, lights illuminated the basement. She jumped back.

"I think they come on automatically," Kevin whispered.

He went to the top of the steps and bent down to look. He stood back up and turned to Maggie. "I can't see anything, but I can hear the hum of his computers," he whispered.

He turned again to face the stairs and bent down. "Hello?" Kevin said. "Anyone there? Dr. Weissman? This is Kevin."

Silence.

"OK, Maggie. Here we go."

He held her hand and they began the descent. With each step, he bent again to look.

"Stay here until I go down a bit further," he said.

"I'm not staying behind," she said, grabbing his shirt.

Two more steps and the music began. Maggie stopped. "What's that?"

"Górecki's Third. Weissman's favorite. I heard it a lot in his office." Kevin pulled her gently. "Keep going. Clock's ticking."

Down a few more steps, she tapped Kevin on the shoulder and pointed to the lettering above their heads: *See my works, ye mighty, and despair.*

"Ozymandias," Kevin said. "It all makes sense. I'll explain later."

As they stepped onto the floor, the hinged door closed above them.

"Oops," Kevin said.

"What do you mean, *oops?*"

"I hope we can get out."

"What do you mean, *hope we can get out?*"

"Well, if we can't, we'll just have to raise our family down here."

Maggie punched him in the back. "That's not funny."

The room was otherworldly: white countertops, white ceilings, white walls, white carpeting.

Kevin and Maggie sat back on the third step and removed their shoes. They inspected their socks to be sure no dirt would deposit on the carpet. Kevin knelt and picked up several specks. They looked at each other and both nodded.

Taking a step, Maggie said, "Boy, this is soft."

"More than that," Kevin said. "It's warm." He knelt down and touched the flooring. "He's got underfloor heating. That's a big draw on his electricity."

Maggie walked over to the computers. "Can you believe this?"

Kevin walked along the table. "Looks like nine on each side," he said. "I told you." He looked over at her. "Didn't I tell you?"

"This place looks like a CIA war room," Maggie said. "All top-notch stuff."

"Built everything himself."

"This explains the huge dish in the junkyard—he's got a broadband satellite connection," Maggie said. "It's all networked. Screaming fast. I'm guessing he's got dedicated bandwidth service so he can control for congestion."

"And the solar power is used for running this system, or at least a backup. Temperature and humidity controls. He's got everything covered."

Kevin radioed Craig. "Craig, we're in. How you doing?"

"Quiet. What about you?"

"Found it. The mother lode. In his basement. Never seen anything like it."

"Copy that. Good work."

Kevin turned to Maggie. "This computer at the near end of the table is the master. There's wrist grease on the lower keyboard."

Maggie pulled out the chair and sat down. As she did, the screen saver dissolved into the image of a crashed commercial jetliner with the tail section torn off. She gasped.

"Look what he's got for background," Kevin said, bending over and pointing at the carnage.

"That's an Airbus A319," Maggie said. Her voice was shaken. "I remember this accident like it was yesterday. LAX. It was foggy. The Airbus taxied across a runway, and a Boeing 737 was coming in on final. Its wingtip sheared off the tail of the Airbus."

"Must be the flight his family died on," Kevin said. Looking at the screen struck Maggie as inappropriate, almost morbid, like staring at a fresh corpse. "Who'd want to see that every day? It would tear my guts out."

"That's not all." She grabbed his arm. "Kevin... Oh, no."

"What? What's the matter?"

"The Boeing was a Peak Air jet."

"Wait a minute. You're telling me that your dad owned the plane that killed Weissman's family?"

She looked up, tears flooding down her face. "Oh, Kevin."

"Maggie, you had nothing to do with this. And, most likely, neither did your father. Weissman blames himself for the accident."

She did not respond.

"Maggie." He pulled her face toward his and looked directly into her eyes. "I know this is a shock. But there's no time for that now. Let's gather as much information as we can and get out. We can talk about this later tonight. Deal?"

She looked back and realized, for the first time, that she had grown to depend on him. She smiled weakly and tried to wipe her tears. "Deal."

He kissed her on the forehead.

He pointed to the screen. "We have to figure out these icons. How many are there?"

"Nineteen," she said softly.

He walked along the table, each side, and read the names printed on each computer: "Communications, computer science, crime, economics, energy, environment, information, international relations, internet, medicine, military, technology, transportation, population/demographics, privacy/surveillance, religion, terrorism, weapons."

"That's eighteen," Maggie said. "They're the same as the ones on the screen. Same order too, alphabetical. The nineteenth icon is different though. It's labeled 'Megiddo.'"

Kevin hurried back to Maggie and leaned over her shoulder, their cheeks almost touching.

"Know what that is?" he asked. "Megiddo is an ancient city in northern Israel. The Hebrew word for hill is 'har' so in archeology this site is called 'Har Megiddo.'"

"I don't get it."

"Say them both together—HarMegiddo. Sound familiar?"

"Armageddon?"

"Precisely. This master computer processes the information from the other eighteen. He's playing war games, and I'll bet he's using tight coupling as the strategy. Do you mind if we switch, Maggie? Let me dig into Megiddo. You go break down one of the topical computers."

They switched quickly, Maggie yielding without protest. She walked along the bank of computers and then came back to Number 4, Economics, and immersed herself in the challenge of thinking Weissman's thoughts after him. Five minutes later she saw it. "He's designed his own search engine. Each computer is dedicated to one topic. It scans news feeds and information sources on that topic from around the world for developments."

"How does it work?"

"He's set up Boolean searches using combinations of keywords that pertain to the topic. This computer is the economics computer, OK? Right now it's searching this combination of keywords: destabilize, terrorism, debt, recession, collapse, default, bankruptcy, threat, crash, radical, conflict, and nuclear. All of these words must be present for a hit. Then he goes to the next search by adding or subtracting a word. Looks like he's using fifty, maybe a hundred, keywords altogether for the economics search. I'm guessing each computer has its own set of keywords."

"There would be millions of combinations using that many words."

"Trillions," Maggie said. "That's why he's using fast equipment."

"He's looking for tight coupling," Kevin said. "Anytime a link between these words is found, the hit is sent to this master computer. As far as I can tell, once they arrive here, the links are broken down into First, Second, Third, and Fourth Order Threats. First Order Threats are sent to the Megiddo file, and the others are sent to the topical file of that computer."

Maggie kept tapping her feet. "We need to keep moving. There's not much time. We need to know what he's planning and when."

"Right." Kevin ran through the First Order Threats and noticed they were further broken down into three more subdirectories: current status, suspended status, and disregard.

After ten minutes of searching, he turned to Maggie. "I don't see anything that looks like a plot. Probably our best bet will be to follow the current status file. Not a lot to go on but it's something."

"Keep looking," Maggie said, growing anxious. "Time's running out."

On cue, Craig's voice came over the radio. "Make it snappy. These dogs are starting to twitch. I don't want to give 'em another dose or they'll be sleeping when Weissman gets back. How's it going?"

"Good. We hacked his system."

"You need to come out soon."

"10-4," Kevin said and set down the radio. He turned to Maggie. "Quick. Come here. Take a look."

"What?"

"He's flagged this file at the top of his current status directory. It's labeled Forest Fires. It's got feeds from two computers: #6-Environment and #17-Terrorism. About droughts in the U.S."

"I want you guys up here pronto," Craig broke in.

"OK," Kevin said. "We're coming."

They covered their tracks as best they could, then pushed away from the table and headed for the stairs.

"How do we turn off the lights?" Maggie asked.

"It'll happen automatically."

"How do you know?"

"I know Weissman."

"Kevin," Maggie said. "Look." She pointed to a bank of small video monitors along the far wall. "There's his surveillance system." They quickly crossed the room for a closer look. "There are seven monitors here," she said, "and that includes a camera on top of the house. See? These are shingles along the bottom of the frame. And these two screens over here are fuzzied out. Good work, Kev. There's no view here of the front door."

"I don't know how I missed that roof camera. That was a dangerous mistake. Do you think it caught us?"

"Don't think so. It's pointing toward the driveway."

"Good. Let's get out of here."

As they sat on the stairs to slip on their shoes, a mechanism above began to open the hatch. "It's working," Kevin said.

"What if it doesn't turn off the lights and music?"

"Don't trust me yet?"

"I trust you to get me 10-to-20."

"Maybe they'll give us adjacent cells."

When they reached the top of the steps, the trap door began to close. They ran out of the room, making sure the door locked behind them. They hurried to the kitchen and peeked out the window. Craig was standing over the dogs with a sturdy stick, the Rottweilers beginning to move.

"Come on guys," Craig said, motioning frantically. "Hurry!"

They stepped out the door and Kevin relocked it.

"Run for it," Craig shouted.

The three raced across the yard. As they were fleeing, Maggie turned back.

"Maggie, just run," Kevin said.

She flailed her arms. Craig stopped mid-stride. "One of the dogs has the dart stuck in his chest," she yelled.

Craig turned around. "Unbelievable!" The Rottweiler's thick coat had folded over when lying down, hiding the dart. As the brute stood to shake off somnolence, the dart reappeared from the middle of his sternum.

As Craig approached the dog, it charged clumsily. Craig sidestepped as before, but getting the dart was another matter. The dog turned and made another staggered run at him. This time Craig gave it a soccer kick and caught it in the side of the face. The dog plowed headfirst into the ground throwing dirt in front of it.

The dog was half-standing, its rear protruding in the air. Craig gave the hindquarters a shove, toppling it to the side, then reached for the dart. Just as he pulled the dart, the dog snapped at his wrist. Craig twisted his arm out of its grasp but a fang caught him in the forearm. Blood spurted onto the dog's snout.

Craig yelled something in an African dialect and delivered a swift, strong blow to the neck. He pushed his bleeding arm into the front of his shirt, careful not to leave a blood trail exiting the property. His shirt quickly turned red.

"I hate that dog," Craig said, catching up to the others.

"It hates you back," Maggie said. The dog was still reeling.

Kevin took off his shirt and gave it to Maggie to wrap around Craig's arm.

"Stay focused, guys," Kevin warned. "Maggie, help Craig get up top without splattering the hill with blood. I'll get the lasers and be up right behind you."

א א א א

Maggie and Craig scrambled up the hill and dropped into the foxhole. "We've got to get you to a doctor," Maggie said, alarmed by the amount of blood that now covered Craig's shirt and the front of his pants as well.

"Kevin knows how to steri-strip."

Just then they both heard a rumble in the distance. "Is that the Land Cruiser?" Maggie asked.

Craig looked in the direction of the mine and spotted a dust cloud headed their way. "Not good," he said. They glanced nervously over the ridge to see how Kevin was doing. He was two-thirds of the way up the hill with fifty yards to go. Carrying a heavy load up the steep incline, he was starting to drag. When he heard the Cruiser, he turned in the direction of the noise and then back with a look of fear on his face. He lifted the duffel onto his shoulder and pounded up the remaining distance, falling across the ridge just as Weissman rolled into the yard. All three lay down, Kevin huffing as quietly as he could, Craig still bleeding heavily. Maggie was petrified.

"You OK to wait a minute?" Kevin, still gasping, whispered to Craig.

"Think so." He squeezed harder on the bleeding site.

Weissman parked the truck as the dogs approached at half speed, wobbly. They looked like they were trying to shake off the effects of an afternoon nap. Weissman bent to give them a superficial pet, when one of them, still under the effects of the drug, snapped at his hand catching him beneath the first knuckle. Blood dripping off his hand, Weissman hit the dog on the side and cursed in Polish. The dog came back growling, baring its teeth. Weissman kicked it over with his boot and stormed into the house.

Minutes later, he returned to the porch with his 30-30 and walked a few feet into the yard. Black and Brown were still tottering about the premises. A shot rang out, the blast ricocheting off the mountains and back again. Brown dropped into a lifeless pile, and Maggie let out a scream.

Weissman's head jerked up, scanning the hills. He walked about the house looking deep into the woods, then through the junkyard. He came back into the front yard, muttering loudly.

He chambered another shell. He put the end of the rifle in his mouth. He kept it there for ten seconds, still looking around the hills.

He pulled the trigger.

This explosion jolted the valley. Weissman stumbled backward and fell.

Maggie again tried to scream but Kevin threw his hand across her mouth.

"Shhh," he whispered. "He took the barrel out before he shot."

"I saw it too," Craig said.

They lay still and watched, afraid to breathe.

Weissman lay motionless. After sixty seconds, he stirred.

Slowly, he pushed himself to his knees. Picking up the 30-30, he used it to prop himself to standing.

"The right side of his face looks horrible," Kevin said, looking through the binoculars. "Man, his face is really bruised."

Weissman shook his head. He put his hand to his ear and pulled on the lobe.

"He's bleeding from his ear," Kevin said. "A lot."

"Blew out his eardrum," Craig said.

Weissman steadied himself. He weakly lifted the rifle and shot four more times against the hills. He stumbled like a drunk, and his aim was random.

All except his last shot. It flew twenty feet over their heads. Maggie heard it whiz past and explode a rock behind her.

Chapter 29

What She Sees

"Doesn't it seem like Weissman stares up at us?" Maggie asked, sitting on the couch.

Kevin placed the last steri-strip on Craig's arm. "That makes seventeen," he said. "A new personal best, isn't it?"

"Can't wait to show it off at the gym. Hey, suppose the gym's still open?"

"Listen you cretins—I think he's on to us. Every time he's in the yard he looks up at the ridge. He shot right above our heads!"

"Coincidence," Kevin said. "If he saw us, he'd yell at us. Or he'd sic the dogs."

"I'm with Maggie on this one Kev. He suspects something."

"You also lost a couple gallons of blood today," Kevin said, "which, no doubt, is why your judgment has shifted in a feminine direction."

"Why did he kill his dog?" Maggie asked with a shiver.

"When a dog bites a person who's a little crazy, it goes dead," Kevin said.

"A little crazy? He's way over the edge," Maggie said.

"Crazy, yes," Kevin said. "But criminal? We still don't have any proof. We found his computers but didn't find anything on them except genius. It's not illegal to be flaky. It's not even illegal to kill your dog. We have no evidence he's done anything wrong."

"If you'll excuse me, I'm going horizontal," Craig mumbled. "You kids behave yourselves." He stood up, then lurched to his left tottering against Maggie.

"Whoa there cowboy," Maggie said.

"I'm OK." He stumbled the rest of the way into the bedroom.

"Don't trip over Cat," Kevin said.

They heard his body collapse onto the groaning mattress.

Maggie followed to close the door. Then she came back and sat down next to Kevin—who found himself suddenly wide awake.

"Let me make some coffee," he said. "I'll be right back."

"Why are you making coffee? It's two in the morning."

His only reply was to switch on the coffee grinder. In the dead of night it sounded like a freight train. "I just thought we could use some coffee."

"You're wired enough. Look at you—you can hardly hold your hands steady."

"Exactly. Caffeine might calm me down."

"You're nervous." She stood up and walked over to him, every inch the temptress, and hugged his arm close to her body. "Talk to me."

"Let's not sit on the couch. How 'bout the table?"

"Sure, the table," she said in a whisper. She playfully kissed him on the forehead.

He felt his knees go weak. For one second, he switched out, parts of his body on high alert while others ceased functioning altogether. He wondered if there was anything he could do, like breathing into a paper bag. *Certainly nothing I can do and be smooth about it. But then, who cares? Whatever she sees in me, it's not smoothness.*

"Maggie," he said as they sat down across from each other, "what're you doing with me? I'm confused. On paper it doesn't add up. Whenever people see the three of us together, they always assume you're with Craig. You need to tell me, and I think I deserve to know."

She paused.

Great. What've I done now? Hesitation can only be bad.

"While you're thinking, I'll get my coffee," said Kevin who saw his chance to buy time.

"To be honest, at first I was interested in you because I was interested in Weissman—you were interesting by association. But then I started to see the same things in you that he did." She reached across the table, took his coffee, drank a swallow, then gave it back. "What do I like about you? Everything. Not to be simplistic, but that's the honest truth. You're a good man. You're real. You're funny. You're smart. You're yourself and not ashamed of who you are."

"Should I be? That's the sort of compliment due the Elephant Man."

"You know how people are. Everyone wishes they were somebody else—stronger, taller, shorter, hairier, less hairy, smarter, more athletic, made more money, musical. The list goes on. About the only exceptions I know are you, Craig, and Cat. Cat makes sense, since he's the age when people stop caring so much about their image. A façade gets to be too much work. But you—you're young, and you're yourself. The three of you aren't perfect, but you're happy being who you are." Her eyes took on an unmistakable look of sincerity. "How do you do it?"

"I always knew I could never be somebody else ... didn't even want to. So I reconciled myself to it pretty quickly," Kevin said. "Even learned to like myself, I guess."

"You're a free man. That's rare."

"Hey, about Craig. I know he gives you a lot of grief sometimes, and the two of you together can be like a carrot peeler on exposed nerves. But underneath it all, he loves you like a brother."

Maggie smiled. "I know. He's sweet, in a really obnoxious way."

Kevin gazed into her eyes, wondering if he could really see her soul. Looking back at him was just a nervous girl. Her eyes betrayed her fears, perhaps the finest test of vulnerability. She was naked like a fawn in the woods found by hikers, waiting to see if they would walk past or kill and eat.

"I still haven't captured what I wanted to say," Maggie said. "To be honest, my feelings for you are different from any I've ever had. When I'm around you, I feel more alive. More positive. More challenged. I guess, in some ways, hopeful might be the word—that my future might be a more hopeful place. I've been running away from my family for so long. Now, with you, I'm finally running *toward* something. That feels good. It feels really good."

She looked at him with a purity of kindness. Kevin had a glimpse of a different kind of beauty in Maggie Foster, a beauty most never have the opportunity to see.

"What is it you like about me?" she asked tentatively.

He was stunned. Now it was his turn to be afraid. That he'd just asked the same question of her in no way prepared him to answer back.

"Wow. Where to start? You're beautiful. Funny, talented, smart. You're athletic. What's not to like? You're the perfect woman."

"Kevin, wait. It sounds as if you like the idea of me, and not me. You checked off a list like you're buying a car—it's blue, got a V-6 and power everything, so you'll take it. I need more than that."

He shifted uncomfortably.

"When I first saw you at the conference, you were gorgeous. You were like an oasis in the desert. I honestly thought if I got close and touched you, you wouldn't be there—maybe a hologram projection or something."

"This was getting good until you referenced Star Wars."

"But there you were: real. Your initial hostility just made things more interesting. And your mind—when we talked with Weissman at the ice cream shop, I loved it! Here's someone I can talk to. Your sense of humor is a bit over the top—like when you made up the story about stabbing that guy. That was totally not funny." He laughed despite himself.

"See—it was too."

"Well, it wasn't funny at the time. Level with me—have you ever seriously injured anyone?"

Maggie mulled over the question. "Once I gave a guy a roundhouse kick to the side of the head and he dropped like a rock. Had it coming though."

"You never told me about that. Are you a martial-arts type?"

"Kickboxing ... and karate. Fosters have that kind of thing in our genes. I did kickboxing for six months, and I have a black belt in karate. Never got into competitions, but let's just say if we're ever accosted in a dark alley, I'm prepared to defend you."

"Maggie, Maggie, Maggie, Maggie..." Kevin shook his head, then took a very deep, long, and deliberately loud breath.

"OK," he finally said, "let me see if I can steer this ship back on course... What do I like about you. Have you ever loved someone in ways that are so intricate, so deep-seated that you can't articulate them? I guess that's the problem I'm having. I'll try, just scattershot. Most girls I've met are needy, requiring constant validation and approval. It about drives a guy nuts. But you stand on your own two feet. You're aggressive yet really fun to be around. I never know what you're going to say, but I always like it—a lot of times I wish I'd said it myself. You've a certain wisdom, a savvy about the ways of the world. I don't know. I can't explain it really." He measured his next words carefully. "I just like being around you. And I'm dreadfully lonely when you're gone."

"That was perfect." She reached for his hand, and together they quietly sipped coffee from their communal mug.

א א א א

It was 10:30 a.m., time for breakfast. Craig looked none the worse for battle injury. Maggie was her usual radiant self. And Kevin—well, Kevin was dragging.

"Can I fix you a bagel?" Craig asked him.

"Skip the bagel. I'm goin' right to coffee. I need coffee. Lots of coffee."

"Long night?" Craig asked. Seeing Kev's face, he turned and looked at Maggie. She winked.

"Right," Craig said. "One large coffee, coming up."

"Where's Cat," Kevin said.

"On a walkabout."

"Did you tell him about the rifle?" Kevin asked.

"No," Maggie said. "I'm sending him home today."

Kevin and Craig looked at each other. "What?" they said in unison. "Why?"

"It's time. This is a long spell for him to be gone. He gets lonesome for Port Alsworth—Kevin, you can understand that. But mostly, it's going to be stressful here. He doesn't need that, and I don't need the stress of worrying about him."

"What was his response?" Craig asked.

"Let me see if I can remember," she put her hand to her temple in an attempt to look studious. "I believe it was 'Yippee.' That's it. He said, 'Yippee.'"

Craig and Kevin laughed. "Good call, Maggie," Kevin said. "But we're sure gonna miss him."

"Me too. You guys ready to talk about Weissman now?" She sat down at the table. "We need a strategy session, or a debriefing, or whatever the FBI calls it."

"Agreed," Craig said.

"First of all, Kevin, you said you'd explain what was written above the stairway," Maggie said. "Something about a mighty despair."

"*Look upon my works, ye mighty, and despair*," Kevin said. "It's from a poem by Shelley. 'Ozymandias.'"

"That's the same poem called in by the bomber after the Mall of America episode," Craig said. "I mean a segment of it."

"What?" Kevin woke up suddenly and nearly jumped out of his chair. "I don't remember that. Where'd you hear that?"

"The TV commentator read it on air. Weren't you there? Where were you? Maybe Cat and I heard it on the car radio."

"I can't believe it." Kevin googled for details of the Mall of America terrain denial device. "Here it is. *To him who has ears to hear ... nothing beside remains ... Round the decay of that colossal wreck.* How'd I miss this? Did I go to the bathroom or something? This could be huge."

"What does it mean?" Craig asked.

"You recognize the first part from the Bible. Jesus said it a lot. He'd finish up telling his parables by saying *to him who has ears to hear, let him hear*. Not everyone understood his parables—they were riddles, sort of."

"But if this is Weissman, why would he be quoting Jesus?" Craig asked. "He's Jewish. That doesn't make any sense."

"Perhaps that phrase was used in the Old Testament too. We should check."

"And what about the rest—you say that comes from 'Ozymandias'?" Maggie said.

"Right. That's where nothing beside remains and round the decay of that colossal wreck come from."

"Why would he be giving clues?" Maggie asked.

"I don't know," Kevin said. "Maybe he's trying to get caught."

They sat pondering this new development. Three minutes later, Kevin jumped up.

"Oh no!"

"What?" Maggie said in alarm.

"We left the shack in such a hurry I forgot to push the boxes over the rug!"

Maggie put her hands to her mouth.

"Is that a problem?" Craig asked.

"He will see it," Kevin said.

"Maybe he won't notice," Maggie said.

"He will see it."

Chapter 30

Fire on the Mountain

JEFF FOSTER KICKED BACK IN AN OVERSTUFFED CHAIR, HIS BOSE home stereo playing smooth jazz while a fire crackled in the fireplace. The sun had been down for hours. He chilled the house with air conditioning so he could have a fire, because he was at the mountain home and was going to have his fire and damn the world.

Ana-Lese walked into the room and asked if she could get him anything: her father looked quizzically at her but said nothing. Ana-Lese had run out of money in New York and didn't want to take any from Jeff on principle, as she was, of course, a self-reliant woman. Something possessed him to respond with a flicker of fatherhood, and he offered use of the Aspen house rent-free.

She leapt at the offer, just a temporary place to stay, she'd told Maggie. Besides, no doubt she could convince some lucky photographer to shoot her for a winter line. That she'd recently met a gorgeous and unhappily-married junior executive from Aspen didn't hurt either. And Maggie had the audacity to call her a homewrecker.

"Who isn't a homewrecker?" Ana-Lese said.

"I'm not," Maggie said.

"For a Foster who's gone to Stanford, you've sure got a lot of hang ups."

There was a loud bang on Maggie's end and Ana-Lese pulled her ear from the receiver. "What'd you do that for?"

"Sorry, just trying to kill a spider. There he is again." Another loud crack and the line went dead.

Ana-Lese felt vindicated about the move. Her powers of seduction were such that Wes, the unhappily-married man, had already offered to leave his wife.

"That won't be necessary," she had told him. "I'm not interested in a long-term relationship right now. Just keep this on the down low, we'll have a little fun, this thing will run its course, and no one will get hurt." He seemed relieved. For the kids, he said.

א א א א

Jeff fell asleep in the overstuffed chair with the aid of a Jack Welch bio, some top-shelf booze, and a few pills. He awoke with a crick in his neck, the morning sun filtering through the blinds. There was a strange man in the kitchen.

"And who might you be?" Jeff said. "And what are you doing in my kitchen?"

"Jake Johnson, nice to meet you," Wes said, a little disconcerted, but repeating verbatim the alias Ana-Lese devised.

"Jack Johnson—that name sounds familiar. Were you recently on the receiving end of a high profile axing from HP?" Jeff leaned toward him, studying his face.

Wes, on the verge of a sweat, was struggling to remember the precise alias—Jack or Jake—and after an awkward pause committed to Jake.

"No, Jack Johnson's a musician. Never heard of a Jack Johnson with HP. My name's Jake." Striving to be companionable, he offered his hand. Jeff ignored it.

"Help yourself to breakfast," he said when Wes's bagel popped up.

"Thanks," Wes said awkwardly.

"What do you do? You're out here pretty early."

"I'm a fashion photographer in town." He shook his thumb in the direction of Aspen.

"Do you always shoot in your boxers?"

"Uh, no, I spilled coffee on my pants so Ana-Lese threw them in the washer for me."

"That's swell of her. Rare, too. I don't think she's ever washed one stitch of clothing in her life. Must be growing up. Keep up the good work." He gave Wes a punch on the shoulder, spilling his coffee. "Just can't keep that stuff in the cup, huh?"

"Does seem I'm having an unusual amount of difficulty, sir." Wes's brain was now locked into stilted and formal language, a stage that in Jeff's experience usually came five minutes before the sort of meltdown tabloids can headline without burden of aggrandizement.

"What's your camera of choice?" Jeff asked. "I'm a photographer myself. Nowhere near as accomplished as you, I'm sure." Jeff didn't own a camera and hadn't wielded one in over a decade, but he had Wes on the ropes and this was too much fun.

Trying to think, Wes finally spit out, "A high-end Canon Rebel," suddenly thankful for all those old Agassi commercials now lodged in his memory.

Jeff rubbed his hands together, now that his prey had turned down a box canyon. "Where is it? Let me have a look. I've always been a Nikon man myself, but I'd love to see your setup, Jack or Jake or Zack or Zeus or whatever your name isn't."

Jeff was advancing forward, ever faster, even as Wes was now in full retreat. Perspiring, he turned to make a run for the door when Ana-Lese saved the day.

"I smell smoke," she screamed, running in half-dressed.

"It's just Jake-the-Ripper burning his bagel," Jeff said, pushing him in the shoulder. "Go get some clothes on before this Casanova pulls out his high-end Canon Rebel and grosses us all out." One more push knocked Wes over a footstool and he went sprawling against the sofa.

She screamed to raise the dead. "Daddy, look out there. Isn't that smoke?"

Jeff was loathe to abandon his prey but alarmed by Ana-Lese's manner. He stepped on the porch and saw two separate black columns of smoke in the west. The air was thick, the winds were gusting the fire directly at him.

"Great. Perfect." He walked back in the house. "You bastard, Jake." He threw a punch at Wes, just missing his nose.

Jeff dialed 911. "There's a forest fire closing in on my house."

"What is your location?"

"You're supposed to have that on file, you incompetent bitch," he shouted. "I don't know my fire number. Get somebody out here right away or I'll sue you all the way to Tijuana."

He slammed down the receiver and yelled for Ana-Lese and Jake. "Come outside you two," he yelled. "There's work to do." He ran onto the deck and rolled up his sleeves. The smoke was advancing.

Jeff sized up the situation swiftly, a talent he'd always had. His only shot was to create a firebreak between the tree line and his house, to move all combustible timber out of the way, and hope the blaze wouldn't jump the distance to his roof.

He rose to the challenge of cutting and dragging the trees closest to the house. This was a battle against nature, man's work, close to the bone. He went to the garage for the chainsaw just in time to see Ana-Lese and Wes backing out in her Mitsubishi Montero.

"Wait!" he yelled jumping behind their Montero. "Where do you think you're going?"

"Daddy, please let us go. The radio's reporting fires all over Pitkin, Eagle, and Gunnison counties. The forest service's been warning about this, and now there're fires everywhere. I'm scared. Please, Daddy."

"No way. I need help. You're not going anywhere."

"Sorry, we're out of here," Wes yelled, swerving around Jeff. But Jeff had an axe in his hand and wasn't afraid to use it. He swung at the passing rear tire, causing a huge gash to rip open.

"Hey, Jake, you owe me! Schlepping my daughter under my roof and lying to me—"

"Sorry, Jeff. Fifty years ago you might've had something there."

"I'll pay you twenty thousand dollars."

Wes slammed on the brakes and jumped out the door. "Done," he said to Jeff.

"I can't believe he thinks he can just buy everything like that!" Ana-Lese was screaming now, beating the dashboard in her rage. She slid over into the driver's seat and floored it, galumphing her way off the side of the driveway and crashing down the hill, leveling bushes. They heard her grind the transfer case into 4Lo and climb the ditch onto the road. The Montero made a clunking sound as it drove away, spraying gravel.

"Know how to use a chainsaw?"

"That's a mortal sin in Aspen."

"Get ready for some serious sinning then," Jeff said, savagely pulling the starter rope. The chainsaw came to life with a two-stroke roar and a cloud of blue smoke. Jeff laid into the nearest tree, disappearing into a cloud of sawdust.

"We need to cut down the trees close to the house," he yelled over the sound of the saw. "Drag them as far as possible. Get anything flammable."

As the first pine crashed to the ground, Jeff handed Wes the saw and ran to the Range Rover. Backing up to the fallen tree, he looped a chain around the trunk then slowly crawled forward in 4Lo. The V8 was hyper-responsive in low gear and a tap of the throttle lurched him forward. He tightened the chain, then gave it some juice, making clawing progress over small flora. After fifty yards he unhooked the chain and returned for the next arboreal corpse. This majestic Ponderosa he could only drag twenty yards.

Then Wes, misjudging the center of gravity on the next cut, made the wrong angle and wedged the blade. "Foster," he yelled, "Chain's stuck."

"Moron!" He threw a hatchet in Wes's general direction. "Chop it down."

With a blast of wind, smoked billowed above their heads. "Maybe it's time to leave," Wes said, not quite sure which represented the greatest danger, Jeff or the looming fire.

There were still twenty trees to go and, despite his testosterone-charged thinking, even Jeff could see the futility of their efforts. He ran and jumped into the Range Rover.

"Wait," Wes said, running to catch up, and just managed to spring open the door as Jeff was turning the vehicle around.

"I really liked that house," he said and cuffed Wes upside the head.

א א א א

Jeff answered the phone in his Denver home, still in a caller-beware mood. It was Ana-Lese needing a place to stay, trying to make amends for the Aspen escape. These apologies were, of course, nothing more than a simple ploy to avoid homelessness.

After making her beg, Jeff said she could stay for a few days. Perhaps it was from kindness, from fatherly protectiveness, from fear that word would circulate about Jeff Foster's daughter lodging in a shelter. In fact, it was because he rather enjoyed Ana-Lese parading half-dressed through the house. He considered asking for more.

Next Wes called for the promised twenty thousand.

"Oh, that's a great idea," Jeff said. "Why don't I pay you twenty thousand dollars for five minutes' work. Tell you what, hang up right now and I promise not to sue you for twenty grand."

"Come on Foster, you promised," Wes whined. "I need it. My wife kicked me out. I wouldn't ask for it otherwise. I need a little walking-around money."

"You and every other poor sucker."

"It's your daughter's fault."

Jeff went ballistic. "What you do with your sex life is your responsibility, not mine."

Call-waiting saved Wes. "Who is it now?" Jeff demanded.

"Sir, this is Jim Gilmore, chief accountant at Foster Enterprises—"

"I know who you are, Gilmore," Jeff said explosively. "What do you want?"

"Well, sir," he stammered, "there are a couple of federal agents here who want to speak to you."

"What're you talking about? What federal agents? Talk to me about what?"

"I'm not exactly sure sir. They won't say. They want to talk to you directly."

"Tell them don't *do* anything, don't *touch* anything, don't *move* until I come down there."

Jeff hung up and ran out the door to his BMW Z3. He roared off to the office, where, to his great displeasure, he found two intimidating men in charcoal grey suits still waiting forty minutes later.

"I'm Jeff Foster, the owner/president/CEO for this company, so I'm the guy you talk to. No one else. We straight on that?"

"I'm William Kinsey from the SEC ... that's the Securities and Exchange Commission—"

"I *know* what the SEC is," Jeff stammered. "Get to the point."

"—and this is Mr. Paul McClosky from the U.S. Attorney's Office for the District of Colorado. Sir, we need to talk."

Chapter 31

The FBI

KEVIN SIPPED MOODILY AT HIS COFFEE. IT WAS A BAD DAY TO BE alive.

"These fires clinch it," he said watching local coverage under the scrolling banner *Colorado Burns*. The field reporter explained how arson was the cause of seventeen separate forest fires in one morning. Then he held up a small lens device found by a property owner.

"It was fortunate Mr. Peterson took a walk before breakfast. Otherwise his beautiful log home (the camera panned out to show a rustic but expensive multilevel structure) would have joined two hundred others in burning to the ground today. While hiking in the back of his property near a state forest road, Mr. Peterson stumbled upon this mechanism (the reporter held up a ten-inch metal apparatus with a three-inch lens) which has now been found in four of the fires. These arsonist devices were apparently placed all over central Colorado. As soon the sun rose high enough, rays struck this lens and ignited highly flammable materials placed on this platform. The arsonist surrounded the device with pine needles and small twigs. With the weather forecast predicting clear skies, ninety degrees, low humidity, and a fifteen mile-per-hour westerly wind, the terrorists knew precisely where the fires would start and what direction they would spread. Twenty-eight thousand acres have burned so far and only five of the seventeen fires are considered contained. National security experts have long feared this scenario, and today those fears have been realized. It's going to be a long, long, long hot day."

"The same scenario we saw on his computer," Maggie said.

"Evidence keeps piling up," Kevin said. "Now this."

"Time to call the feds?" Craig asked.

"Hate to say it—but it's time." He went into the bedroom and came back with his wallet. "I wrote down a tip-line number after the Mall of America event. Guess that's a good place to start."

"How much are you going to say about our involvement?" Maggie asked.

"That's the big question. It's going to be very tricky. Whatever we decide, we all need to stick together. Since I know Weissman best, how about if I do most of the talking. Maggie, you can play my dumb girlfriend from the Bay. You OK with that?"

She picked up her purse, pulled out her switchblade, flicked it open and stuck the point in the coffee table. "Or, I could play whatever role I want."

"That's what I was going to suggest," Craig said.

"I know we have to do this, but I can't believe we're actually doing it," Maggie said.

"Somebody could've died in those fires today," Kevin said.

"I feel like Judas," Craig said. "We're selling out our mentor here. It's probably not a stretch to say we are all he's got."

Kevin finished digging through his wallet and held up a dollar bill. "OK. Found the number." He picked up the phone.

"You wrote the phone number on a dollar bill?" Maggie asked.

"What's your point?" Kevin said.

"You're really clueless, you know that?"

Kevin dialed. It answered on the first ring.

"FBI, this is Jackie, how may I direct your call?"

"I have possible information about the 'benign bomber.'"

"Please hold while I transfer you to an investigator."

Within seconds, there was a voice on the other end: "FBI Counterterrorism, this is Agent Will Dougherty. Just so you are aware, this conversation is being recorded. How may I help you?"

"I believe I know the identity of the man behind the airport bombings and the recent events in Minneapolis and Colorado."

Dougherty became very serious. "I'm listening."

"My name is Kevin Morgan. I've been following these stories very closely. I just graduated from CIMT—"

"Excuse me—you graduated from where?"

"Colorado Institute of Mining and Technology. I had a professor who sounds like the perpetrator."

"May I ask if you had an adversarial relationship with this professor?"

"Just the opposite. He was my favorite prof and I think I was his favorite student." He paused. "This call was not easy to make, and this conversation is not easy to have."

"Understood."

Kevin assumed voice analysis would confirm his sincerity.

"I also worked as an assistant in his office this past year. Anyway, Dr. Weissman taught about the relationship between technology and society. He was a Luddite of sorts but very rational about it. His teaching stirred enough terrorism controversy that the school wanted him to back off. He refused. Push came to shove, he exploded and quit. Dropped out of sight. He's brilliant and he's manic. He's also off his meds. He seems to be very rich, although I don't know that for a fact."

"What's his name again?" Dougherty asked.

"Dr. Anthony Weissman."

"Could you spell that please?"

"A-N-T-H-O-N-Y W-E-I-S-S-M-A-N. Sometimes he uses the first name A-N-T-O-N-I. His separation from the college last month was very controversial. It got a lot of national media coverage. I thought maybe you'd know about it."

"Not right off-hand. Although within an hour I'll know his mother's uncle's shoe size."

"Actually, I think his mother's uncle died in a concentration camp."

"Understood," Dougherty said again. "And your name is Kevin Morgan?"

"Correct."

"Where do you live Kevin?"

"Denver."

Will paused a minute as he waited for his computer. "As you might guess, Kevin, we're taking any leads in this case very seriously. What makes you believe Dr. Weissman would be behind these acts of terrorism? What makes you think he's capable or motivated?"

"He's an engineer with an amazing intellect—degrees from

Harvard and MIT. Probably one of the smartest people in America. But he also is intense and angry. Really, he's a wounded person. A deeply wounded and disturbed person."

"There are lots of people who are angry and wounded. That's not enough to suspect him."

"You're right. Three things make me believe it's him. First, he has always been emotionally unstable and now he's off his medications—it's hard to tell how violent and dysfunctional he might be. Second, many of the things that have happened were exact scenarios we talked about in class. Third, in the past he worked on DOD research, so he'd probably know about weapons and explosives and Terrain Denial Devices, things like that."

"Well summarized," Dougherty said. "Another question: Is he married? Does he have a family?"

Kevin thought about this for a moment. "No."

"You're hesitant."

"His wife and son both died in a commercial plane crash," Kevin said.

"How long ago?"

"Not sure exactly. Maybe five years ago."

"I'll be in Denver to talk with you later this evening."

"Where do you want to meet?"

"Stay in your apartment. I'll arrive sometime after five o'clock. It would behoove you to be there."

"Never missed an appointment with a federal investigator yet."

"Don't make this the first time."

"Want my address?"

"I've got it."

א א א א

The day dragged by like an ant dragging a leaf a hundred times its size. Each glance at the clock bought Kevin only five minutes. There was a relatively exciting hour when they negotiated among themselves what their exact story would be, without, of course, admitting to anything. This despite their broad spectrum of culpability.

It was decided, in the end, that Kevin would indeed do most of the talking. His official storyline would include one attempted visit to Dr. Weissman's mountain home several weeks ago. The contact was unsuccessful, however, because a vicious guard dog chased him off. This story would allow Kevin to discuss Weissman's Gold Dust Trail location without revealing any additional details.

At 4:45 the knock came. Craig was engrossed in a *National Geographic* article about scorpions in Africa, most species he'd had personal experience with. Maggie waited with Kevin. She squeezed his hand before he opened the door. "We're doing the right thing," she said. He gave a weak smile.

Kevin opened the door to a clean-cut man in his mid-thirties, six feet, buzz cut, black suit wearing an official smile. Although not sure why, Kevin liked the man immediately. A few steps behind was a second agent, similarly dressed, without the smile.

"Kevin? I'm Will Dougherty, FBI. This is Joseph Faber." They flashed their badges in a gesture Kevin found strangely comforting. At least it gave the illusion that the proceedings would happen according to a reliable process.

"Come in. Yes, I'm Kevin Morgan. This is my girlfriend, Maggie Foster, and my roommate, Craig Hunter."

They shook hands all around. This was the first time Kevin introduced Maggie as his girlfriend, and the phrase sounded both matter-of-fact and frighteningly complex.

"If it suits you," Dougherty said, "let's dispense with the small talk and get right down to business." The sentence was more a statement than a question and would have sounded unfriendly if not delivered with such a pleasant demeanor. Agent Dougherty, by early appearances, was an efficient yet personable guy.

א א א א

Kevin was fascinated by the speed with which Dougherty and Faber were able to set up a surveillance operation. They got on the phone and planned the time, route, and equipment. By 7:30 p.m., the necessary approvals were granted by superiors.

"We're staying in an area hotel tonight," Dougherty told Kevin. "Here's my number. Call me if there are any questions.

Agent Faber and I are making a visit to Dr. Weissman's house first thing in the morning. We'll just be scouting the place out. No confrontation. Hopefully he won't even know we're there." He looked directly at Kevin. "What I'm about to say is highly irregular, but since you've visited his house before, we were wondering if you'd be willing to go along?"

"Sure. What time?"

"Leave here at 6 a.m. You can get us close to the house, and on the way we'd like to ask a few more questions about Weissman."

"These guys know him too," Kevin said nodding toward Craig and Maggie. "OK if they come?" He shifted his weight, not quite sure how to make his case. "We're kinda like a team—do everything together."

Dougherty looked at Craig and Maggie. "That all right with you?"

Both nodded.

"See you at 6."

א א א

Dougherty and Faber drove a black unmarked Ford Expedition that belonged to the FBI's Denver office. Kevin, Maggie, and Craig slid into the back seat, subdued. Under Dougherty's sovereignty, they listened to Dvorak's *New World Symphony* for the first half hour while half-heartedly drinking coffee and eating an assortment of breakfast snacks. The rest of the journey was filled with color-commentary about Weissman's troubled life. The discussion flowed both ways—Dougherty knew things even Kevin didn't.

When they were only a few miles from Weissman's, Kevin said, "I'm assuming you don't want to park too close to the house. Is that right?"

"That is correct," Dougherty said. "Any suggestions?"

"Slow down up there at the next right turn," Kevin said. As they approached Gold Dust Trail, he pointed. "That's the way to his house, about a mile down. But don't turn. I'd suggest we keep going straight ahead and see if we can find a spot to park off-road. Then we can walk in through the brush. That might be best."

They parked in the usual spot, Kevin taking pains not to recognize it too easily. The five set out walking through the brush on a deer trail. Kevin led the way, followed by Dougherty, then Maggie, Craig and Faber, who had his pistol out. It was hard to know if the agents were buying their pretended unfamiliarity, but at least for the moment their focus seemed fixed on the destination ahead.

"Remember," Kevin said as they closed in, "there's a guard dog on the premises." He led the way to a small clearing, then pointed at the ridge. "That might be a good spot," he whispered. "I noticed it when I was here before. I think it's an old Jeep trail or something." Dougherty looked around, consulted Faber quietly, then agreed. They climbed silently.

It required fifteen minutes of inching along before they were safely on the ridge. Looking down on the shack, everything was quiet. The Land Cruiser sat in its usual location. No sign of the dog.

"Notice any surveillance equipment around the property?" Dougherty asked Kevin. He took out high-power binoculars and started sweeping the premises.

"Yeah. I found out the hard way. When I came to visit him I was walking up to the front door. About thirty yards from the cabin, all of a sudden his Rottweilers ran out from the back ready to tear me apart. I ran as fast as I could and was saved, apparently, by an electronic dog fence. Lucky for me."

"You said Rottweilers," Dougherty said. "Are there more than one?"

"I'm not sure," Kevin said, trying to cover his error. "I was running so fast I never looked back. I think there's only one. But his sign in the driveway says 'Beware of Dogs.' Anyway, my point is that I think there's some kind of system that triggers a dog alarm inside the house."

"Understood. You three stay down." He looked at them sternly.

Faber began snapping pictures while Dougherty continued to scour the squalid compound with his binoculars. He lowered them from his eyes, squinted, then looked again. "Joe, is that a satellite dish in that dump and a solar panel in the bed of that old truck?"

Faber zoomed in with his camera setup. "Looks like it. I'll get some pictures."

"Any idea what those are for?" Dougherty asked Kevin.

"Well, he *is* an engineering genius—probably has something to do with that."

"OK. I'm going down to take a closer look and get a few more pictures around back. Joe, you stay here and let me know if you see anything suspicious." He gave Faber his binoculars and took the camera.

The trio spent a tense thirty minutes waiting, each minute paid for by yet another of Judas' thirty pieces of silver. Dougherty moved in a wide arc around the property with practiced stealth. Faber watched carefully the entire time. No alarms. The Rottweiler stayed inside.

On the return to Denver, Dougherty remembered perfectly the way back to Kevin's apartment. Mumbling goodbyes, Kevin, Maggie, and Craig exited the car. Before Kevin slid out, Dougherty grabbed him by the arm and said "You did the right thing. See you in the morning."

א א א א

Later that afternoon, Maggie called Jeff's house in Denver hoping to talk to Ana-Lese. Fortunately, that's who answered.

"Hello, Fosters," Ana-Lese said in a bizarrely chipper voice.

"Hi. It's Maggie."

"Oh." There was an uncomfortable pause.

"The Aspen house burned down?" Maggie asked.

"Yeah."

"I heard about it on the news. Thanks for calling me."

"Nobody told you? I thought Daddy would call you."

"Jeff doesn't like me much."

"What are you talking about? You're his favorite."

"He doesn't like either of us. He just likes you less than me."

Pause.

"And you wonder why people in this family don't call you," Ana-Lese huffed.

"Actually I know precisely why people in this family don't call me. If I were you, I wouldn't call me either. But, for pretty obvious reasons, I'd never be you. Were you at the house when the fire hit?"

Ana-Lese paused again. After ten seconds, she settled on "Yeah."

"What happened?"

"A fire came and the house burned down."

"Your innate propensity for encyclopedic thoroughness has always been one of your strongest points," Maggie said.

No response. "Could you repeat the question?" Ana-Lese finally said.

Disgusted, Maggie changed topics. "Did you save anything from the fire?"

"Total loss."

"You staying in Denver?"

"For now. I'm staying here with Dad. It's no picnic. He's mad all the time. He keeps getting calls from people, and they're mad at him, then he's mad at me. Now there's some new problem at the office. It's really huge. But he's not talking about it and I'm not asking."

Maggie didn't respond, hoping Ana-Lese would add more details. After a pause, she did. "Maggie, can I ask you a question? Do you think it would help Daddy's stress if I slept with him? I'm kind of afraid to turn him down."

א א א

"Jeff's in deep," Maggie said to Kevin after she hung up the phone. "And when Jeff's pissed, ain't nobody safe."

"Worry about Jeff another day. Tonight we all need a good night's sleep."

"What time did Dougherty say?"

"4:30 a.m., bright and early," Kevin said. "Ouch."

"Poor Kevin," Maggie said.

"In more ways than one. Listen, let's just chill for a bit. Otherwise we're not gonna sleep."

"You're probably right," she said walking over to the laptop. "Give me a minute to check something. After that, I promise to behave."

Maggie pulled up Friday's market report. "Whoa!" she said. "Kev, come here. Look at this carnage yesterday in the market," she said. "Jeff's companies are down all across the board. Peak Engineering down 28%; Peak Air down 33%; Peak Total Communications down 21%. All in one day. No wonder he's on the warpath."

"What's going on?" Kevin said looking over her shoulder.

"Not sure."

Maggie jumped over to Google News where a quick search revealed the problem. A rumor was floating in corporate circles that Jeff was being investigated for fraud by the Securities and Exchange Commission. An anonymous whistle blower sent a packet of incriminating evidence to the SEC's home office in Washington. The same source then alerted *The Wall Street Journal*.

"His house is not the only thing that's burning down," Kevin said.

Craig returned from the gym an hour later, and the trio turned in just after 10 p.m. Kevin lay awake until 3 a.m. He finally drifted off, dreamt the worst, and woke exhausted to the alarm an hour later.

The trio stumbled around in the morning darkness. A gloom hung over the day. Outside it was raining lightly. Kevin bumped Craig out of the bathroom and brushed his teeth but couldn't cleanse his mouth from the acerbic taste of betrayal.

Chapter 32

A Million Little Pieces

AT 4:30 A.M. ON A RAINY SUNDAY MORNING, AGENT Dougherty rang the doorbell. After a perfunctory greeting, the reluctant trio stumbled through a dark parking lot and into the waiting black Expedition. A second counterterrorism field ops squad was already underway and would meet them at the scene.

The vehicle sped through the emerging dawn. There was no music. Dougherty and Faber talked most of the way—they'd learned a great deal about Weissman in the past few days. Craig slept fitfully. Kevin and Maggie could not.

The two SUVs rendezvoused at Gold Dust Trail. Kevin guided the caravan down the gravel road until they reached the choked entrance of Weissman's driveway. They turned slowly into the opening, scraping against the brush and parked just inside the clearing.

The invaders exited the vehicles and moved like ghosts through the shrouded woods, taking up positions around the compound—six agents dressed in dark camo, and three exhausted, frightened betrayers of loyalty, trapped in a double necessity, each true and binding and mutually exclusive. It was an impossible juncture where all roads ended in harm.

Dougherty dispatched Kevin, Craig and Maggie to the ridge. He'd allowed them to come on the mission in the event they might be needed but insisted they stay out of harm's way.

The morning light grew and the rain eased. The Rottweiler heard a muffled disturbance and came to investigate. Two rifled agents with silencers squeezed off one round each. The shots flew straight through the throat of the dog and out the neck, clipping the spine. Blood ran onto his black coat, and he dropped with no death moans. Not so much as a twitch.

Maggie, Kevin, and Craig grimaced from the ridge.

"A lot of artillery to subdue one computer guy," Craig said.

Four of the shadowy figures floated soundlessly to the front door. Between them, they carried a heavy metal battering ram. Dougherty pounded loudly on the door.

"FBI. Open up."

No response.

Repeated, still no response.

He reached for the door. It was locked. Stepping aside, he motioned to the others. They swung the battering ram, and the ancient door splintered.

Dougherty entered. "FBI."

Not a sound. Dougherty put his hand up as a signal for the other three. They stood and listened. It was quiet as a church library at midnight.

"OK, let's go," he said in a hushed voice. "Be careful."

The agents made quick, precise movements room-to-room throughout the house. They finished the search in five minutes. Nothing. Absolutely nothing.

Dougherty called Kevin on the two-way radio. "He's not here. Suppose he's at the mine?"

"No way. He's home."

"How do you know that?"

"The Land Cruiser, for one thing. I just know. He's there," Kevin said. "Is there a basement?"

"None we could find. At least no visible stairway or entrance."

"Any computers?"

"Didn't see any."

"He can't live without computers. You haven't searched everywhere."

"Any ideas?"

"See a device that can input digits or numbers?"

"What do you mean?"

"To enter a password."

"Just the keypad on one locked door. We broke the door and are in that room now."

"Any other devices where you can enter numbers?"

"Not really. A couple phones. Nothing else."

"Pick up a phone and see if it has a dial tone."

Dougherty was silent for ten seconds, then said, "No dial tone. Sounds like a dead line."

"OK," Kevin said. "Try this. Try entering one of Dr. Weissman's passwords from CIMT. I know all his passwords because he gave them to me. Try 1-1-7-3-2-0."

"Hold on."

Maggie looked at Kevin suspiciously and asked in a low voice, "Why did you give him the wrong password?"

Kevin waved her off, then put a finger to his lips. "Wait," he whispered.

Fifteen seconds later, Dougherty came back on. "Nothing."

"OK," Kevin said. "Try another. Try putting a couple letters in that same sequence. Try S-1-1-7-J-3-2-0. The first part is his wife Susan's birthday. The second part is the birthday of his son, Joshua."

"Hold on."

Kevin covered the radio receiver and whispered to Maggie and Craig. "I didn't want to solve this too quickly. It wouldn't look right." They nodded.

Fifteen seconds later, Kevin heard a mechanical noise and knew the trap door was opening.

"I'll get back to you," Dougherty said.

א א א א

Agent Dougherty stood at the top of the stairs, gun drawn, and looked down. The basement was flooded with light.

"FBI," he yelled.

Music was the only sound heard. Weissman had replaced Górecki's Third with *Threnody*, a torturous orchestral piece on the bombing of Hiroshima.

"Dr. Weissman?" Dougherty yelled.

Nothing.

He descended the first step.

"FBI."

The music made him nervous. His brain attempted unsuccessfully to place it.

He descended another step, then another, followed by the other agents. The blazing whiteness of the room nearly blinded him, a room sterile enough to operate in.

A man sat before a computer at the head of a long table. His back was to the stairway. He slowly swiveled his chair and turned around. He looked at them with red eyes. He was dressed in clean white clothes and immaculate white shoes, making his unkempt hair and stubble all the more incongruous. The side of his face was horribly bruised and swollen.

A semi-automatic MAC-9 rested on the table next to the computer.

He was expecting us, Dougherty thought. The pistol is a statement.

Without prompting, Weissman raised his hands, keeping both in plain sight. He nodded at the pistol. "I could have killed you all. I didn't. After you shot my dog, I considered it. But I don't believe in killing."

The calm made Dougherty tense; it seemed veneer and unreliable.

"Lower your guns," Weissman said. "I'm not going to hurt you—though I could at any moment. I have nothing to lose, a condition you do not share."

He ran one hand through his hair. The rookie agent almost shot him. Dougherty could sense the itchy fingers in the room.

"That's all," Weissman said.

Forcing himself to stay calm, Dougherty stepped forward to handcuff the professor. No resistance. Weissman was read his rights, then Dougherty and the rookie escorted him up the stairs. Faber and the other agent remained to collect evidence.

As soon as Weissman entered the kitchen, still ten feet from the front door, he suddenly lost any pretense of orderly behavior. He became irate, screaming curses in Polish and German, fighting his captors, struggling against the handcuffs.

When they dragged him from the house, Kevin, Maggie and Craig stood in alarm. Without thinking and against orders, they began a quick descent down the hill, half-jumping, half-sliding, until they entered the yard.

Weissman, showing surprising strength, threw himself on the ground and kicked at the agents. They grabbed him under the arms and forced him up again. The cuffs cut his wrists, blood smearing on his white sleeves.

From the SUVs, the two agents in charge of controlling the perimeter watched the madman but held their ground. When Weissman spotted his slain dog, he roared with rage and fell to his knees sobbing. The agents continued to struggle, making slow but steady progress at dragging their victim across the compound.

אאאא

Maggie threw her hands to her mouth as Weissman spotted them. Kevin and Craig immediately diverted their heads in shame. Inexplicably, Maggie kept looking straight at him. For a second, their eyes met. Just for a second.

He winked.

Did he wink at me?

But now his bruised face was contorting and his eyes were blinking furiously.

Was that a wink, or was it a blink?

Weissman's hysteria returned so quickly Maggie wasn't sure what had happened. He glared at them, spit in their direction, and swore loud horrible-sounding curses. Her brow furrowed and her mouth dropped open in confusion. She forgot everything else around her and zoned in on his face, looking for a hint, a sign, a message.

אאאא

Dougherty and the rookie, more determined now, jerked Weissman up off his knees, and half-walked, half-dragged him toward the waiting van. He continued to sob, expressing his grief in short foreign epithets. Dougherty was good in languages but couldn't discern among the Polish, German, Yiddish, and Hebrew gemisch. As they reached the SUV, Weissman pulled himself together enough to communicate, his voice still thick with emotion.

"Anyone in the house or mineshaft—leave now."

Dougherty was unsure whether to take him seriously, but then he looked directly into Weissman's eyes.

"No more warning," Weissman said. "Out now."

Will picked up his radio and shouted, "Evacuate! Get out! Get out of there! Now!"

A piercing siren rattled the entire valley, a noise so loud it elicited pain to any within half a mile, except Weissman, who was laughing. The shrill noise came from somewhere inside the building. The two agents came barreling out the front door, holding their ears and racing across the barren yard. After ten seconds, the painful noise turned itself off. The silence was heavenly but short-lived. Five seconds later, a blaring Wagnerian *Tristan und Isolde*, a favorite carried around by Hitler in his knapsack during World War I, replaced the siren pain with detestably loud operatic decibels.

Weissman looked over at Maggie, who stood transfixed. He nodded his head in the direction opposite the house, and with sternness and clarity mouthed the word "Run."

"He wants us to run," Maggie shouted. "Come on!" She grabbed Kevin by the arm and took off running away from the house. Craig took one look at Maggie's face and followed into the trees without hesitation.

The six agents jumped into the Expeditions with Weissman, slamming the doors tight. They watched the cabin through bulletproof windows a hundred feet away.

Nothing. Nothing. Nothing. A seed of doubt entered Dougherty's mind.

Then Weissman said, "I always wanted to blow up Wagner." He put his head back and laughed a long, deep, demonic laugh. As if his laugh had triggered the fuse, the cabin exploded.

The building turned itself inside out with the help of a hundred pounds of high explosives. Millions of fragments, most the size of matchsticks, sprayed the area like so much shrapnel. The percussive blast was deafening, rocking the two vehicles with a jolt.

When the smoke blew away, no fragment over ten inches remained. The decrepit white clapboard shack was now replaced with a massive burning crater thirty feet wide and ten feet deep.

"You can send people back in now," Weissman said to Dougherty. Then he laughed again, deliriously pleased with himself.

Suddenly a huge secondary explosion lit up the sky, causing everyone to wince and cover their heads. The blast, coming from the direction of the mine, was so immense it showered them even this far away with pebbles and dust.

Weissman continued laughing, even louder and wild-eyed.

א א א א

Maggie, Kevin, and Craig were lying flat on the ground behind a thick stand of trees. When they finally peeked up, Maggie started sobbing. Never one for crying, now she did so with abandon. Kevin hugged her tightly.

Craig walked back into the yard and went over to the dead dog. He knelt down beside the fallen warrior and touched its face ever so gently. Then he cleaned some of the dust and wood splinters off its fur.

"In a kinder world," he said, "perhaps we could've been friends."

Chapter 33

Let the Great Axe Fall

"Hello Margaret. Could you come over for dinner tonight? We need to talk as a family."

Great.

"I'd like to bring someone," Maggie said.

"Didn't you hear me? We've got things to talk about as a *family*. No strangers."

"I'll need to change some plans—"

"See you at six-thirty." Click.

אאא

Maggie arrived at the front door simultaneous with the pizza delivery. He ogled her. She opened the door, then slammed it in his face.

"You wait there," she yelled through the heavy oak. "Jeff, someone outside for you."

"Margaret, I swear." Jeff got up from the couch and went to the door. He paid for the pizza and tipped five bucks.

"Was his nose bleeding when he first arrived?" Jeff asked.

"What did you get?" Ana-Lese asked, opening her salad.

"Canadian bacon," Maggie said.

They sat around the table and each pretended, unconvincingly, to be interested in food. Jeff set down his fork. "There's no easy way to say this, so I'll just be blunt. The recent events—the airport bombings, the Mall of America thing, the Aspen fire … It's just destroyed my business."

Jeff's arms tensed, veins bulged in his neck.

"Stock positions in my companies are pretty bad. Some cannibals who'd love to see me destroyed short-traded my stocks. Some issued margin calls. Investors are jittery. My stock prices are volatile—"

"Anything to do with the SEC?" Maggie asked, well aware it would set him off.

"I'll sue for harassment!" He slammed his fist on the table and sprang to his feet. The silverware bounced. So did Ana-Lese. "I'll strangle the pencil-necks with their own ties. I'll bury them in paperwork until they'll need a bulldozer to find their desks!" His face turned red with rage, but his innocence was unconvincing. Especially with these two.

He got up and stormed into the bathroom, slamming the door. He splashed his face and stared at the mirror. Maggie and Ana-Lese heard something break through the closed door, something made of glass.

"Why did you do that?" Ana-Lese said, glaring at Maggie.

"Because if he goes bankrupt, it'll be his own fault. He should learn to tell the truth."

"Just chill, OK? After dinner, you'll get up and leave. I'm stuck here."

"Yeah, well, I'll try to behave," Maggie said sarcastically, "if you'll try to get unstuck."

"Just don't throw any more bombs," she pleaded. "What's the SEC?"

Jeff interrupted them by returning to the room. He poured four fingers of whiskey and slammed it. Then he sat at the table and put his head in his hands.

"Let's try this again. Like I was saying, things don't look good. I still have thirty-two million in assets, but I also have thirty million in debt. The picture changes hourly. I used to be worth seventy million, but right now it looks like we'll probably be wiped out."

Ana-Lese was stunned. She dropped her fork and stared at her salad. Tears surged forth, splashed off her cheek and irrigated the lettuce. Maggie sat quietly. She was not surprised by this state of affairs but didn't know exactly how she should act or what she should say.

"Cindy's still draining whatever's left of my accounts, but I probably don't need to tell you that," Jeff said. Ana-Lese winced. Jeff and Cindy's fighting always made her uncomfortable.

"What's the bottom line?" Maggie asked. She felt slightly guilty for playing hardball, but both Jeff and Maggie were cut from the same cloth.

"First, Cindy's filed for divorce. She'll try to get everything she can."

Nothing's really changed, Maggie thought. A cold day leads to a cold night.

"And second," he said, "I won't be able to support you like before. I'm going to fight to keep the house. Margaret, you're independent now—you've still got some money, right?"

"I'm fine," Maggie said. "I don't think people should mooch off their parents after college anyway." Ana-Lese turned her face as though Maggie had slapped her.

"Ana-Lese, I'll try to help as I can," Jeff said. "You can live here as long as we have this house..."

Ana-Lese's world was coming down around her. Her twenty-five-year-old security blanket was in shreds. Maggie felt more pity than expected.

Chapter 34

Unexpected Visitor

THREE DAYS LATER KEVIN AND CRAIG RECEIVED THEIR FIRST pieces of mail from Peak Engineering. "We regret to inform you that during these difficult economic times, your services will no longer be needed. We hope you are able to find other suitable employment." A few other platitudes followed, but essentially the message was that blunt.

"First job I ever lost before starting," Craig said. "Kev, we'll need to get out of the lease."

"We could pack Dexter and move down to Baja, get a little wooden fishing boat, build a hut on the beach."

"Ah, Shawshank," Maggie said. "Why don't you just dig under rock fences till you find a box of money?"

Craig reached his arms over his head. "Aw, Maggie, let us enjoy our moment of freedom. Personally, I feel like we've been let out of shackles."

"A pretty accurate picture of working for my father."

"Come with us, Maggie," Kevin said. "We'll even let you cook."

The phone rang, and Kevin picked up.

"May I speak to Kevin Morgan?"

"Speaking."

"Mr. Morgan, this is Abraham Jonas of Alcock, Berner, and Fleigle. We're a law firm in Boston. I have a matter I'd like to discuss with you personally if we could arrange it."

"What did you say your name was?" Kevin asked. A concerned look blanketed his face. He quickly shuffled the desktop looking for pen and paper.

"Abraham Jonas of Alcock, Berner, and Fleigle."

"Sorry. Um, thanks. Is this some kind of bad news? What'd I do? I've never gotten a call from a lawyer before."

"Actually, it's good news I'd say."

"That's a relief. What kind of good news?"

"I'm not really at liberty to say over the phone. It really is best if I discuss it with you in person. Are you free tomorrow afternoon?"

"Tomorrow? Yeah, I'm free. I guess." Kevin looked over at Craig and Maggie and shrugged his shoulders.

"Splendid. I'll take a plane in the morning and drop by your place midafternoon. Around 3:00?"

"OK by me," Kevin said. "Can you tell me what this is about?"

"It's best if we wait until we are together. Could you give me directions to your place?"

Kevin gave the directions and they exchanged goodbyes.

"That was weird," Kevin said.

"Who was it?" Maggie and Craig said in unison.

"Some lawyer from Boston who wants to fly out here tomorrow and give me good news."

"Yeah, right," Maggie laughed. "What's the chances of that? Let me see if I've got this right. One week ago, an FBI guy flies out here from the East Coast to talk with you, and now a lawyer from Boston wants to fly out here and talk with you? Who are you? Really, who are you?"

"Oh, Maggie, shut up."

"Sounds suspicious, Kev. You should check him out," Craig said.

An online search revealed the law firm was legit, including one Abraham Jonas, JD, Harvard Law School, class of 1978, specializing in Patent Trademark & Copyright Law, and Intellectual Property.

"This still sounds strange," Craig said. "I bet he has something to do with the FBI. Or maybe the CIA. Maybe they've got evidence that we knew about Weissman and kept it a secret. Maybe they found out we didn't tell them the whole truth about our involvement. You know, *accessory to a crime*, or *aiding and abetting*. Something like that."

"He sounded straight," Kevin said. "I'm a little nervous, but I guess if he's coming tomorrow at 3:00, I'll be here." He looked at the other two. "You guys in or out?"

"In for a penny, in for a pound," Maggie said.

"You two can do what you want," Craig said, standing up. "I smell trouble. I'm heading for the border. When you get out of the slammer—" he looked over at Maggie "—look me up."

Maggie stared up at him in disbelief, then saw the slight smirk. She hit him hard across the patella, sending him crashing to the floor in pain.

"Good," Kevin said. "We'll greet Mr. Jonas as one big happy family."

א א א א

"Hello, I'm Abraham Jonas." He walked through the open door and shook hands with Kevin. "Am I to assume you are Mr. Kevin Morgan?"

"That is correct."

"Excellent," Mr. Jonas said, with a broad smile. "Excellent." He turned toward Maggie and Craig and eyed them with the slightest suspicion. He again introduced himself in the same manor and then asked their names. "Yes, Maggie and Craig. Nice to meet you all."

"Will you excuse us for just a moment?" he asked Maggie and Craig. Then he turned toward Kevin and said, "Mr. Morgan, may I speak with you privately please?" Kevin led him into the kitchen.

"Mr. Morgan," he whispered, "there are aspects of this matter you might wish confidential. Perhaps we should meet alone, just the two of us. Is there anywhere we can go to have that privacy?"

"No need," Kevin responded. "This is fine as far as I'm concerned."

Mr. Jonas paused, evidently considering whether Kevin understood enough to exercise proper judgment. Finally he said, "Are you sure, then, you wish me to discuss this matter in front of the others?"

"Absolutely," Kevin said. "We're a team."

"Fine," Mr. Jonas said. "I didn't mean to imply anything and certainly mean no offense. Just wanted to be sure." He smiled warmly.

"No offense taken." Despite the mystery shrouding his presence, Kevin found it impossible not to trust the man.

They went back into the living room where a space had been cleared on the sofa for the visiting dignitary.

"What I want to talk to you about Mr. Morgan," he said, "is a matter of a transfer of patent royalties to your name. A certain Antoni Weissman—I believe you know him? Yes, good—Dr. Weissman contacted me fourteen months ago and asked me to draft and hold a legal document that would transfer the royalties from some of his patents to your name. This was accomplished according to his instructions. He read and signed it, as I said, fourteen months ago.

"The transfer was written to take effect on July 1 after your gradation from college—a graduation requirement I believe you have now fulfilled? Yes. Good. Therefore today I have a few papers for you to sign that will make this transaction official and legal. This transfer of ownership will continue for life. You should carefully update your will as soon as possible regarding beneficiaries."

Kevin didn't know what to say. "Are you sure there's no mistake? I'm not sure Dr. Weissman even likes me anymore."

Mr. Jonas laughed. His eyes sparkled, and it was obviously a delight for him to be the bearer of good news. "I can assure you, there's no mistake. And quite the contrary, young man—Dr. Weissman has great admiration and affection for you. He told me so just yesterday."

"You talked to him yesterday? How is he? What did he say?"

Mr. Jonas put up a hand: "First, the papers."

"What do you mean royalties?" Kevin asked. "What patents? I mean, how much money are you talking about?"

"The royalties on these six patents have averaged $5.2 million a year for the last eight years. Dr. Weissman believes they should continue at that rate for at least three or four more years. Perhaps longer."

"What?" Kevin shouted. "How much?"

"Of course it will be taxed, but we're still—"

"Did you say *million*?"

"Yes, $5.2 million a year. Which, even after taxes, is still a lot of money." Mr. Jonas produced a small stack of papers that he asked Kevin to sign.

"I can't believe this!" Kevin looked at Maggie and Craig. Maggie's eyes were huge. Craig was grinning, bouncing up and down in his chair, hugging Maggie with one arm.

"Are you for real?" Kevin asked Mr. Jonas. "This is some kind of joke, right?"

Mr. Jonas was sitting back, obviously enjoying the moment. "I can assure you, Mr. Morgan, this is all real."

"Unbelievable." Kevin got up with the papers in his hand and walked to the wall and back trying to calm down. He looked at the top page, then took a deep breath. "I'd like to read these over first. Could we have a few minutes?"

"Of course. If it helps you to know, as I said before, Dr. Weissman has read the papers carefully and found them to his satisfaction."

The trio took the documents and went to the kitchen table. Kevin sat in the middle with Maggie and Craig on either side. They noted Weissman's signature on each document in the appropriate line, dated fourteen months earlier. After ten minutes of study, Kevin said, "Looks fine, but then what do I know? What do you guys think?"

"Looks good," Maggie said. "I'd sign it."

"My thoughts exactly," Craig said.

They returned to the living room and, with a flourish, Kevin signed on the lines indicated by the red X. He handed the documents back to Mr. Jonas.

"Excellent," Mr. Jonas said. "And here are your copies."

"OK now, remember the little people," Craig said to Kevin.

"There was one more thing," Mr. Jonas said. "You asked about Dr. Weissman. He gave me a cassette tape to pass on to you. He said you'd know what it is."

Mr. Jonas handed the tape in a sealed envelope to Kevin. Then he stood and excused himself with a tip of the hat toward Maggie and carried his attaché to the door.

"I'm sure we'll be in touch again," he said. "And you can expect your first check in about two weeks, shortly after July 1." With that, he turned and disappeared down the stairs with a smile.

ℵ ℵ ℵ

"Looks like I'm buying dinner," Kevin said.

"Not until we hear the tape," Maggie said. "I'm starving, but I'm way too nervous to eat until we listen to that thing."

Kevin held the recording up and looked at it. "I can't believe he gave us a tape. Who uses cassettes anymore?" He brought their old boombox into the living room and put in the tape. They all took a deep breath, looked at each other, then Kevin pushed the button.

The tape fizzed for about five seconds. Then a man cleared his throat in the background, and Weissman's unmistakable voice said, "Hello Kevin. Since we first met, you've been like family to me. You have been like my son, Joshua, might have been. I've seen him in you. You're really the only family I've got. As for the royalties, I expect you to share. Oh, and on the other matter, good work."

The three looked at each other, stunned. The tape rolled on blankly for ten more seconds, then Craig pushed the stop button.

"Don't," Kevin said. "Turn it back on. Keep it going. Let's hear if he has anything more to say." He looked over at Maggie. "Can you believe this?" He shook his head.

Craig pushed play and settled back into the sofa. The tape continued for another twenty seconds ... nothing. Then came the muffled motorized sound of a hinge opening a door, followed by Górecki's Third in the distance.

Maggie grabbed Kevin's hand and squeezed. She looked over at him, her eyes nervous and suspicious. Then came a distant, muted voice—

"Hello? Anyone there? Dr. Weissman? This is Kevin."

Kevin and Maggie both gasped.

"OK, Maggie. Here we go."
"Stay here until I go down a bit further."
"I'm not staying behind."

"What's that?"

"Górecki's Third. Weissman's favorite. I heard it a lot in his office."

"Keep going. Clock's ticking."

"Ozymandias. It all makes sense. I'll explain later."

"Oops."

"What do you mean, oops?"

"I hope we can get out."

"What do you mean, hope we can get out?"

"Well, if we can't, we'll just have to raise our family down here."

"That's not funny."

Maggie reached over, hands trembling, and stopped the tape. "I can't listen to this... Not now." She looked over at Kevin. His face had gone pale.

"He knew," Kevin said, choking back tears. "He knew everything."

Chapter 35

Fuel, Meet Fire

LYING ON HIS BED, WEISSMAN LOOKED UP FROM HIS READING and surveyed the surroundings: cold steel bars, cement blocks, stainless steel sink and toilet, metal desk bolted to the wall. About what he expected as a pretrial inmate at the federal detention facility. But he was accustomed to spartan accommodations, and, anyway, it'd be over soon. He'd done what he had to do; now only the waiting remained.

Others railed against their surroundings, against the system and the guards, wasting their efforts. Weissman recognized the futility and refrained. Though he was awaiting trial and considered dangerous, the guards seemed to regard him as old, infirm, and essentially nuts.

He heard the doors open at the end of the block followed by two guards escorting in a new arrival. Weissman lifted his head, cocked it to one side, and listened carefully. As the trio started down the corridor, Weissman shouted, "Round the decay of that colossal wreck, boundless and bare, the lone and level sand stretches far away." Then he listened again.

"What was that?" came the new voice.

Weissman lay back down with a glowing smile. *Ah, life is good.*

"What was *what*?" answered a guard.

"Someone yelled something. Did you hear that?"

"A bit of advice: Stop being so jumpy or you'll wear yourself out."

As they walked past his cell, Weissman glanced up from his book. Jeff Foster looked over but registered no recognition. Foster's Rolex had been replaced with handcuffs, his tailored

Italian suit gone, an orange jumpsuit in its place. His skin glistened with a cold sweat. Jeff's tough guy act was beginning to crack.

The guards continued past two more cells, then stopped across the hall to usher Foster into his new hole. The handcuffs came off, he was given a few cursory words of instruction, and the door slammed shut.

Ten minutes later Weissman stood up, slowly, weakly. He moved to the front corner of the cell where he could watch the new arrival. Several other inmates had already done the same, curious what the newcomer looked like and eager to measure his reactions, to gauge his mettle. Maybe his story would come out, probably not. If they were lucky, perhaps this would be one of those famous federal criminals—the rich, the powerful, the white-collar kind followed nightly on cable news. They might get a front row seat to a spectacular celebrity flameout.

Foster couldn't care less. He didn't look at them and ignored their questions. His spite and hatred for them was evident in his body language. He lay down on his bed and closed his eyes.

Weissman waited until the others, out of boredom, drifted back to their beds. He'd been leaning against the wall for an hour now, smiling, a smile that widened as time passed. Finally he said in a low but clear voice, "I see you got my invitation."

Foster opened his eyes with a start and jerked his head up. He rose quickly to one elbow and then jumped up and went to the bars. "Who said that?" he demanded. Finally, thirty feet away, he saw an emaciated and decrepit man looking at him from the shadows.

"It was a lot of work to plan this party," Weissman said, "but well worth it in the end."

"Who are you? I know that voice." Foster was agitated and shook the bars. "What's your name? Who are you?"

"Welcome to hell."

Chapter 36

Home Lies Beyond the Road Ahead

September twenty-third was cool and clear. Kevin and Maggie sat on the expansive wooden deck of the bed and breakfast where the wedding party was staying. While everyone else lost themselves in the happy confusion of preparing for the wedding, the two lazed on pine chairs, watching the carefree stars a million-million-million miles away. Kevin smoked a pipe with new tobacco Cat insisted he try. The lovers held hands and the world was right.

They'd said what there was to say about getting married and sat in silence. Kevin's smoke kept the bugs at bay.

"There you guys are," Cat said from behind the screen door. He opened it and walked onto the deck. "I've been looking all over for you."

"Sorry, we weren't trying to hide," Kevin said, with a wink in his voice.

"I know better," Cat said. "You two are in love, so you hide. That's what lovers do. But Maggie, you're needed downstairs. They're having trouble with your camera." She glared at him. He shrugged his shoulders. "I don't know."

Maggie got up and gave a tug on Cat's beard, then opened the door and disappeared. Cat smiled and took her chair.

"Liar," Kevin said.

"Actually, more of a fib. I wanted you to myself."

"Maggie's going to be mad."

"I'm not scared." Cat flashed his grandfather/hippie smile.

"You know, Kevin, I love her as my own daughter. I just wanted to say that I'm glad you came along. You're the only person I've ever thought good enough for her."

"Thanks for being there," Kevin said. "I shudder to think where she'd be today without your influence." He paused for a moment, considering his words. "You know Cat ... I think God brought you two together. You're free to disagree, but I feel it's true. In a very deep part of me—a part so deep words can't go there—this is what I feel."

"You might be right," Cat smiled. "You just might be right."

They leaned back side-by-side and drank in the stars together.

א א א א

Maggie was resplendent walking down the black sand beach. Kevin hoped she was not so luminous as to take attention from the bride, but it was wasted worry: Summer was gorgeous in her own right. Corey stood, nervous, waiting. Corey's childhood pastor performed the ceremony and a family was born. Kevin and Craig ushered, which wasn't much since there were no chairs.

The open-air reception was held on the ridge with music by Blips and Bleeps. When Dave, the lead singer, discovered Cat would be at the wedding, he insisted Cat be the front man for this show.

With typical exuberance, Cat plugged in his acoustic and began by saying, "Thank you for inviting us to play this glorious event. We're honored, and now we'd like to start this couple off right with the gift of music."

He counted 1-2-3 and they launched into "Hot Mama in a Cold Car." Cat had written new words and retitled the song "Hawaiian Wedding Blues." Corey loved it. Summer was beside herself.

From all over the Waipio Valley both Hawaiians and tourists congregated, though keeping a respectful distance. Corey sang his song for Summer while Maggie stood ceremonial guard, holding aloft a black combat boot.

The festivities went on and on. Well-wishers danced until the weaker started to drop. After three hours, Cat's sweat shorted out his microphone, which they took as a sign. Corey and Summer fled in a hail of rice, on their way to wedded bliss. They jumped into a mule-team wagon and headed to the Hideaway Cliff House.

The next day Summer's hippie parents led the wedding guests on a horseback ride through the valley, passing lush tropical flowers and lime trees and taro fields and ancient burial caves and wild horses and hundreds of waterfalls.

The bride and groom were nowhere to be seen.

א א א א

The Piper Arrow lifted off from the Anchorage airport and ninety minutes later touched down in Port Alsworth. Maggie, Kevin, Craig, and Cat transferred to her jeep and bounced around Hardenberg Bay to Salmon Ella's. Kevin had purchased the fishing camp the month before and convinced Ella to remain and run the operation with Cat. Maggie took up residence in the little brown cabin, while Kevin and Craig shared the adjacent cottage.

Day after day they tasted the delights of the Lake Clark region: long hikes looking for grizzly, fishing the lake from their fleet of Lunds, fly-fishing the rivers, overnight rafting, climbs on Mt. Tanalian stalking the big horn, fly-in hunts for moose and caribou, trips out to Homer to fish halibut and to Seward to see glaciers calving. Kevin even did a little haggling and procured a 16-foot Lund with a fifty-horse Yamaha outboard, his own personal boat, and life zeroed right in on perfection.

Kevin sent for his Triumph, and while it was being shipped, he and Craig rebuilt Cat's old machine that'd been mothballed for years. Of course the road system in Port Alsworth was limited to a few miles—this was the Alaskan bush after all—but they enjoyed taking their bikes for a spin around the bay and then racing down the runway. Kevin knew his father would've been pleased.

Each afternoon Kevin and Maggie visited a promontory high above the lake. Here, sitting on a cliff and gazing over one of the truly remarkable vistas in the world, they held hands and relished the strangeness and richness of life. Jeff Foster, now a destitute and embattled man, raged upon discovering Anthony Weissman was behind his collapse. Yet Jeff's corruption was real and his empire had been built on threats, intimidation, power, and ultimately fraud, leaving him few supporters as he made his way through the court system. Only highly-paid lawyers consorted with the accused, attorneys who in the end would demand his last dollar as the prison doors swung shut.

It eventually surfaced that Weissman and Jeff shared a contentious history, namely Jeff's intellectual property theft back in their MIT student days. Weissman had been young and trusting and when cheated had no resources to claim back what was rightfully his. It was the beginning of Jeff's fraudulent empire.

Maggie was left with neither name nor wealth. Not that it bothered her, for life had become so much more. Seldom had she known such peace.

Their faith gap kept Kevin and Maggie patiently exploring for answers, as every day they read three chapters together: one each from the Psalms, the Gospels, and C. S. Lewis. Kevin's understanding deepened, and Maggie slowly opened her heart to new spiritual treasures. It was a lush time, a wondrous season of discovery and growth and grace.

The nightly campfire on the shore was everyone's favorite time of day. Cat was in charge of building up the flame, then the others joined by circling their chairs.

"What's the latest on the professor?" Cat asked as he roasted a salmon steak over the fire. "You said the philosopher called?"

"Michael had a great report," Kevin said. "Weissman's not nearly as delusional now that he's back on his meds. His depression has improved. Best of all, it looks like the surgery saved his life."

"You think he might pull through?" Craig asked.

"The doctor puts his odds at seventy percent."

"Cool," Cat said. "I thought he was a goner."

"We all did," Maggie said.

"I had mixed feelings when the judge bought the insanity plea," Kevin said. "But looking back, it's been an answer to prayer. He's done a lot better in the prison hospital than he would've in lockup."

He poked the coals and took a few deep breaths. Everyone waited patiently—they knew how hard this image was for him.

After half a minute he was able to resume. "When the court ruled him not competent to refuse cancer treatment, that was the right call too."

"Weissman sure kicked about it," Craig said. "I'm not sure I blame him. But if he beats the cancer, it'll be worth it."

"Amen," Kevin said.

"As far as I'm concerned, he's a national treasure," Maggie said. "Though I doubt my dad or sister would agree."

"I guess the tumor wasn't as bad as he thought," Kevin said. "With his bleeding and headaches and weight loss, he probably just assumed the worst."

"He *hoped* for the worst, don't you think?" Maggie said.

"Sure acted that way," Kevin said.

Craig's face lit up. "Can you imagine a psychiatrist trying to deal with him? Or his ENT surgeon? Or better yet, his nurse? He'll be lecturing them on radiology and biochemistry and the physics of thermometers."

"Michael thinks pretty soon they're going to approve visits," Kevin said. "They're still concerned I might upset him because I'm the one who called the FBI. But I'm not worried at all. When they give me the green light, I'm there."

"Me too," Maggie said.

"Count me in," Craig added.

"I sure would like to meet him sometime," Cat said. He took a puff on his pipe. "If he ever gets out, why don't you invite him up here?"

The thought of inviting a healthy Anthony Weissman to this little piece of heaven brought a smile to Kevin. Maggie read his mind and reached for his hand.

Acknowledgments

Adam

My deepest thanks to Maureen, my loving and devoted wife who often believed in me more than I did: without her this project would never have seen the light of day.

Thanks also to Katja for being brilliant and loving and the best daughter anyone could ask for. You give me motivation on the hard days. Thanks to Nico for your bravery, for your love, and for the late night talks. I miss you and love you always.

My extended family, church family, and great friends all deserve credit as well. Thanks to Theresa McNiff for believing; thanks to Janeen McNiff for FedExing an early version of this manuscript to a remote village 400 miles north of the Arctic Circle in Norway; thanks to Peter McNiff for giving me my first job in publishing. That job led me to believe that I could pull this off, with the help of friends. Thanks to Matt Swenson for being who you are, and Suzie Swenson for appreciating that.

Thanks to Mike Goslar, Pat Kahnke, Trevis Underdahl, and Mike Devereaux for being great musicians and better friends, for unflagging encouragement, and for accepting me with all my eccentricities and foibles.

Thanks to Nicole Devereaux for being an early reader. Colin Lammie did our cover and is an amazing artist. Thanks to Kendal Marsh for a little tech support at a crucial time.

Thanks to everyone at St. Paul Fellowship: I've never been to (or heard of) a better church.

Finally, thanks to Richard and Linda Swenson—for everything.

Richard

As with any decade-long project, at the end there are many who deserve both acknowledgement and gratitude. Occupying the top rung, once again, is Linda. Thanks for being such an encouragement and for loving our characters and story. Your tireless reading, editing, re-reading, and re-editing of the text suggest your patience is infinite.

Others, too, read parts or all of the manuscript at various stages of development and offered helpful comments, among them Dan Benson, Diana Stimmel, Allison Costello, Don Steffen, Ruth and Fred Menz.

Thanks to our Norwegian friends (especially Mike Elvebo, Marit Holmen, and Olga-Lise Holmen) who allowed Swedes entry into the vast beauty of their fjord district for sabbatical work on this book. Bill and Gail Thedinga, plus Sara and Nate offered Boston area information, Scituate photos, and occasional curbside legal information for those chapters where the delightful Abraham Jonas of Alcock, Berner, and Fleigle makes an appearance. On the technical side, Gary Cowles, Don Steffen, and Philip Cowles provided invaluable help in the areas of publishing, printing, and website development.

Dozens more provided encouragement, prayer, food, cabins, emails, and advice, most especially Caroline Miller, Matt and Suzie Swenson, Marcia Borgie, Karen Swenson, Hazel Bent, Dave and Debbie Bochman, Jack Stimmel, Craig and Linda Wilson, and Donna Knipfer. We are humbly in your debt.

Adam, thanks for the privilege. You're not only a great writer and experienced in the publishing side but also the master of dialogue. I can't wait for others to experience what I've grown so fond of.

About the Authors

Adam Swenson has been involved in writing fulltime for ten years as a feature writer, magazine editor, book co-author and editor. He is a 1998 graduate of Bethel University with degrees in philosophy and theology. He has traveled widely, flying small planes in the Amazon, skinning a bear and picking salmon nets in the Alaskan bush, photographing community development in Nigeria, helping to build a maternal-child health clinic in Zambia, reading Sartre at the Left Bank's Café Les Deux Magots, jogging up the serpentine path to Masada, and working on this novel 400 miles north of the Arctic Circle along the shores of a Norwegian fjord. He lives in Roseville, Minnesota with his wife and daughter.

Richard Swenson holds degrees in medicine and physics and is a futurist, physician-researcher, educator, and the author of eight books. He has presented to a wide variety of professional, medical, educational, and management groups, most major church denominations and organizations, members of the United Nations, of Congress, of NASA, and of the Pentagon. He was an invited guest participant for the 44th Annual National Security Seminar. In 2003, he was awarded Educator of the Year by Christian Medical and Dental Associations. He and his wife make their home in Menomonie, Wisconsin.

Made in the USA
Coppell, TX
04 October 2024